DEADLY CURE

ALSO BY
LAWRENCE GOLDSTONE

NONFICTION

Birdmen

Drive

Going Deep

Dark Bargain

The Activist

Inherently Unequal

FICTION

Anatomy of Deception

The Astronomer

DEADLY CURE

A NOVEL

LAWRENCE GOLDSTONE

PEGASUS BOOKS
NEW YORK LONDON

DEADLY CURE

Pegasus Books Ltd.
148 W. 37th Street, 13th Floor
New York, NY 10018

First Pegasus Books cloth edition November 2017

Interior design by Maria Fernandez

Library of Congress Cataloging-in-Publication Data is available.

ISBN: 978-1-68177-552-4

10 9 8 7 6 5 4 3 2 1

Printed in the United States of America
Distributed by W. W. Norton & Company

For Nancy and Lee

DEADLY CURE

ONE

Noah Whitestone shoved his plate aside. The room smelled of charred meat and cooking fat. Mrs. Jensen would never learn not to overcook pork chops. He pushed himself up from his chair, his hands braced on the edge of the table. His feet throbbed inside his shoes. Before he could step away, a thick hand was on his shoulder.

"No, doctor, you sit right down." Mrs. Jensen slapped a copy of the *Brooklyn Daily Eagle* on the table.

Noah shook his head slowly. "I'll read it later. I've got to go out." The *Daily Eagle* stared back seductively at him from the tabletop. He hadn't read the paper in two days.

"You haven't had your coffee," Mrs. Jensen admonished, her hand not moving from his shoulder. After raising six children, she knew the elements of command. "If you jump up right after dinner, you'll be the sick one." She was a pale woman, a widow of sixty, with tiny red veins snaking across her round cheeks like estuaries. "Your patients can wait ten more minutes. How many did you see in the office today?"

"Fifty, I think. No, fifty-two."

"No wonder," she said with a sniff. "Tomorrow's the first day of autumn. Everybody gets sick. Happens every year."

Was that true? Noah had never noticed. But she was right about the coffee. A few minutes more would do no harm. Gratefully, he settled back into his chair. If he closed his eyes, he would be asleep in moments.

"How many tonight?" Mrs. Jensen asked, after she returned with the coffee. Ribbons of steam rose from the surface. The aroma was strong, acrid. Noah took a sip. Hot. Welcome. Soon the fatigue would begin to abate.

"Only two. But you don't need to wait. I may sit for a while with each of them."

She nodded. "Ah." The evening was generally reserved for patients who could not get out. Many were near death.

Mrs. Jensen cleared the plate and noticed that each of the pork chops had some meat left near the bone. "Was everything all right, doctor?"

"Excellent, Mrs. Jensen, as always." Noah took another sip and unfolded the newspaper. Reading was so much more pleasant by incandescent light. These rooms were his first that did not use gas or oil. The age of electricity.

Mrs. Jensen cocked her head toward the left lead story. "Terrible about Africa. Looks like war for sure. I can't understand why those English won't let the Boers live in peace."

"If you say so."

She tapped the index finger of her free hand on the center column. Her knuckles were broad and puckered, like a man's. "Captain Dreyfus is a free man. He was lucky to get off, if you ask me. All that eyewash about him being falsely accused because he was a Jew. Can't trust any of them."

"Jews or the French?" Noah asked with mock innocence.

"You know what I mean, doctor." Mrs. Jensen brightened as she pointed out the lead on the right. "But at least Admiral Dewey is still on page one."

As he had been for months, thought Noah. The star attraction in Mr. Hearst's war.

"Are you still going to watch the naval parade from Miss Maribeth's yacht?"

"Actually, it's her father's."

"Yes, doctor, I know. Well, are you?"

"If I don't have any patients."

"You can miss one day. They say maybe a million people will show up. Even more the next day."

Preparations for Dewey had been frenetic. The largest naval parade in the nation's history would take place on Friday, followed by the land parade the next day. A huge arch was being hastily constructed specifically for the event at Madison Square, the end point of a procession that would begin at Grant's Tomb. All for a man who had become a hero by defeating the hopelessly obsolete Spanish navy and then putting down a rebellion of barefoot Filipino farmers wielding machetes.

"You promised me the day off. You do remember?" Mrs. Jensen had told Noah she intended to arrive at five in the morning so as not to chance missing the opportunity to view the champion of Manila Bay.

"Yes. I remember."

Mrs. Jensen coughed softly. She always did that before she attempted to elicit a tidbit of gossip. "Miss Maribeth is a lovely girl."

"Very lovely."

"Have you two set a date yet?"

"Not since you asked me two days ago, Mrs. Jensen. Sometime in April, probably, when the flowers begin to bloom. Mrs. De Kuyper wants the ceremony outdoors." So outdoors it will be, he thought.

"Spring weddings are the best."

"So you've said." Noah decided to reclaim the initiative. "Has your rheumatism been acting up?"

"Much bet——" Mrs. Jensen bit off the rest. He had trapped her again.

"Have you been taking Dr. Jordan's Elixir after everything I've said?" She busied herself with the silver.

"Mrs. Jensen, if you insist on taking patent medicines against my express orders, I will be forced to dismiss you and find another housekeeper."

"You wouldn't do that, Dr. Whitestone," she mumbled.

"Oh, wouldn't I?" Noah said forcefully. "How many times have I told you? There is poison in some of those concoctions. I've run into arsenic, wood alcohol, and Lord knows what else. Anya Krakowiak died last month from drinking a bottle of Paton's Vegetable Tonic. It's 10 percent opium."

"But I'd never drink a whole bottle. And there's none of that in Dr. Jordan's. The advertisement says . . ."

"Advertisements can say whatever they want. And Dr. Jordan, if there is such a person, can put anything he wants in his 'elixir.' I checked. There's alcohol and coca in it."

"Very well, doctor. I'll stop right away if you say so." Flatware balanced across the surface of the plate, she moved hurriedly to the kitchen.

Left in peace, Noah sipped his coffee while he leafed through the paper. He would not dismiss her, of course. Despite her limitations on the stove, she was perfect for his needs: willing to work long, irregular hours; always cheerful; could perform well in an emergency; an excellent housekeeper. And she lived only ten minutes away. Besides, if, as a condition of employment, Noah demanded someone who did not take patent medicines, he might go years doing his own cooking and cleaning. Still, it wouldn't exactly do for a physician's housekeeper to poison herself.

Tuneless singing wafted in from the kitchen, punctuated by the clank of dishes against the cast iron sink. The rampant use of patent medicines wasn't surprising, of course. There was rarely a newspaper page lacking an advertisement, often with testimonials, extolling some supposed miracle cure. Ayer's Cherry Pectoral, Mrs. Winslow's Soothing Syrup, Darby's Carminative, Godfrey's Cordial, Dover's Powder—the list was endless.

The hundreds who died each year and thousands more who developed addictions were never mentioned.

Here was one. Noah stopped at the advertisement for Orangeine, The Pocket Physician. On top was a picture of a beautiful young woman. *Miss Hope Ross*, the copy read, *the charming 'Little Rebel' from 'Secret Service' writes, 'Orangeine has never failed me and I have given it severe tests.'* The text went on to promise cures for "headache, hay fever, neuralgia, rheumatism, depression, exhaustion, seasickness, grip, etc." "No reaction," the ad boasted. "Perfectly harmless."

"Harmless?" Noah muttered aloud. "Hardly." The active ingredient in Orangeine was acetanilide. Acetanilide was an industrial chemical, used in dye-making. The substance would reduce fevers, yes, but it was also toxic. It could induce methemoglobinemia, causing the user's skin to turn not orange but blue. As such, it was not difficult to spot devotees of the concoction on the streets, men and women appearing to have just emerged from a deep freeze. The deleterious effects were not merely cosmetic. Excessive use could potentially lead to cardiac failure.

Noah downed the remainder of the coffee and closed the paper. Time to go. Clement Van Meter would be first, poor devil. As Noah stood, there was a knock at the door. Three hard raps in quick succession, and then, when the door did not instantly open, four more. After nine years in practice, he knew precisely what that meant. Not waiting for Mrs. Jensen to reappear, Noah went quickly to respond to the summons himself.

Mildred Anschutz, his neighbor from six houses down, was standing in the doorway. Although sunset had swept a chill through the Heights from across the harbor, she wore neither coat nor gloves. An errant strand of hair had come unpinned and lay curled between her shoulders. A large woman, middle-aged at thirty-six, her chest was heaving. She gave off a strong smell of rosewater.

"Come quickly, doctor. It's Willard." She shifted her hand to her midriff, thick as an ox's under a massive bosom. "He is terribly ill."

"Stomach pain?"

"Yes. He's doubled over."

Willard was her youngest, a rambunctious, perpetually cheerful five-year-old. Ever since he had received a ride on a pumper when he was three, the lad had taken to tearing through the neighborhood dressed in a miniature fireman's suit, single-handedly extinguishing huge blazes and performing heart-stopping rescues of adults, children, cats, and dogs. Noah had often watched the boy's cavorting with amusement and envy. Oliver would have been just his age.

He grabbed his bag off the front table, called to Mrs. Jensen that he was leaving, and was out the door. Mrs. Jensen would understand that he was responding to an emergency, although he would never use the word in the presence of a patient or member of a patient's family. A delicate touch was vital in such situations. One must act swiftly and decisively, but also create a sense of calm. Positive resolution was much more likely when patient, family, and physician kept their wits about them.

"Is it only stomach pain?" Noah asked. "Is there anything else?" He had to slow his pace to allow Mrs. Anschutz to keep up. The streetlights cast angled shadows on her face, rendering her features a grotesque mask.

"He's agitated. Perspiring dreadfully . . ." Her voice trailed off. Noah assumed there were other symptoms too embarrassing to mention.

"Is he choking?"

"No."

"And there is nothing else impeding his breathing?"

"No."

"What has Willard eaten today?"

She shook her head. "He hasn't been able to eat a thing."

"Yesterday?"

"Nothing unusual," she replied. Her fingertips went to her cheek. "I can't remember."

"Don't fret, Mrs. Anschutz," Noah told her. "It isn't important." It was, of course, but he would know what to ask when he saw the boy.

"You must make him well, doctor," the woman exclaimed with a break in her voice that was not caused by exertion. "Pug will be home soon. He hasn't seen Willard in almost two years."

"Pug" was Aldridge Anschutz, Colonel, United States Army. He had been away in the Philippines with Dewey but was due to arrive eight days hence, when the admiral's flotilla made its triumphant entry into New York Harbor.

"You mustn't worry, Mrs. Anschutz," Noah said. "We'll soon find the trouble. He will be well for his father."

And so he would. Noah had waited more than a year for this opportunity, since he had taken his rooms on Joralemon Street. The opportunity, although it embarrassed him to admit it, to prove himself.

Mildred Anschutz was neighborhood nobility, niece to Brooklyn's last mayor, Frederick Wurster. Although Mayor Wurster had lost his official rank twenty-one months before, when Brooklyn had become part of "Greater New York City" on New Year's Day 1898, he remained a power in area politics. Wurster was rumored to be considering a challenge to Governor Theodore Roosevelt, if "TR" opted to run for re-election instead of trying to wrest the presidency from McKinley. Although both the president and the governor were Republicans, TR had once said, "McKinley has no more backbone than a chocolate éclair."

From the first, however, Mrs. Anschutz had made little secret that she considered Noah too young, too inexperienced, too . . . unacceptable . . . to treat her or her five children. She, like most of the wealthy and the prominent, preferred Arnold Frias, he of the white mane and booming baritone, on the board of directors of four hospitals with a vast home on Columbia Heights facing the Manhattan skyline. Frias had recently returned from a holiday in Europe with a new International Benz automobile, the first of its kind in Brooklyn. The richer he got, the more appealing he became to the rich, who, by virtue of their position, assumed that wealth reflected talent and skill.

"Here, doctor." Mildred Anschutz turned into the entrance of her two-story, brick brownstone, a gift from Mayor Wurster to his niece and her family.

When she threw open the door, Noah was hit by a rush of noise. A tall boy, about sixteen with a shock of black hair, was standing halfway down the long center corridor. He was artificially erect, arms at his sides. The boy's back was to the door, and he was yelling at someone in the far room. "Sally, get upstairs and help your brother! Mother said!"

A blur in a blue dress shot across the hall. "I won't!" a girl's voice replied, shrill and indignant. "He's disgusting."

"He's sick," yelled the boy.

"You take care of him," the girl retorted. "Or get Hilda."

"Not me!" shouted yet another female from an unknown quarter. "I was with him before and he soiled the bed. When does Molly get back? She can do it."

"It's Molly's day off, featherhead," yelled the first girl. "Get Annie."

"Annie is a cook, not a maid," retorted the second.

"One of you get up there and take care of Willard," the boy snapped, a colonel's son trying to assume command. But siblings were not privates.

"The doctor will take of care of Willard," intoned Mrs. Anschutz. Her voice was clear and powerful, and the noise ceased instantly. The boy turned. Aldridge, the oldest. Two abashed girls, one about twelve, the other several years younger, appeared in the hall. From the far end, another boy appeared. Daniel, eight.

Aldridge pulled himself up even straighter. His skin was pale, almost white, and his eyes deep brown. "Mother, I was attempting—"

"Not now, Aldridge. I will speak with all of you later." She turned to Noah and motioned toward the stairs. Noah moved quickly toward the second floor, passing a series of photographs of a thick, powerful-looking man in uniform standing in front of a variety of exotic backdrops. In each, be there a pyramid or pagoda, Pug Anschutz stared straight ahead, as if preparing to bark an order to whomever might be viewing the image.

Mrs. Anschutz followed up the stairs, forced to grasp the banister and haul herself up to avoid losing momentum.

Noah formulated a list of tentative hypotheses as he climbed. Toxic reaction was most likely. While food poisoning remained the most likely possibility, animal or insect bite could not be ruled out. Even snakes were not unknown in Brooklyn. If a toxin was not responsible, appendicitis needed to be investigated, as did a bacillus infection.

When they reached the landing, Mrs. Anschutz, wagged her fingers in the general direction of a door to the left. "There," she panted.

In three quick steps, Noah was across the hall. The moment he saw Willard Anschutz, he knew his initial hypotheses had almost certainly been incorrect. The boy did not suffer from appendicitis. Nor food poisoning. Rather than a moaning, prostrate figure lying in pain on the bed, unable to rise, he saw a boy with a mop of black hair—a smaller version of his eldest brother—dressed only in a nightshirt, bent forward, moving from one side of the room to the other, more like a rabid animal than a child. His skin was so pale as to be almost translucent. Drenched in perspiration, the boy was experiencing tremors, mostly of the lower extremities, his tiny feet kicking out, as if to ward off unseen demons. A rancid odor permeated the room.

Willard turned toward the open door, eyes wide, tormented, but seemed to look through Noah rather than at him. Suddenly, he pitched forward on his knees, wailing and grabbing at his stomach. He leaned down until his forehead touched the floor.

Noah moved quickly to the boy, going to his knees as well. He held Willard's shoulder with his left hand, firmly but without pressure, and stroked the boy's sodden hair with his right. Perspiration dripped off the boy's nightshirt to the floor. Willard also exhibited extreme goose flesh and a runny nose. At Noah's touch, the boy began to quiver, but a moment later his agony seemed to abate. Willard straightened and turned to look over his shoulder, for the first time seeming to realize a stranger was in his room. His eyes, dark and brown, were watery, his pupils dilated.

Noah was stunned. The symptoms seemed classic. But in this house? With a boy of five? An Anschutz boy of five?

"Hello, Willard," he said softly. "Can you talk to me?" At the door, Mildred Anschutz stood horror-struck, hands to her mouth.

"I'm cold," the child replied.

"We'll soon fix that." Noah tried to warm Willard with his arms. His shirt sleeves were instantly soaked through. "Where is your pain?"

"Everywhere . . ."

"Anywhere special?"

Willard began to reach for his stomach when, suddenly, a new torment overtook him. He shook off Noah's arms and leapt to his feet. "Mommy," he yelled, and ran to the door.

"He's going to the water closet," Mrs. Anschutz said with anguish. "I must help him."

Mother and son dashed out of the room. Noah followed. He reached the door, just as Mrs. Anschutz was swinging it shut. "I must see the product," he told her.

Her mouth dropped open. "You may not! How dare you? Dr. Frias would never think to violate a patient's privacy so heinously."

The door slammed, followed almost immediately by the sounds of severe diarrhea.

Noah pondered forcing the door open. How could he tell her that he must check for blood or mucus? He reached for the handle, but before he could turn it, heard a rush of water. Mrs. Anschutz had apparently been stocked with modern conveniences. A modern jet-flush toilet had been installed to replace the old wash-outs that dominated in most of the neighborhood. When Noah heard the sound, he knew any further attempt at investigation would be pointless.

Moments later, the door opened. Mother and son emerged. After his bout, Willard was wan, his jaw slack, agitation replaced by exhaustion. Noah dropped into a squat and once more put his arm around the boy. Mrs. Anschutz stood by, shaking and grasping herself about the chest.

"Mrs. Anschutz," Noah told her. "I need some water. Could you fetch a glass?"

She began to protest but then nodded and moved toward the stairs. Activity would help her control her nerves and her absence would be helpful in restoring calm.

"Well, Willard," Noah said with a smile, "I understand you want to be a fireman when you are old enough. Or do you wish to join the army like your father?"

"Fireman," Willard replied weakly, looking up at the stranger. His dilated pupils forced him to squint.

"A wonderful occupation. Very exciting. We'll soon have you well enough to be back to your training. I watch you, you know. Very professional. Your uncle was fire commissioner before he was mayor, was he not? Do you want to man the hose or climb the ladder?"

Willard succeeded in forcing out a tiny grin. "Ladder."

"Why don't you let me play fireman now and carry you to the bedroom?" Without waiting for a reply, Noah lifted the boy in his arms. Willard shivered uncontrollably. Noah placed him on the bed and again stroked his hair.

"I would like to conduct an examination. It won't hurt, and it will help me determine what is making you sick. Once I do that, I will know how to make you feel better. Will that be all right?"

Noah withdrew a stethoscope from his bag. The instrument had been a gift from his father when Noah joined his practice. Willard's lungs seemed clear, although his respiration rate was high. The boy's liver palpated normally. He seemed to have a slight fever. His pulse was quickened and shallow. His abdomen was neither hard nor tender, but Noah detected hyperactive bowel sounds. Both pupils were dilated, and Willard said his vision was blurred. His ears were clear. Willard's lips were dry, as were his oral mucous membranes. His skin exhibited tenting—a lack of elastic response after a soft pinch on the back of the hand. Everything confirmed the initial, if incredible, diagnosis.

When he was done, Noah stroked Willard's hair. The worst, Noah hoped, was past, at least for the moment. His symptoms, however, would undoubtedly return, at least through the night.

Mrs. Anschutz had returned, holding a tall tumbler filled with water. Noah motioned for her to bring it to the bed.

"Do you think you could drink some water for me, Willard?"

The boy shook his head.

"Very well, Willard, but you have to promise to drink when you are able. It is important for firemen to drink lots of water."

The boy motioned for the glass. He took a few sips.

"Bravo," Noah said. "I'd like you to keep drinking whenever you can. Now I need to speak with your mother for a moment. Will you wait for me here?" Noah motioned for Mrs. Anschutz to join him at the far side of the room.

"What is it, doctor?" Mrs. Anschutz asked. Her voice contained the quaver that betrayed the fear of the unknown with which every physician is familiar. "Do you know what is responsible for his illness?" She seemed genuinely ignorant of the cause.

Noah proceeded with caution. "Willard's symptoms seem to point to a toxic reaction. With children, something they have eaten is generally the culprit. Did he partake of oysters, by some chance?"

She shook her head.

"Any meat that was not shared by your family?"

Once again, as expected, the answer was no.

"Has he vomited or just experienced diarrhea?"

"Only the second."

"How long has Willard exhibited these symptoms?"

"He was perfectly fine yesterday afternoon, then began feeling a bit ill last night. He said he had trouble sleeping, but that is not unusual for Willard." She forced a tiny smile. "He has so much energy. This morning he began to feel a bit of stomach pain, although not terribly severe."

"Did you give him any medicine?"

"Bismosal. I always give it to the children for stomach upset."

Bismosal was a patent medicine, bright pink in color, a suspension of bismuth subsalicylate, relatively insoluble and, unlike many patent medicines, had low toxicity. It was generally used for treating infant cholera, but also seemed to provide some relief from gastritis.

"Does Dr. Frias know you treat your children with Bismosal?"

"Certainly. Dr. Frias recommended it. Not all patent medicines are harmful, doctor."

"Of course not. Did it work?"

"It seemed to make him feel better, yes. The pain returned in the afternoon, however, but much more severely. I gave him another spoonful of Bismosal, but Willard continued to deteriorate until . . . until I came for you."

"Has he been given any other medication than Bismosal?"

Mrs. Anschutz shook her head.

"Why did you not call Dr. Frias?"

Mrs. Anschutz dropped her arms and clasped her hands in front of her, in the manner of a schoolgirl giving a recitation. "As I said, his condition did not become radically worse until late afternoon." Her voice had chilled. "When I called Dr. Frias, I was told he had an important personal engagement and could not be reached. Even a physician is allowed a private life, Dr. Whitestone."

"Of course."

"When I saw that Willard needed immediate attention, I presumed to ask you. I chose to fetch you myself because I feared if I sent Aldridge, you might not come."

"Of course I would have come," Noah replied. He had wondered why she had left Willard's side. "I am flattered that you summoned me. One last question. Has Willard had any recent illnesses?"

"He had a cough and low fever some weeks ago."

"Was he given medication then?"

Mrs. Anschutz nodded. "Dr. Frias prescribed some tablets."

"What sort of tablets?"

"Dr. Frias did not say. He told me they would cure Willard's illness and they did. He was markedly improved after three days and has been in superb health since. In even better spirits than usual."

"Until today?"

She nodded.

"And he stopped taking medication . . ."

"Two weeks ago."

"And you are certain that, other than Bismosal, he has not taken anything more recently?"

"My powers of recollection are uninhibited, doctor."

"Very well, Mrs. Anschutz. I feel certain I can alleviate your son's symptoms, at least temporarily, although I would ask you to bring him to my offices tomorrow. I would like my father to have a look at him."

"Very well, doctor," she replied evenly. Noah suspected, when tomorrow arrived, she would take the boy to Frias instead.

"Ordinarily, I would suggest having Willard admitted to the hospital," Noah said. A look of alarm returned to Mildred Anschutz's face. "As a precaution only," he added hastily. "I suspect a short-term illness that will abate significantly in the next forty-eight hours. With the night staff, however, Willard would not receive any better attention than he could get here at home. And, if he needs attention at any time during the night, come to my door.

"For the present, I am going to give him two drops of laudanum. Laudanum is tincture of opium, as I am certain you are aware. I would generally not administer an opiate to a child of Willard's age, but dehydration presents the biggest immediate risk and laudanum will control his diarrhea. It will also ease the cramping and allow him to sleep. You may rest assured that the dose is far too small to do him any harm."

Noah removed the small, dark bottle from his bag. He used a medicine dropper to place the two drops of laudanum into a spoon. He put his free hand to Willard's back to help him sit up and take the medicine. Within minutes, the boy's symptoms began to subside. Soon afterward, he appeared to be resting comfortably.

Noah paused, studying Mildred Anschutz. He should not ask, he knew. Most physicians would leave matters as they were. Let the doctor who caused the problem solve the problem. What was more, this woman had no trust in him, despite her momentary gratitude. But Noah refused to be that sort of physician. There was one diagnosis that fit the symptoms precisely, and he would pursue it.

"Mrs. Anschutz," he inquired, trying to sound matter-of-fact, "might there by some chance be morphia anywhere in the house?"

Her reaction was predictable. She drew herself up to her considerable height and stuck out her chin as if it were weapon. "Certainly not! We are not Chinamen or dope fiends in my home. What would possess you to ask such a question?"

"I am not suggesting that the morphia is here for any nefarious purpose," he assured her. "Perhaps in a patent medicine . . ."

"I told you, no," she insisted.

"I can assure you, Mrs. Anschutz, my motive is simply to eliminate all potential sources of Willard's condition so that we may discover what is actually causing his distress. The tablets that Dr. Frias prescribed. Might you have any left?"

"I don't see why you are interested in medicine Willard has not taken for two weeks."

Why indeed? "The more I know about Willard's history, the more likely I am to find an effective treatment," he offered.

Mrs. Anschutz glowered but, after another glance at her son, left the room. Returning soon after, she held a small, pewter-clasped box with an "A" set in red stones on the top. Inside were about ten small, blue tablets. Noah was certain he had never encountered them before, but as each drug company fabricated its own wares, this was not unusual.

"Might I have one?"

Grudgingly, she extended the case. Noah asked for an envelope, which Mrs. Anschutz fetched, small and cream colored with the omnipresent "A" emblazoned on the back flap. Noah removed a tablet, dropped it into the envelope, and tucked the envelope in his vest pocket.

He was relieved to see that Willard was nearly asleep. Every moment his wracked body could rest would help. "I must make two other calls," he said. "Willard will probably rouse in about two hours, and I will be back no later than shortly after that."

Mrs. Anschutz shook her head fiercely. "You cannot leave. You must stay with Willard. I insist, doctor. If he awakens sooner and his symptoms have returned, I will be at wit's end."

"I can't, Mrs. Anschutz, as much as I would like to. My other two patients are equally acute. One is terminally ill. Both are expecting me. I administered the laudanum to calm Willard in my absence."

Mrs. Anschutz began to protest further, when a young, lank, red-haired woman appeared in the doorway. "I'm back, ma'am."

"And high time, too," snapped Mrs. Anschutz. She then ordered the girl, whom she called Molly, to change clothes immediately.

"Perhaps Molly can sit with Willard until I return," Noah offered, after the girl had hurried off.

"Molly is a maid, not a physician, doctor. You must stay. Get word to your other patients that you are responding to an emergency."

"I told you, Mrs. Anschutz, I will be here before Willard's symptoms return." Noah moved to the bedroom door. "When he awakens, try to persuade him to drink. Small sips, but as much as he can." He took a glance back at Willard. The boy was sleeping peacefully. Then, before Mildred Anschutz could renew her protests, he took his leave.

TWO

C lement Van Meter was a seventy-year-old former mate on a schooner. He had contracted cancer of the colon but, after a lifetime of incompetent care by alcoholic ships' doctors, had not sought treatment until a bowel resection had ceased to be feasible. He had gone comatose two days before. He might linger for days or be dead in hours.

The Van Meters lived in a two-room flat on Pineapple Street, about a ten-minute walk. Noah stepped into a home filled with old furniture, worn carpets, and the slightly musty smell that seemed to settle around the aging like a shroud. A model of a four-masted schooner sat on the mantle. Some of the rigging on the mainmast had come undone and lay hanging over the deck.

Hermione Van Meter, a tiny, desiccated creature, latched on to Noah. "Thank you, doctor. Thank you so much for coming." She dragged him toward the bedroom. Her bony fingers felt like twigs on Noah's wrist.

"You got here just in time. I saw his eyelids flutter. Twice. I think he might be waking up."

Noah thought the prospect unlikely. Loved ones of the terminally ill often cling to the hope that the mere presence of a doctor might prompt a miraculous abatement of symptoms.

"Let's go and see, Hermione." One look at the husk of a once-vibrant seaman, the rhythm of the short rise and fall of Clement Van Meter's emaciated chest, told Noah that there would be no miracle here. "I'll sit with him for a bit," Noah told her, pulling a rickety slat-backed chair to the bedside. "Perhaps it will happen again."

Hermione Van Meter sat on the other side of the bed. She reached out and took her husband's hand. "Is there something you can give him, doctor? So that he might wake up sooner, I mean?" She had endured a half century of extended absences of long sea voyages, sometimes two years at a time, but the prospect of the absence being permanent was unendurable.

"Nothing right now, Hermione. Let's just see how he does."

"All right, doctor," she replied, trying to force a smile to show she was grateful for the visit.

They sat in silence for some moments, Hermione Van Meter stroking her husband's hand. "Clement was going to buy a boat after he stopped sailing. For us to live on, I mean. He was so used to the water, he couldn't get to sleep here. But I was used to the land and said no. Perhaps I shouldn't have been so selfish."

"Nonsense, Hermione. Clement only wanted for your happiness. I'm certain he loved the home you made for him."

She nodded, unconvinced, and they lapsed once more into silence. Hermione Van Meter did not move her gaze from her husband. Noah was certain that, even now, she still saw him as the strapping young merchantman that she had married five decades before.

After about thirty minutes, Noah told her he must leave. "Perhaps I can fetch a pastor." The Van Meters were Lutheran. "I would like you to have company."

She shook her head.

"Any friends I might ask?"

"No, thank you, doctor," she replied with resignation and hopelessness. "I'd like to just be with Clement. Fifty years, but we had such little time, really."

Noah nodded and stood to leave. Mrs. Van Meter reached for her purse on the table at the side of the bed. "I suppose I should pay you now," she said softly.

"I never accept payment in the evenings, Mrs. Van Meter. I'll prepare a proper invoice and have it sent over." He would not, of course. Funeral expenses would come close to breaking her as it was.

She paused for a moment, her fingers on the snap of the purse. Then she replaced it on the table. "Thank you, Dr. Whitestone."

"You're very welcome, Hermione." He took her hand and wished her well as she showed him out, frail and very old, alone with her dying husband.

Medicine taught to avoid personal involvement. Treat with the head and not the heart. Slip into the reverse, and patients suffered. But how could he not feel for Hermione Van Meter? Doomed to pass her remaining years in a two-room flat, abandoned by her husband, her neighbors, even by life itself. What was worse: death or loneliness? Noah had no shortage of opportunity to observe the former, but the latter he had known all too well. Isobel. Oliver. There had been many days when he was convinced death could not be worse. What about now? Would his loneliness finally ameliorate with Maribeth?

Noah arrived at a tenement on Montague Street, the home of his second patient, Thea Harpin, an aging widow with Bright's disease. While she was in no immediate danger, her kidneys were certain to eventually fail, leaving her with the same prognosis as Clement Van Meter. Her rooms, on the second floor, were as crowded as Van Meter's had been empty. Five other widows had crammed their way in to keep vigil, partly in triumph that they would live while their acquaintance would die, partly in despair that one of them would be the next to be chosen in this devilish tontine.

The widow Harpin herself was little changed. But with six women in one room, he was forced not only see to his patient but also to reply to a plethora of inquiries about the various ailments of the others. Then there were the cakes he had to sample and the inquiries as to his marital situation to which he was forced to respond. When the assembled widows learned that he was now betrothed, disappointment filled the room. Various nieces and granddaughters—all beautiful, bright, and vivacious—would now be forced to locate another good catch. With it all, there was scant a moment to reflect on Hermione Van Meter. Or himself. In truth, Noah loved the busiest days. Hard on the body, but easy on the spirit.

By the time he could extricate himself, it was nearly nine. He did not return to the Anschutz home until about a quarter after. Three hours. The laudanum he had given Willard would have largely worn off. Noah hoped that the symptoms would not yet have returned in full force. He wasn't sure what he would do—he was reluctant to administer laudanum twice to a child so young—but controlling the symptoms was most urgent until, if necessary, he could insist that Willard be admitted to the hospital in the morning.

He knocked lightly on the door. The maid answered almost immediately. Molly was a thin, fragile girl, her face spattered with freckles. She seemed to wear a look of perpetual anxiety, no doubt a result of having Mildred Anschutz as her employer. Her lips began to quiver, as if she was trying to force herself to say something, when Mrs. Anschutz stepped through a doorway to the left.

Noah expected to be chastised for his tardiness by an angry and imperious mother. Instead, Mrs. Anschutz seemed surprisingly at ease.

"Come in, doctor." She even smiled at him.

"Willard is well?" Perhaps the boy had been so exhausted by his symptoms that he remained quiescent.

"He's still sleeping. Quite peacefully," Mrs. Anschutz replied. "When I looked in on him a few minutes ago, he did not even notice when I felt his forehead."

"I am pleased to hear that, Mrs. Anschutz. Perhaps his crisis is past." Could it be? So soon? Had his diagnosis been incorrect after all? "I should look in on him for a moment in any event."

"Of course, doctor. Whatever you say."

As they mounted the stairs, Mrs. Anschutz cast Noah an abashed glance. She paused on the second step. "You know, Dr. Whitestone, I must confess that I came to you with some trepidation. Dr. Frias has cared for this family since Aldridge was born. He often says that experience makes the best doctors. But I can now see that some of our younger physicians are more than competent."

Despite himself, Noah was flattered. "Thank you for saying so, Mrs. Anschutz. I was gratified to be able to bring Willard some relief. I am very fond of him. He reminds me of . . . myself, when I was a boy."

"Well, you should visit then. Willard is a great joy. Such spirit."

"Thank you. I will."

They made their way up the stairs. This time, Noah modulated his pace to allow Mrs. Anschutz to keep up with him. When they reached the landing, Noah didn't wait, but moved to the door of Willard's bedroom.

He turned the switch to the electric light. Willard was under the covers, lying on his back, mouth agape. His skin was sallow and pasty and his breathing labored and shallow.

Noah ran to the bed. He had only moments, perhaps seconds. Noah grabbed him by both arms and shook him, first gently, then with ferocity. The child didn't rouse. Noah threw back the covers, pulled up the boy's nightshirt, and dug the knuckle of his middle finger into his solar plexus. There was no effect.

Noah lifted Willard's eyelid. Acute miosis—constriction of the pupil.

"Get me cold water!" he yelled to the boy's mother, who stood stunned in the doorway. Willard's breathing had almost ceased. If Noah could not induce its return, the boy's brain would begin to asphyxiate—if it had not done so already.

Mrs. Anschutz stuck her head into the hall and screamed for Molly to bring water. Noah continued to shake Willard, tried to stand him up, slap him on the cheeks, anything to induce motor function. Finally, Molly appeared with a pitcher of cold water and a cloth. Eschewing the cloth, Noah began to douse the boy's face. No response. He poured some on the child's privates. Nothing.

Don't die, he thought. Don't die. A vision flashed before him. Another occasion on which he had been helpless. A woman. In childbirth. Hemorrhaging. In shock. Don't die. Beautiful. Fading. The baby, Oliver, already dead. Don't die. *Don't die.*

Isobel. His wife. *Don't die.*

But she had.

And so did Willard Anschutz.

THREE

I t wasn't possible. Noah had never been more certain of anything. He could not have been responsible for the boy's death. Willard Anschutz could not have perished from two drops of laudanum. Not after three hours. Not at all. Two drops of laudanum would not have killed a one-year-old let alone a five-year-old. There were any number of cases, certainly, of children dying from laudanum poisoning, but the doses had been exponentially greater.

Noah stared up at the ceiling over his bed. Over and over, he considered every moment he had spent with the child, reviewed each symptom. Had he blundered, misinterpreted some sign, failed to note an item of significance, made a hasty assumption? He could think of nothing. He had taken every precaution, followed proper procedure to the letter.

Why then could he not escape the face of the dead child dancing against the plaster? There were moments that the shimmering image was so real, it seemed the boy was about to speak. As the night had lengthened but stubbornly refused to yield to morning, Willard's features had begun to meld into Isobel's.

Two sets of dark eyes, one holding the innocence of youth, the other the innocence of trust. Whose were which? He had fixed Isobel's face in his memory, immutable and eternal, yet suddenly he could not seem to remember her. Was this to be his punishment for the dead child?

Noah rose from the bed, his joints stiff, his eyelids aching. For a moment, he was light-headed, forced to grasp the bedpost until the feeling passed. When he regained his equilibrium, he walked to the door and turned the switch. The lightbulbs in the ceiling fixture glowed dimly, suffusing the bedroom in artificial twilight. The clock on the side table showed 4 o'clock. Noah padded to the chest of drawers at the wall opposite his bed and removed the framed photograph that sat alone on a lace doily. The photograph that would be guiltily consigned to a drawer, secreted under a sheaf of papers or a stack of appointment books after he was married to Maribeth.

He held the pewter frame delicately in his hands, as if too tight a grip might cause the memories that it held to slip away. Yes, of course. There she was. Isobel. He had not forgotten at all. Beautiful, ethereal, in her high lace collar, her rich chestnut hair piled full and luxurious, framing the face that he would love forever. The face that would no longer age.

One day, he would hold this photograph and be an old man looking at a young woman. Wondering how she would have looked had she lived. Was Mildred Anschutz at that moment staring at a photograph of her son, wondering the same? Would she spend her remaining days seeing a boy perpetually five years old? Had he created that grisly bond between them when he allowed Willard to die?

But he had not allowed Willard to die.

Had he?

Mrs. Anschutz knew that her son was lost even as Noah did. She had gone ashen, and for a moment, he thought she would faint. But Pug Anschutz's wife does not swoon. Instead, she rushed to the bed, leaned down, and held one hand to either side of her son's face. Then she began to rock slowly. A low moan escaped her, eerie, as if it emanated from all corners of the room at once.

Noah had stepped away, but he wanted to examine the boy, even then, to try to determine what had caused his death. He ached to request permission for an autopsy but knew that was out of the question. When Mrs. Anschutz finally looked up, he had instead said how sorry he was. He offered to summon a clergyman, notify the authorities, or see to the arrangements of having Willard's body removed to a mortician's. Anything that Mrs. Anschutz thought might be of help.

But she had just shaken her head, slowly, mechanically, as if physical movement had become disengaged from her core. She would see to everything, she said in a monotone. She had then softly asked Noah to leave.

He walked past Willard's siblings and Molly, the maid, without a word. She was distraught, sobbing into a crumpled handkerchief. Noah considered for a moment whether to try to comfort the wretched young woman, but unwelcome as he now was, he simply had left her in the hall.

Noah replaced the picture frame on his dresser and picked up the envelope that was laying next it. He removed the blue pill and held it between his thumb and forefinger. Could this possibly have any bearing on the boy's death? It seemed impossible. He wasn't even certain why he'd asked for it. Some perverse curiosity about Frias, most likely. But Mildred Anschutz hadn't been deceiving him when she claimed that her son had not taken the medication for two weeks. Of that Noah was convinced. Some people could lie and some could not. After a lifetime of feeling license to say what she pleased to whom she pleased, Mildred Anschutz would never have had need to cultivate such as subtle skill as mendacity.

Yet, something had killed Willard Anschutz. He replaced the tablet in the envelope and left it on the dresser. He padded back across the room and once more lay in bed. He would rest. Sleep was a lost cause.

FOUR

DAY 2. THURSDAY, 9/21—7:30 A.M.

Father, a patient died in my care last night. A child. His mother believes I am responsible for his death."

Abel Whitestone ran his forefinger around the diaphragm of his stethoscope, then placed the end in his vest pocket. He was a large man with small, delicate hands. Lines had given way to pouches along his jaw and under his eyes. He reached up and patted Noah softly on the cheek. "Come into the office."

It was just after seven. Even at fifty-five, Abel arrived early every morning to tidy up, complete leftover paperwork, read medical journals, and prepare the office for the daily onslaught. Noah had tried to persuade his father to sleep an extra hour, but Abel would have none of it. Noah had encountered him in one of the examining rooms, setting bandages, sheets, and instruments in their proper places.

Father and son made their way to the rear. The practice had been here on Adams Street for two decades. Abel had leased office space on the first floor until nine years ago, when Noah announced his intention to enter medical school at New York University in Manhattan. Abel then scraped together the money to purchase the two-story building. Abel, Elspeth, and Noah's sister, Agnes, had moved into the top floor and bottom floor rear, leaving the offices on the street level front. By the time Noah finished school, Agnes had married and moved to Milwaukee. Abel then expanded the offices to the entire first floor. When he extended an invitation to join the practice, Noah had accepted instantly.

Where Noah's private office was bright and modern, Abel's was wood-paneled and dark. It was filled with photographs, letters of appreciation, and plaques from religious and civic organizations, expressing gratitude for some service that Dr. Whitestone had performed in the community. Nothing was more revealing of a doctor's character than his reputation among his patients. Any greed, incompetence, lack of commitment, or professional vanity will soon surface in one who treats his fellows when they are afraid and vulnerable. Abel Whitestone was adored; invited to innumerable weddings and christenings, he had been made godfather to more neighborhood children than Noah could count.

Noah sat in a leather chair opposite the desk, a location from which countless patients over the years had heard that they were pregnant, or tubercular, or in fine health, or dying. Here they had confided, asked favors, or requested an extension on their arrears. This chair had held millionaires, community leaders, the indigent, and thieves. Many had sat and merely sought advice. As now Noah did.

Abel walked in a moment later, letting his hand linger on his son's shoulder as he passed. He settled heavily into the wing chair behind the desk and polished his spectacles with a small handkerchief he removed from a vest pocket. With his glasses off, Abel's eyes appeared sleepy, slightly lacking in focus. Old.

"All right, son. Tell me about your patient."

Noah recited the case history in full, from the first summons by Mildred Anschutz to Willard's death. He restricted himself to a recitation of the symptoms and did not propose a diagnosis. As he spoke, his father sat leaned against one arm of the chair, tugging at his lower lip, looking off to the side. When Noah had finished, Abel sat back in his chair. He never spoke in haste, appearing to give due consideration to even the most obvious question.

"A tragedy," Abel said with a deep sigh. "There is nothing worse than the death of a child." He paused to once again polish his spectacles. "What will you enter on the death certificate?"

"Respiratory failure."

"Seems vague." Abel leaned even farther back, but eyed Noah in a way that had made him uncomfortable since he was eight.

"Should I enter something specific, even if I'm not totally certain?"

"You're not totally certain?"

"How could I be?"

Abel nodded slowly, as if reviewing the diagnosis, but instead he said, "The boy's mother blames you for his death . . ."

"She was distraught. It's natural."

"Perhaps. But do you share her assessment?"

"No. I don't think so." Noah rubbed his forefinger across his thumb. "I'm not sure."

"Not sure if he died from the laudanum or not sure if you are responsible?"

"I can't see how he could have died from the laudanum."

"Then you don't. It was something out of your control. What more do you believe you could have done?"

"Saved him."

"Ah, yes. And how could you have done that?"

"I'm not sure of that either."

"Most men, Noah, if they're worth anything, are responsible for something in their lives. We doctors happen to be responsible for something precious. We are responsible for people's lives. And their health. But the nature of the responsibility doesn't mean we cease being human. We all have our failures. It's painful. And inevitable. Only God is omnipotent. But you know all this. You've lost patients before."

"This seems different."

"Why? Because the Anschutz boy was five?"

Noah didn't reply. From anyone else, he would have been furious.

"Willard Anschutz was not your son, Noah."

His son. For five years, the most bleak of phrases.

Abel heaved out a breath. "Noah, you were not to blame for Isobel's death. Or the baby's. Isobel hemorrhaged. Thousands of women each year die in childbirth. Dear Isobel was one of them. And you were only assisting. Not even the primary physician. A tragedy. A horrible tragedy. But tragedy does not mean culpability."

"I was too slow." The words came out in a whisper.

"You could have been Mercury himself and still not have stopped the bleeding."

"I was too slow," Noah repeated. "Isobel's parents were correct."

"How? How could they have been correct? They aren't doctors. They weren't even in the room. Nor, I might add, was Mildred Anschutz."

"It doesn't matter. They believe my negligence contributed to the death of their daughter. That *I* shouldn't have even been in the room. And they were correct."

Abel shook his head. They had been over this hundreds of times. There were no words left.

"How is Clement Van Meter?" he asked instead.

"He continues to hang on. The man has astounding will. If only he had come to us sooner."

"He's been stubborn for thirty years. Whenever I knew he was in port, I tried to get him to let me take a look at him. Went to his house any number of times. He laughed at me. Thought planning for old age was a joke. 'Aw, doc,' he'd say, 'I'm gonna die at sea. Eaten by sharks, most likely. Or washed overboard in a storm. Ain't no cure for that.' Then he'd throw his arm around my shoulders . . . strong as a plow horse . . . and lead me out the door. 'Now you go and tend to all the shore folk who're gonna die in their beds.' The last thing he figured was that he would be one of them, rotting away, dying by inches."

"I never knew him like that."

"A person just couldn't help liking Clement." Abel paused. "So, Noah? Should I feel guilt? For not convincing Clement to take better care of himself."

"Of course not. Clement Van Meter was a grown man. There was nothing more you could have done."

"I don't see the difference."

"Maybe there isn't any. I don't know," Noah exclaimed. "Don't you feel guilt anyway, father? See their faces? The patients who have died in your care?"

Abel looked off over Noah's shoulder. "Do you remember Rosemary Mangino?"

"From Henry Street? The funny old woman who talked to herself? Of course."

"She had a daughter. Born almost a year to the day after you."

"I didn't even know she ever had a husband."

"Oh yes. A drunk. Ran off after the little girl was born. In any event, the doctor who delivered Rosemary's daughter botched the job. Forceps delivery. He was young and made a mistake. The little girl's skull was compressed. Viola they called her. Grew up to be an idiot, poor thing. Could barely feed or dress herself. But a sweeter or more gentle child never graced God's earth. Viola was always laughing and making other people laugh. Not in a bad way, mind you. It was simply that she was so happy, so easy to please, that people could not help but be happy around her.

"But she was always sickly, of course. Seemed not a month went by when either her breathing or her digestion or something else wasn't out of whack. One day, her respiration went bad. Non-tubercular but clearly degenerative. Everyone knew she was going to die, even her mother. Everyone except me, that is. I decided I was going to save her. I tried everything. Medication, inhalers . . . I read that a tribe in the Amazon ate some mixture of ground-up plants to cure respiratory ailments, so I even tried that. She steadily worsened, of course. I became more determined. At the end, I was spending more time at Viola's house than here. None of it mattered. The little girl died. Six years old."

"I'm so sorry, father. Why did you never tell me this before?"

"Why would I?" Abel heaved a sigh. "I was disconsolate. I even considered giving up medicine. Thought I could never treat patients in the same way again."

"But you did."

"Yes. It took three months, but I did. As will you. And, yes, I still see Viola Mangino's face. Every day."

Abel placed his elbows on the arms of his chair, letting his fingertips fall together just under his chin. "So what will you do now?"

"I thought I might speak with Alan."

"If that will make you feel better. You're seeing him at dinner tonight, are you not?"

"I thought perhaps I would see him this morning. At the hospital."

Abel sat straighter in his chair. "You suspect Arnold had some role in the boy's death?"

"The boy almost certainly died of morphia toxicity. You know that as well as I, father. If it wasn't the laudanum, it must have been something else. Perhaps something Dr. Frias prescribed."

"That is a leap, not a conclusion. I advise you to leave the matter as it is. No one will blame you for the boy's death. Even his mother will come to see that you acted appropriately."

"I can't leave it, father. I have to at least try to find the truth."

"Why? The boy cannot come back. It will make no difference."

"I'm not sure. Maybe I need to prove to myself that it wasn't my fault. Maybe I have to find a way not to feel Mildred Anschutz looking at me the way Isobel's parents did. I just know that I need to. Can you spare me this morning?"

Abel shook his head in resignation. "You never could be dissuaded when you were determined to do something. I suppose that's why you're such a good doctor." He thought for a moment. "I suppose I can ask Pierre Gaspard to help out. He lives only three blocks away, and he loathes retirement. Did you plan on making a condolence call?"

"I thought I should wait until tomorrow. Seeing how Mrs. Anschutz feels."

"Probably wise. Let me go with you."

"No, father. I should do it alone." Noah stood to leave. "Have you forgiven yourself, father? For Viola Mangino? Have you come to accept that it was not your fault?"

"Her dying? Yes, I have."

"No. I meant the forceps delivery."

"Oh, you thought . . . no, Noah. I didn't perform the delivery."

"But . . ."

"Oh no, son. That wasn't me. Arnold Frias delivered Viola Mangino."

FIVE

The pediatric ward was the pride of the sprawling Brooklyn Hospital. Endowed by the dowagers of the Ladies' League, the vast, high-ceilinged room was on the third floor, facing south, so the children could enjoy a light and airy environment. Twenty-four beds lined the walls, twelve on each side, with ample space between. The floors were polished tile, the windows large, and the walls painted a bright off-white. The room smelled of disinfectant and talc. Four nurses were on duty, either sitting at bedside or scurrying between patients.

Each of the beds was occupied. Although the room held both boys and girls, curtains had been set between the beds and could be pulled shut for privacy. The patients ranged in age from two or three to early teens. Some were talking to one another, a few others were attended by visitors sitting in chairs pulled next to the beds, but most of them lay quietly alone. The dowagers could not provide caring relatives, so many children of the poor would receive no visitors for their entire stay. Some would be abandoned permanently by families who could not bear the burden of a convalescing child, then sent to orphanages when they were well enough to be discharged. There, most would languish and molder. Many would die.

Noah stepped inside through the swinging double doors to the sound of dry coughing. Respiratory ailments abounded. More children died from non-tubercular pulmonary infection than from any other cause. He could see just from tone, color, and posture that at least six of the children were gravely ill. Others seemed to be convalescing well. A boy, one of the older patients, was sitting up in bed reading a battered copy of *Huckleberry Finn*.

Alan De Kuyper stood at a bed at the far end of the ward with four younger doctors, three men and a woman. Morning rounds. He was attending a scrawny, pallid, twitchy boy of six or seven. De Kuyper was in his early thirties, a gangly man with robin's-egg-blue eyes, an unlined face, and hair gone prematurely gray. He grinned when he saw Noah walking his way.

"Couldn't wait until tonight to see me?" he asked, then turned his attention back to his patient. "All right, Anson. We're going to play a game. You're going to tell these doctors what's bothering you, and they're going to try to guess what's making you sick."

"I don' wanna play no game," the boy replied.

"No game? Do you want breakfast instead?"

"Not hungry."

"Would you like to get up and play, then?"

"Too tired."

De Kuyper continued to question the boy, eliciting that he suffered from headaches, bad teeth, and that he had difficulty holding things or walking because of weakness in his hands and feet. "Well, Anson," he said, finally. "I'm sorry you won't play with us. We'll leave you alone now."

"Yeah," grunted the boy.

De Kuyper led the doctors to the aisle, out of earshot of the patient. "Well?" he asked.

None of the four responded.

"Review the symptoms. Irritability, hyperactivity, fatigue, loss of appetite, weakness in the extremities, excessive tooth decay . . ."

Still nothing.

De Kuyper sighed deeply. "I'll give you a hint." He bunched his fingers and poked them back and forth toward his open mouth. The four glanced about at one another, but none spoke.

He rolled his eyes heavenward. "Children are known to put anything and everything into their mouths, are they not?"

"I've got it," the woman said, raising her hand as if she were still in class. She was reedy and dark, in her early twenties. "Lead toxicity."

"Very *good*, Dr. Bertelli. And the treatment?"

"Remove the source of the problem."

"Correct," De Kuyper replied. "Easier said than done though. But we'll have a talk with the boy's parents and tell them to repaint their apartment and keep a cleaner house. I'm certain they will run right off and do so."

He excused himself and gestured to Noah to walk to the end of the ward.

"Dolts," he muttered. "Anyone can get into medical school these days."

"They can't be that bad," Noah replied.

"Not like you, old man." De Kuyper clapped Noah on the shoulder. "Actually, they just started. Bertelli's the best. One of the others will be all right, another fair. As for the fourth . . . let's just hope he decides to give up medicine and become a banker."

"Your brother Jamie is a banker."

"Precisely. So, what brings you to my atelier?"

Noah described Willard Anschutz's symptoms, both during his initial visit with the boy and then immediately before he died.

"I'm sorry, old man. Sounds ghastly. My God, I hate to lose patients. It's as if every child is entitled to a life and when one dies, I've denied it to them. Can't dwell on it though. If I did, I'd have to leave the profession."

Noah nodded in mock agreement. This from a man Noah had once found weeping in a closet when one of his patients died of a seizure. "The mother thinks I'm responsible," he said.

"From two drops of laudanum. Ridiculous."

"I thought so, too. But what else could have done it?"

"Was the boy taking patent medicines?"

"I asked and was told categorically by his mother he wasn't. It's a good family. Anschutz. Wurster's niece. The father's an army officer, off slaughtering Filipinos. But I'm convinced the mother was telling the truth."

"Very well. Let's look elsewhere then. You say both pupils were dilated when you first observed the boy?"

"Yes."

"That would eliminate a brain tumor. Could be a strain of encephalitis, I suppose, although the set of symptoms on your first visit work against it. Might be something new. We live near the waterfront, after all. Perhaps an unknown bacillus has been brought ashore from Africa or Asia. One which mimics morphia and only affects the young. You should ask Jacobi."

Jacobi, the oracle. Alan's mentor. In 1861, he had become the first man in America to establish pediatrics as a separate discipline.

"I thought Jacobi doesn't see anybody."

"An exaggeration. Most stories about Jacobi are. He's sarcastic, domineering, a socialist, and a Jew. A man to emulate, except for the Jew part. He's still a revolutionary under the surface, I expect. Although he never talks about it, you know of course that he came to America as a stowaway on a freighter after he escaped from prison in Germany? He was under a death sentence for radical activities."

"Yes. I believe you have mentioned that."

Alan chuckled. "Yes, I suppose I have. In any event, he has no patience for fools or anyone who would waste his time, another of his traits I admire. But he'll be happy to see you if I make an introduction."

"I'd be grateful. He's still at Columbia?"

"Absolutely. Still teaching. At seventy. Amazing fellow. If there is an obscure ailment from which the Anschutz boy died, Jacobi will know it."

Noah reached into his vest and removed the envelope. He held it open to show Alan the small, blue tablet. "Have you ever seen one of these before?"

De Kuyper shook his head. "That doesn't mean much, of course. There are thousands of different medications floating about. The boy was taking these?"

"His mother claimed he had stopped two weeks ago."

"Are they a morphiate?"

"The mother assures me they are not."

"But you suspect otherwise. Quite right. Who prescribed them?"

"Frias."

"Ah! Dr. Dollars." He gestured toward the pill. "Let me have this tested for you."

"I'd like to do it myself."

"Of course. The laboratory will be empty this time of day. Have you used Herold's *Manual of Legal Medicine?*"

"No."

"There's a copy on the front shelf. It's outstanding. If you're going to run a test, follow Herold's methodology." Alan put a finger to his chin. "And why don't I fetch you tonight? You shouldn't be forced to enter the lion's den alone. I'll be by at 6:30."

"I hope eventually I won't need an honor guard to go to your parents' house."

"Give it twenty years." Alan paused. "However the test comes out, you didn't have anything to do with the boy's death."

"How can you be so sure?"

"I wouldn't introduce my sister to an imbecile."

"I'm greatly relieved." When Noah turned to leave, a man who had been sitting at the bedside of a young boy rose to leave as well. Noah held the door as the man passed through. He was sharp-featured and light-haired, in his mid-twenties, clean-shaven, and wearing wire-frame spectacles that framed a prominent, aquiline nose. Behind the lenses lay a pair of quick, attentive eyes. He nodded in thanks but eyed Noah strangely, as if Noah were an acquaintance that he could not quite place.

The light-haired man paused after he walked by, holding the door open and gazing back into the ward. He allowed Noah to pass him and make his way down the hall. As Noah reached the staircase, he looked back, but the man was gone.

SIX

The laboratory was in the basement, accessible only through a staircase at the rear of the lobby. As Noah walked toward it, he heard his name called.

He turned to see a tall, bearded man, wide as a doorway, snowy hair peaked like the back of Melville's whale. A gold watch chain lay across his mountainous abdomen like a garland.

Frias. Walking with him was another man whom Noah did not know, also broad and bearded, but shorter.

Arnold Frias was on him in three steps, speaking before Noah could open his mouth. "Whitestone! I'm pleased to have run into you." He managed to find a deft balance between bonhomie and condolence. "I spoke with Mildred, of course. Dreadful tragedy. Appalling. I know how crushed you must feel. But don't blame yourself, my boy. One cannot practice medicine without such occurrences. But when it is a child . . ."

"Thank you, Dr. Frias. How is Mrs. Anschutz?"

"Beside herself, as you might expect. Willard was such an effervescent lad. He brought joy to everyone. But we cannot anticipate the Lord's plan. Sometimes the best of us are taken far too soon."

"I was planning on waiting until tomorrow to see her."

"I think you might consider waiting a bit longer than that. I'm loath to bear bad tidings, but, unjust as it may be . . ." Frias left the obvious unsaid, then seemed to remember he was not alone. He cleared his throat before making introductions. "By the way, do you know Martin Smith?"

"I don't believe so."

Smith extended his hand. He had a powerful grip. His eyes were gray and his expression even, like a man giving nothing away at a game of cards.

"We've got to be off." Frias forced an ingratiating smile. "I'm giving Martin a tour of the hospital." After a few steps, however, he excused himself and walked back to Noah. This time, he spoke more softly. "I believe you took something last night that belonged to Mrs. Anschutz. I would like it back."

Noah shrugged, then hoped the gesture hadn't appeared as stiff as it felt. "I'm sorry, Dr. Frias, but I don't have it anymore. There seemed no need to keep it."

"You discarded it?"

"Yes, I'm afraid so. Mrs. Anschutz certainly had no further need of it, and I don't like keeping unknown medications about."

Frias considered for a moment whether to press, then glanced over his shoulder at Martin Smith waiting across the hall. "Very well." His face fell into a mien of professional compassion. "Once again, Whitestone, my sympathies."

When Frias was gone, Noah made his way downstairs. He signed in with the attendant at the desk, then set himself up at station. The laboratory, as Alan had predicted, was empty. The space was large and open, with small windows near the ceiling that peeked over the grass of the hospital's back lawn. The room was divided into thirds by work tables, each containing four stations with sink, microscope, burner, and the other tools of the medical researcher's trade. At the near wall, flanking the door on either side, were large shelved cases. One held manuals, journals, and records of previous analyses, the other, behind glass doors, a cornucopia of chemicals that could be used to perform every conceivable pathological, cytological, or histological analysis.

Noah scanned the bookshelves and withdrew the volume to which Alan had referred, Justin Herold's *Manual of Legal Medicine*. Fifteen years ago, Herold had been appointed coroner's physician for New York City at age twenty-four, the youngest man ever to hold the post. Last year, back in private practice, he had published his guide for "practitioners and students of medicine and law."

Part I of the tome was dedicated to toxicology. Chapter 10 was entitled, "Opium and Morphine." Checking for appropriate tests on page 96, Noah found the following:

> *Tests: "Opium itself has no direct chemical test. But, as every watery solution contains the meconate of morphine, well-marked reactions are used to distinguish the alkaloid of opium, morphine, and its peculiar acid, meconic.*
>
> *I. Morphine—The important tests for this alkaloid are the nitric acid, ferric chloride, sulphomolybdic acid, and iodic acid.*

The details of the four tests followed. Since none was certain to be accurate and each had occasions where a positive result might be caused by a compound other than a morphiate, proper procedure dictated that each of the four tests be conducted on the substance. But Noah had only one small tablet. He had been taught in medical school to employ a sufficient quantity of an unknown to ensure a fair result, and so, conducting four separate tests would exhaust the material at hand. Even if a test were positive, he would need to retain at least half the tablet so that it might be tested independently to confirm his findings.

Forced, therefore, to choose one, perhaps two of the tests, he opted for the sulphomolybdic acid test, also known as Froehde's test. It seemed most likely to produce a result unique to morphine. Herold's instructions read as follows:

> *This reagent is prepared by dissolving five or six grains of molybdate of sodium or ammonium in two drachms of strong sulphuric acid. If morphine is treated with this acid, it strikes a beautiful violet color, changing to green, and finally to a sapphire-blue.*

Noah gathered the necessary chemicals. When the reagent was set, he ground one-quarter of the tablet with mortar and pestle, and placed the resulting powder in a test dish. As he prepared to treat the powder with the reagent, he found himself growing excited. If the mixture struck violet, his suspicion that Dr. Frias *had* prescribed a morphiate for Willard would be confirmed. Although the mystery of how the drug had lingered in the child's system would remain, it might well have been the cause of the boy's death. Perhaps the tablet contained some new formulation with an extended half-life.

Noah drew four drops of sulphomolybdic acid into a dropper's neck. He held the instrument over the powdered tablet, unable at first to will himself to the squeeze the bulb. Finally, he did and the reagent dropped into the dish. Noah waited.

Nothing.

No violet at all. If anything, the original blue faded. Noah added more of the reagent. Still no reaction. Noah stared at the mixture in the dish and then at the impotent reagent, as if each had intentionally conspired against him. He reread the instructions, but he had performed the test properly. There could be no doubt. No morphia had been in the sample.

But perhaps the section of the tablet he examined contained only inert matter and the morphia resided in a section he had not tested. Yes. That might be. Unlikely, but far from impossible. He had sufficient material for one, perhaps two more experiments. Should he repeat the sulphomolybdic acid test? Or attempt one of the other three?

Noah chose the nitric acid test.

With morphine and its salts concentrated nitric acid produces a rich orange-red, slowly fading to yellow, or sometimes a brownish-yellow color, which upon standing strikes a light yellow. Nitric acid also produces a reddish color with other organic substances, but these are not crystalline. It strikes a deep-red color with brucine, which upon the addition of stannous chloride is changed to a bright purple; no such change is produced in the case of morphine.

Once again, failure. The powder did not strike red at all. Whatever was in the tablet, it was not a morphiate. No explanation had been provided for Willard Anschutz's apparent morphia toxicity. But if the tablet was harmless, why was Frias so hot about it? Noah dropped the remaining half back into the envelope.

Before leaving, he stopped at the records office to file a death certificate. As he wrote "respiratory failure," he felt like a liar. But was "morphia toxicity" any more honest?

As he made his way out of the hospital, Noah noticed the sharp-featured man with the spectacles that he had seen exiting the children's ward loitering at the far end of the lobby.

SEVEN

Dinner at the De Kuypers combined elements of passion play and farce. Oscar, Maribeth's father, shipper and patriarch, was bluff, generous, pompous, and condescending. Adelaide, his wife, was sharp-featured and sharp-witted, substantially brighter and more venomous than her husband. She constantly sought weaknesses to exploit and generally found them. Alan played the family cynic, the opposite of his younger brother, Jamie, who was crabbing his way up the ladder at the trust department at First Mercantile Bank and who viewed the pursuit of wealth as the highest human calling.

Maribeth, the youngest, was an amalgam. She had her father's fair hair and giving nature, but not his smug superiority; her mother's insight, but not her malice. As the baby of the family and the only girl, she had learned well the tactical use of her femininity. She and Alan adored each other. Jamie was no match for her.

"You're in a bit of hot water, old man," Alan said as the driver pulled the coach away from Noah's door. "What did you tell Frias about the tablet?"

"He asked for it back. I told him I'd discarded it."

"Well, he found out you went to the laboratory and tested it. You shouldn't have signed the log. He came up to pediatrics looking for you, but I told him you had gone. He was hopping."

"I wonder what he was so angry about. The test showed the tablet wasn't a morphiate."

"Maybe he just doesn't like being played for a fool. There are people with that quirk, you know. In any event, it was a big mistake. I wouldn't want Dr. Dollars lurking behind my back."

"I don't see what he can do."

"He can make your life hell, that's what he can do. He can have the hospital deny you privileges, for one thing. Word around the wards is that he's been sounding out the board about some deal. Something that will make him even more money. Never good to anger a bear who's preparing to feed."

"What kind of deal?"

"Something to do with his visit to Germany. When he came back with that automobile he's so fond of."

"Maybe that's why he was at the hospital today. He was with someone named Martin Smith. Looked like a czarist police agent."

"Martin *H.* Smith?"

"Possibly. Do you know him?"

"Know of him. He's a chemist. Formulated Dr. Jordan's Elixir. Made him quite a bit of money."

"I'm sure. My housekeeper takes it. Do you think Frias is going into patent medicines?"

"I wouldn't think so. And if he did, he certainly wouldn't be advertising it at the hospital." Alan patted Noah on the knee. "On a happier note, I think May 15 will be the day. My mother told me to be certain I had no engagements on that day. As if I make plans seven months in advance."

"I'm pleased to be informed thirdhand as to the day of my wedding."

"Welcome to the De Kuyper family. One of the reasons I remain a bachelor is to avoid in-laws. But Maribeth is worth it."

"You remain a bachelor because you would drive any decent woman mad." In truth, Noah had always wondered why Alan eschewed the company of women. He always assumed that a man who chose to work with children would want some of his own. "But Maribeth is definitely worth it."

The previous June, after months of trying to convince Noah that he and Maribeth might enjoy each other's company, Noah had finally allowed Alan to arrange a Sunday outing in Prospect Park. The three of them rented a boat, rowed on the lake, then settled in on the green for a picnic. Alan had kept up a steady stream of conversation, allowing Noah and Maribeth to avoid the awkwardness of a first meeting. As the afternoon moved on, Alan decided that he needed a stretch of the legs.

Maribeth had sat for some moments, not speaking, but not uncomfortable in the silence. Noah realized how lovely she was. Thin and delicate, with a long, swanlike neck. Her eyes were a soft blue and her complexion pale and luxurious.

Finally, she smiled. "I hope Alan takes a long walk. He couldn't be sweeter but subtlety is a trait he has yet to discover."

"He is indefatigable. I hope you are not here against your will."

"The reluctance, I believe, Dr. Whitestone, was on your end."

"I was incredulous that Alan could have a sister so attractive and appealing. Had I known that you bear so little relation to him, I would have forced a meeting sooner."

She had laughed, more of a girlish giggle, but quite infectious. Noah stretched out his legs and, in doing so, moved closer to her. They spoke for an hour, until Alan returned. He had glanced from one to the other, but in tacit conspiracy, neither Noah nor Maribeth let on that they had enjoyed each other's company. Finally, after dropping off Maribeth at Gramercy Park, Alan could bear it no longer.

"Well, Noah? What did you think?"

"I'm sorry, Alan. I found her a bit dull."

"Dull? How can you say—"

"Alan, your sister is an exceptional woman."

De Kuyper had grinned broadly, the pride of the matchmaker.

Noah called on her later that week. At Maribeth's suggestion, they had seen the avant-garde play *The Doll's House* by the Norwegian, Ibsen, at the Empire, with Mrs. Fiske reprising the role of Nora. "Her performance epitomizes the naturalism of the new theater," Maribeth told him later. "She has abandoned the flourishes and melodrama of Bernhardt or Ellen Terry and instead, like Duse, seeks to conduct herself on stage as a genuine person." Over dinner, Maribeth had talked at length about the ongoing evolution in the theater and, in fact, in art in general. "We are entering a new century, Noah. A time of excitement and hope. Experimentation with the ways of our fathers and grandfathers should not be sniffed at but encouraged." She extended a long, delicate index finger and tapped Noah on the back of the hand. "Mark my words, Noah Whitestone. You and I will live to see women get the vote."

"You and I?"

A blush had shot up both sides of her neck.

"I'm sorry," he said, but with a smile. "That is simply my fumbling way of saying that I would be pleased to be able to see you again."

Their next engagement was to upper Fifth Avenue to view the antiquities at the Metropolitan Museum of Art. As they sat over lunch in Central Park, Noah told Maribeth about Isobel. She listened without interruption. How would she take it? What would she say?

"I'm so sorry for you, Noah. You can never forget your past. Nor would I want you to. You should and you will honor Isobel's memory for the rest of your life. And you will love her. But you have a future as well. Trying to make that future as rich and as happy as you can does not sully your wife's memory."

After that, Noah and Maribeth began to keep steady company. He discovered that she wrote poetry, was expert in renaissance art, and volunteered at a settlement house in Hell's Kitchen. Noah asked her once why she saw him instead of one of the many society beaus that would have fought to gain her affection. She replied that she was seeking substance, not wealth. Two months later, he asked for her hand. She had accepted instantly, and as one of the perquisites of their engagement, Noah now attended the weekly family dinners at Gramercy Park.

As they pulled up to the door, Alan sighed. "Well, Noah, as the bard said, 'Once more unto the breach' . . . or was that Wilde?'"

The De Kuypers lived in a three-story, brick town house that faced east on Gramercy Park. Edwin Booth had once lived in the house four doors down. The interior was opulent and overdone, packed with antique furniture and adorned throughout with a series of pedestals upon which sat busts of a variety of ancient Greeks and Romans. Adelaide De Kuyper was the daughter of a merchant and had chosen this décor with the impression that it would convey erudition.

Alan and Noah were the last to arrive, and a servant ushered them into a dining room dominated by a table that could seat twenty, although only seven were present. Instead of placing everyone close together, Mrs. De Kuyper had spaced the chairs so that she and her husband could each have an end.

Either in recognition of the natural split in the family or by chance, Noah, Maribeth, and Alan sat one side of the table, Jamie and his wife, Rosa, on the other. Noah greeted his future in-laws, took Maribeth's hand for a moment, then allowed a servant to seat him. Alan waved the servant off and plopped into his chair. Soup was served almost immediately. Oxtail consommé.

"You're just in time," Jamie crowed, raising his glass, which was emptied regularly. "I was about to propose a toast." Jamie was three years Alan's junior, as wide as Alan was tall. He had taken it into his head that a successful banker must be as immense as Old Man Morgan. "To Admiral Dewey!"

"Here, here, Jamie," extolled his father, raising his glass as well. "To Admiral Dewey."

"Do you also offer a toast when someone swats a fly?" Alan asked.

"Eyewash, Alan," grumbled his father. "A nation needs heroes. They are the glue that holds a people together in common purpose. Promote patriotism. Do you find something objectionable in that?"

"What about Mark Twain?" Alan asked after the glasses had been replaced on the table. "One of the great men of American letters. Didn't he write 'There must be two Americas: one that sets the captive free, and one that takes a once-captive's new freedom away from him, and picks a quarrel with him with nothing to found it on; then kills him to get his land?'"

Maribeth sniffed. "I believe you memorized that passage specifically for the occasion, Alan. Can we expect any other homilies this evening?"

"Mark Twain is a fool," Jamie sniffed, before Alan could reply. "I suspect he is secretly one of those radical socialists who countenance planting bombs in theaters."

"Quite so," growled his father. "What is the matter with you, Alan? Has treating all those immigrants turned you against your country?"

"Never, father," Alan replied. "My country, right or wrong . . ."

"Do you think your country is wrong, Alan?" It was his mother.

"I could never countenance bullies," he replied.

"And you, Noah?" she asked, then blotted her lips with her napkin.

"I confess to being uncomfortable with hero worship." Maribeth's father and Jamie glowered, very much two generations of shared values, but Noah pushed on. "And the Filipinos seem no match for our military. But I hesitate to judge in matters of which, in truth, I know so little."

"That's not what you told me when we were alone," Alan pointed out. "Don't be cowed by these two."

"Leave him be, Alan," Maribeth chided. "You seem to be descending into a bit of a bully yourself."

49

"Hear, hear," Jamie intoned. He raised his glass, with his first smile of the night. "A toast to Alan, the bully."

"How *do* you feel about the war, Noah?" asked Mrs. De Kuyper. "The truth, please. You are going to be a member of the family. You may certainly feel free to be as intemperate as Alan."

"It's as I said, Mrs. De Kuyper. Our soldiers are performing honorably, but it doesn't seem much of a fair fight. There is danger in winning so easily. There are many in our government who itch to join the race to empire that has infected much of Europe. That race, if history is any judge, will surely lead to war. Real war, not like this one. Defeating an old crippled Spain is one thing; war with Great Britain, France, or Germany will be quite another. My complaint, I suppose, is with the people back home who are using the war to increase their own prestige."

"Like TR?" demanded Oscar.

"Enough politics, Oscar," Adelaide De Kuyper told her husband, as the soup was cleared and the lamb served. She was imperious and commanding, what Mildred Anschutz would grow into if Pug was promoted to general. "I prefer to toast our beautiful daughter and her fiancé and their impending wedding on May 15 in the first year of the new century. To long life, happiness, and many children."

Oscar's scowl turned to a beam. "Hear, hear."

"Indeed," Jamie chimed in, although with slightly less enthusiasm. He had always complained that Maribeth got more attention even though she was a girl. "To my sister's marriage to a successful doctor." Oscar had been stunned by Noah's refusal to abandon the family practice and set himself up, with his new father-in-law's help, on Park Avenue.

Alan raised his glass. "To Noah's success. A successful doctor is almost as good as a dishonest banker, right Jamie?" Alan turned to Noah. "But he might not stay successful if he gets on the wrong side of Dr. Dollars."

"And who is Dr. Dollars, Alan?" Rosa asked with a tiny smile. Jamie's wife bisected the continuum between attractive and plain, and had decided shy amiability was the most likely mien to help her husband further his career. At Jamie's insistence, she had attempted to supplement the absence of natural beauty with an expensive trousseau, but lacking grace and self-confidence, the clothes accentuated her lack of appeal rather than camouflaging it.

"That's just what I call this fellow Frias," Alan replied. "He thinks medicine has an obligation to make him rich. Jamie would like him."

"There is nothing wrong with being successful," his father intoned.

"Frias? Arnold Frias?" Jamie asked, ingesting a large bite of lamb and washing it down with a swig of wine.

"Yes," Alan replied. "Do you know him?"

"Customer of the bank. Good-looking man." Jamie grabbed a roll off the tray. "Was in just last week, as a matter of fact."

"What about?" Alan asked.

"Dunno. I'm not in the loan department." Jamie smeared butter on the roll and took a bite.

"He came in for a loan?"

Jamie paused, the buttered roll suspended near his mouth. "That's usually why people come to the loan department, Alan. Went right to see Mr. Dansfield himself. Him and the other fellow." Homer Dansfield was president of First Mercantile Bank, and Jamie breathed his name worshipfully.

"Was the other fellow named Smith?" Alan asked.

"Dunno. I told you. Not my department. Wouldn't have been Smith though. Schmidt maybe."

"He was German, this other fellow?"

Jamie quaffed more wine. "Yes, Alan. German. Schmidt. My, you are obtuse tonight."

Conversation settled in after that, the De Kuypers bickering their way through the next three courses. Noah was grateful that their byplay was so ingrained that no one seemed to notice that he had little to say. His mind was still on Frias and the failed tests in the laboratory.

"You will continue without me," Maribeth said, after dessert was cleared. "I'm going to give Noah a respite."

Oscar and Adelaide watched with approval as their daughter left the table with her fiancé. They didn't totally approve of Noah, perhaps, but what parent is not buoyed by the sight of a happy child?

Maribeth led him to a sitting room. "Noah, what's wrong tonight?"

"I lost a patient last night. Another doctor's patient, actually. I was only there because of the emergency." Noah was grateful to have Maribeth to speak to about it. She was one of those rare people who could make another feel better just by listening.

"I'm so sorry, Noah." Maribeth placed her hand on his. Her skin was always cool. She seemed never to perspire. "Was there something special about this patient?"

"It was a child. A boy. Only five."

"Oh, Noah. How terrible. To have it been a . . . someone else's patient."

"Thank you, Maribeth."

"Noah, I am so proud of you. So proud that I will be your wife, no matter what featherhead Jamie says. Healing the sick, giving comfort to those who are in pain or afraid . . . there is no nobler calling. Mother and father think so as well, although I know they are not free with compliments."

"That is very kind of you, Maribeth. Unfortunately, I don't always heal the sick."

She squeezed his hand. "Noah, if medicine was as easy as all that, everyone would do it. It is the very element of risk . . . and your willingness to take that risk . . . and Alan's . . . that makes what you do so important. So special."

He placed his other hand on top of hers. "You are really quite extraordinary, Maribeth. I don't deserve you."

"Oh yes, you do." She smiled. "You deserve to be taken care of and loved. I intend to do quite a bit of both."

"Mrs. Jensen will be jealous."

"Mrs. Jensen will be just fine. As long as we get someone else to cook."

"She'll be crushed, but I'll break the news to her somehow." He took her hands in his. "I would never want to hurt you, Maribeth. I care for you deeply."

"Do you, Noah? Do you really?"

"Yes, Maribeth. I do." He leaned in and kissed her. Her lips were soft, supple, under his. She eyed him strangely when they pulled apart. Noah knew she wanted more, so he kissed her again, this time longer and more deeply. She smiled afterward. Relief as much as happiness. Why could he not feel more for her? Perhaps real love comes only once.

"We best rejoin the others," she whispered.

Oscar was waiting in the foyer. He called Noah into his study.

"You are determined to remain in Brooklyn?"

"I must stay where my patients are, sir."

De Kuyper nodded perfunctorily. "I suppose I must find that admirable. You will, of course, move to more suitable lodgings?"

"Of course."

"I wish my daughter to live in a proper fashion."

"As do I."

"I'm certain you do, Noah. But I thought perhaps I might help the process along. As your wedding present, I would like to present you with a home on Columbia Street."

"Thank you, sir," Noah said. "Your generosity is overwhelming, but I couldn't possibly accept." I'd have Frias for my neighbor, he thought.

"Nonsense," De Kuyper grunted with a dismissive wave. "Adelaide and I insist. You enter this family and you live like this family. You will face the bay and have an unobstructed view of the Manhattan skyline. In fact, if you look carefully, you might be able to make out my offices on Water Street." De Kuyper puffed up, pleased with himself.

"I cannot refuse then. Maribeth and I are supremely grateful. Perhaps, each morning, we can wave to you from the promenade," Noah offered.

"Well . . . yes," De Kuyper replied. "I suppose you could."

EIGHT

W hen Noah arrived at the Anschutz home the next morning, parked on the street were three horse-driven carriages and another carriage of a different sort. The passenger seat was of gleaming black leather, and the side and front panels were of lacquered wood. The design was similar to a pony and trap, but lacking the pony. In the rear, for locomotion, was a four-stroke, gasoline-powered, flat-cylindered internal combustion engine. A polished brass plate on the inside of the front panel read BENZ & CIE. MANNHEIM.

It was the most sleek, opulent automobile Noah had ever seen. The cost must have exceeded $1,000. Whatever Frias had come across in Germany, he must have believed it would indeed make him a good deal of money if he had purchased this machine in celebration.

The door opened. Noah hoped it would be Frias on his way out, but instead Paul and Lucinda Barksdale exited. The Barksdales were a middle-aged couple who lived two streets away. Paul owned the second-largest clothier in Brooklyn after Abraham & Straus, so he and Lucinda never appeared in public unless impeccably groomed and attired. They walked stiffly, giving the impression of Barksdale store mannequins brought to life. They were also patients of Arnold Frias. When they saw Noah, their gazes lingered for an accusing extra second. Then, in unison, they gave jerky, perfunctory nods and passed without offering pleasantries.

Alan had been correct. Frias was on the attack.

When the Barksdales had made their way down the street, Noah walked to the door. He took a breath, then firmly rapped the knocker against the strike plate.

When the door opened, Noah found himself looking down at a balding man in his mid-fifties with a sweeping, white, handlebar mustache. The man was a shorter, older version of Brooklyn's former mayor, Frederick Wurster. Mildred Anschutz's father, Harold.

Noah took off his hat. "Mr. Wurster?"

The man nodded. His eyes were red, with dark circles underneath.

"Good morning, sir. I wanted to tell you how sorry I am about the loss of your grandson. I was hoping to convey my condolences to Mrs. Anschutz as well."

"Thank you for coming by, sir," Harold Wurster replied. "And you are . . ."

"Noah Whitestone."

Wurster stiffened. "The doctor." The words were uttered in a frigid monotone.

"Yes."

Harold Wurster stepped aside, glaring as Noah passed by.

The vestibule, which had been the scene of such frantic activity two nights before, was now silent. Drapes were pulled shut. The wallpaper, blue and green stripe, seemed to have darkened overnight.

A somber Molly emerged from a doorway on the left, holding a tray laden with half-filled glasses and an empty bowl. When she noticed Noah, she bit her lip, holding back tears. Harold Wurster made a tiny move with his hand in the direction of the same doorway. Noah left his hat on the front table and entered the parlor. The room was filled with furnishings, accessories, and bric-a-brac. Over the fireplace hung the portrait of a young, willowy, surprisingly attractive Mildred Anschutz. Next to her stood a dashing, black-haired Pug, trim and arresting in the uniform of a lieutenant.

Today's Mildred Anschutz, older and haggard, was seated on a divan, dressed in a black crepe dress, her eyes cast down. Her daughters sat on either side of her. Aldridge, wearing a black suit, hair plastered and parted in the middle, stood behind the divan, his hand on his mother's shoulder. Daniel was next to him. No one moved. The scene seemed almost posed, a *tableau vivant*. In the center of the room facing Noah, barring his way to the family, were dual sentinels, Frederick Wurster and Arnold Frias.

Mrs. Anschutz did not look up as Noah entered but Frederick Wurster took one step forward. He was a trim man, a head taller than his older brother, with full beard and mustache only touched with gray. His eyebrows dove together at the bridge of his nose, giving him the look of a prosecuting attorney. He had been mayor for two years, after two years as fire commissioner. In both positions, he had acquired a reputation for ferocious incorruptibility.

"We were wondering whether you would have the decency to come by," Wurster said. His voice was soft, his words measured. Not at all what Noah remembered from when he had heard Wurster speak a year before in Grand Army Plaza. "But don't think for one second that because you have, you will be in any way excused for your terrible act of negligence."

What had Frias said? "I have committed no act of negligence, Mayor Wurster. I encountered a child in deep distress. I treated his symptoms properly. I came to offer condolences to Mrs. Anschutz for the tragedy of her loss, not out of culpability."

At that, Arnold Frias emitted a snort. "Symptoms of what, young man?"

"Morphia deprivation," Noah replied, no longer willing to either lie or equivocate.

"Morphia deprivation?" Frias's voice was mellifluous, and he drew out the words to emphasize the ludicrousness of the idea. "Was that your diagnosis? Based on what, Dr. Whitestone? Your vast experience in treating morphiate tolerance? Just how many such patients have you attended?"

"I am not unfamiliar with the symptoms."

Frias almost sneered. "Symptoms that could be attributed to a plethora of causes. And where did you gain this familiarity? Textbooks?" He tucked his thumbs into the pockets of his vest. "I, on the other hand, have treated hundreds of dope cases. Moreover, I visited Willard just last week. If he were in the throes of morphiate addiction—just the thought is idiotic—I most certainly would have noticed. Unless, of course, you are implying that I intentionally infected the boy and was secretly supplying him with drugs."

"Of course not," Noah said. "And I have treated dope cases as well. But what has caused your change of heart, Dr. Frias? Just yesterday, you expressed to me that Willard's death was a tragedy for whom no one is to blame."

"That was before I realized the full extent of your malfeasance. I was willing to grant you benefit of the doubt, but can do so no longer. It would be a disservice to the community."

Noah turned to Wurster. "I would like to give you the details of the occurrence, Mayor Wurster, but don't you believe, as gentlemen, we should be speaking of this in private?"

"We will speak of it here. I wish my niece to have no doubts about the man who is responsible for her son's death but tries to blame another."

Frias offered a small nod of acknowledgment to Wurster. "Poor Mildred told me that throughout your visit, you questioned both my motives and my skill."

"I did no such thing, sir," Noah protested, although he had certainly done both.

"And how do we know, doctor," Frias pressed, his nostrils flaring as if the scent of blood was actually in them, "that given the abysmal judgment and lack of skill that you demonstrated, you did not give poor Willard three drops of laudanum in error? Maybe even four. Six? Or perhaps it was not error at all, but simply too large a dose, which you later realized and are now attempting to deny."

"Mrs. Anschutz saw me administer the dose."

"She says she did not. She was looking away at the time."

Noah turned his eyes to Mildred Anschutz, but she refused to look up.

"I know your father, doctor," Frias continued, almost rising up on his toes. "I cannot imagine that he would ever have treated a young, helpless patient with the disdain that you apparently showed last night. Disdain and false pride. And the patient has paid for your hubris."

"I treated him properly. I wonder, Dr. Frias, what you would have done had you been at the boy's side." Noah thought about Viola Mangino but forced back the temptation to mention her. "What has caused you to spread this calumny? Is it simply a desire to blacken my name out of spite, or do you have a different motive?"

Before Frias could reply, Frederick Wurster spoke. "You murdered my nephew, Dr. Whitestone. Murdered him just as surely if you had wielded a gun, a knife, or a club. There is no place in the noble profession of medicine for opportunists such as yourself. I have dealt with the corrupt and the incompetent before. The cause of death on Willard's death certificate will be changed to read 'overdose of laudanum.'"

"On what grounds? How can the coroner possibly determine such a thing without a postmortem? Do you intend an autopsy?"

"We are not cutting the boy open," Frederick Wurster said with finality. "The facts could not be more obvious. Moreover, I intend to contact the Board of Regents personally and see that proceedings are initiated to have your medical license revoked. Whether or not I should pursue criminal charges, I have not yet decided."

"Mayor Wurster, you are making a grievous error. I was there and Dr. Frias was not. I encountered a helpless boy in agony, and I took steps to alleviate his symptoms. I have already discussed this tragedy with the head of pediatrics at Brooklyn Hospital, and he has affirmed both my diagnosis and my treatment. I cannot say why events proceeded as they did. I was hoping members of poor Willard's family would want to discover the reasons as much as I do. I see now, however, that you seem more interested in revenge. To Mrs. Anschutz I can only offer my deepest sympathies. I know the terrible pain of losing a loved one."

A hand appeared between Wurster and Frias. Both looked behind them with surprise, then moved apart to allow Aldridge Anschutz to pass. The boy posted himself opposite Noah. He was standing quite erect, taller than he had appeared two nights ago. The beginnings of whiskers were visible below his sideburns and on his chin. His eyes were dark brown, like Willard's. He stared at Noah without fear or emotion.

"Dr. Whitestone, I cannot speak to your motives. Or your ability as a doctor. But my brother is dead. My mother is devastated, and our family will never be the same again. You treated Willard and assured my mother that you would help him. You did not. You are not welcome in this house. I ask you to leave and never return."

For some moments, no one spoke. The only sounds in the room were of breathing and the soft whimpering of Mildred Anschutz. Wurster he could fight. Or Frias. But not a sixteen-year-old boy. Finally, Noah nodded to the boy, retrieved his hat from the hall, and was once again out on the street, wondering how his future as a doctor and even his freedom could have been put in so dire peril from two drops of laudanum.

Noah suddenly had the sensation of being observed. He looked about and saw, waiting at the end of the block, leaning against a wall, the man with the wire-framed spectacles from Brooklyn Hospital. The man smiled slowly and crooked his finger for Noah to join him.

NINE

N ot a successful visit to the bereaved, Dr. Whitestone?" The man spoke with perfect diction, in an accent vaguely British. "I gather they blame you for the boy's death. But I suppose it would have been foolish to expect Dr. Frias to accept responsibility."

"What do you know of it?"

"I was hoping that we might chat," the man replied, ignoring the question.

"About what?"

"Murdered children, of course. I want to chat with you about murdered children, Dr. Whitestone." The man's smile vanished. "Ridgewood, Astoria, Flatlands, Newark . . ." The man was ticking off the names on his fingers. "And now Brooklyn Heights. In each case, a child has either died or been struck gravely ill."

"And?" Noah tried to remain outwardly stoical, but he sensed what was coming and was excited to hear the words.

"And in each case, the symptoms were the same. The same as those from which your patient died two nights ago. Encephalitic asphyxiation brought on by respiratory failure. Symptoms remarkably consistent with morphia poisoning. There was one difference in your case, however." The man waited for Noah to ask.

"And what was that?"

"Each of the other victims came from a poor home. The type of home where they are unable to raise a stink. To be blunt, children who would not be missed. Perfect for experimentation."

"What sort of experimentation?"

The man cocked his head in the direction away from Joralemon Street. "Let's go somewhere where we can talk."

"Just a moment. I've got a few questions first. How do you know me?"

"I've spent enough time in hospitals these past months to know a doctor when I see one. I asked one of the nurses what your name was. Quite harmless really."

"And you have been following me since?"

"My apologies."

"What were you doing there?"

The man shrugged. "A false errand. I had heard that a child had been admitted with the same set of symptoms. It turned out not to be true. But after your furtive conversation with Dr. De Kuyper, I learned my day had not been wasted."

"How do you know what we discussed?"

"Nurse again. Their presence is usually invisible to you doctors, but they listen to everything."

"Very well. I'll hear what you have to say, Mr. . . . . ?"

"McKee. Turner McKee." He extended his hand.

"Mr. McKee." Noah nodded, shaking what turned out to be a heavily muscled and calloused hand. McKee's grip could have easily crushed Noah's fingers.

"I crewed at Yale," said McKee, noticing Noah's surprise. "Swam quite a bit as well. I like the water. Very purifying."

"Allow me to form my own conclusions as to your purity." Noah then suggested a popular tavern on Fulton Street. He had no intention of asking the man to his rooms.

McKee laughed and shook his head. His teeth were straight and well cared for. "Wrong sort of folks go there. I know a more reliable spot. Peaceful. Refined décor. Courteous service. A bit of a walk, but you'll like it." Without waiting for Noah to assent, he turned and started briskly up the street. Noah followed.

They walked through a town in the throes of modernity: macadam where cobblestones had lain, electric lighting instead of gas, brick homes and office buildings in place of wood. On Fulton Street, tracks and overhead wires for the electric trolley cut the thoroughfare in half. Gasoline-and steam-powered vehicles had begun to supplant horses. Even pedestrians strode about with a purposefulness that had been lacking even ten years earlier, as if speed of communication required speed afoot.

During the journey, McKee made no attempt at conversation. Every few blocks, he turned down a side street, always glancing behind him as he did so. Once, he made three rights in a row so that in the end he had returned to his original course. At first, Noah could not help glancing back as well, but they were quite alone. Eventually, he found the intrigue silly, an affectation. It made him more determined to maintain his skepticism. "Murdered children" and "experimentation" were phrases doubtlessly chosen to arouse his curiosity, but curiosity should never be allowed to overcome reason.

They arrived at the edge of the harbor and time once again receded. A series of dilapidated clapboard buildings with peeling paint lined the streets. No electrical wires were visible. Evidence of horse traffic lay strewn in the middle of the road. The smell of brackish water and festering garbage permeated the air.

McKee started down Front Street, the immense span of the Brooklyn Bridge looming over them. Their destination was a seedy tavern,

ARTHUR'S, barely discernible in chipped, faded paint on a grimy window, the sort of establishment that Clement Van Meter had likely frequented in his ports of call around the globe. McKee paused before entering, once again glancing up and down the street. When he was satisfied with what he saw, or didn't see, he opened the door and beckoned Noah inside.

Four kerosene lamps mounted on wall sconces and the soot on the window left the room in constant gloom. Although it was not yet noon, four patrons sat on stools at the bar, one a heavily rouged older woman in a garish orange-and-green dress. None looked up as Noah and his bespectacled companion walked in.

The bartender, bald and hulking, with the flattened nose and perichondrial hematoma—cauliflower ears—of a prize fighter, gave a perfunctory gesture with his head toward the rear. McKee nodded and walked quickly through the bar toward a brown, dusty curtain stretched across a narrow doorway.

The back room was as disagreeable as the front, three unadorned tables set on a sawdust-covered pine-board floor. Heavy shades were pulled across the windows.

McKee swept an arm grandly from left to right. "What did I tell you, doctor? Handsome accommodations, are they not? Can I offer you something? I'm sure you would not favor beer or whiskey at such an hour, but Dolph makes a surprisingly good cup of coffee, seeing how almost no one who comes here drinks it." He then pulled out a chair at a table for two, gesturing for Noah to join him. McKee sat facing the door.

"Coffee would be appreciated," Noah replied, taking his seat.

McKee motioned toward the curtain. How the bartender, Dolph, could see the raised hand remained a mystery.

"Well, Mr. McKee, now that you have dragooned me to this bar, perhaps you might elaborate on the grandiose pronouncement you made earlier."

McKee nodded. "Very well. In the first place, I wanted to tell you that I know you didn't kill your patient."

"Thank you for your confidence. I also know I didn't."

Turner McKee smiled and wagged a finger back and forth. "No. You *hope* you didn't. I *know* you didn't."

"Which implies that you know who did . . . what did."

"Both. But strongly suspect would be more accurate. Very strongly, actually."

The curtain was pulled aside and the man Dolph entered with the coffee. His hands were immense, dwarfing the cups. The smell of java, strong and rich, filled the room. He placed the cups in front of them, then retired as soundlessly as he had entered. Noah wondered if the man could speak at all.

"One of the advantages of proximity to a waterfront," McKee said, gesturing with his head to the coffee. "Access to imports at a low price. Sometimes no price."

They each took a sip, eyeing each other. "By the way," McKee asked, "are you Abel Whitestone's son?"

"Yes." McKee's constant evasions were maddening, but this was a man who required his theatrics. "Do you know my father?"

"I've heard the name, that's all. Fine doctor, your father."

"Thank you. Yes, he is."

McKee allowed the flash of a smile to come and go. "Difficult to find honorable men these days."

"I agree, but might we return to the subject at hand? You distinctly used the word *murder*. That implies intent."

"Or willful negligence," McKee replied.

"So children are dying due to willful negligence. As a result of experimentation. I assume you mean by physicians. Over a wide geographic area."

"Not only physicians." McKee idly scratched his chin with an extended forefinger. "Dr. Whitestone, do you think $75 million is a lot of money?"

"I assume the question is rhetorical. Why that specific figure?"

"That is the sum of profits earned . . . stolen to be more precise . . . by the Patent Medicine Trust just last year."

"I am aware that patent medicines are a scourge, Mr. McKee. I inveigh against their use every day. I have threatened patients, cajoled them, and begged them. Usually to no avail. But patent medicines had nothing to do with the death of my patient. The boy hadn't been taking patent medicines. I was assured so by his mother and I believe her."

McKee shrugged. "Perhaps he hadn't."

"What's more, there is no Patent Medicine Trust. Trusts are legal entities, which I assume a Yale graduate should know."

"Don't be naïve, Dr. Whitestone. Whenever a group of businessmen band together to buy Congressmen, restrict competition, fix prices, prohibit regulation, ensure obscene profits, all to the detriment of the public, that is a trust whether they set themselves up as a legal entity or not. Even Bulldog Roosevelt knows that." McKee gave a sad shake of his head. "The National Wholesale Liquor Dealers Association, the Proprietary Medicine Association, and the American Pharmacists Council spend tens of thousands of dollars each year doing all of those things so that they can continue to poison gullible members of the public with patent medicines. Oh, there's a Patent Medicine Trust, all right."

"In other words, all of these perfectly legitimate trade groups are part of an evil conspiracy."

"Perhaps money means nothing to you, but for $75 million these men will bribe, steal, even murder to maintain their monopoly. Why do you think I duck around corners like a thief? Money is moving everywhere. Not just in the halls of government. Some of your colleagues accept handsome rewards from drug manufacturers to prescribe products without inquiring first what is in them. Or whether they have been tested. Patent medicines. Prescription medicines. Public welfare means nothing. People are dying, doctor. Make no mistake. Usually the poor and indigent. Often the victims are children, or the old, the weak, the infirm."

"And my patient, you are saying, was dosed with a medicine, an opiate, whose properties and effects were untested?"

"Each of the children who died was treated for a cough with what their doctor called a new miracle drug. Other than your patient, they were all poor and uneducated. And your patient was not really your patient, was he? He was Frias's."

"I was only called because of emergency."

"Precisely. Here is my proposal. If I aid you in proving what actually killed your patient, will you help me in exposing the abuses by the drug trust?"

"Tell me first where Dr. Frias fits in all of this."

"I'm not certain. I was hoping you might help in that regard. You certainly have motive for doing so."

"You are obviously a journalist of some sort."

"Of some sort."

"Of what sort, Mr. McKee?"

"I work for *New Visions* magazine."

"The socialists. Radicals. As I suspected."

McKee leaned back. The insouciant grin returned. "Actually, I consider myself more of an anarchist."

"If I am not mistaken, you are the people who featured a cover depicting the flag with the red stripes dripping blood."

"You disapprove."

"Of course I disapprove. Any decent person should."

"My country, right or wrong?"

The same phrase Alan had used. "I can be willing to disapprove of some of my country's policies without disapproving of my country."

"If you say so."

"So let me understand you, Mr. McKee. You have perceived that I am in trouble, so you have hauled me off to a clandestine rendezvous, spewed out a stream of unsubstantiated accusations, indicting businessmen, those in government, and even doctors—the very people you loathe—and now you expect me to be so outraged that, without verifying any of your diatribe, I leap to aid you in trying to uncover some shadowy cabal? To sweeten the mixture, you dangle Dr. Frias in front of me. All of which will help you sell more copies of your magazine. Sorry, Mr. McKee. You'll have to find someone more credulous."

McKee shook his head. "I was wrong about you, Whitestone. You're not as astute as I thought."

"Perhaps. But I'm no naïf, Mr. McKee. Of course, I realize that occasionally a physician will violate his oath. Perhaps, as you imply, Dr. Frias is one of them. But the problem of corrupt doctors is hardly the endemic situation you describe. Your politics have run away with your objectivity."

"You think so, doctor? What if I can prove it to you that my theory is sound?"

"How could you do that?"

"Let us leave that aside for a moment. Let us simply hypothesize that I could."

"I would be extremely disturbed."

"Disturbed enough to help me?"

"But I don't think you can."

"Come by the offices. We're near Cooper Square. If you find my evidence lacking, you may leave uncorrupted, and I will promise never to cross your path again."

"You have no evidence about Dr. Frias specifically, I presume."

"Not yet. Although I adore his new automobile. Don't you?"

"I will not deny that I would be interested to learn what killed poor Willard Anschutz," Noah said despite himself.

McKee's brow furrowed. "Did you say Anschutz? Was that your patient's name?"

Noah nodded. "I thought you knew everything."

"I heard the essentials, but not all of the details. Anschutz as in Pug Anschutz?"

"Yes. That was his house you saw me walk out of. How do you know him?"

"Pug Anschutz is a killer, Dr. Whitestone. A murderer whose crimes are excused because he wears a uniform while committing them."

"You seem addicted to hyperbole, Mr. McKee."

"Hardly. Pug has been serving in the Philippines under General Merritt, helping put down the revolt. Not really a revolt when one understands that Filipinos simply wish for the independence our government promised them if they supported us against Spain. Only after they helped us kick the Spanish out did we inform them that we were now their rulers instead. They then had the temerity to fight back. There have been stories filtering out of Manila about some unpleasant treatment of 'rebels.' Extremely unpleasant. Entire villages have been razed to the ground. Upward of one hundred thousand Filipinos have died. Women, children. The army has made no distinction. Colonel Anschutz is one of the men in charge of 'pacifying' the native population. He approaches the task with enthusiasm."

"Propaganda," Noah replied. "I know their forces are no match for ours, but no American would behave so barbarically."

"Oh yes, Dr. Whitestone. It must be socialist propaganda. Nonetheless, I hope for your sake you have resolved your difficulties before he arrives home."

"Do you believe that threatening me will cause me to break down and throw in with you?"

"No. You are clearly a man of strong, if misguided, resolution."

Noah stood. "Thank you for the coffee, Mr. McKee."

They passed through to the bar, which had acquired two additional patrons. McKee nodded to the ever-silent Dolph, then walked out onto the street. Noah was about to begin the walk to Adams Street, but McKee placed a hand on his wrist.

"Wait. Where are you off to?"

"I have an appointment in Manhattan."

"Very well. We must take different paths. I am prone to attracting the attention of parties you would not wish to meet. You return from the direction we came. Some vigilance on your part would not be misplaced. I will navigate my own course. Perhaps we can meet later at the magazine."

"I don't expect so," Noah said, but McKee had already left, walking close to the buildings of Front Street until he disappeared around a corner.

TEN

Two years before, Columbia College had moved from its home on Forty-Ninth Street and Madison Avenue to Morningside Heights, far to the north and west. The Ninth Avenue line, New York's first elevated railway, had only recently been extended north to accommodate travel to the college. The project had required the tracks to be over one hundred feet off the ground and, at 110th Street, make a sharp ninety-degree turn that was quickly dubbed "suicide curve." The Ninth Avenue line was now the most popular in the city, with New Yorkers of all ages often riding solely for pleasure. There was something remarkable about speeding north on two thin rails, tons of metal roaring so high above the vehicles and populace below as the train hurtled from station to station in a giant game of urban leapfrog.

Noah had not been on the elevated since the extension. Many of his fellow riders, even those seated, grabbed for handholds as the train neared suicide curve. Others, like Noah, stood at the windows, which had been opened from the top so that passengers might lean out a bit to greater appreciate the experience. The excitement in the car was as palpable as on the giant new Tilyou Ferris Wheel at Steeplechase Park in Coney Island.

The train slowed almost to a crawl, but still women gasped as it turned. Noah leaned out as well, not as far as some of the adolescents who rode the train for excitement, but sufficiently that he felt suspended in the air twelve stories above the ground. He was focusing on two men, their hats so far away as to be reduced to dots, when he felt a shove in his back. The window was not open near enough to present danger, but with his attention on the street below, the sensation caused him to reach out blindly for something to grab.

Noah whirled about and was confronted by a ruddy, thick-featured man with a handlebar mustache.

"Sorry, mac," the man said. "The car lurched."

Noah had not felt the lurch, but accepted the man's apology.

"Still," the man added, "I suppose it is best not to take foolish chances." With that, he tipped his hat and walked to the far end of the car.

When the train finally pulled into the station at 116th Street, most of the riders were chattering in exhilaration and relief. As Noah got off, the man who jostled him smiled and gave a small wave. Perhaps there had been something to Turner McKee's tale after all.

Minutes later, Noah stepped inside the wall of Columbia's beautiful, manicured quadrangle. A wonder. McKim, Mead & White's creation had certainly satisfied university president Seth Low's desire for an "academic village" modeled after an Athenian agora. New York University, where he had attended medical school, had consisted of a series of timeworn buildings on which his fellow students had bestowed the epithet The Dungeon.

Abraham Jacobi's office was in the eastern wing on the second floor, guarded by an unsmiling, middle-aged woman with thick spectacles, a severe bun, and the posture of a Prussian colonel. When Noah gave his name, she told him curtly that he was expected and ushered him through the door. Jacobi was standing at the window, looking out over the campus. He turned as Noah entered.

"So what is this mystery Alan De Kuyper tells me only the great Jacobi can solve?"

He was a small man, bald on top, with a wild fringe of white hair around the sides. His jowls sagged and pouches protruded under his eyes. He walked with a slight limp. But even with all these signs of age, Jacobi exuded vibrancy, as if a much younger person lay inside a deteriorating shell.

"A child died in my care. The circumstances seemed singular. Alan feels certain that you are the only man in New York who can help me pinpoint the cause."

The pediatrician emitted a single snort. "Just give me the details, young man. Without the treacle." Although he had been in America for almost four decades, Jacobi's accent, while vestigial, was guttural, distinctly German.

Noah told his story quickly and concisely.

"*Encephalitis?*" Jacobi's face puckered as if he had imbibed pure lemon juice. "Alan De Kuyper suggested that these symptoms were manifestations of *encephalitis?*"

"I think it was more a wish than a suggestion."

"I certainly hope so. The cause of the boy's death seems obvious. Why do you avoid it?"

"Morphia poisoning?"

"Of course."

Noah felt his heart sink. "So you believe my administration of laudanum—"

"No, no. *You* are not culpable. The laudanum you administered could not have caused the boy's death."

"It is kind of you to say so."

"I'm never kind. Except to children, of course. I simply state fact."

"How can you be so sure, Dr. Jacobi? What if somehow I gave the boy more than I thought?"

"How much more?"

"Four drops. Even six."

"You don't know the difference between two and six? Even so, it wouldn't have made a fig of difference. If you had given a five-year-old boy a sufficient dose to cause respiratory failure, he would have died in less than three hours. Children do not have the same responses as adults, you know."

"Could the boy have had an allergic reaction? One that delayed the effects of the drug?"

"An allergic reaction that *delayed* the effect of the drug? Where did you attend medical school, young man?"

"New York University."

"I must make a note to pay them a call and ask about their teaching methods." Jacobi heaved a sigh, then gestured to a chair. "Have a seat . . . Whitestone, is it not? Like the village in Flushing?"

"Yes."

"Have a seat, Whitestone." When Noah sat, Jacobi walked around to the front of his desk and leaned against it. His hands, thick and gnarled, like a laborer's, braced on the top edge. "I realize that you are trying to find an explanation for your patient's death. I am impressed that you are even testing hypotheses that would leave you at fault. All I can tell you is this: There is no pathogen or disease that I have heard of that would have accounted for the array of symptoms you encountered. No published case history anywhere. Any condition that could have been responsible for the first set of symptoms could not have also been responsible for the second.

"Morphia, as I think we agree, seems to be the only answer. First in its absence, then in excess. But as I said, the laudanum you administered could not have been the cause of that excess. I should also tell you that I would have done as you did. If I had encountered a similar pathology on my first visit and if I were forced to leave the patient for a number of hours, I, too, would have administered two drops of laudanum to alleviate the symptoms. In one so young, the risk of dehydration from diarrhea would exceed that of a small dose of the opiate. You were also correct in trying to coax water into the boy. If the authorities are fool enough to pursue the matter, I will be pleased to testify as such."

"Thank you, Dr. Jacobi. I am flattered."

Jacobi waved off the compliment. "Nonsense."

"If it was not the laudanum, what did kill the boy?"

"Only one conclusion is possible. The boy was given another morphiate during your absence. Your faith in his mother's veracity seems to have been misplaced."

"I was with Mrs. Anschutz, Dr. Jacobi. I simply cannot believe she was being duplicitous."

"Have you read any of the writings of the Austrian, Freud, young man?"

Noah had not.

"Freud writes about the mind, particularly how delusion or repressed memory can affect behavior. Fascinating hypotheses. Much of it will turn out to be rubbish, I expect, but there is certainly some truth in his work as well. Freud would assert that this Mrs. Anschutz, racked with guilt over providing the substance that caused her son's death, forced the memory into what he calls the unconscious mind. In other words, she now believes her lie, her delusion and, in believing it, can then convince others that she is not being untruthful at all."

"I am certain I would have spotted signs of madness, Dr. Jacobi, no matter how convincing the delusion was to Mrs. Anschutz."

"But this isn't madness, at least not in the sense we generally think of. The manifestation would be limited to this one incident. In all other aspects, the woman would appear to be quite normal."

"Do you subscribe to this theory, Dr. Jacobi?"

Jacobi shrugged. "He has produced some very impressive case studies to back up his assertions. At worst, my boy, don't rule out the possibility. If correct, you would simply need to confirm that the mother had medicated the child in your absence."

"How would I go about confirming that?"

"They have categorically refused an autopsy?"

"Yes."

"Then I cannot tell you. Detective work is not my province."

Noah stood but did not move for the door.

"Yes, Whitestone? Is there something more?"

"If the child was given a morphiate by his mother, she would have been unaware of the contents. Does that not follow?"

"Yes," Jacobi allowed. "I suppose it does. The mother, unless homicidal or a nincompoop, would not have knowingly dosed her son with an opiate after you had already given him one."

"Then assuming that the family did not use patent medicines . . . and, other than Bismosal, I'm convinced they did not . . . what morphiate prescribed by a physician would she have given her son unaware of the contents? Does that not imply that her physician did not tell her?"

Jacobi tugged at his beard. "An implication I am not pleased to acknowledge. But, yes, that is a possibility."

"Do you believe it equally possible that her son's physician prescribed a medication . . . a new medication . . . something experimental . . . not telling her of the composition because he was part of a test to determine whether or not the drug was safe?"

Jacobi's face darkened. "I am not sure I like the direction of your argument, young man."

"But how else to test drugs if not on subjects?"

"No physician I know would test a morphiate on a child without extreme safeguards. In a hospital, under constant observation, and only in doses so small as to not cause harm. If those doses are tolerated, they would be increased slowly. The notion that a physician would conduct a test as you have suggested is more than harebrained. It is criminal. I am certain you are mistaken."

Having come this far, Noah would not retreat. "Dr. Jacobi, do you believe there is a Patent Medicine Trust? That the liquor dealers, pharmacists, and proprietary drug associations have banded together to prevent government regulation of pharmaceuticals? That they ignore public welfare simply to amass profits?"

"I do not." Jacobi seemed on the verge of asking Noah to leave. "Where did you acquire such a notion?"

How much to tell? There seemed no point in withholding anything. "I was approached by a journalist. From *New Visions*. He wanted me to help him investigate graft he claims is given to doctors by pharmaceutical concerns. I told him that I was already in sufficient difficulty and would not become involved with his magazine."

Jacobi blew out a breath, then took two steps forward and patted Noah on the shoulder. "Very wise, my boy. I've learned that it is a good deal more important—and more difficult—to be among those who build rather than those who tear down. I am still passionate about improving the lot of the poor and the working class, but I no longer subscribe to the notion that to do so one must destroy society. Steering clear of the *New Visions* crowd will stand you in good stead."

The old pediatrician smiled. "I corresponded with Karl Marx, you know. Until about twenty years ago. His children were always afflicted with one ailment or another—Marx never had any money—but mostly we wrote to each other about politics. Karl was a very bright man, God rest his soul, extremely adept at honing in on the flaws of capitalism. His theories on with what to replace it, however, are twaddle."

"So you are not still radical?"

"Radical? What does the word mean really? To some it is merely an excuse to exercise distaste for those who succeed." Jacobi swept his arm toward the window and the magnificent quadrangle beyond. "For me, this is radical. A radical step forward in education. This institution will provide more good than a thousand articles in *New Visions*. Had I only known that in my youth."

"Was it difficult? Escaping from prison? Stowing away?"

"Ah, yes. My hairbreadth escape. My passage across the Atlantic in the belly of a steamer." He smiled wistfully. "Both are somewhat overstated,

I'm afraid. I seem, despite all my efforts to the contrary, to have acquired a legend. But life, I am sad to say, is not nearly so romantic as fantasy. While I did spend two years in prison, I did not exactly escape. Nor was there a death sentence. I was a radical and a Jew . . . the authorities were perfectly content on both counts to allow me to leave. Nor was I forced to work my way over on a tramp, although I daresay my accommodations were none too sumptuous. The irony is that for the past ten years Germany has been attempting to persuade me to return. 'We would be honored if you would come home,' is how the letter read. Signed by the Kaiser's secretary himself. 'Home.' How hypocritical. I have refused, of course.

"So, Dr. Whitestone, the legend of Jacobi, derring-do pediatrician, a pistol in one hand, a stethoscope in the other, turns out to be silly hyperbole. The lesson from this, I suppose, is that when a tale stretches credibility, seems preposterous, it generally is."

ELEVEN

Jacobi had made perfect sense, of course. Turner McKee's tale of the great capitalist conspiracy, rife with heartless, venal profiteers leaving a trail of dead children in their wake in the pursuit of greater and wealth seemed preposterous. But was the notion that Mildred Anschutz had walked around in some sort of trance feeding a lethal dose of a morphiate to her son any less so? And the man on the train was certainly no trance.

In either case, he was back to Frias. And however likely or unlikely the theory seemed to be, Turner McKee and his mysterious proofs had become an itch that had to be scratched.

Noah stopped at a newsstand on Broadway and asked the boy if he might see *New Visions*. The newsboy, small and pimply, wearing a slouch cap, looked Noah up and down. "You, sir?" he asked. When Noah continued to wait, the boy withdrew a copy of the magazine from the rack. "Ten cents," he said, holding his free hand open.

The cover featured a drawing of Admiral Dewey and his Japanese Akita, Bob. Dewey took Bob everywhere and was famous for insisting that every portrait include the dog lounging at his feet. But *New Visions* had placed the Akita's head on the figure in the admiral's uniform sitting in the chair, and Dewey's head on the dog. The headline read, WHO SPEAKS FOR AMERICA?

Noah checked inside for the address of the magazine's offices. Astor Place near the Cooper Union. Of course. Astor Place was notoriously avant-garde: home to artists, theater denizens, and bohemians of all stripes. He tossed the magazine into the trash.

When Noah arrived downtown, the streets were crowded, most of the pedestrians young and moving with an urgency lacking on the sedate streets of Brooklyn. Many were dressed with almost garish ostentation: men in loud, checked vests, and peaked caps; women in flared, peasant-type skirts and low-collared blouses.

The entrance was on Lafayette Street, in an industrial building, a brick rectangle, four stories high, with a dingy lobby and pock-marked wooden floor. A board listing the tenants hung on the left-hand wall, many of the entries written on paper and tacked on. *New Visions* currently shared quarters with a toy maker, an importer of leather goods, a manufacturer of musical instruments, and the Ukrainian-American Society. A large chain-and-pulley elevator was available, but Noah chose to walk up the single flight of stairs. When he reached the second floor, he walked across scuffed black-and-white linoleum to a door with a frosted-glass upper panel that proclaimed NO SOLICITING in letters almost as large as magazine's name.

Noah walked into a scene of controlled chaos. Nine beaten-down wooden desks were spaced throughout, and between them, instead of open floor, lay stacks of paper, cartons, and packing boxes. A dozen men and women, all young, scurried about as if it were one minute before midnight. The men wore no neckwear and were clean shaven. The women were without high collars. Most had hair hanging loose on their shoulders.

Some of the staff were seated in front of Remington Type-Writers; some were reading; some were in fervent conversation with others. No one seemed in charge. Noah's eye was briefly drawn to a poster tacked up on the wall touting William McKinley for president. A gun had been drawn in one of McKinley's hands and a bloody, decapitated head, obviously a Filipino, held by the hair in the other. On another wall was a large drawing of Governor Roosevelt in the guise of a snarling beast.

Although the politics were offensive, the passion in the room, the swirl of raw energy, the . . . youth . . . was intoxicating. Noah leaned forward on the railing that divided the entrance from the remainder of the room looking for Turner McKee, but the reporter was not present. Some of the magazine's employees glanced his way, but no one moved to inquire as to his presence. In his dark suit and carefully trimmed beard and mustache, Noah felt like some stodgy adult breaking in on a party in a university dormitory.

A door opened at the side of the room and a woman emerged. Her skin was dark, but with an undertone of gold. Brown hair, almost black, was loosely pinned so that it fell slightly, framing her face. She was arrestingly, stunningly beautiful.

The woman walked to a nearby desk to speak with a male associate. As she gestured, her long arms and thin fingers moved with kinetic grace. The man to whom she was speaking listened almost worshipfully, nodding occasionally, yet seemed to be rapt only by her words and not her appearance. When she leaned over the desk to point to something on a piece of paper, her blouse, open at the neck, hung down and the sweep of her breast was clearly visible. Noah could not move his eye from the curve of her flesh.

He was unaware of how long he stood gawking. Eventually, the woman sensed his gaze and turned her head. Noah, caught, wanted to look away, but could not. After a second or two, the woman straightened and walked to the railing. She had a loose-limbed way of moving that was at once boyish and startlingly sensual.

"I was looking for Turner McKee," he said. The sentence came out stiff, scratchy.

A look of suspicion fell over the woman's face. Her eyes were large and a striking shade of green, almost aqua. He noticed a fleck of gold in each eye. She gave off a subtle, musky scent.

"He's not here. Why do you want him?"

"My name is Whitestone." Noah cleared his throat but was unable to lubricate his voice. "He asked me to come by. He said he might have some materials I would find of interest."

"Oh, the doctor," she said. She seemed to have moved closer to him, but perhaps he merely imagined she had. Her scent seemed stronger. "Turner mentioned you might come by. That you might be curious to meet the band of wild-eyed revolutionaries who work here."

Noah was stung, jealous at the mention of McKee's name. He was certain just from the way she said it that Turner McKee and this astonishing woman were lovers. A man engaged to be married, jealous of another man whom he had met once, over a woman whose name he didn't know.

"Did Mr. McKee leave anything for me, Miss . . . ?" He had not taken his eyes from hers.

A man appeared at her side, holding a piece of paper. "Miriam, I need you to read this right away," he said. "Mauritz wanted it shorter."

"Mauritz Herzberg?" Noah asked.

"I'll be there in a moment," she said to the man.

"Yes, Dr. Whitestone. He's our publisher."

"Then you're . . . Miriam Herzberg? The Red Lady?"

"An appellation of which I am not especially fond."

"I read about you. You spoke at the rally during the Hampton dress factory strike. Almost caused a riot."

"Yes, Dr. Whitestone. Those women work twelve hours a day, seven days a week, locked inside a sweatbox. Some are only girls, ten years old. I thought someone should speak for them. Don't you?"

"Yes," Noah replied. "Of course."

"Turner left a message for you," she said. "He said that he was out retrieving precisely the information you asked for."

"Retrieving?"

"That's what he said."

"Is he bringing it here?" He hoped she would say yes so that he could wait.

Miriam Herzberg shook her head. Her hair fell onto her face and she brushed it away impatiently, as if it were an annoying insect.

"No. For some reason, he was going home. You might try him there. I'll write down the address for you." She took a pencil and paper off a nearby desk and scribbled down the information.

"Thank you," he said, but made no immediate move to leave.

"I'm sorry, but I can't talk now. We're very busy." She turned on her heel and walked back across the room.

<hr />

McKee lived on Rivington Street, in a Lower East Side tenement, amid the poor immigrants whose rights he sought to secure. People, horses, carriages, and pushcarts filled the streets; Italians in derbies with long, drooping mustaches mixed with thick, fair-haired Slavs in grimy overalls, and Jews with enormous beards, dressed in black. Women in long dresses with shawls pulled tightly about them moved watchfully through the crowds. The smell of pushcart food—onions, sausage, peppers, spices, cheap meat—was everywhere, and everyone seemed to speak at once. Children darted in and out of the foot traffic. Two street Arabs attempted to grab for Noah's wallet, but he dodged quickly and was able to keep it from their reach.

Noah found McKee's building and, heeding the reporter's warnings, looked about before going in. All he could detect was an avalanche of humanity. So many people came and went that the area had an odd sense of anonymity, as a cacophony often seems to engender an odd sense of silence.

McKee's apartment was number six, up a rickety set of steps with a broken banister. The numbers had fallen off most of the doors, but McKee's was fastened on with a single nail. Noah knocked. He waited but got no response. He knocked again, longer and harder. A door down the hall opened. An urchin stuck out his head and, seeing a well-dressed man, stuck it back inside and slammed the door shut.

Noah was about to turn and leave when McKee's door opened a crack. McKee put his face to the narrow opening. "I can't see you now." He turned his head back toward the interior of the room. "I'll be right there, dearie." He smiled and raised his eyebrows. "As you can see, I'm entertaining."

"But what about . . ."

"Your timing is inopportune. Didn't I make myself clear? I'll call you tomorrow. We can meet for lunch. I'll even buy."

With that, McKee cast Noah a stiff, final grin and slammed the door.

Noah muttered his way back to Brooklyn. What an idiot he had been. Traipsing about only to have a door shut in his face by a man engaged in an assignation. Vital information. Murdered children. Melodrama. Jacobi had been correct after all. And perhaps the man on the train had simply been a man on a train.

TWELVE

The following morning, Noah rose early, washed, dressed, and asked Mrs. Jensen to prepare a proper breakfast. Or as proper a breakfast as Mrs. Jensen was capable. Although she had told him that Mr. Jensen had died of a heart attack, Noah had often speculated as to whether the cause had actually been malnutrition.

Noah sipped his coffee as he read the morning edition of the *Daily Eagle*. Dewey's flotilla, led by his flagship *Olympia*, was due to anchor off Tompkinsville, Staten Island, on Thursday, in preparation for its trip up the Hudson on Friday. Noah paid particular attention to the announcement that the official list of instructions for the regiments in the land parade had been transmitted to the army commanders.

"What do you know of Colonel Anschutz?" he asked Mrs. Jensen when she returned with the coffeepot.

Mrs. Jensen filled the space between them with a cough. "Well, doctor, you know how it is with army men."

"No, Mrs. Jensen. Tell me."

"You know. They're trained to fight all the time . . . I guess it kind of gets in their blood."

"Are you saying that Colonel Anschutz is a violent man?"

She lowered her voice to a whisper, thrilled to have the truth dragged out of her. "Hit his wife once. Maybe more. The boys, too. Whole family's terrified of him. Annie O'Rourke, their cook, told Mrs. Hardesty down on Clark Street that the missus whispered to herself when he left that she hoped he didn't come back. She's too afraid even to tell her father or her uncle. Neither of them knows pea soup. Mayor Wurster thinks his son-in-law is the silk."

"Do you know when he's coming home? I mean, will he have to wait until the procession is completed, or will he get leave two days before, when the fleet arrives?"

Mrs. Jensen shook her head. "Dunno. I'll try and find out."

Noah thanked her, then continued to leaf through the paper, trying without success to banish Pug Anschutz and Arnold Frias from his mind.

On page four, he found an item to lift his spirits. The Brooklyn Superbas and Jack Dunn had defeated the Perfectos and the mighty Cy Young by a score of 2 to 0 at Sportsman's Park in St. Louis to bring the season's record to a prodigious 90–40. When all this was settled, he must attend a game with Maribeth. Not Ibsen, perhaps, but great fun nonetheless. And women more and more had begun to be seen in the better seats.

Noah browsed the editorial page, the fraternal society news, the classified advertisements, the stock market reports, and the church page. He was about to put down the paper when an item on page sixteen caught his eye. Right under the account of a policeman shot by a burglar.

"Turner McKee, 24, an employee of *New Visions* magazine, was killed just after 9 P.M. after a fall from Gouverneur Street pier into New York Harbor. Any chance Mr. McKee had of saving himself was lost when he was struck by a passing tugboat, the *Amelia Jane*. Captain Dorn of the *Amelia Jane* succeeded in fishing Mr. McKee from the water, but efforts to rouse him were to no avail. Mr. McKee was taken to the city morgue pending funeral arrangements by his family."

Oh my God.

Noah checked the time. Only nine minutes. He dropped the newspaper, grabbed his coat, and hurried out the door. He had to get to the electric trolley station before 8:30 or he would be forced to wait a half hour for the next departure. Even now, there was a chance the family had already acted.

He turned the corner on Tillary Street, near the foot of the entrance to the Brooklyn Bridge, almost running. The clang of the conductor's bell announced the trolley's departure. Noah yelled for the conductor to wait, but the trolley was already creaking forward. He arrived in a full sprint just as the car was turning on the track to head back to Manhattan. The conductor stared at the figure hurtling toward him as if at a madman. He stood on the platform, blocking Noah's entry, waving for him not to attempt to jump onto the moving car. But on the U-shaped curve, the trolley moved slowly. Noah timed his leap and landed on the bottom step just as the trolley straightened out. As he tried to lean toward the interior of the car, his left foot slipped. His momentum began to carry him out to the street. Noah reached out with his right hand and found a support pole. Pulling hard, he hauled himself aboard, crashing against the conductor's chest, knocking the man's hat askew.

"I ought to call the police, you brainless fool!"

"I'm a physician on an emergency call," Noah gasped. "A matter of life and death."

"Try a stunt like that again and it'll be *your* death," muttered the conductor, but Noah's pronouncement had taken the sting out of his outrage. "All right, then," he grunted, gesturing to the coin box, "five cents."

Fifteen minutes later, the trolley discharged him at City Hall Plaza, and the ride to Twenty-Third Street on the Third Avenue elevated took only twenty minutes more. A quick walk from there and Noah was at the entrance of the squat, gray building that was the repository of the city's dead. At the high desk just inside the door sat a police sergeant with a livid scar that began just below his right eye and disappeared underneath a sweeping mustache. When Noah inquired about Turner McKee, the sergeant tilted his head to one side and pursed his lips.

"You family?" He spoke in a low, official growl, not at all welcoming. McKee's death had apparently attracted official attention as well.

"No. I'm a physician."

"Name?"

"Whitestone."

The sergeant took up a pen and reached for a ledger. He seemed to move with exaggerated slowness. "White-stone," he said to himself as he laboriously formed the letters.

"Could you hurry, please?" Noah finally interjected. "This is urgent."

"Can't go down," intoned the sergeant. "Family only."

"But I told you. I'm a doctor."

"Yeah. White-stone. Don't know the rush. Can't see why he'd need a doctor now." The sergeant smirked at his wit. The scar whitened as it stretched across his cheek.

"Mr. McKee was my patient. I spoke to him just last night, and I'd like to make sure you've got the right man. I think a mistake might have been made in identifying the body."

The sergeant shook his head slowly. "No mistake. Father's there now. He don't seem to have no doubts."

Noah forced an affable grin. "Ah. I was to meet Mr. McKee here."

The sergeant put his right index finger to the point of the scar and rubbed it up and down. "No dice, pal. You ain't family, you ain't goin' in."

Noah reached into his pocket and fingered a dollar coin, wondering whether to risk offering the man money. Then, from a staircase at the end of the hall, another man appeared. He was about fifty, portly, light-haired, with an aquiline nose, and obviously aggrieved. "There's Mr. McKee now." Noah moved quickly past the desk. Before the sergeant could decide whether to chase him, Noah had reached the portly man and whispered, "I'm terribly sorry about your son but I must speak with you, Mr. McKee. Away from the police. My name is Noah Whitestone. I'm a physician."

Beneath the fleshiness, Turner McKee's father had his son's sharp, intelligent face. "About what, Dr. Whitestone? Were you a friend of my son?"

Noah glanced back. The sergeant had left the desk but had paused midway down the hall. He seemed to be trying to decide whether he should accost the interloper now that he was speaking with the father of the dead man.

"I met him only once . . . twice. We spoke of his work. The circumstances of your son's death are suspicious. I'm not at all sure it was an accident."

"Well, I am sure, Dr. Whitestone. I am sure it was not an accident. Of all the ways Turner might have met his end, drowning is the least likely."

"I agree. Do you think I might see his body?"

"Can you learn anything from an examination here?"

"We won't know unless I try, Mr. McKee."

"Then try by all means. Come with me, Dr. Whitestone. He's downstairs."

Noah glanced back over his shoulder. The sergeant had not moved, still unsure how to proceed. He had not been chosen for the tedious job of manning a desk at the morgue because of quick wits. When they reached the staircase that led to the depository in the basement, the sergeant returned to his post and reached for the mouthpiece of his telephone.

On their way down the stairs, Turner McKee Sr. told Noah he was a milliner. He owned three hat-making facilities in the Bronx, an estate in Pelham, and had always known his son's politics would lead to trouble. But he had tears in his eyes as he said it.

When they reached the lower floor, Noah felt the air grow distinctly colder. Halfway down the hall was a set of double doors, across from which stood a coatrack holding giant overcoats. Large wool hats and sets of both thick and thin gloves sat on a shelf on the top. The doors swung open, and Noah and Mr. McKee were hit with a blast of frigid air. The mortuary utilized the same ammonia-cycle commercial refrigeration system that was employed in meatpacking plants. A man in one of the overcoats, hats, and gloves emerged. Even when the doors swung shut, the intense cold remained.

"What are you two doing in here?" the man in the overcoat demanded. Icicles clung to his mustache. Then his ice-encrusted eyebrows rose in recognition. "Oh, it's you, Mr. McKee. I thought you'd gone."

"This man is a physician. I have asked him to look at my son."

"I'm not supposed to."

"Why not?" Noah asked.

"Orders." But he looked furtively toward the stairway, then motioned that they should quickly don the requisite outerwear. The coat was lined with thick fleece, but the moment the attendant ushered them through the doors, Noah felt as if his joints had frozen solid. The attendant seemed unaffected.

The vault was immense, at least one thousand square feet. Stack after stack of sliding cast-iron drawers ran up each of the seven aisles. Every stack held four drawers. The room seemed like a macabre library card catalog. A mist of frost permeated the room, rendering the back indistinct. For all Noah could make out, it might extend to infinity. When Noah asked, the attendant told him that more than three hundred corpses could reside, if *reside* was the word, in this chamber at any one time. Great cities, it seemed, required equally great facilities for its dead.

The attendant led them to the third aisle to the left and then walked to the fourth stack. He grasped the wooden handle of the second drawer from the top. "I'm glad you came back, Mr. McKee," he said before he pulled it open. "I wanted to tell you that I'm an admirer of your son's work. I read *New Visions*." McKee's father nodded, embarrassed that the attendant had misread his politics, but flattered all the same at the reach of his son's articles.

With a sharp tug, the attendant pulled open the drawer. Inside, on the sheet of gray metal that formed the drawer bottom, lay the body of Turner McKee. His clothing had been removed, and the signs of violent death were manifest. McKee's father, who had been forced to view this same sight just moments before, turned his head away.

Noah cast his eyes over the body, his vision obscured by the cloud he created in front of his face every time he exhaled. The most obvious sign of trauma was a broad wound across McKee's left temple, running from the zygomatic bone under the eye, across the sphenoidal, to the parietal almost at the crown of his head. It was matted with dried blood, where he had allegedly been struck by the passing tugboat. There were a number of smaller bruises on the torso and extremities, all of which might have originated from the same source.

Then he saw it. Faint. He wouldn't have noticed at all if he hadn't been looking. He reached out and placed his hand on the dead man's shoulder. To owe his life to someone who had passed him by in a breeze.

Noah felt a pull on his arm and looked up to see the attendant gesturing for him to finish. Noah nodded and let the man push the drawer back in place. The metal track shrieked in the cold. Moments later, they were out the door. The air in the hall felt tropical.

McKee's father thanked the attendant as the three hung their coats. Noah heard noise coming from the staircase and turned to see the desk sergeant and another uniformed man hurrying toward them. The newcomer was shorter but extremely stocky. He walked stiff-kneed, his balled-up hands making short arcs around his hips. A man accustomed to using his fists.

He addressed himself to Noah. "Might I ask who you are and what yer doing here?" He did not need to make an effort to inject menace into the question. It was a natural by-product of his speech.

"I'm a doctor, and I'm looking at the body at the father's request," Noah replied evenly. "Might I ask who *you* are and what *you* are doing here?" He was becoming accustomed to dealing with bullies.

"I'm Lieutenant Laverty, New York Police Department. And I'm used to asking the questions, not answering them."

"I gave you an answer. I was examining Turner McKee's body."

"And what did your 'examination' tell you?" Laverty remained pugnacious but there was a stiffness in his voice as he asked.

Noah shrugged. "Nothing much. It seems as if the blow on the head from the tugboat must have killed him."

Laverty blew out an exaggerated sigh. "A tragedy. If the captain had looked over the side a few seconds sooner, the boy might have been saved."

"Indeed," Noah replied impassively. "But Mr. McKee here has been through enough for one day. We should leave him to make preparations for his son's burial."

As they walked down the hall, Noah glanced at McKee, indicating they should keep silent. Back on the street, Noah waited until they were a block away from the morgue before he spoke. "You must have your son removed to a mortuary immediately. I will give you the name of the one I wish you to use. Instruct the mortician to do nothing else until you hear from me."

McKee grabbed Noah by the arm. "You found something?"

"Circular bruises on both wrists. They had to be made either by ropes or strong hands. Certainly not by an encounter with a tugboat."

"So Turner *was* killed."

"Yes. And I believe he also saved my life."

"How? You weren't with him."

"I might have been, but he wouldn't let me in his flat. There is more to be learned, Mr. McKee, but forensics is not my field and I want to be sure your son's death is investigated properly."

"What do you intend to do?"

Noah felt at the inside pocket of his coat. Yes. It was still there.

"Engage an expert," he said.

THIRTEEN

DAY 4. SATURDAY, 9/23—10 A.M.

Noah instructed Turner McKee to have his son's remains transported to the new Frank E. Campbell Burial and Cremation Company on Madison Avenue and Eighty-First Street. Frank E. Campbell had opened the year before to much fanfare. Its advertising promised to provide funeral services for New York's new breed of apartment dwellers every bit as dignified and intimate as one could host in a private home. Relieved of the burden of providing ceremony and sustenance in confined spaces, New Yorkers had made Campbell's an instant success. McKee was puzzled as to why Noah would choose a mortuary so remote from his home, but promised to do as Noah suggested.

After Noah sent McKee off, he stopped at the Gramercy Hotel on Twenty-Third Street to place a paid telephone call. From there, it was back to the Third Avenue el for a journey even farther uptown.

After leaving city employ in 1888, Justin Herold had taken offices in Yorkville, at 385 East Eighty-Seventh Street. To obtain an audience,

Noah used the same stratagem with which Alan had enticed Dr. Jacobi. He promised to lay out the details of a forensic mystery the likes of which Herold had never seen. Fortunately, Herold was no less curious than the pediatrician.

Herold's office and, Noah assumed, his residence were in a three-story row house in an area populated by German, Irish, and Slavic immigrants. Firmly working class. Why a physician of Herold's reputation and achievements would choose such an area instead of Fifth Avenue or one of the other more prestigious sections of New York was a mystery. Noah hadn't been in Justin Herold's office five minutes before he found out.

"Sorcerers. And alchemists. This is what I'm speaking of, Whitestone. Those who are charged to bring scientific knowledge into our criminal system still believe that the sun circles the Earth."

Herold was pacing the carpet when Noah entered. Without pleasantries, with one brusque sweep of his arm, he'd gestured for his visitor to sit. Herold was thin, clean shaven, almost completely bald, with an unlined and extremely handsome face. The offices were sparsely furnished and incommodious. For some moments, Herold continued to pace, sighing and nodding to himself. Finally, throwing up his hands in frustration, he dropped heavily into the chair behind his desk.

"Whitestone, what do you know of the Meyer case?"

"The poisoner? He's in the penitentiary." The case, six years earlier, had been one of the most lurid of the decade. Henry Meyer, a homeopathic physician, along with his wife, had been accused of killing two acquaintances, Ludwig Brandt and Gustave Baum, by arsenic poisoning. Mrs. Meyer then posed as each man's widow and redeemed the victims' life insurance policies. Meyer's first trial was adjourned when one of the jurors went insane in the courtroom. Rumors of demonic possession had been rampant. Meyer had only escaped the electric chair in his second trial because one juror refused to vote for first-degree murder.

Herold wagged a finger back and forth. "The *alleged* poisoner, you mean. Brandt and Baum may both still be alive. Brandt has even reportedly been seen . . . in Mexico . . . living off the proceeds that Meyer is supposed to have stolen."

"But I thought both Baum and Brandt had been positively identified through their remains."

"After three months? Are you joking, Whitestone? Neither cadaver had been embalmed. I have performed over 2,200 autopsies. It is impossible to render an identification of an unembalmed corpse after three weeks, let alone three months. Four experts testified to that fact at the trial. I was one of them. I copiously laid out the forensics. But did the jury listen? Of course not! Not with the public devouring accounts of the proceedings like pigs at the trough. A conviction; that was all that was important. What did it matter that science disagreed? The judge, the jury, the prosecution . . . all are igno-rant of legal medicine. Or *choose* to be ignorant. A jury would rather convict for the prurient joy of an expected electrocution than to follow science."

"Is that why you left the coroner's office?"

"I was forced out by Tammany Hall. My predecessor, Conway, a physi-cian in name only, had spent three years bristling at my appointment. He found himself unable to secure a living by honest work, so he imposed upon his cronies to get him his old job back. Politics trumps competence, so I am out and Conway is in. The irony, of course, is that the coroner himself employs me as his private physician. I asked him once why he didn't use Conway and he merely laughed.

"So, Whitestone, I now engage in private practice in a neighborhood where my services are appreciated and, as a sideline, have become a con-sulting forensic practitioner. I am flattered to be often solicited to provide scientific evidence at criminal trials. With good fortune, I may advance legal medicine as a private citizen more so than I was able to as a govern-ment functionary." Herold thrust his right hand into his trouser pocket. "Now, suppose you tell me of this extraordinary case you have been so kind as to bring my way."

Noah once again recounted the details of Willard Anschutz's death and its aftermath, omitting, for the moment, mention of murder, Turner

McKee, *New Visions*, or any conspiracy that might be afoot among the manufacturers of pharmaceuticals.

Herold listed attentively without interruption, paying particular attention to the recitation of Noah's failed chemical analysis. "If the sulphomolybdic acid test and nitric acid test were negative," he asked finally, "why not run the others?"

"I was afraid to destroy the remainder of the sample."

"Nonsense. How much of the tablet is left?"

Noah withdrew the envelope from his inside coat pocket and passed it across the desk. Herold peered inside and then glared at Noah as if he was confronting a simpleton. "Half? You used half a tablet for *two* tests? You could perform *ten* tests on this and still have sufficient quantity for a court exhibit. Where did you learn forensic analysis, Whitestone?"

"Medical school."

"Of course," Herold muttered. He pushed himself from his chair. "Now let us go find out what this is." At the side of the office, Herold opened a door and Noah realized where Herold had spent the money he had saved on furnishings. The laboratory inside was more modern and better equipped than the one Noah had used at Brooklyn Hospital.

After some preparations, Herold used a scalpel to scrape a few grains from the blue tablet into a ceramic dish. "This is all you really need, you know. If the test is negative, repeat it, with shavings from a different section of the sample. And again, if necessary. In that manner, if the material is distributed unevenly, you almost will achieve a positive result in one of your tests." Herold reached to the shelf over his countertop and withdrew a small, corked bottle. Withdrawing the cork, he partially filled a medicine dropper. "We shall try the ferric chloride test first. Iodic acid is not as reliable, if have you read my book . . . you did read my book?"

Noah assured Herold that he had.

Herold exposed the scrapings of the tablet to ferric chloride. If morphiates were present, the sample would strike a dark greenish-blue, but the effect might be ephemeral if free acids or alkalis were also present. Noah leaned over the dish, staring, waiting.

There it was! A change in color. Blue. Almost violet. Not greenish-blue, but perhaps the discrepancy was in description. Noah was elated. A definite change.

Herold was not as pleased. "Not morphiates. I'm certain of that. But the result is of equal interest."

"A substance that might have caused the boy's death?"

Herold shook his head. "I don't believe so. Possibly." Herold could not fail to notice Noah's disappointment. "Buck up, Whitestone. I need to check further. It could be carbolic acid, gallic acid, or salicylic acid. But the first would be unlikely to be used in pharmaceuticals . . . in its pure form it is quite caustic . . . nor do I think there is high pharmacological probability of the second. Thus, I think it is almost certainly the third."

"Salicylic acid?" Noah asked. "Wasn't that used as an analgesic and antipyretic some years ago, but then abandoned because it caused severe gastrointestinal pain?"

Herold reared back, as if stunned. "Very *good*, Whitestone. You are not hopeless after all. Salicylic acid is highly effective as a pain reliever and lowers fevers remarkably, but the ancillary effects are so severe as to sometimes be fatal."

"Could this have killed Willard Anschutz?"

Herold shook his head impatiently. "No, no, Whitestone. You don't understand. First of all, the boy would not have died of respiratory failure from salicylic acid. But, more important, I don't believe this is simply salicylic acid."

"What then?"

"We'll soon know. We can precipitate the product and then check melting and boiling points. If my suspicions are correct, we have a very interesting substance on our hands."

Herold was deft, sure, and knowledgeable. His fingers moved with a musician's precision and confidence. Fifteen minutes later, Herold held his hand open toward the substance in the glass tube as if making an introduction.

"Here," he said, "we have a remarkable compound. Salicylic acid has been combined with acetic anhydride to create acetylsalicylic acid, leaving acetic acid as a by-product. Acetylized salicylic acid has a lower boiling point and lower melting point. If the boy took pure salicylic acid two weeks ago, he certainly would not have improved. Or, at least, the gastrointestinal distress would have overwhelmed any analgesic improvement. Someone has apparently discovered, and it seems quite recently, that acetylized salicylic acid retains the therapeutic properties of the pure substance but without the harmful effects. Whoever it was has marketed the substance as a pharmaceutical without telling anyone yet."

"Experimenting then?"

"If you wish. One must determine if the substance works on a large scale. Or at least works without making patients sicker. Or killing them. You can't tell that in a laboratory, or even on test animals, no matter how rigorous you are. Salicylic acid has a notorious history, so this is obviously a secret test of the acetylized version."

"Frias knows. He must. He prescribed this."

"Possibly. Or perhaps he was given these tablets by a third party. Many physicians are so unconcerned by what they prescribe that they do no checking at all. But in either case this Frias certainly has information that may help you unravel the threads of the crime."

"So it was a crime. I didn't believe him at first."

"Who?"

"A reporter."

"He was correct, Whitestone, whoever he was. When a child dies of a foreign substance introduced into his system either intentionally or through neglect, it is a crime. Frias may not be the criminal, but he is a key."

"But how can I turn that key? Frias won't speak with me."

"Perhaps, Whitestone. But I'm confident I can persuade him to speak with me."

"Thank you, Dr. Herold. I was hoping for your assistance. I cannot begin to express my gratitude."

"You are quite welcome, Whitestone. While I am, of course, pleased to provide you aid in extricating yourself from this pickle barrel you've tumbled into, my primary interest is in the science. If forensic practices are to become integrated into our legal system, we must be able to anticipate the new, not simply recognize the old. Here is an opportunity to use science not only to decipher a crime but to prevent further victims."

Now was the time to reveal the rest. "But while I appreciate your help, Dr. Herold, I feel that I must warn you. There may be danger if you involve yourself in this affair."

Noah told Herold of the death of Turner McKee, of the Patent Medicine Trust, of his examination of the corpse, the bruising on the wrists, and Lieutenant Laverty. He even told him of Pug Anschutz, and Frederick Wurster.

Herold listened with growing excitement. "And you say the corpse is just now being removed to Campbell's mortuary?"

"Yes. I was hoping you might to willing to—"

"We must move quickly. Tell me, Whitestone, do you believe you could convince McKee's father to permit an autopsy?"

"I've already done that."

"Excellent. Then we must contact McKee immediately. Or Campbell's. They must postpone embalming until I arrive."

"I've done that, too."

Herold stopped. He looked to Noah and gave one long, appreciative nod. "Fine work, Whitestone. You get better all the time. You are not remotely the dolt I agreed to see on the telephone."

"You weren't interested in my description of the case?"

"I was interested to see who was spewing more hyperbole than a character in a dime-store novel."

"How gratifying."

Herold patted Noah on the shoulder. "Don't take it to heart, man. You have acquitted yourself admirably. That's all that really matters, isn't it?"

"I suppose so."

"No supposing about it." Herold reached for his hat and coat. "We must leave immediately. At the very least, we should be able to determine if water is present in the man's lungs. If not, of course, he would have been dead before he entered the water. Even if water is present, I can discern whether or not he was conscious. The first stage of drowning, 'surprise inspiration,' essentially a deep reflexive breath in which the victim aspirates a large quantity of water, will be absent. And, while I'm sure your examination in the morgue was as thorough as possible under the circumstances, the more significant bruising will tell us a great deal if examined under more propitious conditions." Herold clapped his hands. "Have you ever assisted at an autopsy? Outside of medical school, I mean."

"I would be excited to watch you work, Dr. Herold, but I can't go with you."

"You expect me to go to Campbell's alone?"

"I'm sorry, but I must return to *New Visions*."

"Why? What do you expect to find there?" Herold seemed insulted, like a star performer asked to play to a half-empty theater.

"I realize now that Turner McKee wasn't lying when he said he had vital information. I've got to ask . . . to try to find out what it might have been."

"Very well." Herold grunted. "Telephone me later tonight."

FOURTEEN

DAY 4. SATURDAY, 9/23—12:30 P.M.

Would the Red Lady be in tears? Enraged? Noah pushed open the door to *New Visions*, more eager than he wanted to be to find out.

But Miriam Herzberg showed no outward sign that she was even aware that her lover had died. She was occupied much as she had been the day before: talking with a man at a desk, pointing at something on a piece of paper curling out from a Type-Writer, responding to queries from other members of the staff. Once again, he waited at the railing. She didn't look up although he was certain she knew he was there.

A boy of about sixteen with shiny skin, a broad Slavic face, and smallpox scars sauntered to where Noah was standing. He made a point of looking Noah up and down, as if to snicker at his suit.

"Yeah?"

"I'd like to speak to Miss Herzberg."

"Busy." The boy turned to leave.

"Stay where you are, sonny."

The boy turned back. He wore a smug smile as if to pronounce that he was not intimidated, merely curious. His eyes fixed on Noah's. Small eyes. Hard eyes. Not a boy's eyes at all.

"You will be so kind as to tell Miss Herzberg that if she is interested in learning the true circumstances of Turner McKee's death, she will speak with me."

The boy put his fingers to his chin and rubbed at small patches of stubble that he seemed to be cultivating to hasten his ascent into manhood. Then he shrugged, turned, and walked across the room. He tapped Miriam on the shoulder, gestured with his head toward Noah, and spoke a few words that Noah could not make out. She nodded and returned to what she had been doing. Noah didn't move. After a few minutes, she glanced his way, then walked across the room. She arrived with the same studied nonchalance as the previous day. But her eyes were puffy and red.

"What have you got to tell me, Dr. Whitestone? We're all very busy."

"I wanted first to tell you how sorry I am about Mr. McKee. You obviously thought very highly of him."

"Thank you."

"I've completed a cursory examination of his body. A full autopsy is being done at this moment."

"For whom? The police?"

"For his father."

She let out a breath at the mention of a man whose loss was at least as great as her own. "A nice man. How is he?"

"Aggrieved. And irate."

"Yes. He would be. He loathed that Turner took up with us."

"He's not irate at you, Miss Herzberg. He's irate at the people who killed his son."

"Is that what you discovered? Your great revelation? That Turner didn't drown? There isn't a person in this room who believes he did."

"Perhaps. But does anyone know that he was murdered by at least two men, one of whom held or bound his wrists? Or that the men were in his flat when I went to see him? He warned me off and, I believe, saved my life. I intend to avenge his death."

"How? How will you avenge Turner's death?"

"I can continue his investigation into the Patent Medicine Trust. After all, it is in my interest, too. I'm trying to prove I didn't kill a child. To begin with, I would like to look over his papers. Anything to demonstrate that his death and the death of my patient are linked."

She considered the proposal. Noah could hear himself breathe.

"Come and talk to my father."

She led him toward the door from which he had first seen her emerge. The staff had ostensibly returned to their previous activities, although everyone's eyes were on Noah and Miriam. The Slavic boy stood, hands on hips, glaring.

She knocked perfunctorily, then opened the door and walked in. The inner office was much like the staff room. Untidy mountains of papers, back issues of the magazine, stacks of the *New York Herald*, *New York Times*, and sundry items crammed the bookcases and covered the floor. Across the room, in front of a large window stood a single desk.

A man in his fifties sat behind it. He exuded symmetry; square and short haired, with a pince-nez that sat on the bridge of his nose perfectly parallel to his mouth. His goatee and mustache were precisely cut. He sat perpendicular in his chair, and his head did not tilt in either direction from the vertical.

"This is Noah Whitestone," Miriam said. "He claims he has information about Turner's murder and wants to help." She neither expressed skepticism nor suppressed it.

Miriam's father rose from his chair without bending his torso. Only when he was fully erect did he extend his hand. The only other Jewish army officer that Noah had ever heard of in Europe was Dreyfus. Herzberg's grip was firm but restrained. A cultured man as well.

"Please take a seat." Like Jacobi, Herzberg spoke with an accent vestigially German.

Noah sat in the chair across the desk. Miriam moved around to the other side and stood at her father's shoulder.

Noah related his visit to the morgue and the transfer of McKee's body to a mortuary, neglecting to say which one. He noted that a full autopsy was being performed by an expert, but did not use Herold's name. Herzberg's eyes never left Noah's face during the recitation, nor did he seem to blink, although Noah was certain he must have.

"We are familiar with the circumstances that caused Turner to be in contact with you, Dr. Whitestone." Herzberg was measured but without antagonism. "Your offer of assistance is, of course, welcome, but as you would expect, we are forced to deal with outsiders with caution. The authorities will go to exceptional lengths to infiltrate our movement."

"You think I'm a police agent?"

A wry grin made an appearance and then was gone. "Not likely, I agree, but one becomes accustomed to elevating the unlikely to the possible."

"I can assure you my motives are genuine." Noah's eyes flitted to Miriam and then back again.

"Yes," Herzberg agreed without altering expression. "I suspect they are."

Miriam placed her hand lightly on her father's shoulder. Noah felt the blood rush to his face.

"But you should be aware of the risks, Dr. Whitestone. You will be harassed by the authorities, your career might be ruined, and even prison is not beyond the realm of possibility."

"Thank you for the warning, Mr. Herzberg, but I am already in danger of each of those."

"Perhaps. But you will heighten the probability of each. Any association with us will further inflame the passions of those already aligned against you. Moreover, you will come to the attention, if you have not already, of the same people who disposed of Turner. And, make no mistake. They will attempt to dispose of you as well if you threaten their interests or those of their employers."

Herzberg formed a steeple with his fingertips. His fingers were long and graceful like his daughter's.

"And then there is Pug Anschutz. The man, as I believe you now know, is a disgrace to military officers everywhere. A brute legitimized by a commission. We have information, although not irrefutable proof, that to persuade a prisoner to give information about a suspected arms cache, he threatened to burn down the man's home. With the family inside. The prisoner refused. Anschutz then had the hut set afire. A woman and six children burned to death. The next prisoner Anschutz questioned was more than willing to provide any information the colonel required. The cache was discovered. I might add that Anschutz was cited favorably by his superiors for depriving the rebels of a goodly number of guns and ammunition."

Noah would have scoffed at such an outrageous tale just three days before. Now he couldn't be sure.

"Leaving yourself to the recriminations of such a man," Herzberg went on, "will take a hardy spirit indeed."

"Do you discourage everyone who offers you assistance, Mr. Herzberg?"

"I am not discouraging you in the least. Just ensuring that you do not underestimate the risks. Those who do, regardless of how genuine their motives, tend to become unreliable at the most inconvenient moments. They then become a danger to others. We cannot allow that. The work we do is far too important to permit it to be put at even greater risk."

"And what work do you do, Mr. Herzberg? If I may be permitted to ask."

"It's quite simple, Dr. Whitestone. We attempt to keep the promise of America. The oppressed from all over the world come to this country— as I did—because of that promise. But it is a promise to which bankers, plutocrats, rich idlers, government officials . . . and members of the Patent Medicine Trust . . . feel no obligation. We simply endeavor to remind them. We in the press are in a unique position to do so, Dr. Whitestone. We are not *McClure's* or *Collier's,* but I believe we do our part."

"I respect your motives, Mr. Herzberg, but they are not mine. I'm a physician. I want to know what killed my patient. And what may be killing other doctors' patients."

"But our interests do coincide. Turner's focus, as I believe he told you, had shifted to bona fide pharmaceuticals. He insisted that, for years, your colleagues have been accepting money from pharmaceutical concerns to use their products without first ascertaining whether or not they were safe. Often the medicines prescribed by willing physicians were harmful, addictive, or both. He eventually learned, although I'm not certain how, that two drugs had recently been developed in Germany. One of them seemed to be a new form of a pain reliever and fever suppressant . . ."

"Acetylsalicylic acid."

"Explain please."

Noah told him of Herold's findings, once again not mentioning the pathologist by name.

"Interesting. The other was evidently an opiate, but unique according to the chemist who synthesized it in that no tolerance is developed. The patient feels no craving when deprived of a continued supply. If this is true, of course, it would be a boon since opiates have exceptional medicinal qualities. After some digging, Turner turned up four or five cases of children dying from what seemed to be morphia poisoning. All very recent. The most promising for our purposes was a case last week in Newark in which a seven-year-old girl was given a new mysterious cough remedy and died three days later, although her doctors were quick to claim the girl had a congenital breathing disorder. The search for an effective children's cough remedy has been intense, as I am certain you know . . ."

"Yes. Cough is among the leading causes of death in children."

"And thus whoever succeeds in finding a preventative will garner millions in profits."

"Of which breathing disorder did this girl allegedly die?" Noah asked.

"The details remain vague."

"Yes, I'm certain they would be."

"Turner discovered that the girl's physician . . . Tilson, I believe, was his name . . . had recently returned from a voyage to Europe exultant over the immense progress made there in fabricating pharmaceuticals. He questioned why Americans couldn't formulate the sort of miracle cures that Europeans seemed to produce with regularity. Turner believed Tilson was speaking specifically of Germany."

"Dr. Frias, Willard Anschutz's regular physician, also recently returned from Europe. With an International Benz."

"Precisely."

"Mr. Herzberg, do you have the particulars of the Newark case? The name and address of the family?"

"I have the name and address right here." Herzberg tapped a small pile of papers on the left side of his desk, indistinguishable from the myriad other stacks that rendered the wood top invisible. "Were you planning a ferry ride across the Hudson?"

Noah nodded. "Even if I can't speak to anyone in the family, there might be neighbors about."

"Do you know Newark, Dr. Whitestone?" It was Miriam speaking.

"No, but New Jersey is not equatorial Africa. I'll find my way."

"No need to pioneer, doctor. I know the city quite well. I'll show you the way."

Maribeth flashed in Noah's mind, but then was gone. Noah glanced to Miriam's father. "Do you object, Mr. Herzberg?" he asked.

Herzberg shrugged. "Not at all."

FIFTEEN

N ewark meant a ride on the Pennsylvania Railroad ferry from the terminal at the south end of Manhattan to Jersey City and, from there, a passage west on light rail. With luck, the journey could be completed in less than two hours.

As Noah and Miriam Herzberg walked toward the hansom stand at Cooper Square, a man approached, waving. He was thin without being slight, square-jawed with a pencil mustache, wearing a brown suit and derby tilted to sit on his left ear. He smiled as he neared them. When Noah looked to Miriam, it was clear that this was neither friend nor male admirer.

The man stopped directly in front of them, standing quite close. "Miriam!" he exclaimed. "I am so pleased to see you again."

Miriam stared back at the man as if she had swallowed a piece of rancid meat.

"And who is your friend?" He put up a finger. "Wait. I know. It's Noah Whitestone. Noted physician . . . until a couple of days ago anyway. And how are you on such a fine day, Dr. Whitestone?"

"You have the advantage of me, sir," Noah replied.

The man's smile vanished. "And I will continue having the advantage of you, doctor. You will never, I can assure you, have the advantage of me." Then, just as quickly, the mask returned. The man swept his hand to a gray and overcast sky. "But why should there be bad feeling on such a lovely day? Here we have two young people stepping out for a Saturday afternoon romp. But where could they be romping to?" He turned his gaze back to Miriam.

"Wherever we please," she replied coldly. "This is a free country, I believe."

"It won't be, if you people have your way." He shifted half a step to stand directly opposite Noah. "You've made a fine choice, Dr. Whitestone. I don't know if you realize just how fine. Marriage isn't good enough for the Red Lady here. She believes in free love. Most of 'em ain't so much to look at, but Miriam is . . . ain't you, Miriam?"

Noah hadn't struck anyone since he was a boy. But as his hand came up, Miriam's fingers were around his wrist. She was remarkably strong for a woman. "Well, Officer McCluskey," she said, now matching his smile, "it is nice to see that you're on such good behavior. You usually accuse me of being a Jew as well as a whore."

"I didn't want to shock your new beau." McCluskey smirked. "But now that you mention it . . ."

"We're leaving now," Miriam said. "Why don't you run on home to Mrs. McCluskey? After all you've told me, I would like so much to meet her."

The grin shot off McCluskey's face. "You best watch yourself, little girl. And you, too, doc. Unless you're a very good swimmer."

"You might watch yourself as well, officer," Noah snapped, unwilling to just stand by and do nothing. "Unless you wish to meet some old associates in prison. The police are not above the law, you know."

McCluskey emitted an incredulous guffaw. "You think so, doc? Well, stranger things have happened, I suppose." The copper shook his head in wonder. "Not above the law . . ." He stepped aside, laughing. "Well, you two lovebirds be on your way now. Maybe I'll meet you where you're going." As Noah and Miriam proceeded down the street, Noah could hear, "Not above the law."

Noah and Miriam walked to the hansom stand in silence. As their carriage clattered its way downtown, Noah stared out the window.

"Are you upset because I didn't let you defend my honor with McCluskey? Or because you think I have no honor to defend?"

"That's absurd. Neither."

"What then?"

Noah shook his head and once again turned away. New York street life flickered past as the hansom rumbled over the Broadway cobblestones. The truth was he felt like a coward. He *was* supposed to defend her with McCluskey, no matter what the odds. And then to be dissuaded because of *her* hand on *his* wrist . . .

"Why did you become a doctor?"

"Why do you want to know?"

"I'm curious. It wasn't an accusation."

"Because of my father," he replied. "He's a doctor as well."

"Tell me about him."

Noah turned to face her, placing his left hand on his opposite knee. "He's more than just someone who treats illness. People trust him when they're afraid. He's someone whose advice they seek when they're unsure. He . . ." Noah suddenly didn't want to talk about Abel, although he wasn't certain why. "At first, I thought your father had been a military officer. But as he spoke, I felt as if I was listening to a professor."

"He was both."

"He didn't seem like a . . ."

"Like a revolutionary? A bomb thrower?"

"That isn't what I meant. Please don't confuse me with McCluskey."

"What did you mean then?"

"I'm not certain." He wasn't. "Everything seems a jumble."

She reached over and patted his hand. It was brief, light, and perfunctory, but it felt electric on Noah's skin. "Enlightenment may be your reward, Noah Whitestone."

"That or being thrown off a pier."

"Oh, I suspect you are going to come out of this better than you think."

"That will not be difficult."

"McCluskey's been badgering me for months," she said suddenly. "'If you believe so much in free love, what's wrong with me?' The imbecile. He told me his wife doesn't like relations so he was all saved up. I told him that, first, I don't fornicate with other women's husbands, and second, even if I did, I'd do so with pigs before I would consider it with him."

"You told him that? Weren't you afraid?"

"I'm always afraid." She paused. "You know, free love doesn't mean copulating indiscriminately. It means that we view marriage vows as a means of oppression by the power structure . . . church, government; they're all the same . . . another way to keep the poor and the workers in line. The more laws and conventions we get rid of, the better for society. The rich and those with power talk about the rule of law, but they certainly don't follow it. It's only to keep everyone else down. And they use McCluskey and his ilk to do it. The poor fools don't understand that they're simply tools of the rich."

"You mean the police?"

"Of course I mean the police. What do you think he meant when he said you'd better be a good swimmer? Lord, you don't know anything, do you? There's no one in this city who commits more crimes than the police. The force is rotten, through and through. Always has been. How could you possibly have been unaware of that?"

"Doctors, the police. You people seem to think everyone is corrupt . . . except the poor, of course."

"Not everyone."

The hansom had reached the South Ferry terminal. After Noah paid, they walked toward the slips. After checking the board to determine where the ferry for Jersey City would depart, Miriam took Noah's arm. "Wait," she told him.

They loitered among the throng hurrying about, coming from or going to Brooklyn, Staten Island, Elizabeth, or other destinations in New York or New Jersey. Miriam waited until the Jersey City ferry was announced last call before she and Noah hurried aboard. She waited at the rear, watching everyone who boarded after them. There were only five: a husband and wife dressed in unmistakably Italian garb; two elderly women; and a Negro. None could have been a police agent. The ferryman soon pulled the gate shut and the powerful, deep-throated engine churned the boat away from the slip. Noah and Miriam moved inside, watching to see if anyone at the slip was observing. There was no one.

They spoke very little until the ferry passed Bedloe's Island and the lighthouse, "Liberty Enlightening the World," a gift from France fifteen years earlier.

"A fine ideal," Miriam said, as they passed under the torch that stood atop Liberty's outstretched arm. "A pity it's a hollow one for many who pass here."

"People keep coming though."

"Desperation breeds desperate acts."

"Is that how you got here? Desperation?"

A small smile played across her face. "Papa brought us here in 1880, just after I was born . . . just after he left the army."

"Yes, I thought . . . I didn't know that . . ."

"That Jews could be military officers in Prussia? Papa was conscripted in 1867. His father was a teacher in the Jewish school in Gehlenberg . . . we weren't good enough to be citizens, but good enough to go to battle. He fought with distinction and was promoted to sergeant. Just before Sedan, Papa was promoted to captain."

"From sergeant? How did he manage that?"

"He killed thirteen French and captured another twenty single-handed."

"Thirteen . . . himself?"

"It was guile as much as bravery." Miriam made no attempt to hide her pride. "It was a rainy day. Very difficult to see. Papa had become separated from his unit. Most likely, they had abandoned him. When a French patrol showed up, Papa moved quickly from one place to another behind some rocks. He was the best shot in his division. Every time he caught a glimmer of a Frenchman, he shot him. After he killed one, Papa called out, as if to his comrades, always in a different voice. Papa is quite a mimic. He convinced the French they were surrounded by snipers. After he killed the thirteen, the rest surrendered. He made them throw out their arms before he showed himself. Imagine how they felt when they realized they had been defeated by only one man."

"Quite a feat" was all Noah could think of to say.

"The generals couldn't figure out what to do. The incident was in newspapers all over Germany. Papa would have won the Iron Cross if he was Christian. Eventually they promoted him. Probably from embarrassment. After the war, he went to university and taught philosophy. He was dismissed during one of the purges, and so he brought us here. A desperate act."

"What of your mother?"

"She died of tuberculosis when I was three."

"I'm sorry. He never remarried?"

"No. He said no one could ever replace Mama. I wish I had known her. I only vaguely remember her. I don't even have a picture. Papa tells me I look just like her though."

"She must have been beautiful then."

Miriam chuckled softly, and for a moment, she looked like a young girl.

The Jersey side was approaching, and Miriam said she wished to stand outside. They went out the door to the observation platform, the only passengers who saw fit to brave the icy headwind in the bay. The ferry, squat and stable, nonetheless bounced erratically in the choppy waters. They were forced to hold the handrails so as not to be thrown to the deck. Traffic in the harbor was heavy, and the sound of fog horns was everywhere, muted in the wind. Dewey would sail by this very spot in four days. As would Pug Anschutz.

"And what about you, Dr. Whitestone?" Miriam's voice resonated in the rushing air. "I feel certain you're not married."

"I was. She died."

Miriam placed her hand on his. "Oh, Noah, I am truly sorry for you." She had never before used his given name. "When?"

"Five years ago. She died in childbirth. Hemorrhage."

"You weren't delivering the baby, were you?"

Had she guessed? "No. I was assisting. It was no one's fault. Nothing to be done."

"The baby was lost as well?"

"Yes." He thought for a fleeting instant to mention Maribeth, but did not.

Miriam did not remove her hand. And so Noah Whitestone stood, hand in hand with Miriam Herzberg, as the ferry pulled into the Jersey City slips.

SIXTEEN

The Ironbound was an amalgam of factories and those who toiled within them, all walled in by the curling border of the Passaic River. The variety of industries—paint, lumber, and, of course, iron—were more than matched by the vast array of ethnic enclaves that dotted the streets. Poles, Lithuanians, Italians, Serbs, and Irish all both shared and competed for the space. Few in the Ironbound were abjectly poor—there were always jobs to be had—but, equally, few lived at better than subsistence. Employers saw no necessity of paying the strong and uneducated any more than would keep clothes on the back, food on the table, and a roof overhead. Miriam knew Newark well because it was neighborhoods precisely such as these that were the most fertile targets for those who would forge workers into an organized and cohesive force.

The five remaining Ryans occupied four small rooms on the bottom floor of a row house on Monroe Street. Seven consecutive streets in the Ironbound were named for presidents, perhaps in an attempt to inspire immigrants who would never be among them. Monroe Street was a manageable walk from the Pennsylvania Station, so Miriam suggested she and Noah eschew the ostentation of a cab. Noah replied by asking if it was safe to walk through this district.

"Poor doesn't mean dishonest," Miriam told him, with unmasked irritation. "Don't be so susceptible to propaganda."

When Miriam knocked at a peeling front door, a woman answered. Mary Ryan was bulky, just short of fat, wearing a faded print dress. Her reddish hair was going to gray, and her face was lined and formless. She seemed to sag, as if perpetually warding off collapse. Despite her appearance, Noah realized that this woman was likely no older than he.

"Hello, Mrs. Ryan." Miriam spoke both gently and with authority. She knew the lay of the land as well here as did Noah in a hospital. "We've come because of what happened to Sinead."

Mary Ryan turned her eyes to Noah and shrunk away, biting her lip. He realized that she must think him an official of some sort, and officials of any sort were no friends of the Ryans. Miriam noticed as well.

"We're not with the police, or the city, or anything like that, Mrs. Ryan. This man is a doctor, and we're hoping to prevent what happened to Sinead from happening to someone else's little girl."

"A doctor?" Mary's fear was little abated. After recent events, doctors could be no more trusted than the police.

"Don't worry, Mrs. Ryan," Miriam went on. "He's not going to do anything. We just want to talk to you for a few moments. About Sinead."

Not going to do anything, Noah thought. What sort of place was this where a woman had to be reassured by being told a physician was not here to practice medicine?

"Sinead?" The corners of Mary Ryan's mouth turned up for a moment. "All right. Come on in then."

The Ryans' parlor was tiny and consisted of slat-back wooden chairs and a dilapidated sofa, on which the woman insisted her visitors sit. Mary Ryan offered refreshments, but Miriam and Noah declined.

With gentle prodding, Miriam was successful in eliciting the tale of Sinead Ryan's illness and death. The girl had become afflicted with a dry, hacking cough. Fearing tubercular infection, Mary had taken her to the once-per-week free clinic run by the parish in the basement of Saint Anne's. The doctor that day, a man named Tilson, whom Mary had never seen before, had seemed extremely excited when he saw Sinead and told Mary that he was going to give the girl a brand-new drug that would cure her miraculously.

"And did it?" Miriam asked.

"Oh yes. Sinead was better right away. By next morning her cough was gone. She slept through the night for the first time in a week." Mary Ryan smiled. "Sinead was always so beautiful when she slept. Like an angel was inside her." The smile vanished. "She's with the angels now."

"Was the drug pills or a liquid?" Noah asked.

Mary Ryan jerked her head in Noah's direction. Her eyes went wide, as if he were a sorcerer. She seemed to have forgotten he was there.

"Pills," she said quietly.

"Were the pills blue, Mrs. Ryan?"

She shook her head. "Green."

"Do you have any of these pills left?"

Mary Ryan shook her head. "Dr. Tilson took them. After. Said since I didn't need them no more, that he could give them to someone else."

"What happened next, Mary?" Miriam continued, glancing to Noah to let her handle the conversation.

At the sound of Miriam's voice, Mary Ryan's apprehension dissipated. Noah was envious of her skill. "The day after Sinead was better," Mary said, "Dr. Tilson came here. I was pole-axed, I can tell you. We ain't never had no doctor here before. He wanted to see about Sinead. He examined her and seemed happy. He told me to keep up with the pills and he'd be back in three or four days.

"Day after, Sinead felt so much better still. She stopped coughing and just rested. It was such a relief to watch her. Just breathing easy. Sleeping lots, but she then she needed it, didn't she? I give her the pills whenever she starts coughing, but the next day, they ain't working as good anymore. Sinead starts coughing pretty soon after taking them, and then later starts sweating and moving around like St. Vitus Dance. Can't stop. Asks for the pills. Says they make her feel better. Happy. So, I figured it's just because one pill ain't enough, so I give her two. Couple hours later, I give her two more. Soon after, I went out to take in the washing, and when I come back, I catch her in the sink and she's took some more. I can't say how many. I didn't count them. About ten minutes later, she gets real tired, says she needs to go to bed. She's asleep right away. I was happy to see the medicine was working again. But then she don't get up."

"I'm terribly sorry, Mrs. Ryan," Miriam said. "When did Dr. Tilson come back?"

"Day after Sinead . . ."

"How he did he find out about Sinead?"

"Mrs. O'Bierne . . . she's my neighbor . . . I had sent her to ask the doctor why Sinead was so jumpy. I couldn't leave her."

"You were alone with Sinead?"

"I'm always alone with the kids during the week. There's always one or another of 'em sick. Mike works two jobs at the mill. He runs the saw days, and then five nights doubles as watchman. Pretty easy, he says, the second one, because if anyone tries to mess around the fence, the dogs bark. I guess he sleeps some, but as long as everything's there in the morning, the boss don't seem to mind. And two years ago, Mike caught two dagos tryin' to cut through the fence out behind the curing shed. Boss give him a two-dollar bonus.

"Ain't so bad for me either," the woman continued, losing herself in her tale. "Like havin' Mike work a job where he's gone all week. Sometimes I bring him somethin' hot for supper, but most times we don't see each other except from Saturday night to Monday morning. Ain't bad for the marriage, let me tell you. Mrs. O'Beirne says she wishes she could get her Frank to do the same."

Suddenly, Mary Ryan recalled why her visitors had come. "So Dr. Tilson comes a couple of days later, says that Sinead must have had some breathing disease that didn't show itself, and that he's sorry. Took the rest of the pills back, like I said. Then he told me not to talk about it, so as not to start a panic in the neighborhood." Mary Ryan gave a rueful smile. "Takes a lot more than that to start a panic here."

There was little more to be learned and even less to be said. Noah and Miriam thanked the woman and once more offered condolences. Noah remembered Clement Van Meter and realized how often a doctor leaves a home to nothing but grief and hopelessness.

They were at the door when Mary Ryan stopped them. "You think that doctor killed Sinead, don't you?"

"We're not certain, Mrs. Ryan," Miriam replied. "It's possible."

Suddenly her hand was around Noah's wrist. It was soft and moist, but the grip was strong. In this part of town, women worked as hard as men. "You do, doctor. I can tell."

"I'm not certain either, Mrs. Ryan."

"Yes," Mary Ryan said. "You are."

Noah did not reply.

"If you prove it, you'll turn him in, won't you? You won't just keep quiet because he's another doctor?"

"I won't just keep quiet."

Mary Ryan had not removed her hand from Noah's wrist. "Promise me."

"I promise."

Moments later, Miriam and Noah were on their way back to the Pennsylvania Station. Miriam's eyes shot flames, and for the first time, Noah could imagine her whipping a crowd of strikers into a frenzy. "Seven years old. So what if a girl dies here? She's only a worker's child. Do you think this ever happens to the rich?"

"Willard Anschutz died, too."

"That was an accident. Why are you defending what they did?"

"I'm not."

"Will you keep your promise?"

"If I can."

The passage across the water from Jersey City was silent and peaceful, the last evening it would be so. Beginning tomorrow, giant searchlights placed at the foot of the Brooklyn Bridge, fashioned especially for Admiral Dewey, would blaze each night until the hero of Manila Bay had left New York. Thirty electricians had been working for five days mounting thousands of incandescent lightbulbs in the cables of the bridge, forming the words WELCOME DEWEY. "Welcome" would be lit tomorrow, and "Dewey" on Monday. Special electrical cables had been fashioned to ensure that sufficient current would be available to allow each bulb to burn clear and with intense brilliance. The contrast between the $1 million spent on Dewey's reception and the pittance spent to provide tolerable living conditions for those such as the Ryans was unmistakable. Maybe the Herzbergs had a point after all.

When Noah and Miriam disembarked at South Ferry, daylight had long since ended. The street lamps lighting the terminal did not give off sufficient illumination to eliminate the multitude of shadowy nooks that a facility such as this inevitably provided. Noah peered through the gloom, trying to determine if McCluskey or one of his cohorts was lurking about, but he could make out no one.

Miriam lived in Hell's Kitchen on West Twentieth Street, on the fourth floor of a six-story apartment building. When the hansom stopped in front, Miriam hesitated before getting out. Noah wasn't sure if she was waiting for him to say something or trying to say something herself. The image that was fixed in his mind was of the Red Lady, speaking with such tenderness and compassion to Mary Ryan.

"I learned some things today," he said.

"That's good, Noah." And then she stepped out of the hansom and walked the few steps to her door.

It was after nine when Noah finally arrived at Joralemon Street. Before even doffing his coat, he placed the call through the telephone exchange.

Operators of switching boards were notorious eavesdroppers, but there was little choice. When an operator listened in, there was often a telltale hollowness in the sound coming from the other instrument, which most of those accustomed to utilizing the public exchange learned to recognize. Still, if forced to discuss sensitive topics on the telephone, one learned to be subtle and oblique. But as soon as his call was answered, Noah knew subtlety had been thrown to the wind.

"Whitestone!" Justin Herold barked. "Where have you been? I was worried about you."

"I was checking on another case similar to the one we discussed. In a child. The same ultimate result with the same pathology. But why were you worried? I told you that I would be in touch tonight."

"I completed the autopsy. Your friend didn't die of drowning, as we knew. But nor did he die of the blow to the head. Whitestone, he was beaten to death."

"Beaten?" The line sounded unbroken, but Noah prayed no one was listening in.

"Yes. Slowly and methodically. With blows to the torso that would be difficult to spot unless one was trained to look. He died of asphyxiation, but he had blood in his lungs, not water. The beating would have been extremely painful. Ten of his ribs were cracked. Whoever did this was experienced. The blows were expertly administered. None of the ribs broke through, and the bruising was almost all subdural. If I hadn't opened him up, no one would have known."

"Did his father stay?"

"Yes. He waited in the parlor. Refused to leave until I had completed the postmortem. I only told him that his son died of asphyxiation and that I would complete a detailed written report and forward him a copy."

"That was wise."

"I've dealt with these situations before, Whitestone. Now tell me about the other case."

"Do you think we should be speaking so openly?"

"Nonsense, Whitestone. Just tell me."

Noah transmitted the details of Sinead Ryan's death and its aftermath as broadly as he could while still getting the particulars across to Herold. When he was done, the line was silent.

"Are you still there?"

"Yes, yes, Whitestone. I'm thinking. Was the girl taking acetylsalicylic acid as well?"

Noah had forgotten to ask. When he embarrassedly admitted so to Herold, he expected to be upbraided. But Herold was surprisingly sanguine. "No matter. It's the green tablets we want. There must be something unusual about them."

"Other than the content?"

"Oh, Whitestone. Every physician knows the property of morphiates. No one but a complete idiot is going to give them to a child unless he believed the deleterious effects had been mitigated. That means there must be an additional ingredient that the fabricator believes will prevent acquired tolerance to the active drug."

"That's what Herzberg said."

"Who?"

"The publisher of *New Visions*."

"Right. Of course. I've got an idea, Whitestone. I wonder . . ."

"What? Tell me."

"I'll need a day. Maybe two. Call me then. In the meantime, I'll try to get in touch with this Frias. If I learn anything, I'll be in touch sooner."

Noah was about to turn for his bedroom when he noticed a small, square envelope on the floor. It had been slipped under the door, and he had walked past it on the way in. It was on good stationery, sealed, with no writing on either side. Inside was a short note in a familiar hand.

"You've been summoned," it read. "I'll fetch you after church. Say eleven." It was signed "ADK."

SEVENTEEN

Noah attended the First Presbyterian Church with his parents every Sabbath. He considered it his penance.

Reverend Miller had been droning on about sin and damnation at the church since before Noah was born and seemed sufficiently old to have received his teachings from John Knox personally. His sermons were by this time delivered in a halting croak, but Noah's mother and father never seemed to notice. The aging are rarely cognizant of a similar progression in their contemporaries.

Elspeth in particular took comfort in Reverend Miller's predictable cycle of cautionary tales. She was a tiny woman, gray since Noah could remember, fastidious and pious. Arthritis had struck her when Noah was in his teens, but except on rare occasions when a particularly potent attack laid her low, she refused to alter her routine, to give in to the illness. Even now, she employed a maid to clean only four hours a week. Whenever Noah saw her knobby, swollen knuckles, he was reminded of the power of perseverance.

Neither Abel nor Elspeth had said much before the service, but once they were clear of the church, Abel spoke.

"The police came to see us yesterday." The statement was of concern, not accusation.

"Was it someone named McCluskey?"

Abel shook his head. "Lieutenant Riley. You remember him. His daughter Margot was in last year with mumps."

"What did he want?"

"He came to warn me. He said you might be in some trouble, Noah. I thought you knew well enough to steer clear of Arnold. He also said something about your taking up with radicals."

"How could he know that?"

"What are you talking about, son? He's a police lieutenant."

"What else did he say?"

"That it was never too late for an honest man to save his good name."

"Well at least they're off threat and on to bribery."

"What threat?" Elspeth asked.

"Nothing, mother. I've gotten myself embroiled in an awkward situation. That's all. I'll get myself out."

Elspeth suddenly took his wrist. "Arnold Frias is an evil man, Noah. As your father will attest . . ."

"That is an overstatement, Elspeth . . ."

"The deuce it is, Abel. As you very well know."

"I know nothing of the sort. But Arnold is . . . a dangerous man to cross."

"Do you suggest I apologize, father? Beg forgiveness?"

"Of course not. But you will need allies."

Now Noah understood. "Like Oscar De Kuyper?"

"Strength battles strength."

"And corruption battles corruption," Elspeth added.

"Elspeth, no one said anything about corr—"

"Since he is buying you a new house," she added, "I would think he would want to protect his investment."

"I don't think that's quite fair, mother."

"All right. Protect his daughter then."

"In any case, Noah," Abel said with finality, "he is surely the man to stand up to Wurster and Arnold."

And you are not, Noah thought sadly. The penalty for living a life of virtue and not profit.

The De Kuypers adjourned to the library to demonstrate that this was a meeting and not a social call. Oscar and Adelaide sat across from Noah, he in a leather wing chair, she at the corner of a small divan of muted green velour. Oscar was still in the suit and Adelaide in the plain blue silk dress they had worn to church. Noah was given a straight-back armchair. Refreshments were offered but expected to be declined, which Noah did. Before beginning the conversation, Oscar allowed an extended pause to denote the seriousness of the coming discussion.

"We asked Alan to wait outside to avoid embarrassment." He did not specify to whose embarrassment he referred. "This is a difficult conversation to have . . ." Oscar glanced at Adelaide. She gave a small nod, either in agreement or to tell Oscar he was doing fine. "You cannot help but to be aware that any difficulties in which you find yourself reflect on our family as well."

"I deeply regret any embarrassment that this affair might cause for you, Mr. De Kuyper. I hope you know that. But I assure you that all I did was care for a sick child. Not only will Alan vouch for my behavior, but Abraham Jacobi, the most respected pediatrician in the nation, will as well."

"Yes," Oscar grunted, his nostrils wrinkling for a moment, "Alan has told us of this Jacobi."

"It escapes me how I could have acted differently," Noah continued. "Was I to leave a child in distress because his regular physician might be upset?"

"Of course not . . ."

"Then, Mr. De Kuyper, I fail to see how I can be held responsible because Dr. Frias has attempted to defray responsibility for medicating the child inappropriately."

"Dr. Frias has an impeccable reputation, Noah. How do you account for what you claim is his behavior with the Anschutz boy?"

Noah wasn't about to say "greed" in the De Kuypers' library. "I'm not going to speculate, Mr. De Kuyper," he said instead. "All I can tell you is that I came upon a boy in distress and treated him in a manner that the best professionals in the field have insisted was correct."

"I don't think you understand, Noah." It was Adelaide De Kuyper, smooth, even, and perfectly modulated. "We are prepared to support you, but we cannot afford to be attached to scandal."

"I'm not certain I understand precisely what that means, Mrs. De Kuyper."

Adelaide's eyebrows rose, but her face otherwise remained stolid. "The statement seems plain enough to me."

"Andrew Conklin called on me yesterday." Oscar had folded his fingers and placed his hands in his lap. "You know of him, of course."

"Yes. You have mentioned him." Conklin was a city councilman and friend of the De Kuyper family. Noah had assumed that meant money changed hands during election season.

"You seem to be consorting with some odd . . . characters."

"I am trying to protect my reputation."

"By throwing in with Reds?" Adelaide glanced at her husband. "It seems, Noah, that you are determined to involve yourself deeper in this matter instead of doing what it would take to extricate yourself."

Noah waited, certain that Adelaide was about to tell him what it would take.

"I am told Arnold Frias is a quite reasonable man . . ."

So that was it. But before he could decline to fall on his sword, the door burst open and Maribeth stormed in. "You promised I would be told when Noah arrived, mother."

Adelaide remained unperturbed. Noah wondered if she would change expression in a shipwreck. "I did no such thing, my dear. You insisted on being present, and I didn't reply."

"Well, I'm here now."

Noah had stood, and Oscar rose halfway from his chair. "Please, Maribeth dear," Oscar bleated, "let us handle this. We know what's best."

"For me? And please sit down, both of you."

"We only want for your happiness," Oscar protested plaintively, plopping back into his seat.

"Noah is my happiness. What is all of this worth if the family can't stand up for an innocent man?"

"We never claimed he was anything but innocent, my dear." Adelaide sighed. "But nor are we going to be drawn into a public feud with Frederick Wurster."

"I'm certain you are quite the match for Frederick Wurster, mother."

"I would never ask you to do so, Mrs. De Kuyper," Noah said quickly. "I will fight my own battles. I only wish for you not to prejudge the situation before the truth has had a chance to be made clear."

"That's not good enough, Noah," snapped Maribeth. "Here is what I intend to do, mother. I will marry Noah. I will marry him no matter what. I will marry him if we live in a slum. I will marry him because I love him." She strode to the chair where Noah was sitting and stood behind him, her hand on his shoulder, just as Miriam Herzberg had stood behind her father.

"Perhaps it would then be best if we did as Noah suggests, my dear. He is a level-headed young man." Adelaide stood. "By all means, get the facts, Noah. I only ask that you do so with a modicum of discretion." She glanced to her husband. "Now, Oscar, I'm sure Noah wants to speak with Maribeth. Why don't we leave them?"

Adelaide wheeled and left the room, Oscar trailing behind.

"Your mother is a clever woman." At Maribeth's suggestion, they had left the house and walked into Gramercy Park.

"A generous term. But, yes, she is that."

"She wants me to apologize to Frias and end the matter."

"Yes, I know. Will you?"

"I have nothing to apologize for."

"Then don't."

"It makes no difference. Frias will simply bide his time. As long as I know that he killed the Anschutz boy, I'll always be a threat. But if I refuse to do as your mother . . . suggests . . . among other things, you'll be forced to break our engagement."

Maribeth guffawed. "Forced? Who is going to force me? Didn't you hear what I said in the library?"

"A pronouncement in the library is one thing . . ."

"I think you either overestimate my mother or underestimate me. They will not pressure me, because they know I will do precisely what I say. Unless, of course, there is another factor you are failing to mention."

"There is no other factor."

"The Red Lady . . . Miss Herzberg . . . is always referred to in the newspapers as 'beautiful' or 'glamorous.' I've read 'ravishing' as well."

"She is all of those things."

"But not a factor?"

"No."

Maribeth put her arm through his. "Have you seen the construction in Madison Square?"

Noah had not.

"Come. Let's walk over. I find the spectacle perversely inspirational."

She held his arm for the entire walk. When they turned north on Broadway, they saw before them a scene of frenzied construction. The spectacle justified in every way the *Daily Eagle*'s description of a city "royally robed in the gay garb of patriotism." The pyramids could not have been thrown up with more zeal.

The Dewey Arch, at the junction of Broadway and Fifth Avenue at Twenty-Fourth Street, was near completion. At least one hundred and fifty carpenters, masons, and painters were furiously at work on scaffolding, putting the finishing touches on the grand structure and colonnade leading to it. The arch itself was almost five stories tall and, with four allegorical statues placed on the top of the four piers, exceeded seven. The statues, symbolizing Peace, War, Patriotism, and Return, had been fashioned by the greatest sculptors in the nation, including Daniel Chester French. More than twenty additional sculptures would be placed in the plaza, including eight American heroes of past wars.

The frantic efforts to complete the work on time had attracted hundreds, if not thousands, of gawkers to the plaza. They crowded in from the buildings on Broadway to the nearly completed grandstand on Fifth Avenue. They pressed almost to the edge of the electric trolley track, which wended its way down Broadway to the west of the arch and through the columns. Police presence on the scene was heavy, the officers constantly having to shoo spectators from under the scaffolding and away from the tracks.

Maribeth squeezed his arm. "See? Wasn't I correct? Aren't you inspired?"

"It is certainly grandiose."

Maribeth emitted a soft giggle. "*Grotesque* would be my word. In fact, it was my word. Father was appalled. He comes here at least three times a week to bask in the glow of patriotism. He can't understand why I find the entire display revolting. He told me that these celebrations bring the nation together. Give Americans a chance to revel in our triumphs."

"Defeating Spain? Murdering Filipinos? What sort of triumph is that?"

"I believe I expressed those very sentiments. Father told me I had begun to sound like a socialist. Perhaps I have more in common with your Jewess than you know."

"My Jewess?"

She laughed. "Forgive me. I'm jealous."

"No need."

"Oh, isn't there now."

They walked across the square, toward the arch. Maribeth laughed again, and Noah urged her to be still. At the tracks, a policeman blew his whistle, warning pedestrians of an oncoming trolley. Noah and Maribeth waited, a crush of humanity behind them.

Suddenly, when the trolley was no more than ten yards away, Noah felt a sharp blow in his lower back. A second later he was flying toward the trolley track. Then he was on the track staring at tons of metal hurtling toward him. He clawed with his hands but couldn't move. He was vaguely aware of screams and the banshee screech of brakes. The trolley seemed inches from his head.

Then, just as quickly, a hand was around his ankle, giving a huge jerk. Noah flew off the track as quickly as he had been on it. The trolley came to a stop, ten feet past where Noah's head had been.

Noah couldn't speak. For a moment, he couldn't breathe. He heard a man yell, "He was pushed! I saw it."

Then Maribeth was leaning down. "I saw it, too."

"Thank you, Maribeth," Noah was finally able to whisper. "You saved my life." How had she been strong enough to pull him?

But Maribeth shook her head. "It wasn't me."

Noah thought he hadn't heard properly. Then he noticed a thick-set man with cauliflower ears peering at him over her shoulder. When the man had determined that Noah was all right, he touched his hand to the brim of his cap.

"Thank you, Dolph," Noah said, but Dolph had blended back into the crowd.

Noah got to his feet and brushed himself off. His hands were shaking.

"Who was that?" Maribeth asked.

"An anarchist bartender."

Noah was called to the side to answer questions for a policeman. Other officers sifted through the crowd asking if anyone saw anything. With the rush of the moment past, everyone now denied seeing or hearing anything. Ten minutes later, Noah and Maribeth were headed back to Gramercy Park.

"Where would you go now, Noah? If I wasn't a consideration?"

"I don't understand."

"Oh yes, you do."

"You mean would I go to the *New Visions* offices? I'm not certain. Perhaps."

"Then go now."

"I don't understand. Just a few moments ago . . ."

"If you don't go to her because of some sense of obligation or quaint notion of chivalry, for the rest of our lives both of us would wonder. I'll fight for you if you want me, but only if you want me. Otherwise, we'd be living a lie, and the one thing I cannot abide is dishonesty. I cannot feel or even suspect that you have lied to me, even by omission."

"I haven't."

"But you didn't say you wouldn't."

"I won't."

"All right then. Let's both find out the truth. And in all candor, Noah, it will be something of a relief for me to finally compete with a living woman instead of a ghost."

EIGHTEEN

S o he went.

When he arrived at Lafayette Street, he looked for signs of anyone lurking about the premises. He was conscious of being pathetically obvious, but intrigue was a skill he had never before been forced to learn. Although no one appeared to him to be suspicious, Noah was all too aware that the people to fear most might be those who did not appear suspicious at all.

As he opened the door to the building, a hand was on his shoulder. Noah spun about and found himself face-to-face with McCluskey.

"Don't worry, doc. I'm harmless."

"Stay away from me," Noah told him.

"Or what? You'll call the police? Don't worry, doc. If I wanted harm to come to you, it'd have happened already."

"It almost did."

"That's what I want to talk to you about. Just talk, doc. You got my word."

"Your word doesn't seem to me to be worth much, McCluskey."

"I can see why you'd feel that way, doc. Still, why don't we stroll over to the Union together? I'll say my bit, then see you safely back here."

McCluskey talked as they walked. "So . . . about your little accident in Madison Square."

"Did you do it?"

"Now, doc, I might take umbrage at that, but I won't. I'll even say that I understand why you might think so. But it wasn't me. And it wasn't any of my friends, relatives, or associates. But I know who did do it."

"Who?"

"The same that saved you."

"Dolph?"

"Adolph Graebenfeld. Bartender at *Arthur's*. Prize-fighter. And a good one, by the way. Don't get in the way of his right. Bank robber. Bomb maker. And almost certain murderer. Dolph. The very one."

"Are you trying to tell me that first he pushed me in front of the trolley and then pulled me out of the way?"

"Poetic justice, wouldn't you say? That is the right phrase? *Poetic justice?*"

"Yes. The correct phrase. And I suppose you can tell me why he would do such a thing. A sudden pang of conscience?"

"They ain't got consciences, doc. But you're supposed to be an exceptionally smart fellow. Why don't you tell me why he might have done it?"

The logic, of course, was obvious. "To gain my gratitude?"

"More your services." McCluskey blew out a breath. "Dr. Whitestone, you and me got started wrong. I can see why you'd fall for Miriam Herzberg. She's got more men trotting after her than a bitch in heat. She knows it and counts on it."

Noah was about to protest the metaphor, but McCluskey spoke over him.

"But these people are killers. Don't you know that? In Europe, they put bombs in theaters. In Chicago, they tossed a bomb in a crowd and killed seven police officers."

That incident, called the Haymarket Massacre, was the most notorious in the short history of the labor movement in the United States. During a march in 1886 in support of thousands of workers striking for an eight-hour work day, an anarchist threw a bomb at a crowd of police. Seven were killed. Gunfire broke out, and civilians died as well. Nobody knew exactly how many, but most said the total exceeded one hundred.

"The Haymarket was thirteen years ago, McCluskey. Miriam was not quite old enough."

"Maybe not. But Mauritz was."

"Mauritz?"

"Nobody's sure who threw the bomb. Mauritz was in Chicago, though. He was under suspicion, but he's too smart to get caught. When the Chicago coppers searched August Spies's offices the next day . . . he was head of the anarchists . . . they found some pamphlets. One was called 'Revenge. Workingmen to Arms.' Kind of a blueprint for what happened during the riot. Nobody could ever prove anything, but general opinion said Mauritz wrote it. He got off all the same. Eight of his pals got caught, though. Four were executed. Good riddance, I say."

"I believe the police fired into a crowd of strikers the day before and killed six workers."

"What would you do if five thousand Reds was coming at you and refused to stop?"

"Weren't some of them shot in the back?"

"So the anarchists said. Nobody ever proved that either, though."

"Not surprising, wouldn't you say?"

"Depends on who's doing the telling and who the proving. Anyway, Mauritz came back east after Haymarket. We've been watching him ever since, but like I said, nobody ever accused the old bastard of not being smart. Now his daughter's taking up after him."

"You're saying *she's* the one who had me pushed under the trolley?"

"Not saying anything I can't prove, doc. But answer me this. You told O'Neill . . . he was the officer at the scene . . . that two people saw you get pushed. One of the witnesses was your fiancée. And notice, I ain't saying anything about that one way or another, but I'd certainly think twice if I was gonna be marrying a woman looked like . . ."

"Get to it, McCluskey."

"Okay. So what did Miss De Kuyper and the other chap say the pusher looked like?"

"They didn't. Maribeth didn't see his face. Just the hand in my back. The other witness had a lapse of memory."

"Ah."

"That doesn't prove anything, McCluskey."

"No. It doesn't. Maybe it was just coincidence that nobody saw who pushed you and, right after, Dolph just pops up like McCready's ghost, just in time to pull you off the tracks. Maybe you're the type of fellow who'd stake his life on a coincidence. We coppers though, we ain't so trusting. At least it might mean it's a good idea to keep an open mind, wouldn't you say?"

"Let's say you're correct . . . and I'm not saying you are. Then who killed Turner McKee? Do you expect me to believe they did *that* to gain my services?"

"Course not. Truth is, I don't know who killed McKee. Or why it was done. Man had a lot of enemies, though . . . as you might expect. List of suspects would be pretty long. Folks with a grudge. But I'll tell you what . . . three of the best men on the force are trying to find out who did it. We ain't given that to the newspapers, so I'd appreciate you keeping it in your pocket. But if it'll make you feel any better, I could arrange to have you talk with one of them."

"Perhaps I might do that."

"Any time, doc. Just say the word." They walked on for a few moments in silence. McCluskey sounded perfectly reasonable, every bit as reasonable as Mauritz Herzberg. More, actually. Apparently, whichever side Noah chose—and he would be forced to choose one of them, no doubt about that—he ran the risk of adding "fool" to the growing list of miscreancies of which he had been accused.

"I'll tell you more thing, doc." McCluskey had added a tremolo of sincerity to his voice, sensing a newly sympathetic ear. "There's some on the force who want you arrested for homicide because of that kid. Pretty high placed. But I said no. I said fuck Wurster. It must have been an accident."

"Very decent of you, McCluskey."

McCluskey laughed. "Now you didn't mean that, doc. You think I'm trying to squeeze you. But I ain't. I just wanted you to know we ain't what Mauritz and his crowd say we are."

"So why are you telling me all this, McCluskey? How do I know that it is not you who is engaged in the ploy to secure my services?"

"Fair question, doc. Here's what I propose . . . don't give your services to anybody. Just keep your eyes open until you decide who you think the real criminals are. If, as I figure, you find out it's them, you give us the goods so we can toss them into prison where they belong."

"And if I think it's you?"

"Well, doc. You said it yourself. The police ain't above the law." McCluskey gestured back in the direction of Lafayette Street. "Now you likely want to go and keep your appointment."

Sunday saw no slowdown in activity at *New Visions*. This time, instead of antipathy, Noah was greeted with nods and even a smile or two. The Slavic boy with the pock-marked face—his name turned out to be Sasha—almost said hello. When Miriam saw him, she walked quickly his way. She wore a dark blouse and full skirt and seemed to move with her own special light.

"Are you all right?"

"Considering I was pushed under a trolley, I seem to be fine."

"Yes, I know. Papa wants to see you."

Herzberg asked for details of the incident, then listened to Noah's recitation in stolid silence. "And, until you were pushed, you were aware of no one? Not even Dolph?"

Noah assured Herzberg he was not. Especially not Dolph.

"But did you *feel* a presence, Dr. Whitestone? One does, you know."

"I felt nothing," Noah replied.

"Were you alone?"

Noah hesitated a moment before answering. Herzberg must already have known the answer. Miriam as well. "My fiancée was with me."

"I see." Herzberg rested his elbows on the desk, allowing his fingertips to lightly meet. He spent some moments in that position, but Noah wasn't certain he was thinking about the assassination attempt or Maribeth. "You will have to learn to be more vigilant, Dr. Whitestone," Herzberg said finally. "Survival is a skill honed from experience."

"Is that why you asked Dolph to follow me? Because I'm inexperienced?"

"Once you agreed to help us, you became our responsibility."

"And he has been following me for . . ."

"He began today."

"Excellent timing, Mr. Herzberg. Thank you."

"We were lucky. Let us not confuse good luck with good planning."

"I agree. By the way, do you know Abraham Jacobi? He is German like yourself, I believe."

Herzberg's face darkened. "Why do you ask about Jacobi?"

"I was curious. I asked his opinion about the death of the Anschutz boy. He agrees, by the way, that Willard's death was morphia induced. Perhaps he can be a resource to us."

"Jacobi is a traitor. A Judas." Herzberg turned to the side, and for a moment, Noah thought he might spit. "The worst sort. He believed in the people's struggle until he achieved success and then threw in with the plutocrats."

"He is a fine doctor, however, as I'm certain you'll agree. And he does care for children."

"Jacobi cares only for Jacobi." Herzberg glanced at the papers on his desk. The audience was over.

When they had returned to the outer office, Miriam took Noah aside. "What's the matter, Noah?"

"Someone pushed me under a trolley, Miriam."

"There's something else. You intentionally baited my father."

"Didn't seem to take very much."

"But why do it at all?"

"I just find it interesting that Dolph shows up just in time to save me from certain death."

A slow smile crossed Miriam's face. "Ah, I see. You think it was us. That Dolph, that sneaky Red, pushed you, then saved you. And, of course, he was acting under instructions of the evil, totally unscrupulous Mauritz Herzberg. You've been talking to McCluskey."

"Why would you say that?"

"My word, Noah. We're not stupid, you know. Believe me, there are far better ways to obtain your assistance than pushing you under a trolley."

"Such as?"

She cocked her head to the side. "We can discuss that at dinner."

"I don't think that's a very good idea."

"Why? Because you're engaged and failed to mention it?" She didn't wait for an answer. "Do you have a cook?"

"You want to eat at my rooms?"

"I didn't think you'd especially want to be seen sitting across from the Red Lady at Delmonico's."

"I have a housekeeper who cooks for me. She's off on Sundays, but she'll have left something in the ice box, although it's certain to be dreadful."

"You employ a housekeeper who can't cook?"

"I've grown used to it."

"I've grown used to McCluskey, but I don't enjoy him. In any event, I can cook."

Here it was. The decision he knew would come. "I don't think . . ." But his stab at denial was anemic, even to his ear.

"I'll be there by seven," she said.

He didn't tell her not to come.

NINETEEN

W hen Noah reached Joralemon Street, daylight had faded, but the streetlights had not yet come up. He walked through the gloom to his front door, glancing at the Anschutz house as he passed. He turned the key, stepped inside, and froze as the door swung shut.

He wasn't alone.

Everything appeared as it should, but he was certain someone else was there, waiting in one of the other rooms. He turned silently and grasped the door handle to make his escape. But he stopped. A confederate of the intruder might well be waiting outside. These men were professionals, after all.

Noah decided to make his way to the rear. Use the back door. It seemed less of a risk, although he could not be sure why. He reached ahead with his right foot and placed it soundlessly on the carpet. Then his left.

There was a noise, a soft clink of metal on metal. A gun? Knives? The source was in the very direction in which he was headed. Noah began to pivot, to go back the way he had come. Before he could move, he heard singing, soft and tuneless.

"Mrs. Jensen?"

"Dr. Whitestone? Is that you?"

"What are you doing here?"

Noah's housekeeper appeared in the doorway to the kitchen, her bulk near to filling the opening. She wore her apron and an expression that was at once maternal and abashed.

"Oh, doctor, I'm sorry if I startled you, but I just couldn't bear the thought of you being alone and having to cook for yourself. With all that's been going on, I mean. I thought to give you a little company and a good meal. I bought some bass right from the pier, and I'm cooking it up now. With some potatoes and vegetables. Would you like a glass of port?"

Noah repressed the urge to throttle her and glanced at his watch. "I'm not very hungry, Mrs. Jensen. I actually thought I would skip dinner tonight. Thank you for the gesture, but you can get on home."

"Pshaw!" She gave a wave that caused the flesh on her forearm to quiver like aspic. "You've got to eat, doctor. Just proves how much you need to, when you don't feel like it."

The woman would be as immovable as Kronos. "All right, Mrs. Jensen. But I've got to go out again. If you can serve me very quickly, I'll have some supper. But then you must promise to go home and relax. We will have a busy week ahead, and I want you rested."

The old widow beamed. "You just sit right down, doctor. I've never told you this, but bass is my specialty."

Oh Lord, thought Noah.

Mrs. Jensen scurried into the kitchen and returned moments later with a fish that had been skinned but not filleted, surrounding by carrots, onions, and potatoes. Noah put a tiny morsel on his forked and tasted it. He was stunned. It wasn't wonderful—that would be too much to hope for—but nor was it bad. Perfectly edible. Even tasty. He cursed the day he had told Mrs. Jensen that he preferred meat.

Noah tried to eat quickly, but Mrs. Jensen was having none of it.

"Dr. Whitestone, please stop gobbling your food. Not very healthy, if you ask me."

Noah moved some fish around the plate, making it appear he had less to finish.

"And here I thought you'd want to know what I heard from Mrs. Tumulty."

"What is that, Mrs. Jensen?"

"About Dr. Frias and Mayor Wurster."

Noah put down his fork.

"Mrs. Tumulty works for the Hearns. You know. The boat maker."

Zechariah Hearn constructed the finest yachts in the east. He was rumored to have a waiting list five years long, on which the names Vanderbilt, Astor, and Roosevelt appeared. Hearn lived in an immense mansion, the largest in the Heights, three stories sitting on the bay, with, of course, a private dock.

"Well, Mrs. Hearn gave a dinner Tuesday last week. And two of the guests were . . ."

"Yes, Mrs. Jensen. Mayor Wurster and Arnold Frias." She so reveled in gossip that Mrs. Jensen might not finish the guest list before Miriam arrived.

"No, doctor. Mayor Wurster wasn't there. The second person was a German. Very friendly with Dr. Frias."

"Mrs. Jensen, Dr. Frias has recently returned from a holiday in Germany. Perhaps this was someone he met on his trip."

"And went into business with?" Mrs. Jensen was now smirking in obvious satisfaction. There can be no more pleasing circumstance for a gossip than to know something that someone else does not.

"What sort of business? Who was this German?" But Noah knew. He was the "Schmidt" that Jamie De Kuyper had seen at First Mercantile.

"Well, doctor, I'm surely pleased to have finally gotten your attention. His name was Hafstaengel. Mrs. Tumulty got the name off his place card."

"And the business?"

"Mrs. Tumulty couldn't be sure. She caught only bits of the conversation when she was serving. But this Hafstaengel fellow seemed to think it was important. Even made a toast. 'To the future,' he said. 'The twentieth century.'"

"I don't see how that has any meaning, Mrs. Jensen. The twentieth century is only a bit more than two months away."

"He also said, 'To making the world a healthier place. With our American partners.' He tilted his glass at Dr. Frias before he drank."

"Did the wonderfully observant Mrs. Tumulty remember any details of the German's business? Its name, for example."

Mrs. Jensen shook her head sadly. Mrs. Tumulty had apparently not done as good a job as Mrs. Jensen would have herself.

"Did this Hafstaengel say where he was staying?"

"It was his last night in America. He sailed back to Germany Wednesday morning. That was the reason for the dinner. To wish him off."

And Willard Anschutz died that night. So that was Frias's important personal engagement. "So where does Mayor Wurster come in if he wasn't present?"

"He was supposed to be present but seems not to have been able to get back from Philadelphia in time. He's one of the partners, though. So is Mr. Hearn."

"Partners in what?"

Mrs. Jensen shrugged.

"Did any other names come up?" De Kuyper, for instance.

"Not that Mrs. Tumulty told me."

Noah looked down at his plate. He had succeeded in eating a sufficient amount of Mrs. Jensen's fish to be able to beg off the rest. He told her he was stuffed and tried to hustle her off to clean up, but the woman would not move.

"Is there something else?" he asked.

Her eyes dropped. "Yes, doctor. I did hear something else."

"Do you wish to share your information with me?"

She obviously did not, but eventually forced herself to speak. "It will be in the *Daily Eagle* tomorrow or the next day. Admiral Dewey's fleet is due at Sandy Hook on Tuesday, two days early. Colonel Anschutz will be here on Wednesday. He already knows about his son."

TWENTY

Noah finally had succeeded in persuading Mrs. Jensen to leave at 6:45. It occurred to him that the widow, living alone, her children grown and moved away, was lingering simply because she did not have all that much to go home to. But if his housekeeper and Miriam met at the door, all Brooklyn would know by the next morning that he was dallying with the Red Lady. As would certain people who lived on Gramercy Park.

He waited in the sitting room as the clock ticked and took stock. Heavy furniture and dark colors. The décor of an old man. When the clock chimed seven o'clock, he drained the port, repaired to the kitchen to deposit the empty glass, then returned to the front room. Five past.

When the crack of the door knocker came, it sounded like a gunshot. He swung open the door, and her smell filled his nostrils. Miriam didn't move for a moment, remaining on the doorstep, holding a canvas sack

144

filled with produce, a loaf of bread, and something wrapped in paper. The top of a bottle of wine peeked out the top. She reached up with her other hand and touched him on the cheek. He could hear his heart throb in his chest. Could she?

"Are you going to invite me in?"

Noah stepped aside and let her pass. She wrinkled her nose. "It smells of fish in here. Have you eaten already?"

Noah told her of his surprise visit by his housekeeper. His voice sounded to him stiff, mechanical.

Miriam laughed. Throaty. "I don't have to cook this, Noah. It's only a chicken. Anarchist coq au vin."

"What's the difference between anarchist coq au vin and the regular version?"

"No formal recipe. Just use whatever seems to work at the time. And, of course, everyone present gets a share." She reached into her bag and withdrew the wine. It was a bottle of Chateau Margaux. Even Noah, who knew next to nothing about fine wines, was aware that Chateau Margaux was one of the most expensive wines in the world.

She saw him stare at the bottle. "A case of this was contributed to our cause from Henry Clay Frick through the stevedores who unloaded his latest purchases from Europe. The case will be reported as, alas, damaged in transit. He will be furious, but what can he do? Search the hold for spilled Bordeaux? This isn't stealing, you understand. This is justice. Petty justice, perhaps, but justice all the same."

He located a corkscrew among the kitchen utensils, uncorked the bottle, and poured them each a glass. She lifted hers before she drank. "To drinking a murderer's wine. Your first act of revolution."

"My second."

"What was your first?"

"You."

Miriam looked around room, just as Noah had done a few minutes before. She saw what he had not.

"These furnishings are anonymous, Noah. They reveal nothing. This might as well be a hotel room."

"I don't pay much attention to accoutrements."

"Nonsense. No photographs? Keepsakes? I still have my favorite toy from when I was small. A little carved duck. All the paint is off it now, but I wouldn't part with it for anything."

"I have a photograph of my wife in my bedroom."

"What was her name?"

"Isobel."

"And of the fiancée of whose existence you are so possessive?"

"I don't feel the need to trumpet my affairs."

"In your own home?" She waited, but Noah didn't reply. "Well, do you? Of Miss De Kuyper?"

"No." Noah noticed that his glass was empty, although he had no memory of finishing it.

"Then let me see your wife's."

"No."

"Let me see it."

The door to the bedroom was closed. Noah realized he always kept it so, an odd affectation for man who lived alone. But all right, he thought. You want to see it. See it.

In a moment, they were inside. Noah turned the switch to engage the dim electric lights, then led her to the chest of drawers. He flipped his hand toward the frame, dismissively as he would to a bill collector. Miriam ignored him, but simply lifted Isobel's photograph and studied it. She tilted the frame slightly, as if to see a two-dimensional image from a different angle. Finally, she replaced the photograph on the doily, handling it gently, almost caressing.

"I can see why you loved her so."

Noah felt his eyes fill with tears, but he willed them back. Miriam padded softly from the chest of drawers to where he stood. She raised her hands to his face. Held him. Pulled him to her. Their lips touched.

Maribeth's lips had been stiff when they kissed, like Isobel's, but Miriam's were supple. She pulled back for moment, looked at him for a moment, brow furrowed, and then leaned in again. This time, the tip of her tongue flicked against his lips. Then it was inside his mouth.

Suddenly, they were kissing wildly. He raised his hands to her face. Her skin was warm, almost liquid against his palms. Their tongues darted back and forth. He had never kissed anyone like this. No matter how ferociously their mouths pressed together, Miriam's lips remained soft. He grabbed her around the back, pulled her close. The instant he felt the fullness of her breasts against him, he was fully aroused. More than four years. Too long for any man.

She began tearing at his clothing. He was tearing at hers. They staggered toward Noah's bed, hitting the side with their legs and tumbling down. Noah's vest was open, his tie askew. Suddenly, Miriam pressed a hand against his chest. Again, he was stunned at her strength.

"Wait!"

Noah felt a wave of horror that she had changed her mind. She stood up, standing before him. She lifted her blouse over her head. Her breasts swelled in her pale brown camisole. Never taking her eyes from his, she dropped her skirt to the floor. Then her slip.

Miriam paused. Noah lay on the bed, transfixed, wanting to throw himself at her but feeling as if he were pinned by a great weight. The air was filled with her.

Suddenly, she was naked, undergarments in a silken pile at her feet. Dark hair against golden skin. Breasts, full and round, with a pink silver-dollar sized center. She moved to him. Began opening the buttons of his shirt, one at time. Then of his trousers. He lifted his hand to reach for her breast, but she stopped him. "Just a moment more," she whispered.

She made Noah undress until he was naked as well. With Isobel, they had always made love under covers. She had never seen him erect.

Miriam pushed Noah to the bed and then placed herself astride him. She lowered herself, used her hand to guide him into her. Noah closed his eyes and felt a moan escape. She rocked slowly, forward and back, as he felt himself rise off the bed, his back arched.

A feeling came over him, new in its intensity, beginning at his center and radiating outward. His entire body tingled and was transformed. He heard a loud, deep-throated cry and realized it was him. Suddenly, there was an explosion within him and then without, a release as he had never known. Miriam's hands on his shoulders seemed all that prevented him from rising ethereally from the bed. Instead of ending almost instantly, as it always had, the release lasted, lingered, aftershocks trembling through him for a magical eternity.

And then he was done. Spent. Exhausted. He opened his eyes to see Miriam smiling down at him. Her face held great tenderness. She moved her hand to his cheek.

"Thank you," he whispered.

She laughed softly. "You're welcome." She rolled off, laid next him, and took his hand. "But we're not done yet. We've just started." She placed his hand on her. Moist and warm. She pressed down on his middle finger to push it inside her. "Where I come from, the woman gets to make some demands as well."

"I'm not sure I know just what to do," he said.

"Don't worry, Noah. I'll show you. I'm hardly shy."

That began a night of lovemaking the like Noah had never known. They laughed; they cried out; they used their hands, their lips, their tongues. It seemed every time Noah drifted off to sleep, she woke him by stroking, kissing; one time he opened his eyes to find that he was in her mouth.

Miriam had no inhibitions. None. She violated every rule of proper womanhood. Her passion was boundless, her appetite insatiable. Even more astounding, in one of their few moments of passivity, she told Noah she was hardly unique. Most of the women in her movement felt no compunction whatsoever about enjoying sexual relations in all their permutations.

Finally, closer to dawn than midnight, Miriam, nestling against him, drifted off. Noah was exhausted but wide awake. He played the entire, astonishing night through his memory. At the end, he knew.

Maribeth had told him to be sure of his decision. Now he was. Finally. Only then did he drift off to sleep.

TWENTY-ONE

Noah's eyes blinked open to the sound of activity on the street outside. For a moment, he didn't know where he was. He looked about for Miriam. She was gone. He felt the bed where she had slept. Still warm, but perhaps from him. Her clothes were gone as well, and his were folded neatly in the chair under the window.

He heard sounds from the other room. Distinctly those of breakfast being prepared. Noah stretched his arms full and smiled.

"Miriam?" he called.

Seconds later, the door to his bedroom swung open. "You're still in bed, doctor? Were you dreaming? And who is Miriam?"

"Hello, Mrs. Jensen."

She wagged a finger at him. "It's already past eight. I was surprised to arrive and find you still lazing about, I'll tell you. I was going to wake you, but I thought perhaps you were up late with a patient." The last sentence was delivered as a question.

"Past eight? My Lord, I've overslept." Mrs. Jensen arrived at six-thirty. When had Miriam left?

"Coffee is in the pot," she said. She stared at him for a moment before going back through the door.

Noah dressed quickly. As he walked in to drink his coffee and check the morning paper, Mrs. Jensen was poised near the door to the kitchen. A choice item of gossip was to be had, not from one of her friends but right here in this very room, and she would have it.

"So *who* is Miriam?"

"No one, Mrs. Jensen."

Mrs. Jensen waited, a dramatic pause. "If you say so, doctor." She turned to leave, then stopped. "I found a strange bottle of wine in the kitchen, doctor. Looked French."

"Very perceptive, Mrs. Jensen. It is French."

"I didn't know you went in for French wine, doctor. Was it in the house?"

"It was a gift from a patient."

She wanted to ask which patient, but could not force herself to violate the snooper's creed and be direct. "You have patients who give you French wine? Oh, doctor, your practice must be looking up."

"Yes. Perhaps it is."

"It was opened, but there were no dirty glasses."

"I washed my glass myself."

"Ah. There was a chicken in the ice box as well. And some vegetables."

"I went shopping." Thank the Lord, Miriam had not gotten to cook. "Mrs. Jensen, I would like to ask a favor."

She stood and waited, wondering what the favor had to do with the chicken and the French wine.

"Would you go to Abraham & Straus for me today? I would like to change the wallpaper. Perhaps some of the furniture as well."

"I don't understand, doctor. You'll only be living here another six months."

"Something brighter, more cheery. Not so . . . old. And, oh yes, one more thing. Would you buy me a picture frame? Suitable for a photograph."

Mrs. Jensen stood in stunned silence.

"These are perfectly reasonable requests, Mrs. Jensen. Now, would you please get me the newspaper? I'm already late."

She stood her ground for a moment more, unsure of what to do. Finally, thinking of no way to elicit the information from someone so erratic, she fetched the *Daily Eagle* and trudged out of the room.

He leafed through to page three and the headline DAY OF TROLLEY ACCIDENTS. Underneath, it read CONDUCTOR'S SKULL CRUSHED BY FALLING FROM HIS CAR—DEATH SOON FOLLOWS, then ONE MAN JUMPS FROM A MOVING CAR, WHILE ANOTHER TRIES TO BOARD ONE—INJURED MAN FOUND ON TRACK; and, finally, HAIRBREADTH ESCAPE—LOCAL MAN PULLED FROM PATH OF CAR NEAR MADISON SQUARE.

Noah read down the article to a description of the last episode. All the circumstances precisely matched his brush with death: time, the nature of the rescue, even the number of the trolley. But the man pulled from the path of the trolley had been identified as one John J. Coughlin. And there was no mention of anyone being pushed—the article claimed the near-victim had been "celebrating on the Sabbath."

Before he could come up with a reason why the police would release a false account to reporters, the bell on his telephone sounded. A singularly annoying noise. A mechanism to inform subscribers of incoming calls was necessary, of course, but why couldn't the telephone companies develop a less intrusive device? Mrs. Jensen started for the instrument, but Noah waved her off. He lifted the earpiece and heard a familiar voice.

"Whitestone? Herold here. How far away are you from 40 Stone Street? It is in lower Manhattan." Herold's voice had the distinctive hollowness that indicated a third ear was on the line. Noah hoped that Herold would not transmit any sensitive information.

"I know where it is," Noah replied. "No more than an hour, certainly."

"Excellent! I want you to meet me there."

"When?"

"Now, Whitestone. Now. Why do you think I asked?"

Noah arrived fifty minutes later to find Justin Herold waiting for him at the entrance of a four-story brick building. Stone Street was a narrow thoroughfare, two blocks long, tucked between two main arteries, South William Street and Pearl Street. The district was home to New York's major financial institutions, but Stone Street consisted of a series of unprepossessing structures housing other businesses that wished to benefit from proximity to money. Number 40 backed Hanover Square. Delmonico's was a mere twenty yards to the north and west.

"Very punctual, Whitestone. Come inside."

Herold led Noah to a directory of the tenants. "Any of these strike a chord?"

Noah scanned the names but could find none that appeared to have any relation to the problem. There were two lawyers, a dentist, and a bondsman, plus a variety of other businesses of various nationalities he could not identify.

When Noah admitted to being at sea, Herold aimed his finger at one of the listings. "What about this one?" It read FARBENFABRIKEN OF ELBERFELD CO.

Noah tried to recall his medical school German. "*Fabriken* is factories, is it not?"

"Very good, Whitestone. How about *farben?*"

"Uh, colors. That's it. Colors."

"And what do you think *colors factories* means?"

Noah had it. "Dye makers."

"Correct. And the significance?"

"About twenty years ago, dye makers discovered that some of the products they use had medicinal properties as well. Acetanilide is one of them. It was formerly marketed as Antifebrin, until the side effects were discovered and it was discontinued as an ethical drug. Now it's the active ingredient in Orangeine. A number of the agents discovered by dye makers are now used in patent medicines."

"Excellent, Whitestone. But not just patent medicines. Dye makers are spending thousands—many thousands—developing new ethical drugs as well. The beauty for these companies is that the substances, once discovered, are remarkably inexpensive to produce in bulk. This particular firm has recently synthesized a substance we recently encountered."

"Acetylsalicylic acid?"

"Precisely. Only in order to ensure that these simple and inexpensive substances are not made available at a less-expensive price, the dye makers, now drug companies, have begun to assign trade names and take out patents. Since American patent laws are more stringent than those in Europe, only the patented version of the drug will be available for prescription. And, since patenting assures a virtual monopoly, the profits will be immense. In the millions. Perhaps millions each year. With stakes such as these, it is not difficult to imagine the lengths to which these firms will go to discover new drugs to patent. Acetylsalicylic acid will be marketed under the trade name Aspirin. We just happened to come across it in the test phase. But, as you will see, that phase is ending."

What Herold had just told him reminded Noah of McKee's investigations. Had the murdered reporter stumbled onto this very place?

"Which company is this?"

"They do business in this country simply as Farbenfabriken of Elberfeld, but in Germany it's Bayer Dye Works. Aspirin, I have discovered, was synthesized by one of their chemists. A man called Hoffmann. But we are interested in another substance that Hoffmann synthesized. He did not restrict the acetylization process to salicylic acid."

"What else?"

"Let's go up to their offices and find out."

Their destination was on the third floor, a simple wooden door with a brass plaque. Herold walked in without knocking. Inside was a counter, chest high, behind which sat a buxom young redhead. She broke into a huge grin as Herold and Noah entered.

"Good morning, gentlemen. Can I help you? You are from the Smith Company, are you not?"

Noah was about to ask if that was Martin H. Smith, but Herold nudged him with his foot. "I'm afraid not," the pathologist said. "We're physicians."

The woman looked disappointed. "Do you have an appointment? Mr. Onderdonk will be tied up this morning."

"I'm Justin Herold. I've attended many of the city's high office holders." With a flourish, Herold took a card from his vest pocket and placed it on the countertop. "This is Noah Whitestone, a very prominent physician from Brooklyn. We are extremely interested in your line of products. We presumed to drop in without an appointment to hear something of your remarkable assortment of new pharmaceuticals." He gestured to a placard propped up on the counter. "This is it, yes?"

The woman took the card, read it, then glanced up at Herold. Her eye went back to the card and then to Herold once more. "Perhaps I should ask Mr. Onderdonk if he's got a few moments to speak with you." The woman put up a finger and then darted through a door to an inner office.

"Look at the placard, Whitestone," Herold said. "Notice anything?"

Across the top left, it read BAYER PHARMACEUTICAL PRODUCTS; across the top right, SEND FOR SAMPLES AND LITERATURE TO. On the bottom right was FARBENFABRIKEN OF ELBERFELD CO., and on the bottom left 40 STONE STREET, NEW YORK. In the center was a display of Bayer's wares, arranged like a piled set of child's blocks. The array contained the names of twenty products, although only four were featured. One of the four, at the top of the pyramid, was ASPIRIN. The substance was billed as THE SUBSTITUTE FOR SALICYLATES. Noah understood immediately why Bayer had sought a patent on the name. Aspirin *was* a salicylate.

When Noah indicated that portion of the placard, Herold shook his head. "No," he whispered. "The other one. Beneath Aspirin on the left."

Noah saw it, THE SEDATIVE FOR COUGHS, just as the young woman emerged.

"Mr. Onderdonk will see you," she announced operatically, as if President McKinley were behind the door.

As Noah and Herold entered the office, a man moved forward to meet them. He was short and round, and wore a dark blue wool suit that, even to Noah's untrained eye, had certainly been custom tailored. His hand was extended, his right arm rigid. A salesman's sincere, toothy smile was frozen on his face.

"H. Bryce Onderdonk," the man exulted. "It is a pleasure to make the acquaintance of two esteemed members of the medical profession." The man gave a small wave with a pudgy hand. The opal on the ring on his little finger flashed in the light. "Your fame precedes you, Dr. Herold. The coroner's office has not been the same since your departure. And I watched your testimony in the Meyer trial with fascination."

Herold gave a short bow, trying without success to appear modest.

"So," Onderdonk went on, not waiting for a comment, "what brings you to our offices?"

"We are interested in obtaining samples for some of these new medications," Herold said. "And I, as a medical researcher, would be fascinated to hear something of their development."

"I thought you were more interested in the dead than the living," Onderdonk said, but in a manner that left no doubt the remark was in jest. He removed a handkerchief and dabbed at his lips.

"True, Mr. Onderdonk. But in order to correctly analyze the dead, I must be aware of any new medications they might have taken while they were alive."

"Of course. Are you interested in any in particular?" Onderdonk remained affable, but a note of disquiet had crept into his voice. He emitted a small cough to cover his unease.

"Well, let's start with Aspirin," Herold replied. "A substitute for salicylates. Does that mean it has analgesic and antipyretic qualities?"

Onderdonk regained his full measure of enthusiasm. "Indeed. Aspirin will be a wonder. All the benefits of salicylates without the excruciating aftereffects."

"What are the ingredients? If you don't mind my asking."

"I don't mind at all, Dr. Herold, if you don't mind my not answering. In truth, I'm not certain myself. All I can say is that this medication was developed by the very best chemists in Germany and then tested for safety. It is a compound that represents a vast improvement over salicylates."

"Why is Aspirin not yet on the market then?"

Onderdonk offered a small, conspiratorial chuckle. "That was a decision of the home office. We are going to bring it out slowly at first, then launch a major advertising campaign. A copy of the placard you saw on the way in is to run as an advertisement in both the *New York Medical Journal* and the *American Journal of Insanity*, both highly prestigious publications."

"But are there samples available?" Herold pressed. "As a physician, I would be excited to be able to prescribe a new wonder drug."

"Alas, we have nothing on hand," Onderdonk replied. "We are expecting a full supply of samples from Germany very soon. I have your card. I will personally see that each of you is placed at the very top of our list of recipients."

"Thank you so much." Herold beamed. "Medicine is indeed poised to leap into the new century."

Onderdonk beamed wider. "My very sentiments, Dr. Herold."

"Can we obtain samples of your other three featured drugs as well? I noticed on the placard out front you have a uric acid solvent . . ."

"Lycetol. Yes, a remarkable new treatment for kidney ailments."

"An antineuralgic and antirheumatic . . ."

"Salophen. Another remarkable innovation."

"And a sedative for coughs."

"Yes. The best of all. Not only will this drug relieve coughs in children—as you know, Dr. Herold, perhaps the most pernicious problem facing medical science today—but it has shown great promise both in the relief of other respiratory ailments . . . asthma, even tuberculosis . . . and as a general mood enhancer. The drug is even a remarkable sleep aid. It received its name because test subjects in Germany were so uplifted after its use. *Heroisch. Heroic* in English. So our marketing director thought to keep the sentiment and called the drug Heroin."

"Very deft."

"And," Onderdonk proclaimed, "the preeminent feature of this new substance is that it is perfectly safe! No harmful effects whatever!"

"Truly a boon," exulted Herold. "I suppose you are not at liberty to discuss the ingredients of this medication either."

"I would be completely at liberty if I knew myself, Dr. Herold. Given the intense competition to develop new pharmaceuticals, I'm sure you can understand why the home office would be reluctant to publicize the details of a new discovery."

Noah was about to say that the details would have needed to be divulged in order to gain a patent, but a look from Herold caused him to hold his tongue. Onderdonk was ignoring him anyway.

"Of course," Herold agreed with a nod. "Parents across America will sing your praises for having developed a cough remedy for children that does not contain opioids. I assume that is what makes this discovery so revolutionary."

Onderdonk shifted his weight. "As I said . . ."

"So no one in New York has had the benefit of samples of your wonderful products?" Noah was speaking for the first time.

"Not from this office. We have been so recently established, you see. And you are . . . Dr. Whitestone. Are you in practice with Dr. Herold?"

"Dr. Whitestone has been engaged on a research project with me," Herold said.

"You're a fortunate man, Dr. Whitestone," Onderdonk said, glancing toward the door to his office. He was either wishing Martin Smith would arrive or that his current visitors would leave. Probably both.

"I must confess, Mr. Onderdonk," Noah went on, "we are not here by coincidence."

"Oh no?"

"No. We heard of your amazing products from a prominent local physician: Dr. Arnold Frias."

"Frias? I don't think I know the man." Onderdonk rubbed his hands together as if friction would improve his memory.

"Are you certain? We were at a dinner with Herr Hafstaengel."

"You met the director?"

"Only in a casual way. Dr. Frias was by far more effusive. Herr Hafstaengel seemed almost embarrassed at the praise."

"He is a modest man." Onderdonk's forehead had begun to glow.

"Dr. Frias has had such remarkable results with Aspirin, and I believe other of your medications, that we thought to visit you today."

"Frias you say?" Onderdonk dug into his vest pocket and withdrew his watch. After checking the time, he looked up and forced a smile. "I would love to chat further with you, doctors, but my next appointment is due momentarily."

"Martin Smith?" Herold asked.

"Yes. How did . . . well, no matter." He moved to the door. "Thank you both for coming by."

"Our pleasure, Mr. Onderdonk," Herold replied. "The visit has been most enlightening."

"Exceptionally so," Noah added. "Thank you for being so helpful, Mr. Onderdonk. We will not forget to mention your extraordinary cooperation."

"To whom?"

"To whoever asks, of course."

Once they were back on the street, Herold grabbed Noah by the arm. "Whitestone, I'll wager anything that this Heroin product they're so excited about is nothing but acetylized morphine. When we get hold of one of those green tablets the girl in Newark took, we'll know for sure."

"Then you're not upset? That I used Frias's name? And Hafstaengel's?"

"It's your getabout, Whitestone, not mine. This Onderdonk fellow will be in touch with Frias, of course, and word that you are getting closer to a solution will undoubtedly be passed to your enemies. So, I suppose, if you are willing to put yourself in greater danger by flushing them out, who am I to disagree?"

"My only hesitation was that I didn't want to put you in danger as well."

"Oh, I doubt I'm in any danger, Whitestone. I'm a prominent person with, if I may say so, not inconsiderable influence. TR and I even got to be friends when he was superintendent of the Board of Police Commissioners. He often consulted with me because he believed the official occupants of the coroner's office were corrupt political hacks. No, Whitestone, I suspect if your enemies feel the need to toss someone else into the river, they'll start with you."

"Thank you for the comforting thought, Dr. Herold." Noah wasn't sure that Herold should be quite so sanguine. With millions at stake, not even TR's friendship would prevent mayhem. But Noah had come to know Herold too well to try to press the point.

"Our main goal now, Whitestone, is obtaining a Heroin tablet. I don't think Onderdonk was lying about not distributing samples through this office. No one would trust a dolt like him with anything sensitive. I'll warrant they come from Germany and go directly to the doctors in their employ. Unfortunately, one of the by-products of our last conversation is that, when Onderdonk speaks to Frias, our names will be linked. I was intending to seek him out as a disinterested party. Ah, well, every investigation has its challenges. What you need to do is go and see your Red friends and find out who else might have one of those tablets."

"Perhaps you should visit the *New Visions* office, Dr. Herold. I had thought to check with Dr. Jacobi. If there are the beginnings of an epidemic about, he's the man who would know."

"Don't be silly, Whitestone. Jacobi is a good man, of course, and I don't hold with the Reds any more than you do. But you already have their trust. And, one has to admit, they've definitely been out front on this."

"I suppose so."

"No need to suppose. This is science. Let me know as soon as you can lay your hands on one of those tablets. In the meantime, I've got some things I wish to try on my own."

TWENTY-TWO

The door on Lafayette Street swung open quickly, almost striking Noah in the face, and Sasha, the dour Slavic boy with the pockmarked face, burst out. The boy looked up at him for a moment, glowered, then hurried past and down the street. Every errand these people run they think is urgent, Noah thought.

Noah walked up the stairs to the second floor. Just before he reached *New Visions'* door, a series of odd events occurred in rapid sequence.

The glass on the door seemed to bulge out and then break; the hall seemed to lose its orientation to the horizontal; Noah felt pressure on his chest, as if he had been caught in some great wave at the seashore; and, most frighteningly, he could no longer hear. Just after these singular phenomena, the hall went black.

Noah opened his eyes. His lungs were choked with dust. Glass and plaster littered the hall. The door to *New Visions* was gone, as was a good deal of the wall. His vision was blurred, and the scene floated in front of him, as if in a dream. He still could not hear, although a buzz of background seemed to ring in his ears. He was confused. He was aware of where he was, yet unaware at the same time.

He tried to stand but pitched back to his hands and knees. Sounds had begun to penetrate the buzz. Sharp sounds, although they seemed to be filtered through liquid. Then Noah knew. They were screams. Awareness returned, slowly at first, then faster.

Bomb. The offices of *New Visions* had been bombed. The vision of Sasha running away from the building stuck in his mind for a moment, then was replaced.

Miriam.

Noah tried once again to stand, but once again fell. Finally, he succeeded in forcing himself to his feet. He began to stagger through the plaster and glass to the destroyed offices. He realized his clothes were torn, his jacket almost shredded. Warm liquid flowed down his forehead. His own blood. He continued through the hall, his steps still unsteady. The screams became clearer, louder, more persistent.

He reached the yawning opening in the wall and braced himself against a stud. The devastation inside was staggering. Plaster, broken furniture, hanging wires, torn papers, twisted metal, shards of glass and wood were everywhere. Interspersed with the inanimate wreckage was the wreckage of men and women, sometimes whole, sometimes in parts. A man's leg, still in its trouser, was at his feet. He scanned the room but could not see her. He continued to hear the screams but could make out no one screaming. To his left, he saw that Mauritz Herzberg's office was completely blown out.

Noah began to make his way through the room. The first three people he encountered—two women and a man—were dead. One of the men was the owner of traumatically amputated leg. Another man was unconscious with a fractured humerus. Noah propped him up and placed his arm on a piece of desktop. A woman, her clothes in tatters, lay muttering to herself. Noah sat her up as well. Both would survive until ambulances arrived. A bit farther on, Noah saw the door to Mauritz's office. It had been blown, almost intact, halfway across the main room. Noah was about to keep searching when he saw a foot protruding from underneath. He reached down and flung the door to the side.

Miriam.

She was lying half-turned to one side. She seemed conscious. Noah knelt by her and reached for her wrist. Pulse was weak and rapid. Thready. Difficult to palpate. Her skin was pallid; her gaze unfocused. Hemorrhagic shock. Blood loss. Internal or external. If the former, he would be unable to save her. Like Isobel.

Noah rolled Miriam over. Blood underneath her. As large as a rain puddle. Leg wound. Not pulsing. Venous, not arterial. Warm. Elevate. Pressure. He grabbed for the door that had pinned Miriam to the floor— and very possibly had shielded her and saved her life. Her father's door. He rolled Miriam onto it and placed one end on some debris, forming an incline. Trendelenburg position. Head below the heart. Maximize blood flow to the brain and lessen it to the wound. He covered her torso with whatever was available. Her eyes—those wonderful eyes—were glazed.

Noah ripped off his vest, folded it into a compress, and held it to the wound as tightly as he could. Pressure. More effective than a tourniquet, even with major trauma. Would not present the danger of cutting off blood flow completely and mortifying tissue.

After a few seconds, the bleeding was under control, but Noah dared not release the compress. Miriam's eyes had cleared slightly. Her brain was getting more oxygen.

"Noah?" she whispered. "Is that you?"

"Yes. Be still."

"Where's Daddy?"

"In the other room."

Noah sensed movement and looked up to see a man in the doorway, likely from one of the other offices in the building. "You! Come here!" Noah yelled. For the first time, he noticed that his shirt front was covered in blood.

The man did not move at first, so Noah yelled again. The man finally began to pick his way through the rubble, looking back and forth in disbelief, as if he had entered the Ninth Circle of Hell.

"Hold this tight right here!" Noah commanded when the man arrived. Noah showed the man how to keep pressure on the wound. The screaming had stopped, replaced by a soft moaning emanating from many quarters at once. He must help the others.

"Don't leave." Miriam's voice was still weak, but her articulation had improved.

"Don't worry. I'll be right here."

As he stood to look around the room, Noah heard bells in the distance. Ambulances. As he combed through the rubble, he located three more dead. He made comfortable another four whose injuries could wait until medical personnel arrived in force, removing shards of glass, supporting broken limbs. He discovered one man bleeding from multiple cuts whom he also placed in the Trendelenburg position. A number of men had begun to appear at the scene. Noah employed them, one after another, directing each to perform whatever emergency function might keep the injured in stasis until professional help arrived. As he moved back and forth through the room, he checked on Miriam often. She seemed no worse. Lacking internal injury, she would survive.

Finally, when he had done all he could for the living, Noah made his way to Mauritz Herzberg's office. The room had been reduced to a pile of odd sizes of wood, glass, plaster, and paper, piled together as if at a town dump. The window was gone, completely blown out. What remained of Herzberg's desk, half a top and one leg, rested against what once had been a side wall.

Noah saw a right hand protruding from the pile. Although his own head wound seemed to have stopped bleeding, he suddenly felt light-headed, dizzy, vaguely faint. He lowered his head between his knees for a moment, then pushed forward through the debris. Throwing off the larger pieces of flotsam and scraping off the smaller, he uncovered a head and torso. Mauritz would have been unrecognizable to a stranger. His face was largely gone. His left arm had been torn off at the elbow, and massive thoracic trauma was apparent. At least he would be able to tell Miriam that her father had died instantly. The concussion had been so close, so severe, that Mauritz would not have had even a second's recognition.

Noah's fatigue was returning quickly. He staggered out into the main room to see that ambulance attendants had begun to fill the room. His legs suddenly felt like jelly, and the room was moving before his eyes. Voices lost distinction, became hollow, distant. Noah tried to move to where Miriam lay, to instruct the ambulance attendant precisely what care to take of her wound. After his first step, his other leg could not follow. The room began to spin. He was vaguely conscious of a man in white gesturing in his direction. The man seemed to be yelling something, but Noah could not hear him.

The effort to stand had become overwhelming. Noah leaned backward, coming to rest against a denuded joist. He slid slowly to the floor. He felt his eyes closing, as if drifting off into a deep sleep.

TWENTY-THREE

DAY 6. MONDAY, 9/25—5 P.M.

Welcome back, Dr. Whitestone."

Noah blinked and looked about. White walls. Overhead lights.

"Where am I?"

"Bellevue Hospital."

Noah's vision began to clear. A man was looking down at him. Young. Smiling.

"You'll be fine," the man said soothingly. "I'm Bradley Kerr. We've sutured your head wound. Other than some superficial bruises, you're in remarkably good condition. Drink a lot of water and fruit juice. Of course, you would know to do that already."

"How are the others?" Noah was in a private room. He wondered why.

Kerr frowned. Doctors generally disliked treating other doctors. As patients, physicians tended to be pushy and inquisitive. Nor could they be put off by evasions or platitudes. "Nine dead in total. Out of twenty, we think. Of the eleven, only two will likely not make it. The others will be all right over time. No small thanks to you."

"There was a woman . . ."

"With the leg wound? Yes. She's the one who told us your name. She's going to be fine. Miracle, really. Being as close to the blast as she was. We transfused her. Two pints so far. Seemed to take."

"Did you mix the blood first?"

Kerr fought back the urge to be curt. "Of course."

Transfusions were dangerous, hit-and-miss affairs. Sometimes, an unpredictable incompatibility seemed to exist between donor and recipient, which caused the recipient to fall critically ill or even die. Surgeons had discovered that mixing the donor's blood with the recipient's before transfering back to the patient seemed to radically lessen the number of adverse reactions. There was a theory running around that blood could actually be "typed"—analyzed for properties—but nothing had been proven.

"You know, Dr. Whitestone, if you had been thirty seconds later treating that wound . . ."

Noah nodded. The movement sent a dull pain through his skull.

"You saved her life." Kerr crossed his arms. "The Red Lady."

What was that supposed to mean? "Can I see her?"

"Soon." Kerr had seen him wince. "We've got something for the pain. New drug. Amazing analgesic properties."

"Aspirin?"

"Yes. How did you know?"

"Doesn't matter."

Kerr lifted a small cloth off the table top to reveal two blue tablets. Noah wondered whether Kerr was aware of the ingredients in the medication he had just recommended. Noah considered for a moment whether to decline the tablets. But he had encountered no adverse reactions from Aspirin, and what better way to learn about new drugs than to take them himself?

"Do you have Heroin as well?" Noah asked after he swallowed the tablets with a glass of water. "I believe they are marketed by the same company."

"The cough remedy? Where did your hear about that? We just received a memorandum from the chief of medicine this morning."

"I have a friend at Brooklyn Hospital."

"Really?" Kerr walked to the doorway and leaned for moment against the side. "But no, I don't believe so. I'll ask for you, if you like."

"That's all right. I was just curious."

"Of course. Well, I suppose I should give you the talk." Kerr then advised him in professional monotone to rest until the medication could begin to take effect. Then he left the room, switching off the electric light as he went.

Within fifteen minutes, the pain in Noah's head had begun to substantially subside. A marvelous sensation of relief. Whatever the benefits or detriments of Heroin, if Noah's experience was any test, Aspirin was destined to reap the enormous rewards that Herold had predicted.

The door opened and the light switched on once more.

"Feeling better?" McCluskey wore concern uneasily.

Noah pulled himself up and propped his back against the pillow. The pain remained moderate.

"Who's Sasha, doc?"

Noah didn't reply.

"You must know him. The doc out there said you called out his name . . . more than once . . . and even stuck 'bastard' on to it."

"I was delirious. I don't remember doing anything of the sort."

"He remembers. Want me to call him back so he can say so?"

"Sasha worked at the magazine. He was running out just before the explosion. When I said hello, he looked at me strangely and kept going."

McCluskey nodded. "Aleksandr Cviec. Belonged to a different group. Communists. We'd been watching him on and off. We watch all of them on and off, except the big fish. Mauritz. Miriam. Them we try to watch more often. So many of them, it's like keeping track of cockroaches. Can't say I can really tell them apart . . . socialists, anarchists, communists . . . but they sure seem to hate each other. Somebody had it in for old Mauritz. Took thirteen years, but justice is done at last."

"Eight others died as well, McCluskey. And I could have been nine."

"Woulda been sad about you, doc. As to the others . . ." McCluskey shrugged.

"You seem to know a lot about these groups, McCluskey. Dolph. Sasha. If you are so clued in, how come you can't stop any of the violence?"

"Oh, we stop plenty, doc. Those stories just don't make the papers."

"Are you going to be able to catch him? Sasha?"

McCluskey shrugged. "We'll try, but word is his friends already got him out of town. It's a big country, doc, to try to find one lousy kid. Oh yeah, the dicks on the McKee case figure the communists did that one, too."

"Why? What do communists care about the Patent Medicine Trust?"

"Don't know nothing about that," McCluskey replied. "But we do know he was working on a story saying the communists were betraying the workers. Lot of folks out there talking about the workers. Ain't none of them workers themselves, though. Notice that, doc?"

"Why was John J. Coughlin in the newspaper article about the trolley?"

McCluskey shrugged. "That was me. Thought I was doing you a favor. I figured you'd had enough publicity for one week."

Noah tentatively swung his legs off the bed. He was in a hospital robe. His clothes were nowhere to be seen, although his shoes had been placed at the far side of the room.

"Wait a minute, doc. Where you going? You're not supposed to move around."

"I'm a physician, McCluskey. I know when I can move around and when I cannot." In truth, he should have remained in bed. If he had suffered a mild concussion, no small possibility, movement could exacerbate the effects. But rest was a luxury he could scant afford.

The policeman put his hand on Noah's arm, although lightly, without force. "You don't think we had any hand in this, do you, doc?" He did sincerity better.

Noah looked up wearily. "Of course not, McCluskey. How could you think I would judge you so unfairly?"

"Good. Glad you still got your humor, doc. Go and see your girlfriend then. But don't forget our conversation."

"I never forget anything you say, McCluskey. And she's not my girlfriend."

Noah pushed himself tentatively to his feet. Good. No sharp pain. No dizziness. No blurred vision. Cranial trauma had obviously been minimal. He was sore, his joints ached, and his forehead throbbed where he had been sutured, but under the circumstances, he was in excellent fettle. He wondered how long the Aspirin would remain effective. When the effects waned, he intended to ask for another dose.

Noah took some tentative steps as McCluskey looked on. His balance was good. He touched a finger to his nose.

"What's that for?"

"Coordination test."

"Guess you passed. Unless you was trying to poke yourself in the eye."

"Sorry to disappoint, McCluskey. I hit where I was aiming."

"And that's it? You touch your nose and figure that you're okay after getting knocked silly by a bomb? You're eroding my faith in medicine, doc."

"Well, McCluskey, since you are so concerned with my welfare . . ." The copper had succeeded in making himself almost likable, although Noah was not altogether certain how he had turned the trick. "If I had the time, I'd check my pupils for focus and dilation, my reflexes, and my heart and lungs. I'd perform a number of hand and arm move-ments to check for tremors, unilateral or bilateral motor weakness, coordination, and position sense. I would whistle, smile, and clench my teeth to check the trigeminal nerves, which, as I'm sure you know, branch off the cranium and control facial muscles. I would turn my head from side to side, slowly and then more quickly, then palpate the muscles that control head movement. I'd open a bottle of alcohol to test sense of smell, one nostril at a time, to check for frontal lobe damage. And finally, I'd conduct an ad hoc test of my hearing. But I don't have the time, so I'm simply going to leave it at touching my nose and get about my affairs."

McCluskey threw up his hands. "Okay, doc, you've won me over. You do know what you're doing, after all. But before you go roaring on down the hall, I should tell you that you got visitors."

"Who?"

"De Kuypers."

"Which ones?"

McCluskey smirked. "Brother and sister."

"Who told them? The explosion couldn't be in the newspapers this soon."

"I did. I thought you'd want your fiancée to know."

"What about my parents?"

McCluskey shook his head. "No need to worry them. I'll get word to them on the sly . . . now that I know you touched your nose. And don't worry about reporters. I think I'll tell them John J. Coughlin was at the scene."

"Thank you, McCluskey. I sink deeper into your debt. Can I see Marib—them now?"

"Sure, doc." McCluskey started for the door, then turned back. "You know, if Maribeth De Kuyper was ever my fiancée . . . I should be so lucky . . . I'd sure think twice before messing it up."

"Thank you for the marital advice, McCluskey. The breadth of your acumen stuns me."

"I'm assuming that's a compliment, doc." Almost as soon as the policeman left, Alan walked through the door carrying a suit of clothes over one arm. He was alone.

"My fair sister isn't certain that she wants to see you," Alan said, preempting the question. "She has entrusted me to assure her that you're no threat to die."

"Why doesn't she want to see me?"

"You have to ask?"

"But, Alan, she told me to see Miriam. That I should be sure. That she could abide anything but dishonesty."

"And you believed her? My word, old man, I don't know much about women, but even I wouldn't have fallen for that." Alan handed over the clothes. "Your housekeeper sends her love."

"Her love?"

"That's what she said."

"Please, Alan, go fetch Maribeth. I must speak with her."

A few minutes later, Noah was dressed and Maribeth was at the door. She stayed beyond the threshold for a moment, then walked stiffly into the room. Her eye went to the sutures on Noah's forehead. She started toward him, but then pulled back.

"Alan tells me that you are in no danger. I'm very pleased."

Noah moved across and took her by the arms. "You must trust me, Maribeth. I love you and want to marry you. You asked me to be certain and I am."

"But now I'm not. Competing against a living woman turned out not to be as simple as I imagined."

"You're not competing against anyone, Maribeth."

"Alan told me you saved her life."

"Would you have been convinced if I had let her die?"

"Of course not. You know what I mean."

"No. I'm not certain I do."

"Do you intend to see her again?"

Yes, Noah thought, that was the question. "Only to help solve the puzzle," he said. "I'm very close. The reporter was right. They're murdering children."

"Who?"

"German pharmaceutical makers. Martin Smith. And Frias. I can't stop now. But the moment I've got my proof, I'll never see Miriam Herzberg again. I swear to you."

"But will you never think of her again?"

Noah moved forward and put his hands on either side of Maribeth's face. She pulled against him for a moment, then placed a gloved forefinger near the sutures. "Does it hurt very much?"

"No. I've taken a wonder drug. The Bayer Company seems to have produced an endless supply of miracles."

"Well, then, I'll hope for one more."

He leaned in and kissed her. Suddenly, he wanted her terribly.

"Alan has something for you," she said.

"What is it? He didn't say anything."

"He was waiting to see . . ."

"I understand. I'll be downstairs soon."

"I'll be waiting." As Maribeth turned to leave, she added, "She's in room 224."

TWENTY-FOUR

H ello, Noah."

Miriam had been placed in a room with three other patients, all post-traumatic, none of whom had been in the explosion. A woman with severe facial contusions and a fractured left orbital, a result of a beating by her husband, was asleep, sedated. A prostitute, no more than fifteen, had been treated for a gunshot wound to the abdomen. Another young woman, recovering from a mastectomy, lay staring at the ceiling, biting her lip, tears running down the sides of her face. Noah had wiped her cheeks and tried to speak with her, but the woman had refused to acknowledge him. Noah had also encountered two policemen in the hall on the way to her room.

"How are you feeling, Miriam?" he asked when he returned to her bed. "You are looking well." She was, surprisingly. The pallor was gone, and her face had regained crispness. Her eyes were sharp and focused. He took her pulse. Strong and regular.

"What did they do for you other than the transfusions?"

"Saline solution. That's what the doctor said. And some tablets for pain."

"Blue?"

Miriam nodded. Aspirin was fast becoming the analgesic of choice.

"All quite right. If you continue to take liquids and nourishment, you should be able to leave tomorrow or the next day."

"And go where?"

"Home. I'm certain there is no shortage of friends to care for you."

"Papa is murdered, Noah. If I go home, I suspect I will be as well."

"I'm terribly sorry about your father, Miriam." She was correct, of course. If a rival faction had planted the bomb, as McCluskey thought, none of her acquaintances could be trusted. "But I can assure you at least he didn't suffer."

Miriam glared at him. What had he said?

"Papa suffered his entire life. He suffered for himself. He suffered for my mother. He suffered for people he did not even know. But mostly, he suffered for me. It is only scant consolation, I'm afraid, that he did not suffer as he died."

"I'm sorry." He could think of nothing else to say.

"Papa was a great man, you know, despite anything the coppers say. He was kind, compassionate, and gentle. The most intelligent man I ever knew, but the wisest as well. And, despite what you may think, he understood that violence would simply breed violence."

"Even in Chicago?" The words were out before Noah could stop them.

"The Haymarket? Where did you hear that? McCluskey? It's a lie. Papa was in Chicago before the riot, yes, but to try to stop the violence. He had been in war. He told me, 'No man should die by the hand of another.' He had terrible arguments with Spies. He said riots would only bring repression, not freedom. Spies responded by threatening Papa with a revolver. Afterward, the Chicago coppers tried to involve him, but everyone they questioned insisted Papa had nothing to do with it. Except Spies. Spies swore the riot was Papa's idea. That he had written the incendiary pamphlets. The coppers wanted Papa, but they weren't about to legitimize Spies by using him as a prosecution witness. So they had to let him go. The coppers have been after him for thirteen years. I suppose they finally decided if they had no cause to arrest him, all that was left was to murder him."

"But the police didn't murder your father, Miriam."

"Of course they did."

"No. I saw who did it."

Miriam pushed herself up in bed, then winced. "You saw?"

Noah told her of Sasha's hurried exit.

"I can't believe it. Father rescued him. Took him in. Sasha was living in the streets. If it was anyone but you who told me . . ."

"McCluskey told me that Sasha was a communist and that the communists hated your father. Is he right?"

Miriam heaved a sigh. "As much as I hate McCluskey, it's possible. The communists do . . . did . . . hate Papa. He refused to ascribe to violent revolution. Sasha could have been planted in our office, I suppose. Now that I think about how we met him . . ."

"How?"

"He was always on the street in the same place. In front of a clothier on Broadway. He didn't beg per se, but was always available for odd jobs. For some reason, or so we thought, he took a liking to Papa. Papa didn't trust him right off but eventually began to give him errands to run or messages to deliver. He was fearless, eager . . . too eager, I suppose . . . and very bright. Eventually, Papa gave him a job." She began to breathe more rapidly and lost color.

"You need rest now, Miriam. I'll try and return tonight. Certainly tomorrow morning. Then we can discuss your living arrangements. You're safe enough here for now." He ventured a smile. "And please, Miriam. The doctors and nurses are not revolutionaries. Just do what they tell you."

As Noah turned to leave, Miriam reached out and grabbed him by the wrist. Her grip was still strong. "Papa always took care of me," she said. "You'll have to take care of me now."

"Of course."

Alan and Maribeth were waiting for him in the lobby.

"How is she?" Maribeth asked evenly.

"My Jewess?"

"How is Miss Herzberg?"

"She's doing remarkably well. She appears to have the constitution of a horse."

"Perfect, then, for a man with the temperament of a mule."

Alan placed his hand on his sister's arm. "Has she been told about her father?"

"She didn't need to be told."

"The police say he was a murderer."

"He was nothing of the sort. He was a philosophy professor and a war hero. He cared for others. You would have liked him, Alan."

"One can like a man but not what he stands for."

"I believe he stood for the same things you do. In any event, Maribeth said there was something you wanted to tell me."

"Show you, actually. Feel up to a trip to the hospital?"

"I'm in a hospital."

"My hospital. Assuming Dr. Dollars isn't about."

Noah turned to Maribeth. "Can you trust me a little longer?"

"I don't trust you now." But then she waggled her fingers at him. "Go. Find out what's killing those children. It will infuriate my parents and Jamie."

TWENTY-FIVE

A lan led Noah to a bed in the children's ward, about halfway down the corridor on the left. In it lay a girl of about ten, pretty and slight, with flaxen braids. At the side of the bed sat her mother, a larger, older, beaten-down version of the girl. The girl was sleeping, although Noah could tell instantly that she had been sedated.

"This is Magda Szysarska," Alan said, indicating the mother. "And this is her daughter Wanda. They are from Canarsie. Mrs. Szysarska is a cleaning woman. She and Wanda live alone. Her husband ran off two years ago. She speaks almost no English. When we first saw Wanda, she was exhibiting all the symptoms of morphia deprivation. Her mother brought Wanda all the way here by carriage about seven hours ago."

"Why did she do that?"

"You'll see." Alan motioned to a nurse who was tending a bed at the far end of the ward. "Rutya speaks Polish," he explained to Noah as the woman hurried over. When she arrived, Alan said, "Tell Mrs. Szysarska to repeat what she told me before."

The nurse said something unintelligible to the woman in the chair. Noah could not even get the gist; Polish seemed nothing like German. Mrs. Szysarska looked quizzically to Alan. She had just told the story. When the pediatrician indicated she should do so again, the woman let loose with a torrent.

The nurse nodded throughout the rendition. When the girl's mother had finished, she gestured with a backhanded flick of her wrist for the nurse to relate the account to the doctors.

Rutya, the nurse, spoke in a thick Slavic accent. "Mrs. Szysarska say Wanda get sick 'bout four days 'go. Bad cough. Dry. 'Stead of free clinic, she go to local doctor. Molk. Dr. Molk very 'cessful. Big house. Two nurses. But Mrs. Szysarska know cough very dangerous and want to make sure Wanda get right treatment.

"Dr. Molk see Wanda and right away get very friendly. Mrs. Szysarska surprised. Dr. Molk usually charge two dollars for visit an' poor people don' come. But Dr. Molk say he know Mrs. Szysarska can't pay. Then he say he got jus' the thing to help Wanda."

"What was it?" Noah asked. He looked to the Polish woman at the bedside. She was staring back at him and nodding, as if they were part of an unspoken conspiracy.

"Pill," said the nurse. "Secret pill, doctor say. Very new. Mrs. Szysarska can't tell no one. Dr. Molk say he come by in two days to check on Wanda. Mrs. Szysarska can' believe. No doctor in America ever come to her house before."

"And did he?"

"Ja. Wanda had got better by then. Cough stopped. But after doctor examine her, he's not happy 'bout something. Asks how many pills Wanda took. Mrs. Szysarska says she got to give more pills 'cause they stop working sooner. Dr. Molk get upset and tell Mrs. Szysarska to give back rest of pills, 'cause they won't work no more."

Tilson, in Newark, had demanded the pills back only after the poor Ryan girl had died.

"After Dr. Molk leave, Wanda get sicker. But different. Stomach this time. Diarrhea, cramp, heavy perspiration. So Mrs. Szysarska bring Wanda here."

"Why here?" Noah asked again. "Why not a hospital nearer her home?"

"Mrs. Szysarska don't want to go anywhere that Dr. Molk might come. She say Dr. Molk turning Wanda into dope fiend."

"How would she know that?"

Magda Szysarska looked up at Noah. "In . . . Poland . . . my . . . father . . . doctor."

"When Wanda arrived here," Alan said, "her symptoms were as acute as you described in the Anschutz boy. And, Noah, if it will help set your mind at rest, I also administered laudanum to deal with the immediate problem. Now that I know with what I am dealing, I intend to wean Wanda off her craving slowly."

Noah turned to the nurse. "What color were these pills?"

Rutya wrinkled her forehead. For a moment, she thought she had misunderstood the question. Then she turned to Magda Szysarska and uttered a short phrase. Mrs. Szysarska replied with a one-word answer.

"Green," the nurse said.

"If we only had one of those pills," Noah said to Alan.

Noah felt a tap on his arm. He turned to see Magda Szysarska looking up at him from her chair, a thin smile on her face. The woman reached into the pocket of her dress. When she opened her hand, it contained two green pills. Mrs. Szysarska placed them in Noah's hand. Then she said something to the nurse.

"She say she learn from her father which doctors to trust and which not."

Noah did not need to wait for Justin Herold. He went quickly to the laboratory in the hospital basement, withdrew Herold's text, and prepared the reagents. This time, he used only a few grains and performed all four tests. Each was positive. The green tablets that had sickened Wanda Szysarska, killed Sinead Ryan, and likely killed Willard Anschutz were a morphiate. Acetylized morphine almost certainly.

He returned to Alan's office and handed him the tablet he had used for the test. "Alan, could you seal this in an envelope and engage a messenger for me?" Noah gave him Justin Herold's address. On one of his cards, Noah wrote, "The sedative for coughs," and asked Alan to place it with the tablet. Herold could perform the tests to confirm the composition of the tablet, although Noah had no doubt of what he would find.

Heroin. The new wonder drug. Safe. Tested. Without risk. The drug with which Arnold Frias had murdered Willard Anschutz.

TWENTY-SIX

Mrs. Jensen's hands were clasped against her bosom. "Oh, doctor. I'm so pleased you're home. I was so worried." Her body tilted ever so slightly his way, as if she had wished to embrace him but was restraining herself.

"Thank you, Mrs. Jensen. I would very much appreciate a cup of tea."

Noah lowered himself into the parlor chair, put his feet up, and closed his eyes. He opened them to the sound of a knock at the front door. The clock on the mantel told him he had slept for an hour.

He started to get up, but Mrs. Jensen popped out and gestured for him to remain seated. Noah heard the door open and then conversation. He couldn't make out what was said, but it did not sound as if Mrs. Jensen had extended a warm greeting to whomever had come calling.

"Hello, doc. How are you feeling?"

Noah pushed himself straighter in his chair. "Reasonably well, McCluskey. What are you doing here?"

"Well, doc, if the truth be known, I was worried about you."

"I'm touched."

"There you go again, doc. But I mean it. You saved at least four lives today. Even though I got little use for any of the four, I got to admire you for doing it."

"Thank you, McCluskey. But any doctor would have done the same."

"Not like you did. You kept your head. You made passersby help. You moved fast, doc. If I'm ever in trouble, you're who I'd want."

Had he really done all that?

"Also, I brought you something." McCluskey removed an envelope from his coat. "This ain't such good news, I'm afraid. We arrested Carl Seitz this afternoon. Know him?"

Noah shook his head.

"Anarchist. One of them we watch closely. Pretty sure he killed at least two, and he's been known to get involved with explosives himself. After he heard about Mauritz, he took off for the International Workers Party headquarters. Those are the communists. We got him with two pistols, a knife, and four sticks of dynamite under his coat."

"A rather impressive arsenal."

"That's what they do, doc. Sooner you realize it, better off we'll all be."

"Perhaps. But what does this have to do with me? It's no secret that there are violent people among the anarchists. Miriam told me that her father was constantly trying to discourage violence. That it made him unpopular and might even have been the reason he was killed."

"Don't know about that, doc. But I do have an idea what prompted Seitz to take off with mayhem on his mind." McCluskey brandished the envelope. "He had this letter on him. I'm sorry to do this so soon after . . . but I thought you should read it before you get yourself in any deeper."

Inside the envelope was a single sheet of paper.

"My dearest comrade," it read, "if you have been given this, I must be imprisoned or dead. We have spoken often that our struggle does not depend on any one man or woman. In war, my dear Carl, as I know so well, casualties are inevitable. There are always those who do not survive, who can only hope to be remembered with honor. And we are at war, Carl. There are no lines of battle, perhaps, no hill to be taken or fort to be stormed. Our war is not for territory but for the dignity of men, women, and children everywhere. We seek food for the hungry, shelter for the homeless, and equity for the downtrodden. We must root out the pestilence of greed and class distinction. Destroy it wherever it is found. Ruthlessly, viciously, and forever.

"If I have fallen, I ask for the honor of the fallen, that another grasp the standard in my place. If there is another, and another, always another, the forces we seek to destroy must inevitably fall before us. They fight for luxury; we fight for freedom. The latter will inevitably overwhelm the former, if only we have the will.

"So you are left, dear Carl. Miriam, if she has survived, will be your most valued ally, as you know. She is single-minded and resourceful. She shares our loathing of unearned privilege and will take any risk, perform any task, to rid the world of the vermin who toss away day-old bread while others starve. Trust her and use her well.

"With eternal affection and hope,

Mauritz."

Noah handed the letter back to McCluskey. "It's fake."

"No. It isn't."

"It must be."

"Doc, does this sound like something one of us dumb coppers could write?"

"Perhaps one of you is secretly Stephen Crane."

"It's real, doc. You know it is. You wanted proof. Now you got it. What do you intend to do about it?"

"I'm not certain, McCluskey."

"I can't protect you if you throw in with them. Now that you know. There's them who think I've been giving too much rope already. That first you killed a kid and then you turned on your country, they say. I don't believe that, doc, but if you ignore this letter . . ."

"Give me until tomorrow."

"It's her, ain't it? You fell for Miriam and can't see through. I warned you, doc."

"Nonsense. A day, McCluskey. That can't be asking too much."

The policeman considered the proposition. "All right, doc. I'm pretty sure I can do that. But don't come back tomorrow telling me you need more time."

"I won't."

TWENTY-SEVEN

Noah arrived at Bellevue Hospital, fed, bathed, and rested; anointed a hero by the *Daily Eagle* for his valiant efforts in the wake of the bombing of *New Visions*, especially since, according to the newspaper, he had simply "chanced by" the carnage. The article had neglected to mention that the very same Noah Whitestone was under suspicion in the unnatural death of a five-year-old boy. Perhaps Frias and Wurster had thought better of their campaign to ruin him, in light of his actions on Lafayette Street.

Or perhaps not. Parked on First Avenue, in front of the hospital entrance, was a shiny, new International Benz.

He should have turned around right there, he knew. Miriam had already gotten him into enough trouble with her lies. But he simply could not let it sit.

Noah made his way through the vast lobby, looking carefully for the outsized figure of Arnold Frias, but whatever business Frias had in the hospital, he was evidently attending to it. It was possible, of course, that Frias's destination was the same as his own, but he thought it unlikely that a prominent society physician would wish to sully his reputation being seen in the company of the Red Lady.

When Noah reached the nurses' desk on the second floor, Bradley Kerr appeared, walking quickly down the hall.

"I asked to be told when you arrived," Kerr said, his tone doctor-to-doctor.

"Why?"

Kerr did not seem to find the question accusatory. "To see how you are," he replied with a brief shrug. "I assumed you'd be back to visit . . . Miss Herzberg."

"Thank you. I seem fine."

"Drinking your fluids?"

"Amply. I seem to urinate every twenty minutes."

"A hazard of the cure. Anything else?"

I would appreciate more Aspirin. I took the last two this morning."

"You're supposed to wait at least four hours between doses. Any adverse gastrointestinal effects?"

Noah shook his head. "Should there be any?"

"No. But we were told by the manufacturer to watch for them."

"Are they a salicylate?"

"Supposedly not. I'm not sure what's in them, to tell you the truth. But they were extensively tested in Germany."

"I'm sure it's fine then."

"All right. I'll give you twelve before you leave."

Kerr led Noah to Miriam's room. Noah told him he could find his own way, but Kerr insisted. When they arrived, two of the beds were empty. Only the woman with orbital fracture remained, and she was again asleep. The prostitute with the gunshot wound had been discharged. The woman recovering from the mastectomy had, after being helped to the bathroom, slashed her wrists with a razor she had somehow obtained from the supply closet. By the time the nurse decided to check on her, the woman had died.

"She must have had help," Kerr told him. "She could never have gotten the razor by herself. One of the nurses, most likely. We'll never find out which one, though. The rate of post-mastectomy suicides is the highest we have. Many women prefer death to deformity. I'm not certain I blame them. Their husbands abandon them, they become pariahs in society, and many relapse and die anyway."

"We treat victims as though they were criminals."

Kerr nodded. He stepped into the hall, but Noah noticed him waiting just around the bend of the door, pretending to be occupied. Who was he reporting to? Frias, McCluskey, or both? No matter. After this, at least one of the threads that bound him would be cut.

Miriam was asleep. The golden hue had returned to her skin, and her breathing was deep and even. He touched her wrist. Her eyes opened. She smiled when she saw him, then used her elbows to push herself back against the headboard. The smile vanished.

"What's wrong?"

"Nothing. I was worried about you. But you look quite well. And beautiful, as always."

"You're not telling me the truth."

"Who is Carl Seitz?"

"A friend of Papa's."

"He was arrested."

A veil dropped over Miriam's face. "When?"

"Yesterday. He was carrying more munitions than a regiment."

Miriam sighed but did not change expression. "Papa told him, but Carl would never listen."

"He was carrying a letter as well. From your father."

Miriam sat full up in the bed. "What did it say?"

"You need to be careful," Noah said, from physician's reflex. "The wound could begin to bleed again."

"I'm perfectly fine. What did the letter say?"

"That now that your father was gone, Seitz was responsible to 'root out the pestilence of greed and class distinction and destroy it wherever it is found. Destroy it ruthlessly, viciously, and forever.'"

"And you think destroy meant violently destroy."

"That is the generally accepted meaning of the term. And he was carrying four sticks of dynamite when he was arrested."

Miriam shook her head, patiently, as if speaking to a child. Noah felt the blood rush to his face. "That's just the way people in the movement talk, Noah. Hyperbole is their stock-in-trade. Papa's loathing of violence was well-known."

"And how about, 'Miriam will be your most valued ally. She will take any risk, perform any task, to rid the world of the vermin who toss away day-old bread while others starve. Trust her and use her well.' Was that hyperbole too?"

"I see. I am to be condemned on the strength of a letter. Very well." She slid down in the bed. "For your edification, Papa recommended Carl to me because I could ride herd on him. Keep him from losing his head. Which he seems to have done in my absence. But I think you should go now. I suddenly feel quite tired." She turned on her side, her back to him.

Noah wanted to slam the door behind him as he stalked out, but this was a hospital. He should have been relieved, but he only felt more the fool.

Kerr watched Noah emerge with a look of studied nonchalance. "Difficult visit?"

Noah merely glared. He spun on his heel to leave, but Kerr called him back. "Don't forget your Aspirin."

When he reached the street, Frias's automobile was gone.

McCluskey worked out of the 13th Precinct House on Twenty-Second Street between First and Second Avenues, just a short walk from Bellevue.

Noah was none too pleased to give the policeman the satisfaction of being correct, but in fairness, the man had earned it.

The lobby of the station was bustling, filled with hatless, uniformed patrolmen moving about, the top buttons of their long frock uniform coats undone. Some men in plain clothes loitered. Two youths, recently apprehended, hands manacled in front of them, were at the desk in the center of the room, each held by the arms by patrolmen.

A sergeant emerged from the rear, tall and dark haired, with an impressive handlebar. "Excuse me," Noah said to the man, "I'm here to see Officer McCluskey."

"You mean Sergeant McCluskey."

"Sorry. Yes. My name is Whitestone. He's expecting me."

"Not here."

Had he been at Bellevue as well? With Frias?

"When is he due?"

The sergeant shrugged.

"Can I wait?"

The man nodded. "Long as you stay up here." Without inquiring further, the sergeant walked through to the other side of the room and disappeared through a door.

For the next ten minutes, Noah watched with fascination as a parade of human flotsam was marched through the station house. Most were eventually taken through a door at the right, which Noah assumed led to the cells. Some, complainants probably, gave information to the officer at the desk and left. Through it all, a steady stream of patrolmen came and went through the series of doors that led to other parts of the station.

Standing idly, Noah felt the need to urinate yet again. He asked a uniformed officer where the water closet was, but the man simply kept walking as if he didn't hear. A similar request to a second officer elicited the same response. Finally, Noah approached a man in plain clothes lolling against a pillar near the front door.

"Could I use the water closet, please?"

The man eyed him up and down. "Waiting for someone?"

"I'm a friend of Sergeant McCluskey. He's meeting me here but must have been delayed."

The man considered the response. "Okay. Through the door to the left of the desk. Then third door down on the right."

As Noah walked to the door, the desk officer seemed about to challenge him, but the plainclothesman gave a nod and the desk man went back to his duties. Noah walked through and found the lavatory. Seven tall urinals lined one wall, and a row of five wash-out toilets lined the other. Wash-outs needed to be cleaned constantly, and these had not been. The smell of urine and excrement was overpowering, even for one as inured to bodily function as Noah. He relieved himself quickly, then washed his hands in a stained sink at which only the cold water tap worked and yielded but a trickle.

Noah hurried out of the foul room. As he did, the door to the room opposite opened and a plainclothesman stepped through. He almost bowled Noah over. He growled something unintelligible about watching where he was going and headed to the front. As the door swung shut, Noah had a peek inside the room.

He froze, unable to breathe.

Oh God. What have I done?

Important decisions demand time to consider the options. But when time is an unaffordable luxury, instinct must take its place. Without hesitation, Noah pushed the door open.

"Hello, Sasha," he said, walking through. "McCluskey said I'd find you here." He nodded at the two other men in the room. One was swarthy, the other ruddy-faced and thick-featured with a handlebar mustache. An old acquaintance. "Gentlemen."

The boy leapt up, his tiny eyes gone wide. "What are you doing here?"

"I told you," Noah replied casually. "Same as you. Waiting for Sergeant McCluskey." If McCluskey came back, he was sunk. But perhaps fate would favor him, just this once.

Sasha glanced around the room. The other policemen were suspicious but disarmed, at least tentatively, by Noah's ease of manner. "You don't think you were the only one working against the anarchists, do you, Sasha?" Noah gave a guffaw. "Sorry, but you're not that important. If it makes you feel any better, I didn't know about you either. I should have guessed, though, when I saw you running out of the building."

Noah gestured to the chairs. "Are we going to sit while we wait or stand here staring at one another until McCluskey comes back?"

The swarthy detective motioned to the chairs. "Have a seat, doc."

"And I don't trust him," Sasha said.

Noah lowered himself into one of the slat chairs. "Well I don't trust you either. Something we can agree on."

No one spoke. Noah felt three sets of eyes on him. Silence was his enemy. It led to doubt. "Why is everyone so somber?" he asked. "Didn't McCluskey say I was coming? I left word at the hospital."

The ruddy-faced detective nodded. "McCluskey said you might be working with us, not that you were."

"Well, I wasn't at the start. That's for sure. Miriam Herzberg got to me first." At the mention of Miriam's name, three heads nodded. "But when McCluskey showed me I was throwing in with a bunch of murderers . . . showed me the letter from Mauritz Herzberg to Carl Seitz . . . I'm not a traitor, you know. Murderers deserve to die."

"Well, I guess I'm glad I didn't push you out the train then."

Noah smiled at the detective. "Me as well." Sasha had turned stolid; Noah pressed his advantage. "You must be the star of the day. After thirteen years."

"Star, my left foot," the swarthy detective muttered. "Dumb Hunky. Can't count to two."

"Wasn't my fault," the boy bleated. "And I told you it was all still there. Blown up with everything else."

"It?" What was Sasha talking about? "Wasn't much left of the office," Noah said. "I was in there."

"We was there, too, doc," the mustachioed detective said. "After you was carted off. Looked through everything."

"It got blown up, I tell you," Sasha said.

"If it didn't," the swarthy detective growled, "and we read it in the papers, we're gonna come get you in Albany or wherever you end up upstate. We'll take one of those sticks of dynamite you didn't use, shove it up your ass, and light it."

Then Noah knew. Mauritz Herzberg hadn't been the target at all. Just a bonus. He stood up. The two detectives tensed in their chairs. Noah grabbed for his abdomen. "Where's the lavatory, please? The medication I'm taking for my head gave me diarrhea."

"We don't need the details, doc."

"Right across the hall," said the other.

Noah moved to the door. "You won't get lost," the swarthy detective added.

"Physicians are supposed to be able to find their way to the toilet," Noah said. The detectives didn't budge. He had gambled neither would want to stand and wait while he moved his bowels in the vile-smelling place.

As soon as the door clicked shut behind him, Noah darted down the hall, opened the door to the main room, and sauntered through. The desk officer gave him a glance but nothing more. The plainclothesman at the pillar had left.

He walked toward First Avenue as quickly as he could without running. He had very little time. He would have none if McCluskey returned in the next ten minutes.

TWENTY-EIGHT

"Get up! You've got to get out of here." Noah rushed into the room, closed the door behind him, and threw back Miriam's covers.

Miriam propped herself up, perplexed. "Why?" The sedated woman with orbital fracture was vaguely awake, blinking her unbandaged eye at the proceedings.

"Just come. If you don't leave before the police arrive, you never will."

"The doctor told me my leg might hemorrhage at any time."

"It isn't true. They're just trying to keep you here." Noah quickly checked the bandage. Dry. No oozing from the wound. "The sutures will hold. You can walk quickly, but try not to run or twist."

"What about this?" She gestured to her hospital gown. "I can't very well go running about on the streets in this."

"You'll have to." Noah glanced around the room. "No, wait." The clothing of the woman who had slit her wrists after the mastectomy

195

had not yet been removed from the closet. Noah lifted the slip and the faded, plain blue wool dress off the hook and handed them to Miriam. "Put these on."

Miriam gingerly swung her legs over the side of the bed and stood up. Her leg briefly gave way, but she caught herself and took a few steps. She limped only slightly. She threw on the dress on over the hospital gown. Noah laced up her shoes.

"Let me check the hall, then walk with me out of the room. If we run into that doctor, Kerr, let me do the talking. He's in with McCluskey or Frias or both. You might have a bit of trouble on the stairs, so hold on to my arm. We need to move with haste but can't appear to be fleeing. With luck, no one who knows us will see us leave."

Noah opened the door and looked up and down the hall. Kerr was nowhere in sight. He beckoned to Miriam. She could not move quickly, but with each step, her limp dissipated. Noah could see she was in pain, but she refused to give in to it. They had almost reached the staircase when, from around the corner, a policeman appeared.

"And what do you two think you're doing?" The copper was young, fresh-faced, and spoke with the forced growl of a rookie.

"Sergeant McCluskey's orders," Noah said curtly.

"She's not supposed to leave. He didn't say nothin' to me." The rookie didn't even think to ask Noah who he was.

"McCluskey clears his orders with you now, does he?" Noah did not stop moving.

"No, but . . ."

They had reached the top of the stairs. "Then we're going to the station house." Noah gestured to Miriam's other arm. "You might help, you know."

Almost by reflex, the young patrolman raised his left arm. Miriam took it. Thus, supported on one side by Noah and the other by the rookie copper, Miriam was able to make it down the stairs. Noah thanked the man when they reached the ground floor.

"Need help from here?" the patrolman asked. "I should go with you anyway."

"I'm going to put her in a carriage, even though it's only a few blocks. If the wound opens, she could hemorrhage. If you're willing to be seen on duty riding in a hansom, come on along. They'll love that at the station house."

The young policeman considered the prospect. A more experienced man would not have let them leave alone, appearances be damned, but the rookie was every bit as afraid of looking foolish as of making an error. While he was still pondering the choice, Noah had led Miriam out the door and helped her into the first carriage at the stand.

"Thirteenth precinct house," he said loudly to the driver.

The hansom pulled away from the curb, moving south on First Avenue, leaving the perplexed patrolman to stare after it. At Twenty-Third Street Noah instructed the driver to turn right. After he had done so, Noah had the cab pull to the curb.

"Did anyone go through Turner McKee's room after he died?"

"Why? What is this all about?"

"Just tell me."

"Yes. I did."

"Did you find anything? About the drugs?"

"No. We didn't find anything at all. But the coppers had been there first."

"They didn't find anything either. They thought it was at the offices."

"I don't understand."

"Sasha was working for the police, not the communists. He set the bomb for them. The target wasn't your father at all, although I'm sure they're pleased he's dead. They wanted to destroy whatever material Turner McKee had amassed on the Patent Medicine Trust. You were correct the first time. That's who McCluskey is working for. Specifically, I think they are interested in suppressing any incriminating information on a new drug from Germany called Heroin. It's made from morphine.

That's the drug that killed Sinead Ryan and my patient. They tortured McKee before they killed him, trying to get him to reveal what he had and where he had it. McKee was too tough. He died without telling them. After they searched his room, they assumed the information was at the office, so they had Sasha blow up the place. Two detectives came by afterward to search for anything that remained but didn't find any evidence one way or another."

"There was nothing to find. Turner never kept anything important at the office. At his rooms either. The chance of burglary or a raid by the police was too great."

"Where then?"

Miriam sized up Noah for a moment; *she*, he realized, was deciding whether to trust *him*. "Do you think this driver will take us to Pelham?"

"His parents' house? Are you certain or guessing?"

"Certain. He told me. I even know where they are in the house."

"Let's go then. For a price, this driver will take us to Paris." Noah knocked on the trap. When the driver opened it, Noah gave him the destination and asked for a rate. "You will have to move as speedily as you can."

"Let's see," the driver replied, taking on an expression of extreme studiousness. "That's up Second Avenue, across the Macombs Dam Bridge, on through the Bronx . . ."

"I know were Pelham is, driver."

"I expect you want me to wait and bring you back."

"Two hours. Possibly less."

"Back to Bellevue?"

"Brooklyn Heights."

"Whole day gone then. I can do that for fifteen dollars."

"Absurd. I'll offer you seven."

"Twelve.

"Ten."

"Eleven."

"Ten."

The driver agreed with a scowl, as if he had been forced to have a tooth extracted. In fact, ten dollars for a day's work was a windfall to a cabbie.

"And what about me?" Miriam asked, as the driver urged the horse north.

"You would have been found to have died from the complications of your wound."

The driver turned out to be extremely adept. They reached Pelham, on the shore of Eastchester Bay, in ninety minutes.

The McKees lived on a long tree-lined dirt road that meandered through the wooded countryside. Most of the houses on the road were behind high walls and gates, which rendered the area at once beautiful and forbidding. The driver pulled up at a high, squared wrought-iron gate with black bunting woven between the stiles. A weather-beaten man of about fifty in work clothes stood just inside. The sort who hires on to a family and remains with them for life. He wore an expression of profound sadness.

"Are you here for the funeral?"

"Turner McKee's funeral is today?"

"At three," he said. "You are supposed to go directly to the cemetery and then return here afterward. Mr. and Mrs. McKee don't wish to be disturbed until after the ceremony."

The retainer eyed them curiously through the window of the hansom, paying particular attention to Miriam's garb.

"You must be Conrad," she said. "I worked with Turner. He told me you taught him to swim. We need very much to speak with Mr. McKee immediately."

The man's expression softened. "You're Miriam Herzberg then. Turner spoke of you as well. I was sorry to read about your father."

"Thank you. This is Noah Whitestone. We are trying to learn the true circumstances of Turner's death and make certain that those responsible are punished."

The gatekeeper rubbed his face. Stubble rasped against the calluses on his hands. "I got to warn you, Miss Herzberg, you may not be welcome in the house. The master and the missus are of the opinion that if it wasn't for you and your father, young Turner would be alive."

"Turner came to us, Conrad. We did not seek him out. He believed in the work he did. Allow us to attempt to gain him a measure of justice."

Conrad thought for a moment, then cocked his head up the tree-lined path. "Quarter mile up on the right." As the carriage began to move through the gate, he added, "Good luck."

No other homes were visible from the path. The house was fashioned on an English country estate, broad and sprawling, three stories high, eight windows on either side of the portico. Three other carriages, shiny and black, all horse drawn, waited in the driveway. They looked at each other before pulling the bell, Noah with the freshly sutured laceration across his forehead and Miriam, limping in the plain, one-dollar dress of a dead woman.

The maid who answered the door looked them up and down and seemed on the verge of closing the door in their faces.

"My name is Whitestone," Noah barked, as if to a wayward orderly. "I'm a physician. I need to see Mr. McKee immediately. He knows me. Tell him I'm terribly sorry to intrude, especially today, but I have vital information. He will know on what subject."

The maid hesitated. But she had been trained to take orders and Noah had given her one. Without replying, she closed the door almost all the way and went off. Some moments later, the door again opened and Turner McKee Sr. stood inside.

"I am burying my son in ninety minutes, Dr. Whitestone. What is so vital that it cannot wait?" He turned to Miriam. "Miss Herzberg. I am terribly sorry about the death of your father, but still, I should have thought you would have been embarrassed to come here."

"You have lost your son, Mr. McKee. I have lost my father. Both were murdered by the same men."

"The same men? Your father died in a bombing by a rival radical group."

"No, Mr. McKee," Noah said. "The bomb was set at the behest of the police. I saw the man who placed it, laughing in a police station with two detectives. I suspect those two are the same men who murdered your son."

"Ridiculous! I was willing to indulge you at the morgue, Dr. Whitestone. I was even willing to allow my son to be cut open on your say-so. But all that Dr. Herold found was death by asphyxiation."

"From blood in his lungs. And his ribs were broken."

"Nonsense. Dr. Herold told me—"

"Dr. Herold wished to spare your feelings. We can telephone him if you wish. He will confirm what I just told you. Your son was beaten to death by two New York City police detectives."

McKee placed his hand against the door jamb for support. He didn't want to believe Noah, but he did.

"You knew yourself your son had died by violence when we first met," Noah went on. "Now I've discovered who killed him and why. What's more, information that may well lead to the exposure of his killers is in this house."

"Here?"

"Your son left his evidence here, Mr. McKee," Miriam said. "He always feared precisely what occurred."

McKee swung the door wide. "You should come in then."

TWENTY-NINE

Once they were inside, McKee took in their appearance more fully. "Can I offer you something? You must be thirsty after your ride."

"Perhaps some water while we speak," Noah replied.

McKee pulled a cord on the far wall of a vestibule that was furnished expensively but without ostentation. A man appeared in a doorway at the far end. "A pitcher of water in the study please, Dodson." The man nodded and disappeared.

"Come this way," McKee said, extending his arm to the left. "If you wish, Miss Herzberg, some of my oldest daughter's clothing is here. Her dresses should fit you admirably."

"Thank you, Mr. McKee, but I have grown attached to this one."

McKee's eyebrows rose.

"The woman who owned it killed herself. Her husband and society would have treated her as a criminal because her cancerous breast had been removed. It isn't much, but I can honor her anguish by wearing this for a while."

McKee sighed and shook his head. "I admit I never did understand Turner's attraction for the downtrodden, Miss Herzberg. Nor did I understand yours. I always thought it was akin to those who feel compelled to take in stray animals. I never believed my son when he railed on about endemic injustice. Society always seemed perfectly just to me. Oh, I saw flaws, certainly, but I simply assumed that flaws were the price one paid for freedom. But since I visited the morgue . . . and now . . ."

"Turner!" came a voice from up the curved center staircase. "What are you doing down there?" A woman came into view from the second floor. She was tall and lean, about fifty, attractive with sandy hair gone mostly to gray. She wore a black dress and a veil pulled back over her head. Her face was lined, but the lines seemed recent, as if they had been etched on. She eyed Noah and Miriam at first with surprise. Then her gaze settled on Miriam and her expression turned to disgust.

"I must speak with Miss Herzberg and Dr. Whitestone, Leticia," McKee said to her. "Please wait for me. I promise we will leave with time to spare."

"I want her out of my house," Leticia McKee said icily.

"I said wait for me, Leticia. We may have made an enormous mistake. If we wish to honor Turner's memory, I must hear them out."

At the mention of her son's name, the woman's eyes filled with tears. Her head began to shake back and forth. "I don't . . ."

"Trust me, Leticia. Our anger at Miss Herzberg may have been grievously misplaced. If so, please allow me to attempt to right an immense injustice."

Leticia McKee, now thoroughly confused, nodded perfunctorily. She seemed about to speak once more, but instead turned about and disappeared up the stairs.

"You must forgive her," McKee offered.

"Nonsense," Miriam said. "Her feelings are perfectly understandable."

McKee smiled briefly in thanks and then directed them down the hall to a wood-paneled room lined with bookshelves. "Before we do anything," McKee said when they were all seated, "you must give me some details."

Noah provided McKee with a brief rendition of the events that had transpired since his son's autopsy. He made particular reference to the Patent Medicine Trust, the new drug Heroin, Arnold Frias, and the rogue policemen's role in the deaths of McKee's son and Miriam's father.

"So you see, Mr. McKee, your son died a hero," Miriam told him. "He won't be a hero to those who lined their pockets at the expense of the helpless, but he will be a hero to the families of the children who are saved from death or drug compulsion because of his efforts."

McKee let out a slow breath. "If what you say is true, I will be greatly gratified. I freely admit I want to believe you. I am tempted to believe you. But I cannot do so on your word alone. Now what is the information Turner left here?"

"We're not sure. But it was sufficiently inflammatory to have cost him his life."

"You said you knew where it was in the house."

Miriam spoke. "What was Turner's favorite book as a child? He said you would know."

"Oddly enough, it was a dime-store novel by Horatio Alger Jr., *Brave and Bold; or, The Fortunes of Robert Rushton*. He reread it many times. Why?"

"In your library is a copy of that book. There is a packet behind it."

McKee led them back across the main hall. The library was two stories tall, filled with books of all sorts. The value of the collection fairly screamed out from the shelves. A section was devoted to natural history, one to travel, one to the history of the Americas. Many of the volumes were antiquarian, some dating from as far back as the fifteenth century. Some volumes were in French, others in German. Many were in Latin. A section devoted to contemporary literature was stunning. Beautiful leather-bound sets of Dickens, Trollope, Twain.

Noah stood awestruck, as if he had walked into a cathedral. He wondered how Miriam felt, being in the presence of such splendor. Here were the trappings of wealth, it was true, but wealth used to preserve a great intellectual heritage. The countervailing forces of her father's life.

"My father was a bibliophile, Dr. Whitestone. I have enhanced his collection. I was hoping Turner . . ." McKee shook his head. "I have an excellent selection of works tracing the history of medicine. I wish there was time so that I might show you. But, as it is, our interest is in one of the least impressive volumes in this room. Except to me, of course. But first, I must show one of my acquisitions to Miss Herzberg."

McKee strode across the room to a section in the far corner. He withdrew a volume bound in gleaming red leather from the bottom shelf. He returned and handed it to Miriam. She gasped when she opened the cover, then collapsed into a chair and cried.

McKee was distraught. "I'm so sorry, my dear. I thought you would be pleased."

Miriam looked up, her face blotches of crimson. "I am, Mr. McKee. Thank you so much. I thought they were all gone." She caressed the title page as if it were her child.

McKee gently took the book from Miriam and handed it Noah. It was entitled, *Eine Kritik der Empirismus von Occam nach Leibniz*, "A Critique of Empiricism From Occam to Leibniz." It had been published in Berlin in 1879. The author was Mauritz Herzberg, professor of philosophy at Georg-August University of Göttingen.

"It is evidently quite brilliant," McKee told Noah. "I sent this to William James himself. He pronounced it a groundbreaking study of the evolution of scientific thought. I never told Turner I had purchased it. I was ashamed, I suppose, to admit that I was sufficiently curious to spend three hundred dollars on a rare book written by a man of whom I never spoke well. I wish now I had said something." He took the book from Noah and gave it once again to Miriam. "This is yours if you want it, my dear."

She sniffed loudly and shook her head. "I have nowhere to keep it where I know it will be safe. Papa belongs here, I think. In a fine library, in the company of all these wonderful thinkers."

"Very well." McKee returned the book, then grabbed one of the sliding ladders that allowed access to the upper shelves. "Now to the subject at hand." He slid the ladder halfway down the wall and climbed a few steps. He pulled a small, ragged volume, bound in paper from a shelf, fondled it gently, as Miriam had the philosophy text, then removed a few books on either side. McKee poked his hand into the opening, nodded, then withdrew a rolled-up sheaf of papers tied with ribbon. After he replaced the books, he climbed down.

"Let us return to the study and see what Turner gave his life to tell us."

Moments later, Noah was leafing through the material. He was astonished.

"Your son was correct, Mr. McKee," Noah said after he had finished. "His research is superb and the magnitude of the conspiracy immense. Many millions are at stake. Heroin, diacetylmorphine chemically, is to be marketed throughout the nation in elixirs, tablets, pastilles, and powders. It will be prescribed for asthma, dysentery, nervous disorders, respiratory disease, and, most ironically, as a treatment for morphine addiction. Its most widespread application, however, will be as a cough suppressant, particularly for children.

"The Bayer Company has recruited a number of physicians in America and Europe to both test the substance and provide testimonials. Bayer will soon begin to advertise extensively within the medical community, although not to the public at large. Whether or not any or all of these physicians are aware they are dealing with a morphiate is uncertain. But Bayer certainly knows. Felix Hoffmann, the chemist who synthesized the substance, was quite open to his superiors as to process. Heinrich Dreser, the head of his section and the man responsible for testing new drugs, attempted to claim credit for the process when he saw the potential value of the discovery. Dreser, Turner discovered, negotiated an agreement with Bayer in which he shares in the profits of any new drug discovered in his section.

"Dreser tested the substance in the laboratory, on animals, and on a number of Bayer workers. He insisted this research demonstrated that Heroin creates no tolerance. In other words, the user develops no craving for the drug at shorter and shorter intervals. Turner could not determine whether Dreser's testing was fraudulent or simply incompetent. One of the researchers may have called Heroin an extremely dangerous poison but was ignored. Dreser also seems to have sampled the substance himself. Heroin is four times as powerful as morphine but inexpensive to synthesize from the base substance. Thus, if a user develops a tolerance, the profits of his craving will be far greater. And as we have seen from the children who died, tolerance is certainly developed and it seems to be quicker and more profound than with ordinary morphine."

"Then the testing had to be fraudulent," McKee exclaimed. "This Dreser knew he was dealing with a product made from morphine. How could he have missed that it created tolerance?"

"Tolerance in adults takes a good deal longer to evolve than in children. With morphine, it might take weeks. Even with the increased potency of Heroin, Dreser might well have given the drug to test subjects, noted it was efficacious, and then discontinued usage before they developed a craving. Or he and researchers are continuing to take it without awareness that they are developing a tolerance.

"After the laboratory phase, Dreser presented the drug to the Congress of German Naturalists and Physicians. He told his audience that Heroin was ten times more effective in suppressing coughs than codeine—which, as you may know, is also a morphiate—but was only one-tenth as toxic. Most of all, he insisted Heroin, given in prescribed doses, was completely safe.

"This year, Bayer will produce a ton of Heroin. They will send the product around the world, but fully half of the production will come to the United States. America has restrictive patents, but almost no safety standards for pharmaceuticals. That combination means that nowhere in the world will Heroin be more profitable. Drug companies will simply purchase the substance from Bayer and fabricate it any way they wish.

"Turner tracked down some examples of the manner in which the drug will be sold in the United States. For example, the Martin H. Smith Company . . . that's the firm that had the appointment on Stone Street . . . intends to market an elixir called Glyco-Heroin. Heroin mixed with glycerin, which likely will improve the taste. To ensure that the drug is widely prescribed, Smith has followed the widespread practice of purchasing testimonials that will run in medical journals throughout the nation. Here's an editorial for the *Southern Practitioner*.

"'Of all the remedies and drugs in our experience, which would tend to ameliorate and suppress cough, we find in Glyco-heroin an agent that to all appearances is a remedy par excellence.'

"A doctor named Levian in the *Buffalo Medical Journal* will say the following: 'The combination that makes up the Glyco-heroin should appeal to anyone who is treating patients afflicted with pulmonary and laryngeal diseases. The composition of Glyco-heroin is in our opinion quite a happy one. It is an excellent stimulating expectorant without producing nausea. A teaspoonful of this preparation, I found to be a definite dose, the effects of which lasted for three to four hours. Two weeks' trial on six patients convinced me of its utility.'"

"Do these men have no shame?" McKee asked. "They are willing to abet the deaths of children?"

"You don't understand, Mr. McKee," Noah told him. "It is more a case of turning a blind eye than of open malfeasance. These doctors know they are being asked to endorse a product—paid to endorse a product—so, like the Bayer chemists, they simply see the positive results and nothing else." Noah tapped the pile of papers. "Here is the worst of the lot. Arthur B. Smith of Springfield, Ohio. He will write this for the *Texas Medical Journal*: 'Recently, my attention was called to a preparation composed of a solution of Heroin in glycerin, combined with expectorants, called Glyco-Heroin (Smith). Each teaspoonful of this preparation contains one-sixteenth grain of Heroin by accurate dosage. It is of agreeable flavor, therefore easy to administer to children, for whom the dose can be easily reduced with any liquid, or by actual measurement. It possesses many advantages not shown by any other preparation I have used, and has none of their disagreeable features.'

"He includes five case studies. Three are for children. Of a sixteen-year-old with severe bronchitis, he says, 'Prescribed Glyco-Heroin (Smith) one teaspoonful every two hours, decreased to every three hours. After a few doses were taken there was a decided improvement, the respirations were slower and deeper, the expectoration freer, and the temperature normal. In a few days, the patient was practically well and able to return to school. No medicine except Glyco-Heroin (Smith) was given, and the results from its use were excellent.'

"Then he cited a six-year-old boy. 'Capillary bronchitis with pains over chest, cough, and difficult expectoration. Glyco-Heroin (Smith) administered 15 drops every three hours. After taking a few doses the condition was much improved, and a speedy return to perfect health followed.'

"Finally, this Dr. Smith will discuss a girl, only five. 'Whooping cough. Spasmodic paroxysms of coughing, sometimes being so severe as to cause vomiting. Tenacious mucus was present, requiring great expulsive effort to loosen it. There was little fever, but the patient was much prostrated and weakened by the cough. Glyco-Heroin (Smith) was given in 10-drop doses every two hours with good results. In a few days the condition was much ameliorated, the cough under fair control, expectoration was freer and easier to raise, and convalescence uneventful. The case was discharged cured and there were no unpleasant sequela, the patient at present being in perfect health.'"

"My son uncovered all of this?"

"There is more, Mr. McKee. Much more. Your son was a hero, as Miriam said. He died trying to save the lives . . . and the souls . . . of countless children who would otherwise have been victims of this poison."

Noah removed another sheet of paper. "This says that the Fraser Tablet Company has contracted to produce five million Heroin tablets per year, beginning in three months. They will be marketed as a treatment for asthma. Fraser's factory is in Brooklyn, on Prospect Hill. They will be sending salesmen throughout the nation to sell Heroin tablets to pharmacies. There is no telling how widely this poison will spread unless someone speaks out."

Turner McKee Sr. flopped back in his chair, his hands hanging over the armrests. "Horatio Fraser. I know him. Not well, but we served on a committee together. To raise money for a children's home on Delancey Street. A *children's* home. There are no words."

"This nation is blinded by greed, Mr. McKee." It was Miriam. "Only through people like your son can we hope to protect those caught in its wake."

"I never approved of Turner's politics," McKee said softly. "Thought he was agitating against his country out of spite. I told him more than once that I could not understand what had made him so . . . angry. He tried to tell me that I did not understand. That injustice was being perpetrated under the guise of freedom of commerce. That America much more resembled a crooked card game than a fair deal. I told him he had been corrupted." He turned to Miriam. "I hated you and your father for despoiling my son. I was convinced that he had been led astray by seductive arguments and a beautiful woman. I hated you even more when Turner died. I thought his death a waste. Useless. But I see now that not only had Turner made his own decisions, but that his decisions were correct. He was not corrupt at all. I was. A fool. I am proud to own your father's text, Miss Herzberg."

"Thank you, Mr. McKee," Miriam replied. "But how could you be expected to believe tales of injustice that seemed so outlandish?"

"I should have believed my son." McKee looked at his watch. "I must go to the cemetery now. But I thank you both. Deeply and profoundly. I am forever in your debt. Whatever help I can provide, whatever risk must be borne, for as long as I live, you need only to ask."

"Thank you, Mr. McKee," Noah replied. "We will not hesitate to ask if the need arises."

"You are both welcome at Turner's service, but I don't think it would be wise to give away your whereabouts. Neither of you is safe. You both must remain here. I could not live with myself if what befell Turner happened to you. I'm not without influence. I'll see that this information reaches the proper authorities."

"You're very generous," Noah replied. "But we can't stay. I wish we could attend the service . . . your son has earned that . . . but there are elements of the problem that require immediate attention. There is no better way to honor his memory than to see that justice is done. If you could supply a pen and paper, I would, if I may, copy some of this material. Then I will return it to same spot on the shelves. If anything should happen to me, or Miss Herzberg, you are then free to use it as you wish. For the moment, however, just keep it safe. I'll need it in the future."

McKee considered for a moment trying to dissuade them, but instead stood and put out his hand. "I will leave you then. Godspeed in your endeavors."

THIRTY

DAY 7. TUESDAY, 9/26—2:30 P.M.

W e should have taken his offer, Noah. He has powerful friends." Pelham and wealth had been left behind as the cabbie made his way quickly toward Manhattan. "Yes, I know. But even if his friends believed him, I expect they would be of little use. Frias has friends, too. I have someone else in mind."

"Your fiancée's family?"

"Hardly. Oscar De Kuyper is much more likely to be an investor than a savior."

"Who then?"

"I'm not certain you would approve."

When the carriage reached the center of Morrisania, Noah instructed the driver to pull over at a hostel. Morrisania was a working-class town near the railroad, an immigrant community, where the citizenry and the police were on uneasy terms. The inn was two stories, a frame house, which, like the neighborhood that surrounded it, showed age and wear.

"I want you to place a telephone call to my home," Noah told Miriam. "Tell Mrs. Jensen that you're Mrs. Tumulty. Ask if she enjoyed the bottle of wine and the chicken you gave her. Speak quickly so that she doesn't interrupt and give the game away. Then remind her of the dinner at the Hearns. Tell her, oh, that you heard from Annie O'Rourke that one of the men who was there is stepping out on his wife. You can't say who over the telephone, but since you and she have a date at her home at six, you'll tell her then. You'll need to sound like a gossip. Spice up the conversation as much as you can. Someone will certainly be listening at the telephone exchange to any calls placed to my telephone, so if Mrs. Jensen doesn't know to play along, you've got to tell me. Can you do that?"

Miriam sniffed. "What a question. I am hardly a stranger to conspiracy, Noah."

The woman at the desk of the inn was of indeterminate age, blond and hugely corpulent. She was pleased to let two strangers use the telephone for, say, twenty-five cents. She initially seemed to be of the opinion that, for her consideration, she should be allowed to stand and listen in, but after a glower from Noah, she retired to the rear, or at least out of eyeshot.

Miriam placed the call. When Mrs. Jensen picked up, she slipped into a perfect brogue. She even managed to age her voice to sound like a fifty-year-old.

"Helloo, Mrs. Jensen," she began. "This is Mrs. Tumulty . . ." Miriam was perfect. She clucked, cooed, and chortled. At one point, she exclaimed, "Ooooh, you don't say. No, of course not. You know me, Mrs. J. I won't tell a soul."

After a few more minutes, Miriam ended the conversation. The woman, who had doubtless been listening to every word, returned to the desk. Noah thanked her and gave her an additional two bits. Miriam said nothing until they were back in the carriage.

"She understood instantly. There is no possibility that anyone listening in would have known. Your housekeeper is very clever, you know."

"Sometimes too clever."

"Not this time. She managed to tell me that the police came by looking for you and that a copper in plain clothes is loitering down the street watching your house."

"I expected as much. Do you think he'll follow Mrs. Jensen home?"

"Not if she's correct and there's only one. If he leaves, your house will be unguarded. Besides, I expect your Mrs. Jensen will spot a copper right off. She'll think of some way to signal us."

"All the same, I'm going have the driver leave us a few blocks away. We'll be able to see for ourselves before we approach her house."

The carriage arrived in Brooklyn just before six. As with the woman at the inn, Noah gave the man extra, in this case two dollars. The cabbie scratched his head, unable to figure out why Noah had bargained him down only to give him extra. But a tip carries a message an unsuccessful negotiation does not, and so Noah could be confident that the details of their journey would remain unpublicized. The last thing he would wish was to bring the authorities down on the kind and generous man whom they had visited that afternoon.

Noah and Miriam checked both Mrs. Jensen's block and the side streets before knocking on her door. She opened it and rushed them inside. She took Noah by the wrist, squeezing so hard that blood flow to his fingers was constrained. "Oh, Dr. Whitestone, I'm so happy to see you. I was so worried. They're all after you. You'll be safe here. Stay as long as you like."

"Thank you, Mrs. Jensen," Noah replied, gently prying her fingers off his arm. She realized what she had been doing and pulled her hand to her chest, like a child caught stealing a piece of candy. "You are a true friend to put yourself at risk on our behalf."

She waved off the compliment, making little effort to hide how pleased she was to receive it. Her reaction to Miriam was less effusive. "And you must be 'Mrs. Tumulty.'"

"Yes, Mrs. Jensen. And thank you. I've heard wonderful things about you."

"And I've read a good bit about you." But Mrs. Jensen's disapproval, be it for Miriam's politics or for Maribeth, was tempered. A genuine celebrity had just entered her home.

"The newspapers, as I believe I've mentioned, Mrs. Jensen, can be unreliable," Noah pointed out nonetheless.

"And," Miriam added, never turning her glance Noah's way, "the notorious Red Lady has no designs on Dr. Whitestone. He saved me from being murdered. When all this is resolved, I have no intention of interfering with his betrothal." Despite himself, Noah felt a pang of . . . what? Regret? Jealousy?

Mrs. Jensen cocked her head to one side, weighing the elements. Then she smiled. "You both must be hungry and tired. Why don't you freshen up while I make you some dinner?"

"First, I need some information," Noah said. "You told Miriam on the telephone a policeman came inquiring about me. What did he look like?"

"Well, he wasn't very tall, but big in the chest. Like a bricklayer. Dark. Dark eyes, dark hair, dark skin."

Noah nodded. "I know him. He works for McCluskey. Interesting that a detective from Manhattan had to come to Brooklyn. And that he was alone watching my house. There seems to be only a small group involved. Perhaps just the three. That might work to our advantage."

"Why does it matter?" Miriam asked. "The other coppers will help him whether they're in on it or not."

"It depends on how comfortable McCluskey feels broadcasting details of what he's doing. We might be able to move about somewhat freely."

"I'm not sure we can just go parading on the street, Noah."

"Mrs. Zeeland's nephew was gunned down by the police for spitting on the sidewalk," Mrs. Jensen noted.

"John Zeeland was a housebreaker, Mrs. Jensen. He pulled a gun when he was cornered."

"Oh, doctor, you know what I mean."

"And besides," Noah said, "I won't be as easy to spot as you think." He fingered his beard. "I'd grown rather fond of this. But I'm told beards make a man look older. Perhaps, Mrs. Jensen, first thing tomorrow, you might go out and purchase me a razor and some shaving soap."

Mrs. Jensen bubbled. "No need, doctor. I still have Mr. Jensen's things. Fine straight razor, soap, and even a strop."

"If you will entertain the Red Lady then, Mrs. Jensen, I will retire to perform my facial transformation."

"Don't call her that. And what about your forehead? You look like you've just risen from the grave."

"I can remove the sutures. I'll cover the wound as best I can with woman's face powder. I can wear my hat low."

"I've a better idea," Miriam said. "The Brooklyn Academy of Music is on Montague Street. That's only about a five-minute walk from here. There is bound to be a theatrical supply house nearby."

"There is," said Mrs. Jensen. "Heinemann's. Just down the street from the theater. Jake Siegel runs it. Lives in the back."

"Then tomorrow we'll purchase stage paint," Miriam continued. "While we're at it, a set of workingman's clothes would also be a good idea. With you a clean shaven workman and me in this dress, no copper will look at us twice."

Any man would look at you twice, Noah thought, even in sackcloth. But he held his tongue.

Mrs. Jensen fetched the shaving kit. When she returned, she had regained her funereal look. "Your father came by your rooms earlier. He and your mother are terribly worried. They asked me to telephone them the second I heard of your whereabouts."

Noah shook his head. "We can't risk it. The telephone exchange is not to be trusted. Nor can you visit them this evening. Perhaps, however, tomorrow, you can go to the office. Even if a copper is outside, he'll simply assume you're a patient. Tell my father that I'm in fine health and will contact him when it is safe to do so." Then he whispered in her ear the other errand he wanted her to run.

A few moments later, Noah was staring into the glass in Mrs. Jensen's lavatory. He cut away the sutures, then took a few practice snips with the scissors with which he would trim the beard before shaving off the remainder. He had worn it for nine years. Camouflage.

Removing a beard seemed to take almost as long as growing one. When he was finally finished and washed off the remaining lather, Noah once again appraised himself in the glass. His skin tingled and was pale where the whiskers had been. The face looking back *was* him, but at the same time unfamiliar. His mouth, full and mirthful as he was growing up, seemed to have grown thinner, tighter. He now had lines that stretched from the sides of his nose down past the corners of his mouth, almost to the jawline. His eyes, he observed, were lined in the corners, with just the beginning of puffiness above and below. He had simply never noticed. All in all, a disconcerting picture of a man aging quickly and not well.

The stigmata on his forehead, however, only about three inches long, was far less prominent with the sutures gone and his entire face exposed. The stage paint would certainly mask it from all but close view and equalize the tones on his face.

Noah found himself unwilling to leave the lavatory. He felt exposed, vulnerable. A castle with shattered walls. After a few moments, however, he straightened his clothes and forced himself to step out into Mrs. Jensen's parlor. Instead of astonishment, or even fright, both women were quite effervescent.

"Why, Dr. Whitestone, you look ten years younger. And *very* handsome. Don't you agree, Miriam?"

"I do indeed, Madeline." Madeline? Where had that come from? Noah was uncertain if he had even known his housekeeper's Christian name.

Mrs. Jensen demanded they eat. Miriam insisted on helping. "I'd love to see how you do it," she said, straight-faced.

After the two had disappeared into the kitchen, Noah went to the telephone, mounted on the wall in the foyer. Although he did not expect the call he was about to make to be the subject of police eavesdropping—they were, he was certain, unaware of the recipient's role in the case—he nonetheless wished to disguise his purpose.

He gave the number to the operator at the exchange and waited. A few minutes later, a familiar voice at the other end was saying hello.

"This is H. Bryce Onderdonk, Dr. Herold," Noah said quickly, before Herold could greet him. "I'm certain you remember our meeting."

"Ond—oh yes, of course, Mr. Onderdonk, how could I forget? To what do I owe this unexpected pleasure?"

"I was hoping to elicit a small favor."

"Have I ever denied you?"

"You mentioned when we spoke that, after your days in the coroner's office, you struck up a friendship. Do you remember?"

"I struck up many friendships."

"This one was of particular import insofar as it was with the head of a sister agency. This friend has gone on, I believe, to even greater triumphs."

"I believe I now know to whom you refer."

"I want to meet with him. Tomorrow."

"Tomorrow? You must have lost your reason, Wh—Mr. Onderdonk. Dewey's flotilla sails up the Hudson on Friday. I'll wager . . . my friend . . . hasn't slept in days. You expect him to stop what he's doing to see us?"

"That is precisely what I expect. I have some fascinating material to show him. I have sent you a parcel. You will be quite interested as well. Now, of course, if you don't think you can . . ."

"I can. But how will we meet, Mr. Onderdonk? I cannot wait to greet you again in person."

"I'll place another call to you tomorrow, doctor. Will 10 A.M. give you sufficient time?"

"I believe so. Until then, Mr. Onderdonk. I count the hours." With that, Herold rang off.

THIRTY-ONE

DAY 8. WEDNESDAY, 9/27—7 A.M.

Noah slept in the spare room, while Miriam shared a bed with Mrs. Jensen. He awoke early, before seven, but his housekeeper was already awake and puttering about. More than that, a denim shirt and pants along with a dark wool jacket and cap lay across the chair, with a pair of workingman's boots underneath. On the dresser sat three jars, in which Noah assumed was the stage paint. Jake Siegel at Heinemann's, an early riser this day by design or demand, was apparently another in Mrs. Jensen's extended circle of friends.

She had purchased a copy of the *Daily Eagle* as well. The newspaper had become Noah's personal bulletin, so he looked through it before dressing. Today, two items were of particular interest.

The first occupied the entire front page, under the headline DEWEY ARRIVES AHEAD OF TIME: THE FLAGSHIP OLYMPIA NOW AT ANCHOR INSIDE SANDY HOOK. The *Olympia*, with the admiral remaining aboard, would, for the moment, remain anchored at the south end of Raritan Bay, twenty miles from Tompkinsville, Staten Island, where the fleet was to dock until Friday's procession up the Hudson. Once the fleet docked, Pug Anschutz would certainly commandeer a small vessel to head for home. And revenge on the doctor whom he believed murdered his son. That left Noah two days, perhaps only one.

The other item was on page 2. SUSPECT IN BOMBING BECOMES VICTIM OF REVENGE KILLING. RADICALS KILL ONE OF THEIR OWN IN POWER WAR. The details were straightforward. Aleksandr Cviec, twenty, was found dead of multiple knife wounds in an alley off West Forty-Sixth Street. Pinned to his shirt was a note, soaked with his blood, on which the figure of a red clenched fist had been drawn. The fist was well-known as the symbol of the Free Workers Party, the anarchists. The newspaper went on to note that Cviec, a communist, had insinuated himself into the staff of *New Visions*, the anarchist weekly. Then, taking advantage of their trust, he planted the explosives that resulted in Monday's spectacular bombing. Ten had been left dead, including the magazine's founder, Mauritz Herzberg. Herzberg's friends had apparently learned of Cviec's treachery before the authorities and taken matters into their own hands. The murderer or murderers currently remained at large, but the police promised an intense investigation to apprehend the culprits.

Even if Noah hadn't stumbled on him in the station house, McCluskey would never have allowed the boy to roam free. Sasha had signed his own death warrant the moment he agreed to place the explosives in the *New Visions* offices.

Noah slipped into his workingman's garb. The clothes fit him poorly, which was ideal. The stage paint turned out to be quite easy to apply and, with a moist cloth, blended invisibly with his skin. When he was done, Noah did not recognize himself.

At breakfast, he learned that Miriam had her own plans for the day. In the Jewish religion, it seemed, a funeral must take place within forty-eight hours. Mauritz Herzberg's was at two o'clock. All the arrangements had been made in advance—to Mauritz Herzberg, the prospect of sudden death was a constant companion. The service was at Congregation Bnai Jacob Anshe Brzezan on Rivington Street, a tenement, as the congregation lacked funds to build a synagogue. Herzberg would then be buried at Beth Olam Cemetery on Cypress Hills Street in Brooklyn. As if they were not already in sufficient peril, Miriam announced that she intended to be present.

Both Noah and Mrs. Jensen did their best to dissuade her. McCluskey's men were certain to be near, and for the Red Lady, he would be able to recruit as many of his fellow coppers as he wanted. Once Miriam was in custody, it would be a small matter to dispose of her as they had Sasha or Turner McKee. And Noah had no doubt that Miriam would suffer some terrible indignities before she was killed.

But Miriam would not be moved, not by the threat of rape, not by the threat of death. "I will be at my father's funeral. Whether or not McCluskey can do anything about it remains to be seen."

"I'll come with you," Noah said.

Miriam shook her head. "You do your errands, Noah. I'll do mine."

Her position was clearly not open to negotiation, so at ten precisely, Noah placed his telephone call. "This is Onderdonk," he said when Herold lifted the earpiece.

"City Hall. One hour." With that, the line went dead.

When he arrived, he spotted Herold immediately, standing in the center of City Hall Plaza, perusing the passersby. His gaze swept past Noah more than once without a spark of recognition. Noah was relieved. A disguise, after all, cannot be trusted until it actually fools someone.

He continued to walk Herold's way, and Herold continued to pay him no mind. Finally, unable to resist, Noah ambled past, jostling the pathologist as he went by.

"Excuse me, sir," Herold barked angrily. "I believe you should pay more heed to where you walk."

Noah turned back. "What a disagreeable fellow. And why are you lolling here? Are we going inside or aren't we?"

Herold froze and then squinted, as if trying to detect a blood particle on a piece of cloth. "Whitestone? By George, it is Whitestone. I never would have recognized you. Why on earth did you do yourself up as a laborer?"

"Better a live laborer than a murdered physician. Come, Herold, I'll fill you in on our way inside."

Herold told the copper at the entrance who he was and that he was expected. The guard eyed Noah with curiosity, but after he checked his log book, he summoned a page.

The page led them to a meeting room on the second floor on the other side of the building from Mayor Van Wyck's office. He knocked and was told by a man inside to enter. The page opened the door and held it, allowing Herold and Noah to pass through.

"All right, Herold. What can I do for you gentlemen with old Bulldog Dewey sitting out in the harbor like Neptune, waiting for all of us to pay him homage and kiss his trident?"

Noah had seen innumerable drawings of TR and even a number of photographs. He had read descriptions of the bluff manner, high-pitched voice, and, of course, the famed crocodilian grin. The badlands of South Dakota. San Juan Hill. Scaling Mont Blanc. All part of the TR legend. As superintendent of the Board of Police Commissioners, a post he held for only two years before moving on to an appointment as assistant secretary of the navy, TR had established a reputation as a corruption buster that far eclipsed that of Frederick Wurster. All in all, a man who would be as content ramming down a door as turning the handle and walking through.

The man himself proved quite different. Distortion slipped away, and what was left of this Cheshire cat was not a grin but bearing. Theodore Roosevelt wore wealth and privilege the way other men wore a watch chain. He exuded a patrician's ease with power. His enunciation was precise, and his voice was nowhere near as tinny as the newspapers indicated.

Roosevelt also bore little visual similarity to the caricatures. Except for rather small eyes, which were obscured by the pince-nez perched on his nose, his features were regular and pleasing. He was actually quite handsome. The walrus mustache of San Juan Hill was trimmed to the top of his upper lip. He was tall, just under six feet, with the thick chest for which he was famous and short brown hair.

"You do not share in the current mania of Dewey worship, governor?" asked Herold. Traces of a grin wrinkled the corners of the pathologist's mouth, which TR acknowledged with a nod.

"Herold," said the governor, "Dewey is the most ambitious man I have ever known. And I have known myself. And his crust. He has been grousing to all his commanders that I was not there to greet him when he arrived. According to the admiral, I was supposed to be docked off Sandy Hook waiting to yell 'Huzzah' as he came into view. It has slipped his mind entirely that it was on my recommendation that he received this fortuitous appointment. The public may genuflect, but anyone who knows pea soup about warfare is aware that the great Dewey's miraculous feat could have been equally achieved by a talented Annapolis midshipman. The Spanish have not had an effective navy since the armada. In fact, I suspect they were using some of the same ships."

TR grinned. He did actually smile with his teeth clamped together. The effect was not one of ludicrousness, but rather of a man enjoying a joke more than anyone else in the room. "Of course, the reason I could not meet Dewey was because I had a previous engagement with you gentlemen. Now, perhaps you will begin by telling me . . . Dr. Whitestone is it not . . . like the village in Flushing . . . I've sailed there often from my home in Oyster Bay . . . why you appear more to be the man to repair a broken steam pipe than a broken leg."

Noah recounted the events of the previous week. Throughout the rendition, TR paid full attention, his gaze never wavering. That his eyes were small made them seem even more penetrating. Noah wondered if TR's focus was as acute as it appeared, or if the stare was a politician's ploy, cultivated to flatter and deceive.

When Noah was done, TR stroked his mustache with his right index finger. His hands were thick and powerful. "A vast web of corruption in our pharmaceutical industry," he said finally. "Fascinating. You have done a fine job, Dr. Whitestone, although I cannot say I approve of your bedfellows. Herold excepted, of course. Nonetheless, we must stamp out corruption wherever it is found."

TR paced across the room and back again. "But scandal casts a broad net. Generally too broad. We must take care not to sweep into the same basket those firms that do business fairly and honorably. The mere garnering of profit is not a crime. Only doing so by deceit, felony, or chicanery."

"I agree wholeheartedly, governor," Noah replied. "But we cannot allow children to be poisoned."

TR's eyes turned into beads behind the lenses. "I do not need to be lectured on the protection of children, Dr. Whitestone."

"Of course not, governor. I simply meant—"

Herold cleared his throat. "Do you not believe Heroin is a poison, governor?"

TR rolled on his fingertips the green tablet that Herold had given him. "I have no reason to doubt your research, Herold. You know the esteem in which I hold your work. But I am not a chemist or a toxicologist. At this point, you have no solid evidence to conclusively prove that the research this Dreser fellow performed was faulty. The testimonials that Smith and the others obtained were not necessarily bought. They may have been legitimate expressions of praise for a product that achieved the results its manufacturer promised it would. Your evidence is persuasive that this drug, Heroin, should be more rigorously tested, but how can I intercede officially when all I have been given is anecdote?

"As to the Anschutz boy, neither you nor Dr. Whitestone can say for certain that this unfortunate lad was even given this drug. His mother denies it. The doctor denies it. I've heard of this Frias. Prominent man. Good reputation . . . for a Democrat. The woman in Newark . . . even if she was in my jurisdiction . . . will not, I am sad to say, be terribly credible as a witness. Nor, I fear, will the Polish woman. You gentlemen have done a superb job in building the beginnings of a case, but you have brought me nothing on which I can yet act. Even this tablet cannot be definitively traced back to this German company." He handed the pill back to Herold, who accepted it with surprise. "No, gentlemen. I'm in your debt for the risks you have taken to protect the innocent and vulnerable among us, but much of what you have so far obtained seems more to me like trawling than precision. But, by all means, continue your investigation. The moment you obtain even a grain of hard evidence, you need only to contact my office."

Herold began to protest, but TR silenced him. "I have not yet finished. Corrupt police, on the other hand, is a matter I can and will do something about. I didn't spend two years supervising the department to see it fall back into corruption. McCluskey, you say? I will see that this man and his cronies are investigated thoroughly, and not by his chums either. The commissioner himself will handle it."

"Thank you, governor," Noah replied, trying to sound grateful. Leaving McCluskey on the loose, investigation or no, would achieve nothing.

"Nonsense. I will send a messenger to police headquarters the moment we are done here."

TR coughed and, even though he carried a watch, glanced to the clock on the mantel.

"Thank you, governor," Noah said, taking Herold by the arm. "We are supremely appreciative that you would see us in such a hectic week."

"Think nothing of it, Dr. Whitestone. I repeat . . . the moment you obtain evidence on which I can act, I want to see you. I will leave instructions with my secretary that your calls are always to be put through."

"We are grateful."

"Once I get this McCluskey off the street," TR said as they were leaving, "you might choose to leave those clothes at home."

THIRTY-TWO

For the first time since Noah had met him, Herold had lost his effer-vescence. "Ambition . . . I would not have believed it."

Noah placed a hand on the pathologist's shoulder. "He was right to be skeptical. Why should he take on faith what we say and dismiss the findings of a seemingly reputable researcher in Germany?"

"No, Whitestone. The TR I knew, the man who was determined to sweep out the corruption in the police department by bull force, would have seized on what we presented to him. This man . . . the one we just met . . . has his eye on Washington. His greatest concern is that Dewey has similar aspirations."

"Still, Herold, if we can hand him some solid evidence . . . material whose publication he thinks will grease his path to the presidency . . . he may well yet make a valuable ally."

Herold perked up. "Yes, he might at that. My, but you have turned quite pragmatic, Whitestone."

"By necessity."

"Very well. Let's find him something he can't dismiss. I think I know where to look next."

"As do I," Noah said. "Forty Wall Street. And it's less than a mile from here."

But Noah's destination was not the First Mercantile Bank but rather a cafeteria favored by working men and clerical employees. Through the front window he saw, waiting at a table, someone dressed incongruously for the surroundings, shifting uncomfortably, glancing frequently at the entryway.

He moved inside, walked toward the rear, then sat suddenly at her table.

"I'm sorry, sir, but this ta—my God! Noah."

"Hello, Maribeth."

"Why in the world . . ."

"It's my new mode. What do you think?"

"I think I might prefer different clothes, but I'm pleased to see you out from behind the shrubbery."

"That's what everyone seems to think."

"Who's everyone?"

"Uh, my housekeeper . . ."

"And your Jewess?"

"Yes, as a matter of fact."

"How is she? I can't wait to meet her."

"Her wound is healing remarkably quickly. But she takes terrible risks."

"She's not alone. You seem to be recruiting all your female admirers in your conspiracies."

He shrugged. "Women make the best conspirators."

"No. We're just smarter than men."

"I'm beginning to agree. Still, I wish I could spare you involvement."

"Why? Do you think Miriam Herzberg is the only woman who wishes to right a wrong? That one has to preach from street corners to announce one's commitment to decency?"

"No, I don't think that at all."

"Good, because I'm no preacher."

Noah grinned. After a moment, Maribeth grinned as well.

"All right. Maybe I am. And yes, I suppose it's true. I'm jealous of her, and not just because you find her irresistible."

"But—"

"Please, Noah. And I can hardly blame you. I find her sort of irresistible as well. I can't say I agree with everything she does, but at least she's *doing* and not simply primping or serving tea . . ."

"That hardly describes you, Maribeth."

"Doesn't it? Discussing Gainsborough's brushstrokes doesn't foster social justice. Well, I'll be doing now."

"You don't have to compete with Miriam Herzberg, Maribeth. Certainly not on my account."

"It's not on your account. Now let's go. Jamie is waiting for us."

"Was it difficult getting him to agree?"

"Not in the least. He harrumphed for ten minutes and absolutely refused to help. He asked me what I took him for. I assume the question was rhetorical."

"How did you change his mind?"

"I told him I might be indiscreet about some of his indiscretions. Jamie is very impatient for success and doesn't always adhere strictly to the proper etiquette of his profession, such as it is. Then he feels the need to brag about what he considers cleverness but others would consider violations of trust."

"Would you really have informed on your own brother?"

Maribeth smiled. "Well, Noah Whitestone, you'll never know, will you? Nor will he."

The offices of the First Mercantile Bank fanned out from a central corridor past the public area inside the filigreed brass double doors at the entrance. The trust department, in which Jamie toiled with a constant eye on the vice president's office in the corner, was on the right, the last turn before the two unsmiling guards at either side of a gleaming white marble staircase that led to the executive offices on the second floor. But Homer Dansfield and his immediate circle never climbed those stairs. A small custom electric elevator designed by Rudolf Eickemeyer himself had been installed at the rear of the staircase six years before, its use restricted to the five top executives and customers of the bank deemed of sufficient importance to rate mechanical conveyance. It was Jamie's great dream to one day ride that elevator.

The loan department was to the left of the corridor, about halfway down from the entrance. The files, Jamie had told Maribeth, were housed in a room just off a conference room, in which a huge mahogany table, sixteen chairs, and full bar were placed to ensure that those most in the bank's debt could discuss rates of interest in comfort.

About ten yards from the door, Maribeth stopped. "You wait here," she said.

"I will not," Noah snapped. "Do you think I'm letting you go in there alone?"

"You don't have much choice, Noah. Have you forgotten?" She gestured to his attire.

He had forgotten. The plan had been for him and Jamie to look through the files while Maribeth waited in the trust department, but that was no longer possible. But if Maribeth was caught, particularly because she was trying to live up to Miriam . . . Before he could say anything, however, she was through the door. Noah followed quickly but remained in the public area where tellers' cages lined either side of the aisle.

Maribeth walked past the tellers' windows, spoke briefly to the guard, then was allowed to pass through the trust department door. Noah made a show of withdrawing a deposit record under the askance gaze of the guards—not too many laborers had accounts at First Mercantile. A few seconds later, he saw Jamie and Maribeth emerge and walk across the hall. Maribeth was as relaxed as if she were strolling through the Botanical Gardens, but Jamie could not have appeared more furtive. He glanced about constantly, and his head seemed almost pulled into his body, like some overstuffed turtle. When they disappeared through the door, Noah felt himself break into a sweat.

Noah laboriously wrote on the deposit record with one of the three pens left on the counter for customers' use. He made a show of dipping the pen into the inkwell excessively, then made to mumble a curse at a blot. He crumpled the deposit slip and threw it in the trash. Maribeth and Jamie had not emerged. Noah withdrew another slip and again wrote slowly. The door to the loan department remained closed.

Suddenly, a portly man of about fifty wearing a dark-blue suit emerged from an office on the right and hurried across the hall the toward the door where Maribeth and Jamie had slipped inside.

They'd been found out. Or would be. Noah tried to decide what to do. He certainly wasn't going to overpower a roomful of bankers and guards. A diversion. Kick up enough of a rumpus that everyone would turn their attention to him? Yes. It might be their only chance. The portly man was at the door.

Noah lifted his hand to knock over the inkwell. As he did, the door opened and Maribeth and Jamie emerged. Jamie and the portly man spoke for a second or two, then the man ducked inside the room.

Noah put his arm down, just before he felt a tap on his shoulder. He turned to see a guard glowering at him.

"You got business here, bud?"

"Uh, I was thinking of opening an account."

"With what? Yer shoes?" The guard clapped a beefy hand on Noah's shoulder. Maribeth walked past them toward the front door, never giving him a glance. "G'wan," the guard growled. "Git outta here." The guard turned toward the door, his hand never leaving Noah's shoulder. The man's fingers dug in and felt as if they would be imprinted there. Walking stiff armed, the guard bum-rushed Noah until they were at the front door, then with a short flick, sent Noah off into the street. Making a show of wiping his hands, the guard turned on his heel and went back inside.

Maribeth was waiting up the street, her hand in front of her mouth, little crinkles in the corners of her eyes.

"Not a word," Noah muttered, but Maribeth giggled anyway.

They went to Trinity Church on Broadway and sat on a bench in the courtyard that faced away from the street. Maribeth retrieved three hand-written pages from her bag. "Jamie got cold feet about taking the actual files. He made me copy the names instead. That's why we took so long. It turned out to be the right thing, actually. Someone came afterward looking for the same file."

"Yes, I saw him. Who was he?"

"I'm not certain. But he was senior to Jamie. I could tell by Jamie's obsequiousness."

"The wind must be up. If you hadn't gotten to these when you had, they'd have disappeared into someone's desk, where I'm confident they reside now." Noah glanced at the notes, written in Maribeth's flowing script. He scarcely breathed as his finger moved down the list.

"They're all here," he said finally.

"Not quite all," Maribeth replied.

Noah stood to leave. Maribeth rose from the bench as well, but Noah put up his hand. "It isn't a good idea to be seen with me in public, even dressed like this. Even if the people on this list don't know that I've got it, they're certainly aware that I'm getting closer. They will be even more desperate to prevent any of what I've learned from being made public." He folded the papers and handed them back to her. "If anything happens, I trust you to use these properly. The material at McKee's as well."

Maribeth nodded. "When will I hear from you?"

"I'll get word to you tonight. I promise."

"And now?"

"I've got to pay my respects."

"You're going to Mauritz Herzberg's funeral, aren't you? I'm coming along."

"You certainly are not."

"Why? Are you trying to keep your women separate?"

"She is not my woman. And you can't go for the same reason I couldn't go to Jamie's office." She began to protest, but he put up his hand. "It's much more important that you remain safe. Once you become publicly involved, you're lost to me as a resource."

"Well, we couldn't have that now, could we?"

THIRTY-THREE

DAY 8. WEDNESDAY, 9/27—NOON

The coachman refused to enter Beth Olam Cemetery. He stared at the tall, wrought-iron gate flanked by two pillars with the strange six-pointed stars as if Semitic phantoms would tear at his soul if he crossed the threshold. Noah handed the man two bits and alit. A swarm of mourners, their backs to the entrance, was visible on a rise about fifty yards away. The actual burial seemed to be on the other side of the hill. The sound of chanting, rhythmic and mysterious, guttural and ancient, cut through the wind.

Noah walked up the path toward the place of interment, past row after row of graves, most topped with the same six-pointed star, others with two hinged tablets with rounded tops festooned with the odd, exotic characters of the Hebrew alphabet. When he reached the edge of the crowd on the back side of the rise, he looked for men who didn't belong. It wasn't hard to spot the coppers salted among the Jews.

The chanting continued, stopped, then began again. What bizarre rituals these people had. After a few moments, he succeeded in working his way sufficiently through the throng to reach the top of the rise. He halted, stunned.

The gravesite was still at least fifteen yards away. He had been aware that both Mauritz and his magazine had many admirers but had been unprepared to encounter a crowd that radiated out into the other rows of graves in every direction almost as far as he could see. Five hundred men and women—possibly as many as one thousand—of every age and, surprisingly, every economic stratum, stood in the cool overcast to pay last respects to Mauritz Herzberg.

In the hub, a rabbi stood at the coffin, a plain pine box, unfinished and unstained. Did Mauritz Herzberg choose such a lack of adornment as a statement to egalitarianism, or was plain pine mandated by his religion? The rabbi was a large man, with an enormous, untrimmed beard, dark, dappled with gray. He had large, sad eyes that angled downward from the bridge of his nose, as if the burdens of history's oppressed now resided in him alone. A skullcap was perched on a mane of graying hair, and his shoulders were wrapped in a long white shawl.

At his side was a group of men, mostly young, dressed in the manner Noah recognized as that of the Hebrew ultra-devout. Long black coats, wide-brimmed black felt hats, yellowing white shirts, black trousers and shoes. Each had a full beard and a set of side curls set behind his ears. A prayer book was open in front of the rabbi, and he rocked each time he read from it.

The knots of coppers thickened closer to the gravesite, but neither McCluskey nor his henchmen were among them. Had TR actually kept his word?

After the coffin had been lowered into the ground, some in the crowd moved forward to form a line to drop a small shovelful of dirt into the hole. This seemed to be a sign of affection and respect. Noah looked about, wondering where Miriam was hiding herself. She would certainly at some point join the ritual.

Oh no.

Across the way, moving to the front of the crowd, wearing a black dress, her head covered in a black shawl, was the distinctly un-Semitic figure of Mrs. Jensen. Next to her was a young man. He was dressed in a long black coat, a wide black hat, and a full beard. The "young man" was slight, with dark skin. He wore thick glasses. Apparently, during her visit to Heinemann's, Mrs. Jensen had not restricted her purchases to Noah's disguise. How could Miriam have thought she would fool anyone with this insane charade? Noah wanted to run across and grab her. "No stranger to conspiracy," she had said. Idiocy.

Each of Herzberg's intimates stood for a moment in silent contemplation before passing the shovel to another. Eventually, Mrs. Jensen stepped forward. Mrs. Jensen was apparently to be Miriam's surrogate. She tossed the small amount of earth, then stood back and, incongruously, crossed herself. Noah found the gesture shocking, but neither the rabbi nor the other mourners seemed to mind.

Then, astoundingly, Mrs. Jensen's companion stepped forward. Miriam in that silly disguise. She accepted the shovel from Mrs. Jensen, tossed some dirt, and mouthed what seemed to be "Goodbye, Papa" through the thick stage beard.

As soon as she was done, the two women turned and began to make their way back through the crowd. The rabbi asked that a space be cleared for them. The coppers began to move as well.

About five yards from the gravesite the coppers moved in, five surrounding Miriam and Mrs. Jensen, not letting them move. As if he were a wraith, McCluskey materialized and stood in front of them. He mouthed something Noah couldn't hear to which Mrs. Jensen replied angrily, "How dare you?" McCluskey brushed her aside, then with a backhand swipe, knocked the hat off Miriam's head.

McCluskey's jaw literally dropped. He stood gaping at a figure who, other than the side curls, had hair that was cropped nearly to the skull. He reached tentatively forward and tugged at the beard. A yell of protest. Then a torrent of epithets. From a young man.

The rabbi had by then pushed his way through. He began to scream at McCluskey and the other coppers in a mixture of English and some incomprehensible tongue. He gestured wildly and at one point seemed as if he might strike one of them. Members of the crowd began to gather around. The police glanced at the gathering knot of angry mourners with obvious distress.

The rabbi, still yelling, began to make backhand motions, gesturing for the interlopers to leave. The coppers looked to McCluskey. Hundreds were standing in angry silence, watching the scene play out.

McCluskey looked at Mrs. Jensen and a slow smile crossed his face. He nodded as if to say he'd remember her, then he and the other coppers began to slowly back away. With every step they took, the crowd sullenly matched it. A few minutes later, the entire police contingent had disappeared over the rise.

Another young man in the garb of the devout then stepped forward and dropped some dirt onto the casket. This young man bore a remarkable similarity to Mrs. Jensen's companion. Noah worked his way toward him. The young man had blended into the group of similarly dressed mourners who had stood at the rabbi's side during the ceremony. As Noah came upon them, they closed ranks and stared at him threateningly.

"It's all right," Miriam said. "That's no copper." She smiled through the beard. "He's a friend."

The men allowed Noah to pass, but one of them whispered in Miriam's ear. She nodded. It was time, certainly, for her to leave.

"Very deft," Noah said. "I shave a beard and you grow one."

She fingered the horse hair. "I don't know how anyone can stand these. Mrs. Jensen was superb, was she not?"

"She shows additional talents with every passing day."

Miriam tugged at the edge of the beard and slowly peeled it away. It came off with a raspy sound, but she grimaced only slightly. She removed the hat and shook out her hair. Noah was again struck at how astonishingly beautiful she was. He felt a wave of lust and hated himself for it. But self-loathing did little to diminish the feeling.

"Don't you think McCluskey might still be lurking about?" he asked, desperate to say something.

"No. He'll have slunk away by now. In any event, I've got friends watching."

"Where did the rabbi find Mrs. Jensen's companion? I thought it was you in a bad disguise."

"That was the idea. His name is David Rubenstein. He was the most like me physically of all the students in the seminary. They don't usually involve themselves in such intrigues, but they made an exception today. Rabbi Ben Eleazer violated the funerary laws to allow me to mourn my father. He didn't end with Psalm 91, the mourners didn't form two lines for the family . . . me . . . to walk through, and we didn't wash our hands afterward. I was surprised he was willing to do all that, but he said that God loved my father and so did he. Each would be willing to bend the rules for a great man."

"Your father was a man who elicited great passion one way or another. Perhaps that's a sign of greatness in itself."

"Greatness lies in persuading others to work for good."

Noah thought of Abel. "Yes, I suppose that's true."

"And your venture this morning?"

"Not as conclusive as I would have liked. But I'm off to see if I can remedy that."

"Can I help? I'll come along if you like."

If he liked. . . . But he shook his head. "Thank you, Miriam, but this is something I want to do alone."

THIRTY-FOUR

DAY 8. WEDNESDAY, 9/27—1 P.M.

S o now, finally, inevitably, to Frias. A careful and clever man. Two
traits that, with luck, might just prove his undoing.

If Frias was presented with a list of American investors in
the Bayer Company's Heroin venture, he would think only to save his
own skin. Of that, Noah was convinced. He wouldn't stop to find out
that Noah did not actually possess documentary evidence but merely
names, illicitly obtained, scrawled on a piece of paper. He would leap at
the opportunity to claim he had been hoodwinked by the Germans into
believing the drug was safe—likely a half-truth anyway. Noah could
then present Frias's *mea culpa* to TR, and the web he had fallen into
could finally be disentangled.

There had been a line of hansoms in front of the cemetery, but by the
time Noah arrived, only one remained. He hurried toward the door only
to have another man, well dressed and in his thirties, beat him to it. Noah

looked up the street, but no other cab was in sight. He was trying to decide whether to wait or walk toward Jamaica Avenue when he saw the other man walking away. The cabbie had refused him for some reason.

"Are you waiting for someone?"

The cabbie was younger and more clean-cut than most of his breed. "Not at all, sir. He changed his mind. Please get in."

Noah climbed in and gave his destination as Joralemon Street. His tenure as a workman had served him well, but to confront Frias, he needed to clean up and rejoin the higher classes. And he didn't fear McCluskey, at least for the moment. Miriam had been correct. The copper had already overplayed his hand and was unlikely to now make himself even more conspicuous. Noah grinned to himself. The police, after all, are not above the law.

The cab slowed almost to a stop. Noah was about to lean out the window to see what was causing the delay when the door flew open. Another man leapt inside. Clean-cut like the driver. Then Noah knew. Military.

Suddenly his breath was gone. He was heaving forward. A pain in his stomach and chest. Terrible. It shot to his throat. He tried to lift his head. A blow to the back of his neck. He almost retched. Couldn't see in front of him. A hand, powerful, held his head down. The hansom began to move. He was gasping, breath still spasmodic from the blow to the solar plexus.

Noah bounced along with the cab for about fifteen minutes, never allowed to straighten up. No one looking in from the street would see him. The cab stopped, and the door was again flung open. The man next to him in the cab pulled his left arm up behind his back. Pain shot through his shoulder. He was hauled out of the hansom, then half dragged, half marched forward. He was pushed through a door that closed behind him. Hands on his shoulders pushed him down into a hard chair.

A moment later, Noah was in a bare room, about ten by twenty. Gloomy. Heavy drapes masked the windows. He struggled to focus.

"Good afternoon, doctor. Thank you so much for accepting my invitation." The voice came from behind him. Noah heard the click of heels on the hard wooden floor, and a moment later, standing over him, was a man of about forty in an army uniform. He wore shiny boots but no cap. He stared down with the same expression that Noah had seen in the photographs that lined the stairway the night Willard died.

Anschutz.

The two other men from the hansom walked around to face him. Anschutz glanced to one of them and another chair was brought immediately. The colonel sat in it, facing Noah.

"Yes, doctor. I'm early. Admiral Dewey himself prevailed on General Merritt to grant me emergency leave. Bereavement leave. My youngest son died, you see."

Anschutz waited, but Noah knew better than to respond.

"Not talkative? Well, that's all right. I'll talk for a bit." Anschutz seemed larger than in the photographs. Denser. His neck was as wide as his head, his jawline straight, not a trace of jowl. His hands were large and muscled, but his fingernails were manicured and perfectly cut. Like TR's. He sat leaning slightly forward, a forearm resting across his thigh. Casual and comfortable in the promise of violence that fell about him like an aura.

He ran his eyes up over Noah. "A very nice job of disguise, doctor. Captain Bright and Lieutenant Van Nostrand here would certainly not have recognized you. We leave on Sunday for Washington. If you had simply gone about your business in that outrageous outfit, you might have avoided this meeting. For a time, in any event." Anschutz paused, drawing out the moment, making no effort to hide his gratification in the torment of another. "Well, doctor, don't you want to know how we were so fortunate to be able to make your acquaintance?"

Noah refused to speak.

"Not curious? I'll tell you anyway. We couldn't find you, so we were watching Dr. Herold. When Van Nostrand saw him escort a laborer into

City Hall, well . . . we're only soldiers, not a brainy doctor like you . . . but we're smart enough to figure that out. They followed you, and you eventually stepped into the cab the lieutenant had borrowed from its driver. Want to know how we found out about Herold?"

"Frias," Noah said.

"Bravo. Yes, Dr. Frias was more than a bit suspicious when a man he'd never met developed an overwhelming desire to speak with him. Herold telephoned his office three times, you know. Far too eager to be innocent. How you persuaded a reputable man like Herold to help you in your fraud is a mystery. Convincing my nincompoop of a wife to allow you to treat my boy was one thing, but Herold seems intelligent."

Noah had returned to silence.

"So now we get to the subject at hand. You. And what is going to happen to you for murdering my son." Anschutz slowly leveled his index finger at Noah's chin. "And how long it will take to happen. Bright and Van Nostrand are highly expert. I'd even call them virtuosos. We've served together for two years. We would die for one another, and we would kill for one another. They are anxious to begin." The two men stood by, each without expression.

Anschutz remained seated, leaning on his arm in studied casualness. The comfort with which he embraced the captor's role made McCluskey pale by comparison. Everything McKee, Mauritz Herzberg, and even Mrs. Jensen had said about Pug Anschutz was true. He had burned a family alive. He had murdered other helpless Filipinos. He had struck his wife and his children. And he would murder Noah without compunction, hesitation, or fear of consequences. Pug Anschutz killed because snuffing out the life of other human beings gave him pleasure.

Noah's heart was pounding. His arm socket throbbed, and his neck and abdomen ached from the blows. Still Anschutz sat, silently waiting. For what? A response? There was no response he had any interest in hearing. Then Noah realized he must speak. Anything. This was an interrogation, entertainment to Anschutz. Theater. A game requiring give and take. A game to which Anschutz had developed a craving every bit as powerful as that of a dope fiend to opiates. If Noah continued to remain mute, Anschutz would use his thugs to force him to play his part in the burlesque.

But what to say? A torturer will continue his sadistic rituals until his victim confesses. The veracity of the confession is beside the point. Only the act matters. The acknowledgment of self-abasement. With the confession, the victim loses all right to respect and dignity. After the torturer achieves that, the game has ended. The victim is then merely so much detritus and can be dispatched.

Noah spoke evenly. "Colonel, you have proven yourself precisely what your detractors say you are. A mindless brute." The colonel's shoulders stiffened, and he blinked twice in rapid succession. One of his men moved menacingly at Noah, but Anschutz put up his hand. A dull sheen of perspiration had appeared on his forehead.

"I didn't kill your son," Noah went on. "But someone did. Every competent physician to whom I gave the facts of the case has agreed. Poor Willard died of morphia poisoning, but not by my hand. But do you take the time to try to determine the truth? No. You simply decide to make someone suffer. Anyone. You call your wife a nincompoop, but you are more than willing to take her word when it will justify brutality. You are so blinded by your need for vengeance that not only will you commit an injustice by making me the object of your rage, but you will let the person who is responsible walk free."

Noah paused. Had he gone too far?

Anschutz grinned and brought his hands together in mock applause. His bottom teeth were crooked, and the asymmetry was jarring. "Very good, doctor. The counterattack. An excellent response strategy. Fernando Aquino used that very same technique in Luzon. I was so impressed with his resolve that I had his feet cut off. Perhaps I should cut off yours."

Perspiration had by then formed on Anschutz's upper lip. He blinked quickly again. Noah looked more closely and noticed some yellowing of his skin. The remnants of a tropical fever.

"You think I'm going to kill you right here and now, Dr. Whitestone, don't you? You believe you are not going to leave this room alive. That is why you employed this silly, what-have-I-got-to-lose gambit." Anschutz's skin suddenly seemed to be glowing, making the yellowing more pronounced. "I may kill you here, but I may opt against it. Punishment for murdering my son should be more profound than a quick soldier's death. So I might . . . might . . . decide to let you leave here a free man. If I do, soon, perhaps very soon, perhaps not, I will find you and end your life. There is no recourse, no reprieve. After Washington, I will be home for one month, and during that month, you will die . . . if I don't have you killed now, of course. Every moment between now and then, I leave you to ponder your death.

"I'm a soldier, Dr. Whitestone. Death is my business. And, if I may be so modest, I know my business well. I can assure you that waiting for the inevitable is excruciating. Do you know your Greek parables, doctor? The Sword of Damocles?"

Anschutz snapped his fingers, a single sharp crack. "Actually, I've a better example. Among the Rif tribes of Morocco, there is a fascinating method of dealing with an enemy. The man is strapped facedown to a board, with his head protruding over the edge. The board is placed projecting out over a very deep well. All that keeps the board from toppling into the abyss is a large urn, filled with sand, placed at the prisoner's feet as a counterweight. But a small hole has been made near the bottom of the urn, allowing the sand to run out. While the prisoner stares into the pit, the women of the tribe sit around him and inform him of the progress of the sand leaking out of the urn. Some tell him not to worry—hours are left before he will plunge to his death. Others advise him to say his prayers—the sand has almost run out. I'm told that by the time the sand has finally leaked out sufficiently to send the prisoner over the side, he has gone mad and is screaming wildly, begging for the women to push him over and end his agony. He falls to his death screaming. As someone who has been forced to deal with many prisoners, I must confess to be in awe over the utter genius of the technique."

The perspiration beaded. Anschutz was apparently still febrile. "So, doctor, I cannot strap you to a board, but I feel confident that, when I finally do show myself to commit the act, you will welcome it." Anschutz made to consider an alternative. "Unless I kill you now."

Anschutz licked his lips, then suddenly barked out a single laugh. The sound startled his men, although each barely flinched. Whatever fever he had contracted in the Philippines had gone to his brain. How could his superiors not have known? Or perhaps they did. Perhaps there was more to his leave than bereavement.

An unhinged Pug Anschutz was even more dangerous than a rational one, but also more vulnerable. Must keep the dialogue going.

"That will not help you find out why your son died."

"I know why my son died."

"No, you don't. I understand how a credulous old fool like Frederick Wurster can be gulled by a gold watch, an International Benz, and a baritone. But you? You, colonel? I didn't think you would be quite so easy to take in."

Anschutz stared at Noah. His pupils had dilated and he squinted to focus.

"Your son was an experiment, colonel. Willard died in a test that your trusted Dr. Frias was paid to perform . . . of a new drug, a morphiate called Heroin."

Anschutz exhaled deeply and quickly drew in another breath. "Marketed by the Bayer Company of Germany. A drug that Dr. Frias prescribed for Willard two weeks before you saw him and which he carefully monitored until Willard had finished the entire prescription three days later."

Anschutz continued hyperventilating. "Dr. Frias was quite open with me. He did not feel the need to shave his beard and scurry about like a Chinaman. So, doctor, please tell me . . . how could a medicine that

Willard had not taken for two weeks have caused his death? A medicine that the best scientists in Germany pronounced as safe."

"But Heroin is not safe. Did Dr. Frias also mention that he is one of the Bayer Company's largest American stockholders? That he personally invested fifty thousand dollars? And that another investor is your wife's father and still another is his brother, Frederick Wurster? And that a drug manufacturer named Martin Smith, with whom I saw Dr. Frias in Brooklyn Hospital, is also part of the cabal, as is a doctor named Tilson in New Jersey whose patient . . . a little girl . . . died precisely as Willard did? Did he tell you any of that, colonel?"

Anschutz didn't answer. He was staring, but over Noah's shoulder, his mind seeming to have wandered someplace else. At one point, he seemed to whisper, "My wife?" His gaze again fell on Noah. "My wife?" he asked, making no effort to hide his distaste. "She knew?"

"What? You mean about the money?"

"About anything."

"I . . . I'm not certain what you're asking."

Anschutz pushed himself to his feet; he had to put his hands to his thighs to do it. His collar was soaked, and his breathing had become more shallow. "All right, doctor. You've convinced me."

Bright and Van Nostrand glanced at each other. One of them—Noah didn't know which was which—gave a small confused shrug.

"You mean I can go?" Noah asked, hoping not to sound incredulous.

"No, doctor. You're going to come with me and pay a house call."

THIRTY-FIVE

M olly opened the door. When she saw Noah standing with Pug Anschutz, her eyes bugged.

"I wish to see my wife," Anschutz barked. Molly opened her mouth to respond, but no sound came out. She spun about and ran off up the stairs to do as she had been told.

Anschutz stepped into his house and Noah followed. Bright and Van Nostrand remained outside, sentinels on either side of the short path that led to the front door. Noah glanced at the photographs lining the wall of the impassive, clear-eyed soldier, more and more distant from the erratic, unstable killer with whom he seemed to have unwittingly struck some sort of bargain.

Mildred Anschutz appeared at the head of the stairs, even more drawn and haggard than when Noah had made his ill-fated condolence call. Whether the cause was Willard's death or her husband's return was uncertain, but like Molly, she seemed panic-stricken to see her husband

246

and Noah together. She slowly descended, then, as directed by her husband, went into the parlor and seated herself on the divan. Pug Anschutz waited until she was settled, then sat next to his wife, but with about a nine-inch gap between them. He sat with forced rigidity, a hand resting on either knee.

Anschutz addressed his wife while looking straight ahead. "The doctor has something he wishes to say."

This was the moment Noah had been hoping for, to finally be able to force Mildred Anschutz to confront her own missteps, but now that it had arrived he was unsure how to proceed. Noah had no doubts that Mildred Anschutz was now in the same peril that he had just avoided and that he had put her there. But she was also the only person who could definitively clear his name.

"I thought we might finally resolve what happened to Willard." He addressed himself to the woman on the divan in a tone as gentle as if she were a child.

At the mention of her son, Mildred Anschutz raised her eyes to Noah, her brow wrinkled in anguish. As she did so, her gaze flicked for a second to Pug.

"Let's review," Noah began. He thought of his own Oliver. "Two weeks before I was summoned, Willard had taken ill and you took him to Dr. Frias. After an examination, Dr. Frias prescribed two new drugs. One was for fever and pain. Those tablets were blue. The other was for cough and general malaise. They were green. Am I correct so far, Mrs. Anschutz?"

"Of course. You know you are." She tried to answer him dismissively, but her voice held a quaver.

"After Willard's recovery, you noticed his behavior had become strange . . . isn't that correct, Mrs. Anschutz? He seemed more nervous."

"I noticed nothing of the kind. He seemed to me the same as always, as I told you . . . until that last day."

"He exhibited no further symptoms? Was in need of neither the green pills nor the blue?"

"That is what I said." For the first time, Pug Anschutz glanced briefly to his wife, exhibiting the same rapid blinking as he had with Noah.

"And Dr. Frias came by to see Willard?"

"After three days. He said the crisis had passed, but I should remain vigilant to a relapse."

"Vigilant? You?" Anschutz sneered.

"Yes, Pug," Mildred replied, drawing herself up. "Someone must remain vigilant with the children. Someone who is with them more than one week in two years." Noah stiffened. This was a dangerous moment to show backbone.

Anschutz snorted. "You did your usual fine job." He turned to Noah. "I married an imbecile, Whitestone. Why is beyond me."

"Because my family could help your career. Because you wanted to be a general before you were forty, and you needed a push to get there. I was good enough for that."

Anschutz's jaw clamped shut, and Noah jumped in before the colonel could open his mouth again.

"Are you certain, Mrs. Anschutz, that Willard wasn't behaving oddly and you once again consulted Dr. Frias?" Noah was aware that he was speaking too fast, but the words seemed to pour out of their own volition. "That Frias also noticed the changes and gave you an additional supply of the green tablets. And that your supply ran out on the day Willard became ill? And when Dr. Frias wasn't available, you engaged me?"

Mildred Anschutz leaned her head at him as if she were peering into a cage at the zoo. "Are you accusing me of lying, Dr. Whitestone? Again implying that I have covered up the circumstances of my child's . . . death. Of allowing you to be accused when I knew you to be innocent? What sort of person do you think I am?"

"Perhaps you did not do so intentionally, Mrs. Anschutz."

"What? You're saying I lied without realizing it?"

The notion did sound half-witted but Noah pressed on. There was little choice. "Are you familiar with the works of Dr. Freud, the Austrian brain specialist, Mrs. Anschutz?"

"Certainly not. I have no need for a brain specialist." She turned briefly to her husband, but Anschutz had again become expressionless.

Noah repeated Jacobi's hypothesis that Mildred Anschutz had dosed her son with Heroin and then, when the terrible, unbearable result became manifest, repressed the memory of the act. He stressed the amazing results Freud had obtained. Noted that, despite the skepticism with which such a seemingly outrageous theory would be received, Freud was destined to become one of the great medical scientists of the age. He concluded by saying, to Pug as much as to his wife, that she would in no way be responsible if such was the case. The responsibility would lie completely with the doctor who had prescribed the medicine.

As he spoke, Noah scrutinized her carefully, convinced that if the Austrian were correct, some spark of recognition would be detected. But Mildred Anschutz sat tight-lipped, her hands folded in her lap for the entire rendition.

When he was done, she stared at him for some moments. "Young man," she said finally, "are you completely an idiot? That is the most absurd thing I have ever heard. I can assure you I have never been less than in full control of my faculties." She stood up, pulled to her full height. For the first time since the night of Willard's death, she appeared the matriarch. "You will leave my house this instant. You will never return, no matter what the circumstances." She pointed toward the door. "I thought you merely an incompetent doctor. But now I realize, in addition, you are an unfathomably stupid man."

When Noah didn't get up instantly, she looked down at her husband. "Pug, throw this fool out." But Anschutz didn't move, except to look up at his wife with contempt.

THIRTY-SIX

Arnold Frias had offices on Fulton Street, an elegant suite of rooms with a separate entrance on the first floor of a newly built office building. A brass plaque on the door identified the occupant. As a condition of his lease, Frias had obtained an agreement with the building's owners to allow him to park his automobile in front of his door.

The offices themselves were as opulent as the International Benz outside. The waiting-room furniture was leather and plush, the wallpaper silk, and the desk at which the receptionist sat mahogany. The receptionist herself did little to diminish the image. She was twenty, dark-haired, prim, and lovely, dressed in a ten-dollar frock.

The waiting room had not an empty seat. Most of the roughly dozen patients were women, all well dressed, ranging in age from early twenties to over sixty. Three were accompanied by children. Two men, elderly, one holding a gold-headed cane, filled out the roster.

Noah told the receptionist his name, and that he was a physician who had come on a matter of great urgency. She looked him up and down, began to open her mouth to question, then excused herself and ducked into the inner office. Her hips swiveled as she walked, enough to hint but not enough to be suggestive. Noah wondered if she was Frias's lover. The receptionist returned a few moments later.

"Dr. Frias will see you." She was cool, professional, and curt.

Frias's private office was at the rear, as elegant as the waiting room. Frias stood at the side of his desk as Noah walked in, large and imposing. The fingertips of his right hand rested on the desktop, forming a small tent. He could not have appeared more affable.

"Come in, Whitestone. I was expecting you. Mildred telephoned and said you might be by. You shaved off your beard, I see. You look younger." He observed Noah's garb. "Interesting get-up. Practicing for poverty?"

"You may be the one needing the practice, doctor. I expect you to lose fifty thousand dollars."

"You mean my investment in the Bayer Company? Hardly. I'll make millions."

"Not after I publish my findings."

Frias heaved an exaggerated sigh. "Whitestone, you are truly a fool. Not only will your . . . 'findings,' as you put them . . . have no effect on my net worth, you will have been the agent that ensured the success of the venture."

"I hardly think so. When Heroin is exposed for the poison it is . . . poison you prescribed to a child . . . it is difficult to imagine how your seamy enterprise will succeed."

"On the contrary. It is difficult to imagine it failing. The range of applications for the drug is immense. Even greater than for Aspirin. Heroin, as I'm sure you know, is a drug whose safety and efficacy is supported by the scrupulous research of one of the foremost chemists in Europe. He presented a paper to an august body of scientists that was received with acclaim."

"The acclaim will evaporate when documentation is produced that children were sickened or killed by the drug."

"What documentation? You have no proof at all. Not a single case where Heroin can be shown to have produced deleterious effects. I thought that had been made clear to you by TR." Frias let the pronouncement settle. "I also have friends in the governor's office, you see."

"But *you* know the drug is harmful. Have you no scruples at all?"

"Any difficulties that might have been encountered are strictly a matter of dosing."

"So you used poor children as subjects of an experiment."

"Someone has to be. Oh, Whitestone, can you not be just a bit less callow? Every new drug needs human testing. Or would you prefer medicine to freeze in place where we are now?"

"I'm not certain helping the advance of medicine will be a comfort to the Anschutz family."

"I will tell you again, Whitestone, although you seem to have incurable problems with comprehension . . . I prescribed Heroin for Willard for three days a full two weeks before he died. There was not a single tablet in Mildred's possession when the course had been completed. I visited Willard the day after the prescription lapsed and noticed a mild set of symptoms the details of which I'm certain you can guess. Still, the boy seemed to have no lasting effects. As I said, a dosing problem. I have not prescribed Heroin since and will not until the dosing problems are solved. If the report you intend to publish can explain how a mild, acetylized morphiate can lie dormant in a child's system for two weeks, then suddenly be aroused to cause symptoms, I'm certain you'll be immortalized in the annals of medicine. Far more likely, as you have hypothesized, was that Willard was given morphiates subsequent to those I prescribed. And the only other morphiate I am aware of Willard ingesting was the dose of laudanum you administered."

"He did not die from the laudanum."

"You need to believe that, I know. It runs in your family."

"What does that mean?"

Frias drew himself up. He loomed over Noah, nostrils flared, his face suddenly gone crimson. "You are so sanctimonious. So facilely quick to accuse. The evil Frias. Uncaring. Avaricious. Sacrificing his patients' lives and well-being on the altar of profit. Not like the Whitestones, father and son. *They* work for higher motives. *They* would never sully themselves. Frias would poison children for a few pieces of silver, but the Whitestones would *never* accept money to administer an untested drug to unwitting innocents. Not *them*.

"Well, doctor, would it surprise you to know that your father is guilty of the very crime of which you accuse me? Of course, he did not kill *a* patient. He killed five. Ten years ago. For two thousand dollars. Four hundred dollars per death. Then after it was done, he tried to avoid responsibility. Place it on me. We have not spoken since."

"You're a liar."

"No. I'm not. And what's more, you know I'm not. I can see it in your face. How do you think he paid for that building he lives in?" Frias thrust an index finger forward, a weapon to shoot Noah's illusions dead. "With the money he received from the Schweinert Company. To test a new analgesic. Are you interested in the details, or would you prefer ignorance to truth?"

Frias took Noah's silence as assent and plowed ahead. He made no effort to hide his satisfaction, sounding as if he were recounting the tale of saving a patient.

"Schweinert was another dye maker. Bayer's competitor. I needn't tell you that, for reasons no chemist has been able to divine, products used in the dying process often have pharmaceutical properties. Schweinert was experimenting with salicylic acid. The gastrointestinal consequences were well-known, of course, but Schweinert's chemists thought buffering the substance with glycerin would ameliorate the impact. And, of course, glycerin made the medicine more palatable to ingest.

"They applied for a patent under the name Glycosal. They had tested the substance on animals but had either ignored the results or misread them. Schweinert's managers were terrified that a competitor would market glycerin-buffered salicylic acid before they could get Glycosal to market. So, instead of conducting human testing in Germany, they decided to introduce the drug immediately in the United States.

"You can guess the rest. Your father and I were two of the physicians they chose to purvey the drug. Schweinert's representatives misrepresented the test results. Your father and I were friends at the time. We had been ever since he cared for one of my patients when we were young."

"Viola Mangino."

Frias nodded in surprise. "He told you? Yes. It was my first forceps delivery, and I botched it. I mean my first ever. Medical schools are different today. When your father and I attended, there was no practical work at all. Neither of us ever delivered an infant until after we had obtained our medical degrees." Frias sighed. "Horrible. What a tragedy.

"In any event, the tests for Glycosal were disastrous from the first. I stopped using the drug almost immediately, but your father persisted. Such a stubborn man. Five of his patients died. Internal bleeding mostly.

"Your father could not or would not believe that his patients died from complications from a drug he administered. Died in agonizing pain. First he insisted that some other medication was to blame. Then that *I* was to blame. For talking him into participating in the test. Eventually, he had no choice but to believe the truth . . . as will you." Frias put his hand to his belly, two small, caressing pats. "And of course he kept the money."

Frias removed his watch and checked the time. The instrument was gold. Swiss. Eighty dollars at the minimum. He absentmindedly rolled the stem between his thumb and index finger. He raised his eyes to Noah.

"Now you will leave. We shall not speak again. You best spend some time considering what you will do once your medical license is revoked. If you are not in the penitentiary. Then, of course, there is Colonel Anschutz. Once I inform him of our chat, he will be even less well disposed toward you than he is now. On the whole, Whitestone, I would say that your position has become totally untenable. It is simply a matter of what calamity befalls you first. You might consider moving far away from here and very quickly. A shame, considering you were about to marry into a good family.

"I also wish you to remember how much you've helped me. When your wild accusations are discredited, my reputation will be more spotless than ever, and Bayer's introduction of the drug should encounter no difficulties whatever." Frias rolled the stem of his watch once more. "Now get out."

There was a knock on the door. The receptionist stuck her head in. "Mrs. Anschutz would like to speak to you again."

Frias indicated to the young woman that he would take the call. "On second thought, Whitestone, wait a moment. Mildred likely wants to find out the results of our interview. I will be happy to tell her that you are ruined." Frias lifted the earpiece off his telephone, his other hand resting comfortably on his watch chain. After a moment, his hand slid off and hung limply at his side. He said, "I'll be right there." Then he replaced the receiver and mumbled, half to Noah, half to himself. "Pug Anschutz is dead."

"The fever . . ."

"No, Whitestone. As always, your diagnosis is incorrect. The colonel didn't die of fever. He died of a gunshot wound. A single bullet in the heart."

"A bullet . . . Who . . . ?"

"Aldridge, his son."

THIRTY-SEVEN

N ot two minutes after Noah had walked through the door, Mrs. Jensen related the story.

"Just after you left, there was a terrible row. Annie O'Rourke told me Colonel Anschutz seemed to have lost his mind, raving and waving his arms about. He had taken it into his head that somehow Mrs. Anschutz had given those pills to Willard after all. Something about pretending not to remember. He was yelling something about 'fraud' . . ."

"Freud."

"What? In any event, Annie had never seen him like that, and she was terrified of him before. Molly Fitzsimmons, the maid, was so frightened that she ran from the house. The colonel accused Mrs. Anschutz of conspiring against him with Dr. Frias. He insisted that Dr. Frias had issued a second prescription and his wife was feeding morphia to his son, and then that she and the doctor had gotten together in a pact to keep the truth from him. Then he began to mutter that killing two doctors was not a great deal more difficult than killing one. Mrs. Anschutz cowered in the corner, denying everything, but that seemed only to enrage the colonel further. When the children came to the doorway, the girls were in tears, but Colonel Anschutz screamed for them to get out. Aldridge refused. He rushed to his mother's aid. Brave boy. Colonel Anschutz whirled about and struck him. One backhand blow. Aldridge fairly flew across the room.

"Annie said then Colonel Anschutz approached his poor wife. She hadn't budged from the corner of the room. He put his face right up to hers and screamed. 'Tell me the truth, you fool!' He grabbed her by the front of her dress. 'You murdered your own son. Admit it!' Mrs. Anschutz was too terrified to speak. She whimpered and shook her head. She began to sink to her knees. The colonel screamed louder. 'Talk, I say!' Annie said it was almost as if he thought he was back in the Philippines. He raised his arm to strike her, but before he could deliver the blow, Aldridge called to him from the doorway. He had left and returned with his father's revolver. 'Make one move, father, and I will shoot you down,' he told the colonel. Annie said the boy was remarkably calm. Colonel Anschutz began to advance on the boy. 'You wouldn't dare,' he said. 'You don't have the fortitude.' Aldridge did not say another word. He simply pulled the trigger. His father fell dead to the floor, shot through the heart."

"My God," Noah whispered.

"Then Mrs. Anschutz called her uncle instead of the police. Mayor Wurster handled everything. Just a little while ago, a detective showed up to take Aldridge's statement." Mrs. Jensen lowered her voice to a whisper. "Annie overheard him say that he left his coach two streets away so no one would know. Two other detectives snuck the body out in a plain carriage."

"That poor family. I wonder what will happen to poor Aldridge now."

Mrs. Jensen looked surprised. "Nothing, doctor. He has already been cleared. The police have called it self-defense."

"That's impossible. Colonel Anschutz may have been a soldier, but he was still unarmed."

"When Mrs. Anschutz finally told her uncle what the man she married was really like, Mayor Wurster was aghast and furious at being taken in. 'Good riddance to bad rubbish,' he said. He told the police detective what to report. I'm not certain anyone outside the family will ever know Aldridge was even involved."

Mrs. Jensen had seemed to overlook that, between Annie O'Rourke and herself, the story was already spreading faster than the Chicago Fire. "And Annie heard all this?"

Mrs. Jensen appeared more surprised still. "Of course. Annie hears everything."

"As do you, Mrs. Jensen?"

The housekeeper instantly turned full red. "No, doctor. Never. I can assure you—"

Despite himself, Noah smiled. "That's all right, Mrs. Jensen. You are one of my most valued friends."

"Oh, doctor . . ." She quickly recovered, then placed a beefy hand on his forearm. "I forgot the most important news of all. Mayor Wurster's main goal is to protect Aldridge, so in order to ensure that tongues don't begin to wag," Mrs. Jensen uttered the phrase without irony, "he's decided to drop any proceedings against you. He told his niece, 'Mildred, we must lay to rest Willard's death along with your husband.' Isn't that wonderful news?"

"Under the circumstances, I can hardly celebrate."

"Of course, doctor . . . I know that . . . I didn't mean . . . but I can't help but be pleased that you've been exonerated."

"I haven't been exonerated. They're burying the affair. It's hardly the same thing."

"But, doctor, you're innocent. What does it matter?"

Innocent? Was he? Perhaps *he* was the one who repressed a painful memory.

"And it means you can go back to your practice. Work again with your father."

"Yes. My father." Noah turned and headed for his bedroom. "I'm going to get some rest now, Mrs. Jensen. I won't be needing you anymore today."

THIRTY-EIGHT

DAY 9. THURSDAY, 9/28—10 A.M.

She'd been knocking on the door all morning, first every half hour, then every twenty minutes, then every ten. But the door to Noah's bedroom remained locked. At first, he told Mrs. Jensen to go away; eventually he refused to respond. This time, however, she yelled through the door, "Miss De Kuyper is here. She said she's not leaving until you come out." Then Maribeth's voice came through the oak. "You will stop being ridiculous. Open this door, Noah Whitestone. I intend to camp out if I have to."

She would, too. "Please, Maribeth, just leave me be. I need some time to myself."

"That's the last thing you need."

It was a test of wills Noah would ultimately lose. And in truth, he wanted to be with her, wanted to desperately. He put Isobel's picture back in the top drawer of his bureau, then turned the key and swung the door open.

Maribeth waited across the threshold in a pale-blue dress and white hat. Her eyes seemed to radiate in the morning light. Behind her and to the side, Mrs. Jensen stood like a penitent, hands clasped in front of her, eyes cast plaintively.

"Why are you still in those clothes?"

Noah looked down at the workingman's outfit he had yet to take off. "I slept in the chair."

"Utter foolishness." Maribeth strode past him into the room. She glanced for a moment at the top of his bureau, then turned her gaze on him.

"Tell me," she said. "Right now."

He let the words come out without preamble. "My father is a fraud." When Maribeth asked what in the world he was talking about, Noah laid out the entire sordid affair.

Maribeth listened without seeming at all shocked. "You've yet to speak to your father, I presume. To ask if the story is true."

"It's true. Frias had too many details right to have been making it up. My father did suddenly have money to the buy the building when just the year before he had lamented that he couldn't afford to; he did stop talking to Frias at precisely the moment Frias said; and he did lose patients then as well, although I didn't know it was as many as five. Turner McKee knew as well. I thought it odd at the time that he asked about my father, but didn't pursue it."

"And on the basis of that, you condemn him without a hearing? A man you revere?" Maribeth heaved a sigh. "Perhaps it's because you elevated him to a state that no one can live up to. I never had that problem, you see. I love my parents . . . I do, actually . . . but the only thing on pedestals in our house are those phony statues my mother pays so much for. I've never been forced to confront some appalling, unsuspected bit of scandal because I'd never be surprised. But you weren't so fortunate. So now, when the unshakable conviction that your father is a saint is shattered, it leads to the equally unshakable conviction that he is a craven murderer. Two endpoints with no middle. And on the word of a man you've spent the last week trying to prove is a murderer himself. Can't you see how absurd that is?"

"Perhaps."

"Then put on some real clothes and let's go ask him."

Noah began to refuse. To sit across from Abel and hear confirmation of Frias's terrible accusation—of all that had befallen him in the past week, that would be the worst. Still, what choice was there? He wasn't going to spend the rest of his life in his bedroom, as tempting as it felt at the moment.

"Give me ten minutes."

When they arrived at Adams Street, Noah looked up at the building that until today had only evoked the best of memories, connoted only warmth, honesty, and integrity. Now it bore the stigma of five innocent patients who had died horrible deaths.

The waiting room was full, but instead of getting into his white laboratory coat to assist, Noah would force the patients to wait while he spoke with his father. At least Pierre Gaspard, who diagnosed and treated with same frenetic speed he did everything else, would keep the line from stretching to the street. Abel saw immediately that the subject was not pleasant and beckoned Noah to the office.

Maribeth made to wait, but Abel shook his head. "This concerns you as well, my dear. Especially if you're considering becoming part of this family."

So he had guessed.

In the office, Abel settled heavily into his leather chair, while Noah and Maribeth sat across the desk; division by preference rather than by blood.

"Would you mind letting me know precisely what Arnold told you? Or have I already been irrevocably condemned?"

"Of course not, father." Noah repeated the tale, speaking evenly and without judgment, thereby communicating judgment all the more.

When he had finished, Abel nodded, an incongruous wry smile on his face. "Yes. The basic facts are there. They always are with Arnold.

He rarely leaves himself vulnerable to the letter of the truth. Its spirit is something else again."

"You are not culpable then?"

"That would depend, I suppose, on who was doing the judging. To me, I will never be anything less than fully responsible for the suffering of those poor people."

"I would prefer to decide for myself."

Abel barked out a laugh. "Would you? Very well." He opened a desk drawer and withdrew a bottle of brandy and a shot glass. As he poured, he looked across at his son. "Yes, I've had the occasional brandy in the morning. Usually when I've been awake all night." He downed half of what he poured. "What Arnold neglected to mention was that he did not come to Glycosal as an innocent. As with Heroin, he had been to Germany. Whether by coincidence or design, he arrived in Munich just before Schweinert planned to announce the fabrication of the drug. He visited the company and spoke to the directors. Glycosal had not yet undergone human testing. Arnold agreed to undertake the tests in America. *Asked* to do it. The Schweinert directors jumped at the offer and appointed him their representative. Paid him a handsome retainer. I never did find out how much.

"When Arnold returned, he solicited a number of area physicians. I was one of them. He knew I was strapped for funds, that you had begun medical school and I wanted very much to purchase the building in which I then rented space. He told me that he had reviewed the laboratory results carefully while in Germany and consulted at length with the chemists. He even claimed to have spoken with test subjects. There were, of course, no test subjects, as I found out later. Arnold was, as he is now, in high repute. He would pay me two thousand dollars to participate in a marketing campaign . . . that's what he called it, a 'marketing campaign.' When he offered me such a fortune with his assurances that the drug was safe, I accepted. For that alone—for taking his unverified word—I should be damned.

"I prescribed Glycosal to thirty patients, and at first, the results were promising. One or two reported some gastric distress, but nothing untoward. After two weeks, however, patients began to complain of symptoms more severe. I ceased use of the drug immediately and told Arnold. He appeared stunned. He said no one else had reported similar difficulties.

"At the time, an epidemic of food poisoning was running rampant in Brooklyn. Eventually, it was traced to embalmed meat. There are no better government standards for food than for pharmaceuticals. Arnold hypothesized that my patients had been made ill by the beef and not the drug. In fact, he insisted Glycosal had likely prevented them from becoming even sicker."

Abel downed the remainder of the brandy. "Once again, I accepted his word. Perhaps I wanted to. Was blinded by the prospect of more money than I usually make in three months. So for two more days, I continued to prescribe Glycosal to my patients. As you know, five of them eventually died."

"But how could only your patients have become ill?"

"It wasn't just my patients. Arnold had neglected to tell me that he ceased his own testing even before I spoke to him, that others in his pool had communicated suspicions as well. I've never been able to understand why he withheld the information only from me. Perhaps he simply wanted to ruin me." Abel rubbed his forehead hard with his fingertips. "But whatever his reason, I killed five of my patients.

"Then, to my everlasting shame, I didn't return the two thousand dollars. I'd already purchased the building, and I would have been ruined, just as Arnold planned. So I kept the blood money. I have loathed myself for it ever since."

Abel heaved an immense sigh. "In some ways, I'm relieved you found out. I've carried the burden of your adulation for too long. Once again, I have no one to blame but myself, but how can anyone resist the awe of their child?"

"Rubbish!" Noah lowered his voice. "You might have been guilty of not plunging yourself into financial devastation as a result of being duped, but no more. Your doctoring was not motivated by greed. You proceeded honorably with your patients. I would have done the same."

"I disagree."

Both men turned to Maribeth.

"I'm sorry, Dr. Whitestone, but you were correct. You allowed your judgment to be compromised by the promise of easy money. I'm all too familiar with such occurrences, except in my family there is no subsequent regret."

Noah began to protest, but Maribeth would not have it. "You do your father no good, Noah, by excusing behavior he knows is inexcusable. That just continues the burden you've already placed on him."

"Thank you," Abel said softly. "The burden of five unnecessary deaths is enough."

"But how could my father have had any way of anticipating the consequences? If he had, he certainly would not have accepted either the money or the assignment."

"He distrusted Dr. Frias and he ignored his distrust. That same distrust, Noah, that caused you to test the tablet you obtained from Mrs. Anschutz. If you hadn't, you would be practicing medicine right now, and the boy's death would be considered simply a mystery that would never be solved."

"Perhaps. But I can't be certain whether my actions were motivated by distrust or . . . I suppose jealousy is the right word."

"Jealous? Of Arnold?" Abel asked.

"Of his success. Of the unquestioned trust people like Mildred Anschutz showed in him. Trust I was convinced was undeserved—that they were impressed more by his trappings than his skill—and I was determined to prove it."

"But he did prescribe Heroin to the boy. And that's what certainly killed him."

"I don't see how."

"One day it will all come out. These things always do."

Maribeth interjected once more. "So what will you do now? Anschutz is dead, and Wurster is letting the matter drop."

Noah looked across at Abel. "Right now, I think I'd like to stay and help clear some of the backlog in the waiting room. Be a doctor again."

Maribeth stood. "I'll be going, then."

Noah saw patients in one examining room, Abel in the other. Pierre used Noah's office to consult with patients whose conditions did not require immediate intervention. They worked smoothly and efficiently, and soon the waiting room contingent began to thin out. Noah saw patients complaining of respiratory distress, conjunctivitis, dyspepsia, edema, dizziness, cough, paresthesia, tinnitus, and goiter, all within ninety minutes. Patients ranged in age from twelve to eighty-six; about two-thirds were women. He examined, diagnosed, counseled, and prescribed. In many cases, he merely assuaged fears of a condition worse than that which existed.

He was so happy, he had to remind himself not to whistle.

He had indeed been intensely fortunate, drawn to the brink, then pulled back. He could safely fade into the obscurity that most of the best physicians enjoyed. He could marry a woman he had come to treasure, his infatuation with Miriam Herzberg either overlooked or forgiven.

As for Heroin, what could he actually accomplish? Frias had built his fortress to withstand whatever meager assault Noah could mount. He had recruited a phalanx of doctors and drug purveyors who would override any medical objections, and a sufficient number of the wealthy and influential to ensure that ethical issues would be shunted aside. Eventually, of course, the drug would come to be seen for what it was, but by then Frias would have made his millions and would merely express shock that he had been mislead by his associates in Germany. "Terrible tragedy," he would lament as he emerged from First Mercantile.

And Willard Anschutz . . . Frias would escape blame for his death as well. Proof of malfeasance would be impossible to establish. Even Noah could not figure out how the Heroin prescription had done the boy in. Jacobi's notion about that Freud fellow's theory had turned out to be as moronic as it had first sounded. But it was not the laudanum. Of that Noah was certain, and that was all he had really needed to establish.

His next patient was Millicent Faircloth. Noah chuckled. He adored the Faircloth girls, all four of them. Millicent was the oldest, sixteen. She was tall and gangly with a shock of rust-red hair, skin awash with freckles, a long face, and emerald eyes. None of the sisters was attractive in a classical sense, but each was so vibrant as to appear to be moving when standing still. Millicent had taken into her head to be a writer, and Noah was certain she would succeed. Whenever she saw him, she badgered him to read the works of Edith Wharton, whom she described as "sub-lime." Noah always promised he would but, in truth, had little interest in reading anything made up.

And what malady would she complain of today? Another streak in the Faircloth family was hypochondria. Millicent had, at various times, insisted she was tubercular, had a brain tumor, or had contracted psittacosis—parrot fever—an ailment whose name she decided was suitably exotic. She always seemed disappointed when Noah told her she was about the healthiest person he knew.

Noah poised himself near the examining table as the door opened, trying to stifle his grin. But walking in, instead of Millicent Faircloth, was Maribeth.

"Alan has disappeared."

"What?"

"He wasn't at the hospital. I was told he placed a telephoned call and said he had an emergency and would be delayed. I spoke to the woman in hospital administration who received the message, and she said Alan sounded . . . different. She couldn't explain it but said it wasn't the way he generally spoke. I asked if it was simply the sound from the receiver, and she said no, it was more than that. And when the woman asked where the emergency was and how long Alan would delayed, Alan said some emergencies take a long time. Then he hung up the mouthpiece. Alan would never leave his patients without offering an explanation. Something is wrong. I know it."

Noah remembered Turner McKee, speaking to him through the crack in his tenement door. "It's McCluskey."

"I thought you said McCluskey wasn't a threat anymore."

"After the cemetery, I thought he wasn't. But he's obviously cleaning up loose ends for Frias and his investors. Or maybe just for himself. They're taking no chances."

Maribeth went white. "You mean you think Alan is dead?"

Noah thought for a moment. "No. If they'd done away with him, there would have been no call. He would simply have turned up somewhere like Turner McKee. It seems that McCluskey is holding him. For what purpose I don't know."

"We've got to do something. Try to find him."

"How? He might be anywhere."

"Well, I don't intend to just sit here."

"There's always McCluskey himself, I suppose. If we can locate him, he might lead us to Alan. We can start at his precinct, although he's unlikely to be just lolling about."

Maribeth held open the door. "Let's go, then."

"Let me use the telephone first. We're going to need some help."

Five minutes later, Noah left the offices on Adams Street. He glanced back at the building from the window of Maribeth's hansom. He had the distinct feeling he would not be back here again.

THIRTY-NINE

W e can no longer count on Herold."

"I'm surprised. He didn't sound like a man who would lose his nerve."

"He didn't. But Frias is clever. He contacted Herold, claimed the entire brouhaha was a big misunderstanding and offered to share the research notes from Germany proving Heroin is safe."

"But Heroin isn't safe."

"As Herold will likely find out for himself. But by the time the notes arrive and Herold has a chance to go through them—even assuming they haven't been altered—Heroin will be a fait accompli. And with Herold unavailable, the chance of enlisting official help through TR is gone as well."

"So Herold as been gulled. He didn't sound like the man for that either."

"He isn't, not really. Herold's interest was always in the forensics, the science. He enjoyed the amateur sleuthing, but getting back to the lab will be irresistible, as I suspect Frias understood." Noah smiled thinking of the indefatigable pathologist. "I'm relieved in a way. At least Herold is not in danger, and that's one less person to worry about."

"If we can find Alan, that will be one less still."

Noah had directed the driver to Lafayette Street. The best people to help them locate McCluskey—and the most motivated—were the Reds. Noah assumed that even with the offices destroyed, one or another of them, perhaps even Miriam herself, might be poring about to see if any papers or records could be salvaged. Maribeth had eagerly agreed.

"I will at least enjoy watching you squirm with the two of us in the same room."

"I have no reason to squirm," Noah replied, lamely even to his hopeful ear. After a snort from Maribeth, he added, "I expect the two of you to get along famously."

"As do I," Maribeth said. "Perhaps we'll decide to dispense with you altogether."

When they neared Lafayette Street, the forced banter ceased. Ten had died in the offices they were about to visit, and Alan might well be about to be added to the toll.

Two large wagons were parked at the side of the building. Workmen were tossing chunks of wood and plaster from the offices into chutes that ran from the blown-out second-floor windows to the wagon beds. Soon, empty wagons appeared to replace the two being filled.

Noah told Maribeth to wait while he went to check if any of the *New Visions* staff was about, but she refused. They walked up the flight of stairs in silence. The second-floor hall had been cleared, the glass swept up and temporary joists placed throughout to support the floor above. Noah stood and looked, the sight of disremembered bodies and smell of explosives branded in his memory.

The offices themselves were deserted. Eight workmen were hauling the last remains of *New Visions* to the chutes at the window opening. The job was almost complete; a few hours of work remained at most before the carpenters, plasterers, and glaziers would undertake the room's rebirth. The room seemed much larger denuded of furniture, stacks of papers, and scurrying workers.

Noah stood in the doorway for a few moments, surveying what had, just a few days prior, been a hive of youthful idealism guided by a soldier and philosopher. All gone now. It occurred to Noah that he had no idea how to find Miriam. She would have submerged herself somewhere in the vast Red underground and might reemerge anywhere in America or even in Europe.

There was one place he might check, however. The ride took only twenty minutes. Once again, Maribeth refused to wait in the carriage.

"Is Dolph here?"

The man behind the bar stopped wiping the countertop, but his left hand remained leaning on the bar towel. He was thin and coiled to Dolph's hulking menace—a snake for a bear. After an exaggerated pause, he shook his head.

"Will he be in?" There were three patrons in Arthur's, each of whom Noah recognized from his previous visit. None so much as looked up.

The bartender shook his head once more. Could none of them speak?

"I'm a friend of Miriam Herzberg. I'd like to get a message to her."

"I know who you are. And I ain't Western Union."

"But this is important."

The man began to methodically wipe the bar, creating little curlicues of moisture that evaporated and then were replaced in the next cycle. He raised his head to stare back at them, now more bird of prey than snake. Noah took Maribeth's arm and led her outside.

"We appear to be on our own."

"Then we must make do with our own resources. Where does this McCluskey fellow work?"

"In Manhattan, but as I said, that's the last place he'd be if he has taken Alan."

"Someone will know. I can be quite charming."

"McCluskey is a killer, Maribeth."

"How can I be in danger in a police station?"

But Maribeth emerged from the precinct house looking defeated, the first time Noah had ever seen her so. Noah assumed no one would talk to her, but just the opposite turned out to be the case.

"McCluskey has been suspended from duty. Two other police detectives as well. Evidently the suspensions were ordered by the police commissioner himself on instructions from Governor Roosevelt. That's all anyone in there is talking about. And I heard the phrase, 'That son of a bitch of a doctor,' more than once."

"But where is he? Someone must know."

"No one seems to. McCluskey was pretty secretive. No one is even certain where he lives."

"They just weren't telling you."

"No, they would have. Especially after I told them why I wanted to see him."

Noah's eyebrows shot up. Maribeth and Miriam were becoming more alike by the hour.

"Well you did want to know, didn't you? But it made no difference. I'm at wit's end."

"We shouldn't lose hope. If McCluskey is holding Alan for some reason, perhaps he'll make contact with us."

"You mean, don't you, that he's using Alan as bait for that son of a bitch of a doctor."

"It's possible."

"So I'm to lose a brother or a husband. Perhaps both."

"And perhaps neither. Speculating has gotten us nowhere."

"Not yet. But speculating allows you to prepare."

FORTY

With no way of locating McCluskey, Maribeth and Noah had little choice but to go about their business as normal in the hope that McCluskey wished to locate them. That meant meeting at the pier at 8 a.m., from whence the De Kuypers' sixty-foot yacht, *Excalibur*, would sail into the harbor to join Dewey, the *Olympia*, and the rest of the fleet making its way up the Hudson.

When Noah arrived, the family had divided along the De Kuyper fault line. Maribeth stood next to her father, looking ravishing in an eggshell-colored boating dress and parasol. Jamie and Rosa had taken their places next to Adelaide, Jamie in full glower, quite clearly standing as far from his sister as he could manage. Jamie may have told his mother of the caper at First Mercantile, because Adelaide shot Noah a frosty glare as he emerged from his carriage. Or perhaps she was simply expressing an ongoing opinion. It wasn't about Alan, because Maribeth and Noah had agreed that they should pretend to be surprised when he failed to make an appearance.

The *Excalibur* herself was decorated, as would be all of the thousands of yachts that joined the procession, with American flags and red, white, and blue bunting. The flag Oscar had purchased for the mast was immense, and even the strong harbor wind could not lift it more than a few degrees from the vertical.

Why the family didn't simply go aboard and wait for Alan, Noah could not discern, but stand on the dock they did, gazing at the carriages scurrying to deliver passengers to the many other boats along the slip. Oscar complimented Maribeth on her dress two or three times, and Adelaide told Jamie to stop fidgeting, but otherwise they waited in silence. Drumbeats punctuated by the occasional blast from a cannon followed by cheering drifted in from the harbor.

"We can't wait any longer," Jamie protested finally. "We'll be stuck at the back of the flotilla." Adelaide looked to Oscar, who coughed and then moved to toward the metal stairs that would take them aboard. A jacketed seaman stood at the bottom, waiting to extend a hand to aid the De Kuypers in mounting the first step. Maribeth once more looked up and down the pier, then, with resignation, she nodded and followed the others.

"Hello! Aren't you missing someone?"

A carriage had clattered to a halt and Alan De Kuyper had emerged, wearing a wide grin and waving a small American flag. He came up short at the six gaping people before him.

"Why the shock? I can wave the flag as well as anyone. We are here to celebrate a great American hero, are we not?"

"Where have you been?" Adelaide, Maribeth, and Oscar asked the question at once.

The grin shot off Alan's face. "I had business to attend to. I left word at the hospital."

"I know," Maribeth said. "I went there looking for you."

"Why would you do that?"

"We were concerned for your welfare . . . with all that's occurred."

"As you see, there was no need."

Noah had never before seen Alan belligerent. "In any event, we are very pleased to see you."

Alan's demeanor returned as quickly as it had left. "And I you. Well, let's be on board then. I hope the decks have been polished, so we don't dirty our trousers when we kneel."

Oscar harrumphed and stood aside to allow the family to board. As they moved to the stairs, a face appeared in the carriage window. It was a man in his late teens or early twenties with blond hair, a full face, and large eyes. He smiled at Alan, more of a smirk, and quickly leaned back, pulling out of view. His appearance returned the scowl to Alan's face.

"Who is that?" Oscar asked.

"Francis Contreve. He's a medical student. I was at his parents' house in Ossining, if you must know. His mother suffers from cardiac arrhythmia."

Adelaide's cheeks sucked in as if she had downed a glass of wine turned to vinegar. She turned away, grabbed Jamie by the arm, and dragged him up the stairs.

"Shouldn't you have just brought her to the hospital?" Jamie asked before Adelaide hissed at him to just get aboard.

The carriage in which Alan had arrived rode off, neither Alan nor Francis Contreve saying good-bye to the other. Alan stood facing his family, challenging any of them to speak. Maribeth moved in and planted a kiss on his cheek. "You can hardly be upset that people love you enough to worry about you."

Alan looked tentatively at his sister. He started to form an aggressive reply, then stopped. "No," he said, "I suppose not."

Noah clapped Alan on the back, although his arm felt stiff in doing so. "Most certainly not."

"Very well." Alan sighed. "Let's go and be patriotic."

Before Noah could move to the stairs, however, he felt a tug at the back of his sleeve. "Not so fast, doc."

Noah turned his head. It was the swarthy detective from the precinct. "McCluskey wants to see you."

Noah pulled his arm away. "I have neither the time nor the inclination to ever see Sergeant McCluskey again."

"Too bad, because he's playing host to a friend of yours, and I'm not sure how long his spirit of hospitality will last."

"What friend?" Noah asked, although he already knew the answer.

The detective smiled. His teeth were a dull shade of yellow. "The kind of friend we're happy to entertain."

"You're lying."

The man shrugged. "Mebbe so. Willing to take that chance? Just think how you'll feel when you read the newspaper tomorrow and find out I wasn't."

"And what if it's a trap?"

"What if it ain't?"

Maribeth had moved to Noah's side. "Go, Noah. You've got to."

"Best listen to the lady, doc."

"All right."

FORTY-ONE

DAY 10. FRIDAY, 9/29—8:45 A.M.

The detective, whose name was Radovic, was annoyingly chipper during the ride. He did everything but offer Noah a beer. And why not? He held all the cards, and Noah was hardly likely to leap to the street when he was going of his own volition.

"You shoulda really come in with us, doc. Woulda been definitely worth your while. Big mistake going over our heads instead, even to TR. Not that it'll make a difference. We'll all be at the precinct in a week or two. McCluskey has a lot of friends. Soon as nobody's looking, everything will go back the way it was. But he is pretty peeved with you. No getting around that. Wish he wasn't. I kinda like you, doc."

"Where are we headed?" Noah asked during one of the infrequent lulls in Radovic's conversation.

"No need to worry yourself about that, doc. Someplace where we can all transact our business undisturbed. You 'n' me 'n' Boyle 'n' McCluskey

. . . 'n' the Red Lady. Hey, that's going to be a good name for her . . . Red Lady." Radovic snickered at his wit.

They had driven north, the Hudson on their left awaiting Dewey. The sound of cheers and explosions wafted over the buildings. South of Fourteenth Street, Radovic paid the driver, and he and Noah got out. The streets were deserted. A few blocks away, they would be packed.

They walked north a bit more, then turned into a narrow alley. Another carriage was tied to a post, and at Radovic's instruction, Noah got in. "Sorry, doc," Radovic said, as if with genuine regret. "Gotta do this." Seconds later, Noah was blindfolded. "Don't touch it, doc. If you do, the deal's off 'n' the Red Lady will have to take her chances with us."

"I won't touch it."

They didn't travel far, but the carriage made almost constant turns. Noah tried to time the distance and note the direction of the turns in order to have a sense of their destination. The booming cheers from the river helped with orientation. He thought he had done a good job until the carriage stopped. If he was correct, they were back virtually where they had started.

Radovic helped him out and into a building. He could tell when he was indoors by the change in temperature. A door creaked, then a second. He was led down a set of stairs. At the bottom was another door, which when opened let in a surprising amount of noise from the parade. They must be very near the river.

A hand on his shoulder pushed him into a chair. Then the blindfold was whipped off and he was face-to-face with McCluskey. Radovic stood on one side and the red-haired copper with the handlebar, Boyle, on the other. It was a replay of his encounter with the soldiers. He had merely traded Anschutz and his cronies for McCluskey and his. If he'd been asked three days ago, he'd have sworn that with McCluskey he'd drawn the easier hand. He knew now that just the opposite was true.

The room was about twenty feet square and smelled of mildew and urine, probably animal, possibly human. Four small windows sat just below the ceiling on the left. Filthy drapes were stretched across each. Light came from bare windows on the right that seemed to open onto the walkway of an alley, so they were indeed below street level. Noah looked around, but they were the only four in the room.

"Where's Miriam?"

"Close, doc. Very close." McCluskey lacked Radovic's affability.

"I want to see her."

"You're not in a position to be making demands, doc. Or haven't you noticed that yet?"

"Then why did you bring me here?"

"That's a pretty stupid question, coming from someone who's supposed to be as smart as you. But what if I told you I brought you here to offer you a choice? Your life for hers? Would you do it?"

Noah didn't hesitate. "Yes."

McCluskey pursed his lips and nodded. "Well, you got moxie, doc. I'll give you that. But why do I need to give you a choice when I've got both of you?"

"So we add liar to your list of virtues."

"Oh, doc. Name calling? Is that all you've got? Well, doesn't much matter. I don't blush." He nodded to Boyle. "So you want to see your lady friend?"

"Yes."

"Then come along."

McCluskey led Noah to a door at the back of the room. Boyle came along, but Radovic stayed where he was. McCluskey took the knob but didn't turn it.

"Ready?"

Noah nodded.

McCluskey turned the knob and threw open the door.

Noah felt a choking sound come out of him as he looked across the room. Tied to a chair, her head dropped to her chest was Miriam. She wore only a slip, on which one of the shoulder straps was torn. It was also torn down the center to below her breasts. Her hair was disheveled and hung forward.

"We've taken a little of the sass out of her since you two had your romp."

Noah whirled and lunged for McCluskey. As he reached for the vile copper's throat, he was aware of being surprised that McCluskey hadn't moved. As he saw his fingers almost find their mark, there was an explosion inside his head. His next awareness was staring at McCluskey's shoes.

"You got to be more careful, doc," the voice came down to him. "Seeing as you just got out of the hospital."

Noah looked up to see Boyle drop the blackjack back into his jacket pocket. As Noah blinked and pushed himself to his feet, he tried to banish the ache at the base of neck.

Then he heard a soft moan. McCluskey had moved to the chair and lifted Miriam's head by grabbing her by the hair. A large bruise was under her left eye, and her lips were swollen and red. A dried trickle of blood was at her nostril. When Miriam realized it was Noah, she tried to form words but couldn't.

"You filthy detestable coward." Noah felt himself start to move to McCluskey again, but Boyle had him by the arm.

"Uh-uh, doc. Next one you won't be getting up."

McCluskey let Miriam's head fall again to her chest. "Well, doc, you'll be happy to know that we dumb cops finally found out what free love is all about. And, I gotta say, we can see the appeal. Miriam here does it all sorts of ways, sometimes with two or three at once. Bet you don't believe that, but it's true. Know what? We'll prove it to you. As they say, seeing's believing."

McCluskey reached down and stroked Miriam's shoulder. She emitted a small, gurgled wail. McCluskey withdrew a revolver, then nodded to Boyle, who produced a pair of handcuffs from another pocket.

Noah was not going to be party to the spectacle. He'd rather die. Daring McCluskey to shoot, he spun and launched a right at Boyle's jaw. Ordinarily, the copper would have parried it with ease, but he was so surprised at Noah's move that he remained still long enough for Noah's fist to reach its mark. Boyle staggered backward—Noah lacked the force to knock him off his feet—but he dropped the handcuffs before starting back at his adversary.

Then the gunshot Noah expected came. One sharp retort. He waited for the stunned sensation of being hit to overwhelm him, but it didn't happen. Instead, it was Boyle who dropped to the floor. At the same time, McCluskey fired as well, but not at Noah.

Noah turned. There were two men in the door, both with revolvers leveled at McCluskey. Behind them, just past the doorway, was Alan De Kuyper.

Maribeth had done it—speculating allows you to plan. Of course, it was her brother and not Miriam Herzberg she'd thought the Pinkertons would be saving, but she'd been bull's-eye in assuming that McCluskey had intended to establish bait to lure Noah.

Boyle was bleeding from the shoulder but had rolled behind a packing crate. A pistol was in his hand aimed at the invaders. The two Pinkerton men retreated into the doorway for cover as Boyle fired. McCluskey eyed the door at the far end of the room, then hunched down behind Miriam. He hesitated only for a second before leaping for the door while Boyle's fire covered him.

McCluskey swung the door open and was about to duck through when one of the Pinkertons, risking being hit by one of Boyle's bullets, leaned into the room and took aim. McCluskey saw him, then grabbed the chair that held Miriam and pulled it in front of him just as the Pinkerton fired. The center of Miriam's chest exploded in a gush of blood. Radovic had been correct. The Red Lady.

The chair toppled backward, McCluskey dashing in a crouch through the doorway behind. The Pinkertons would not be able to give chase; Boyle was between them and the door. But Noah could. And he did.

As he passed Miriam, he glanced down and confirmed what he already knew. She was dead. He whispered a farewell and swore McCluskey would pay if it took him the rest of his life.

A stairway lay just past the door. Noah could hear the clatter of McCluskey's footsteps and followed. After a left-hand bend, another doorway became visible, this one leading to a small pier. Sounds of revelry grew louder with every step closer to the river. When he reached the entrance, a small white launch was just pulling away, belching steam from the stack. A police boat. McCluskey certainly did have friends.

McCluskey himself was at the helm, so Noah assumed he was alone on the boat. Neither Boyle nor Radovic would be joining him. Noah ran and leapt from the end of pier, falling into the launch as he landed. McCluskey spun about at the sound, but he couldn't leave the helm. He leveled his revolver and fired, but with the pitch in the river, the shots didn't come close.

Noah had reached a part of himself he had not known existed. He had a clarity of purpose that was undiluted by doubt or fear, not even death. He knew, knew absolutely, that he would be the instrument of justice for Turner McKee and Miriam Herzberg.

He grabbed a boat hook and advanced toward the cabin. McCluskey was making for the flotilla in the middle of the river, but Noah would not let him reach it. Music, cheering, and cannon fire surrounded them, as if he and McCluskey were a sideshow act.

McCluskey fired wildly until his revolver was empty. After the last round had been spent, Noah advanced with the boat hook. McCluskey's head swiveled from the path of the launch back to Noah. He was goggle-eyed. The last thing Noah had expected was panic.

"What's the matter, McCluskey? Can't swim?"

"As a matter fact, I can't," McCluskey replied, continuing to glance about.

"Then you shouldn't have picked a boat." Noah suddenly lunged forward, the point of the boat hook aimed for the center of the copper's chest.

McCluskey was remarkably quick. Just before the hook reached him, McCluskey dodged, sending Noah stumbling forward. In the next instant, the positions had reserved and McCluskey was swinging a marlinspike at Noah's head. But with the wheel unattended, the launch pitched and McCluskey flailed at the air.

This would be Noah's only chance. As McCluskey lurched toward the open end of the cabin, Noah swung his leg into him, catching McCluskey just below the knee. The copper spun toward the stern, tried to regain his balance, then grasped desperately for a handhold. But he missed and plunged over the side.

The commotion had been visible to the boats in the flotilla, and a yacht, small by De Kuyper standards, was sailing quickly in their direction. McCluskey bobbed up and reached for the side of the boat, but it remained just past his fingertips. He went under, came up, then again grabbed fruit-lessly for the gunwales. The scene continued to repeat itself, McCluskey growing more fatigued each time.

"Help me, doc," McCluskey gasped between dips under the surface.

"Why should I?"

The yacht would be there in minutes.

"You took an oath," McCluskey managed to wheeze out. "I know you did."

Noah watched McCluskey flail. He had taken an oath, of course—to heal and comfort the sick.

But McCluskey wasn't sick.

Noah stood on the deck and watched as exhaustion and the weight of McCluskey's clothes eventually pulled him down.

Two minutes later, the yacht pulled up next to the launch.

FORTY-TWO

Alan, Maribeth, and the Pinkertons were waiting when Noah managed to ungracefully steer the launch to the slip. The owner of the yacht had refused to help, promising instead to call the police as soon as he reached land. Noah didn't bother to mention that the police wouldn't come within miles of this affair. Nor would anyone else.

One of the Pinkertons tied up the launch, and Noah stepped tentatively to the pier. He was spent and not only because of the physical exertion.

Maribeth came to him first, Alan waiting a pace behind. "We're both terribly sorry about Miss Herzberg," she said. "I know I've teased you, but I'm genuinely sorry never to have known her."

Noah nodded thanks. There was nothing to say.

Alan stepped up and handed Noah a flask. "I was saving this for when I saw Dewey, but I think you can use it more."

Noah took a long swig of the brandy. The burn felt good on his throat.

Neither Maribeth nor Alan pressed him but instead waited silently on the pier. Noah gazed out at Dewey's fleet making its way up the Hudson surrounded by countless private boats, each displaying an American flag. The sound of a military band drifted across the river, but he couldn't pinpoint the source. Downriver, the *Olympia* herself was coming into view. A moving steel city, a monument to America's foray into bullying might. Whatever attention the episode with the police launch had created had long dissipated, no one else willing to tear themselves away from the pageantry to investigate why one man stood by while another drowned. Noah wondered if there would even be an attempt to retrieve McCluskey's body or if the authorities would simply wait to see if it eventually washed up somewhere to the south. It was as if by mutual consent, the deaths of Turner McKee, Miriam Herzberg, and her father, Sasha, McCluskey, and the others were deemed never to have happened. Just as the police had rendered invisible the shooting of Pug Anschutz. And poor Willard—his death would now be invisible as well. Arnold Frias was beyond Noah's reach.

There was nothing to do now but close this book and try to decide how to move forward.

"How did the detectives get in so quietly?" Noah eventually asked Alan. "Radovic was standing guard in the first room."

"Believe it or not, he was asleep . . . sitting on the floor, leaning against the wall." Alan hesitated. "Apparently they'd been up most of the night. In any event, by the time he woke up, there was a pistol against the side of his head."

"What happened to him?"

"He's dead . . . although he was alive when I left him. One of the Pinkertons said he tried to pull a derringer when the coppers came to take him away, but the Pinkertons had searched him before. I suspect the derringer was a fantasy, that the coppers preferred a silent Radovic to a talkative one."

"Yes, that they would." Noah turned to Maribeth. "I owe you my life."

"Not me," Maribeth replied. "My father. He hired the detectives." In response to Noah's incredulity, Maribeth added, "My father is no more two endpoints with no middle than yours. At first he thought he was saving Alan, but even when he knew it was Miss Herzberg—and you—he had them go ahead. After I told him how much I admired Miss Herzberg, he said anyone who could evoke those feelings from me was worth rescuing, even if he abhorred what she stood for. He also told me that since it was apparent that I was in love with you, he intended to protect you as if you were his own son."

"Your father said that?"

"And even more unfathomable, my mother agreed."

"She didn't look like someone who agreed."

"It was grudging, I admit. But she doesn't have to like you, Noah. Only respect you. And I've made certain that she will."

"Take it, Noah," Alan added. "Grudging acquiescence is the best you're going to get from Lady Macbeth. As I think you've noticed, you're not alone in that."

Noah wanted to ask Alan, but he didn't. That part of the story would remain a piece of an unspoken bond between them. Alan would be happy with that, and Noah realized he would as well.

"Jamie, I take it, was unaware of any of this," Noah asked instead.

"Jamie needs to be told that the sun has risen," Alan replied. "He doesn't notice anything that isn't green and made of paper."

Suddenly, Noah's legs seemed profoundly heavy. His body seemed to throb as fatigue overtook him. "I think I'll go home now," he said.

"I'm coming along," Maribeth said instantly. "Alan can wait for my parents at the pier."

"Yes, I suppose I can do that. I'll finish the brandy."

"Thank you," Noah said softly. "Thank you both."

The hansom they engaged clopped along on streets that appeared as they might after a holocaust. Instead of the hundreds who would be scurrying about on De Kalb Avenue, there were less than a dozen. Noah

wondered how many of them had avoided the waterfront for political reasons. Had all of inland Brooklyn been left to the Reds?

Finally, on Clinton Street, he spotted a familiar face. No need to wonder why *she* had avoided the parade. Noah casually watched her move up the street. Another life that had changed in the past week, although hers likely less than most. The girl turned and entered a shop.

Then Noah knew.

"Stop!" he commanded to the driver. "Stop, I say! I'm getting out. Wait for me here."

"What is it, Noah?" Maribeth asked.

Noah didn't reply. He leapt from the coach, hurried into the shop, and then to the counter. He arrived in time to see the apothecary hand the girl a small package.

She sensed eyes on her and spun about.

"Dr. Whitestone," she stammered, "I . . . I . . ."

"Don't try to lie to me," Noah said. "I know the truth. You know it, too. You've known it all along. You've been trying to tell me but you were too afraid."

Molly burst into tears. Noah gave her his handkerchief and waited until she had calmed herself. "I didn't want you to take the blame, truly I didn't, but I couldn't get myself to speak."

"Tell me now." She started to protest, but Noah spoke over her. "I want to hear it right from the beginning. From the day Dr. Frias first treated Willard for his illness."

Molly gulped once or twice, trying to begin. Once the first words were out, the remainder came in a torrent. When she was done, she begged Noah not to say anything, that she was terrified of losing her job. Noah was tempted to reply that because of her he had almost lost his livelihood, his freedom, and his life. But what was the point? He simply retrieved his handkerchief and left the store.

Back in the carriage, he found himself growing more and more furious, but not with Molly. "What an idiot I was. So obvious. How could I have

missed it? Even if I didn't think of it at first, the girl fairly screamed it out at me every time I went to the house."

"Screamed what?" Maribeth asked.

"That was Molly, the Anschutz's maid. She was the one who gave Willard the morphiates that killed him, not Mildred Anschutz. She was blameless. So was Frias, at least in this. Willard didn't die from an overdose of Heroin. He died from a patent medicine, Paton's Vegetable Tonic. The same concoction that killed Anya Krakowiak. I told you, it's 10 percent opium. Willard drank a good bit of the bottle. He'd already taken the laudanum. The combination overpowered his system."

"But why would she give him such a concoction at all?"

"She'd been doing it ever since Willard had taken the Heroin tablets. Among her many other duties, it seems, Molly was responsible to keep Willard in line. No mean feat in the best of circumstances. Unbeknownst to Mrs. Anschutz, Willard became agitated whenever the tablets wore off. Molly felt certain that if his mother continued to encounter him in that state, she would be held to blame. Molly's older sister also cares for children and gives them Paton's to keep them quiet. So Molly began to give Willard small doses of the stuff between the prescribed intervals. But after three days, the tablets ran out and Willard became impossibly unruly and Molly was forced to increase the dose.

"Once again, all seemed well. Every time Willard took Paton's, his demeanor improved. Whenever the morphia began to wear off, he became overactive, but Molly dosed him before he could become too boisterous. He was such an energetic little boy, no one noticed the irregularity . . . that this activity was not the same as his usual behavior.

"The longer Willard used Paton's, of course, the more dependent on it he became. More frequent doses became necessary to maintain his equilibrium. After a week, Molly realized that she had made a grievous error, but was too panic-stricken to own up to it to Mrs. Anschutz. And to make it worse, Colonel Anschutz was coming home and she had seen the way he treated his own wife and children. What might he do to a mere maid?

She became so terrified of leaving Willard alone that she canceled her day off the week preceding the one in which I treated the boy. As Molly's fear escalated, her own doses of Paton's increased . . . she had been taking it along with the boy. Mrs. Anschutz had two patent-medicine dope fiends under her roof.

"The day I treated Willard was Molly's regular day off. She had meant to cancel it once more, but she received an urgent call from her mother who had been taken ill. Molly had no choice. She went to tend her mother, praying that Willard could get through one day without Paton's. She rushed back as quickly as she could, but it was too late. Willard's symptoms had already set in, and I was present. Willard had begged his mother for medicine, but Mrs. Anschutz, ignorant of the true nature of Willard's illness, had merely given him Bismosal.

"When Molly returned, I suggested that she tend to Willard whilst I visited my other patients. Not the best choice in retrospect. When Mrs. Anschutz realized I was committed to leaving, she grudgingly agreed. Willard's tolerance for morphiates was by then such that he awakened within thirty minutes of my departure. Molly knew the state he would be in, so she fetched the bottle of Paton's and gave him two spoonfuls. He awakened again just before I returned. Molly again fetched the Paton's and was about to give Willard another dose. Before she could, Mrs. Anschutz called to her from the hall to ask if Willard was still asleep. Molly ran to the door and replied that Willard was resting comfortably. But she had left the open bottle on the table next to Willard's bed. When she returned to his bedside, Willard had drunk most of the bottle. You can surmise the rest. Molly hid the bottle, and Willard slipped into respiratory distress. When I encountered Molly, I saw how upset she was, but I merely assumed that the pressure of working in the Anschutz home was responsible."

"So what will you do?"

"About Molly? Nothing."

"But then Mrs. Anschutz will continue to employ a woman who killed her son."

"Molly can have no effect on the other children. And if I do say something, she will be arrested and sent to prison. A maid. A poor ignorant maid. That would be as unjust as if I had been. Molly was no more responsible for Willard's death than the privates in the army are responsible for the Philippine war. Whoever sells Paton's Vegetable Tonic is responsible, and they will remain unsullied no matter what I do. So I choose not to throw Molly to the wolves."

"I don't know . . ." Maribeth mused. "She did cause the death of a child."

"Yes, I know. But she was merely a coincidental instrument. I'm sorry, Maribeth, but that's how I see it."

"And Frias? What about him?"

"That is the question, isn't it? What can you do about the man who is proved innocent of a specific charge but is guilty of bigger crimes? In Molly's case, I choose to do nothing; in Frias's, I can do nothing."

Maribeth considered that for a moment. Then she placed her hand on his. "Not in the immediate term perhaps."

Noah placed his fingertips against Maribeth's cheek. Then he smiled. "I sense that I am not wholly about to return to the tranquility of private practice."

EPILOGUE

P resident Roosevelt loved to conduct ceremonies outdoors. He had decided to use the lawn of the White House to sign "An act for preventing the manufacture, sale, or transportation of adulterated or misbranded or poisonous or deleterious foods, drugs, medicines, and liquors, and for regulating traffic therein, and for other purposes." The law, which he had strenuously urged Congress to pass, had already become popularly known as "The Pure Food and Drugs Act." The weather was balmy. Chairs had been set up to allow dignitaries, congressmen, and members of the press to watch the signing in comfort.

Many of the men—and occasional women—who had stirred the conscience of the nation with articles, petitions, and indefatigable appeals, both public and private, had been invited to witness the historic event, the first effort by the United States to ensure that the food Americans ate and the drugs they took were safe.

Some, however, had not been invited. Socialists. Anarchists. Men like Upton Sinclair, whose novel *The Jungle*, published the year before, had created a sensation, exposing the medieval conditions under which men toiled and died in the meatpacking plants of Chicago. Samuel Hopkins Adams, whose series in *Collier's*, The Great American Fraud, had laid bare the cupidity of the Patent Medicine Trust, also failed to be issued an invitation.

But Roosevelt considered himself an open-minded man and, barring outright radical politics, had chosen to honor those who risked their reputations, and sometimes lost their lives, in such a worthy cause.

The Whitestone family was among a select few whose invitations had been handwritten by the President himself. "To the man who first alerted me to the dangers to society that we address today," read the salutation. Noah, Maribeth, and even the children had also been invited to a special luncheon afterward, reserved for only the most special of guests.

Turner was old enough to rate a seat of his own, but Miriam curled up happily in her mother's lap. TR sat at a long table, members of Congress behind him, all smiling broadly. He gave a short speech about the deep responsibility elected officials bore to protect from unscrupulous operators those who had placed them in office. The president mentioned no names.

The words washed past Noah is if in a foreign tongue. He would have paid more attention, been more in the spirit of the celebration if not for the note he had received just before his departure for Washington: "Congratulations," it read. "No man deserves this honor more. And please extend my greetings to the President and tell him I look forward to seeing him again when he is next in New York."

It was signed, "Arnold Frias."

AUTHOR'S NOTE

Although I slightly distorted the time line, the Heroin story was as portrayed. Heinrich Dreser was, in fact, the head chemist at Bayer, and his role in the development of the drug and its testing is as described. He profited handsomely from the drug, as well as from Aspirin, but may well have died addicted to the product he swore was safe. The placard referred to in chapter 21 was indeed run as an advertisement in the publications mentioned. (*The American Journal of Insanity* is now *The American Journal of Psychiatry*.)

That ad is reproduced here:

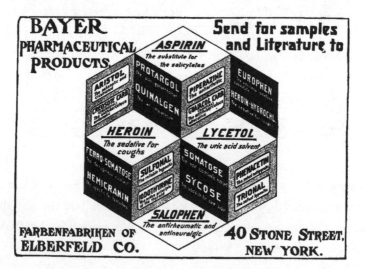

The Martin H. Smith Company did market Glyco-Heroin and the testimonials in chapter 29 are genuine. An advertisement run by the Smith Company:

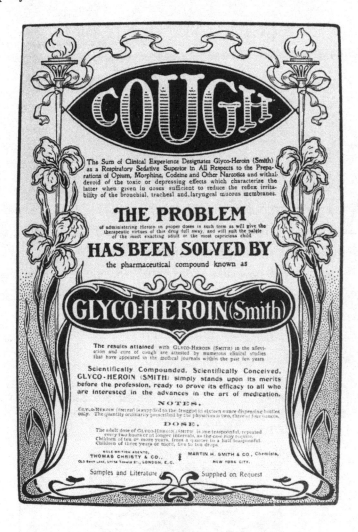

Fraser's tablets were real, as was Orangeine. Horatio Fraser's factory in Brooklyn burned down in 1905, with the loss of 200,000 Heroin tablets. The ad for Orangeine referred to in chapter 1 appeared in the *Brooklyn Daily Eagle* on September 23, 1899.

The celebration for George Dewey was as described. Five million people were said to have lined the parade route—on a per capita basis, the largest crowd ever to applaud a military leader in the nation's history. Dewey ran for president twice but failed to secure the Republican nomination. The Dewey Arch, thrown up as quickly as described, deteriorated almost as fast. By 1903, it had begun to crumble. A campaign to raise funds to repair the structure failed, and the arch was torn down in 1906.

Justin Herold was a real person, a fascinating man who joined a number of progressive causes. He was seriously hurt in a trolley accident in 1906, remarried in his sixties, and fathered a child in his seventies. Abraham Jacobi was also real. He remains a legend among pediatricians. The Jacobi Medical Center in the Bronx is named for him. Frederick Wurster was indeed the last mayor of Brooklyn. He never again ran for public office. The antipathy between Dewey and Theodore Roosevelt existed.

The Anschutz family is fictional, although the atrocities committed by American soldiers in the Philippines are not. Arnold Frias, the De Kuypers, and Noah Whitestone are all figments, but the representation of the practice of medicine in 1900 is accurate.

Heroin became a scourge, but its manufacture was not outlawed until 1914. Sale and possession, however, did not become illegal until 1919.

IMAGES ON PAGES 293 AND 294: *Advertisements for Heroin, circa 1900. Published in the U.S. before 1923 and public domain.*